FLARE

The Firebrand Chronicles Book 2

FLARE

The Firebrand Chronicles Book 2

J.M. Hackman

ISBN: 979-8-9921251-2-2

Cover by C.S. Hackman

Second edition printing November 2025

This book is dedicated to the Most High King.

Author's Note

BRENNA JAMES IS YOUR typical teen. She likes to hang out with friends, enjoys time off from her studies, and dreams of acing her history exam. But she struggles with impulsivity, time management, and poor choices. Why does she do the things she does? When is she going to "grow up?" Welcome to ADHD, Attention Deficit Hyperactivity Disorder.

ADHD is usually recognized as the child running around the classroom, yelling out answers without raising their hand, or incessantly picking on the classmate in front of them. But it's also the quiet, withdrawn kid in the back row, distracted and unable to focus on their classwork. It's called ADHD, Predominantly Inattentive (It's a sibling to the better-known ADHD, Combined—which includes a hefty dose of hyperactivity—and the lesser known ADHD, Unspecified). ADHD, Predominantly Inattentive affects girls more often than boys. In all three types, there's a lot of "noise" or extra information in their head, so that concentration becomes impossible. They have trouble focusing on tasks, tracking or managing time, and making (and keeping) friends.

But this condition is real—it's not an excuse for laziness or bad behavior, or something kids can control or grow out of. (ADHD children grow into ADHD adults who use techniques, coping mechanisms, exercise, and/or medication to help them focus.) These children are also bright, creative, and determined. They're not broken—they just learn and process the world around them differently.

If you'd like to learn more about ADHD, check out https://www.additudemag.com or https://chadd.org/.

EAST JASPER TERRITORY

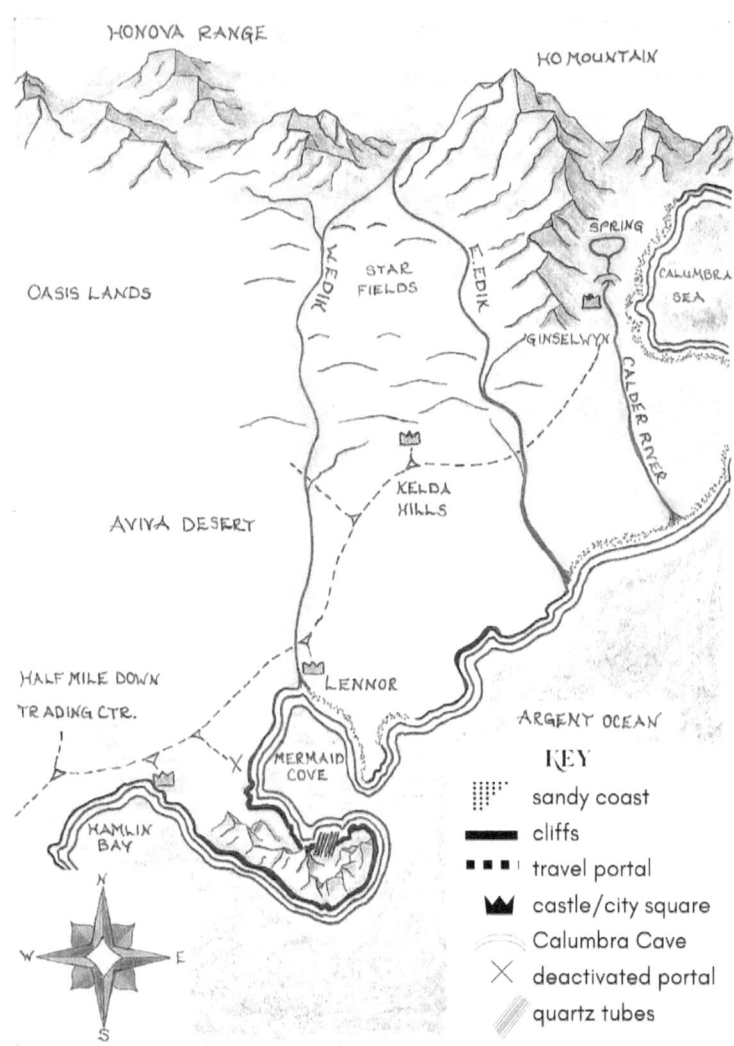

HONOVA RANGE

HO MOUNTAIN

SPRING

CALUMBRA SEA

OASIS LANDS

W. EDIK

STAR FIELDS

E. EDIK

GINSELWYN

CALDER RIVER

KELDA HILLS

AVIVA DESERT

HALF MILE DOWN TRADING CTR.

LENNOR

ARGENT OCEAN

MERMAID COVE

HAMLIN BAY

N
W   E
S

KEY

- ⦙⦙⦙ sandy coast
- ▬▬ cliffs
- ▪▪▪▪ travel portal
- ♛ castle/city square
- 〰 Calumbra Cave
- ✕ deactivated portal
- ⫽ quartz tubes

Close-up of Mermaid Cove

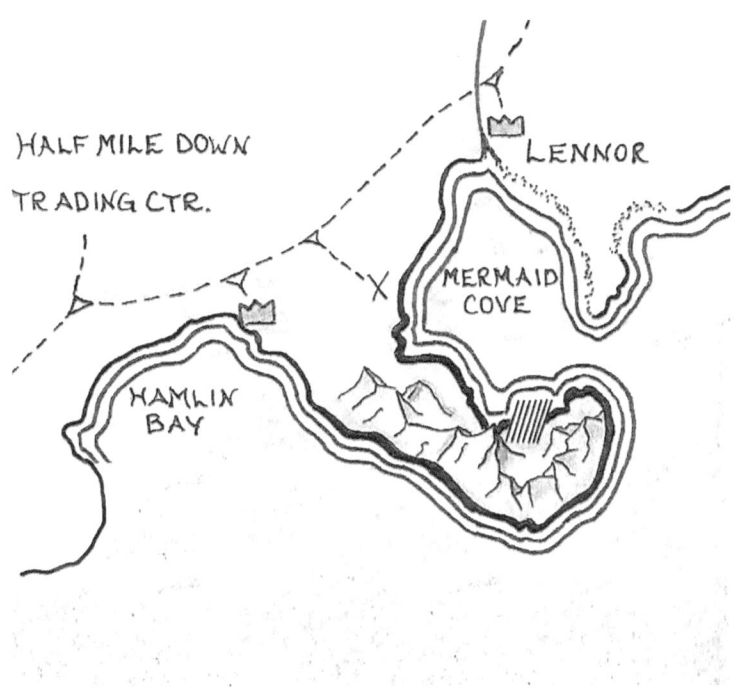

HALF MILE DOWN
TRADING CTR.

LENNOR

MERMAID
COVE

HAMLIN
BAY

Chapter One

Tiny waited at the portal to Linneah. This had become a routine for me. On any available weekend or holiday, one or both of us would use the portal to travel to Linneah.

I breathed deeply. Fall had arrived a bit late this year, and I was loving the crisp air and colored leaves. As I approached, Tiny crouched and poked at the ground.

"Everything okay?"

Frowning, she looked up. "Look around."

That was when I saw them—more than half a dozen burned spots surrounded the portal spillway. Some were a faded brown, while others were crispy and black. My stomach twisted.

I'd forgotten about the strange guy lingering near the spillway months ago. I hadn't seen him since. Maybe he was just a drifter...who appeared misty at a certain angle. Who disappeared in the blink of an eye. Who left burned circles behind in the grass.

I grimaced. I should've mentioned the weird guy to my mom during one of my previous visits. But school, daily life stress, and visiting my second home had wiped the unsettling encounter from my mind.

"Did you ever mention this to your mom?" she asked like she could read my mind.

"No, I kept forgetting. And I haven't seen that guy again."

Standing, she dusted off her pants. "Mention it to her this time, okay?"

I nodded, hoping my ADHD wouldn't bury the thought.

"So are you ready to surprise Baldwin?"

I couldn't help my sigh. "That's the plan."

Although Baldwin and I had been dating for over a year, the last visit hadn't gone so well. Happiness had flashed in his green eyes, but then he'd remained quiet and withdrawn. By the time the visit was over, I was certain something was wrong. Dating someone from an alternity wasn't easy, but we did the best we could.

A giant fist squeezed my heart. What if our best wasn't enough?

"I'm not sure this is a good idea." Neither Baldwin nor my mother were expecting me, after all. I could just turn around, go back—

"Don't second guess yourself. It's genius. Annnd"—Tiny drew the word out—"there's more."

"More?"

She grinned. "I heard from Anna last night."

My ADHD instantly grabbed onto the news and conveniently threw away every doubt I'd been obsessing over. "Really? How is she?" I didn't see my shapeshifting friend as often as I'd like. She lived in the Jasper Territory, same as me, but on Matana Island, not Linneah. Half the time I visited, she was grounded.

"She's free this weekend. She sent the letter via fo-li."

My eyes widened. "For real?" I'd never seen a foslykos, but I'd heard stories. They *glowed*.

"Yeah. Luckily, it was after dark."

So cool. Foslykos, or light wolves, were used by citizens of the Jasper Territory to send messages. They were pretty much the alternity's postal service, but their multicolored, glowing bodies made them one of the best things about my other home.

"At least we know they can get through the portal," I said.

"True. Anyway, she wants to get together this weekend. Cool, right? It's like a girls' weekend, one last hurrah."

I raised an eyebrow. "What're you talking about? Is someone dying?"

Her smile tightened. "No, never mind. Just being weird. So anyway, Anna said to meet her outside the Golden Pickle."

The words were like a dash of cold water. Linneah's hot spot. I bit my lip. "Can't we meet somewhere else?"

Tiny rolled her eyes. "It's just a place to meet. We don't have to stay."

Right. Of course not. Like being there wasn't bad enough.

We walked to the middle of the spillway. I turned away from the mysterious dark circles as water lapped past my boot soles. They still creeped me out. After a few seconds, my vision went hazy. Tiny vanished, and the cobblestones disappeared under my feet.

This was the worst part.

My knees wanted to buckle, but I'd learned to keep them slightly bent if I wanted to arrive in Linneah still standing. The air changed from cool to freezing, its arctic teeth biting through my soft shirt. Another gust of air, this time like a furnace blast, before my vision cleared. The cobblestone dais of the Linnean fountain solidified under my feet, and water droplets sprayed ice cold on my skin.

"Ugh." Tiny put a delicate hand to her stomach. "I should've had more than a granola bar for supper."

I frowned. "Didn't you eat anything else?"

"Uh, a few grapes?" She shrugged. "I'll get something at the restaurant."

"Please don't remind me," I grumbled.

I stepped toward the inside rim of the platform and raised my hand. With a quick flick of my fingers, the fountain spray ceased, opening like a doorway. After we stepped through, I turned, and with the same gesture, the fountain's spray was complete again.

Inside the castle gates, silence and early evening light settled into nooks and crannies. The stone and wood buildings stood like quiet statues, sentinels over my second home. In the distance, patchwork farms and treehouses disappeared over a hill toward the griffin house. The roar of the sea murmured its timeless song, its white-capped waves a sliver of dark gray in the distance.

A guard lounging by a vendor's cart stepped forward. "Passes?"

I smiled. "Hi, Reggie."

"Lady James." He bowed. "Forgive me. I did not recognize you or Shaynedel right away. Welcome back."

"Thanks." As he headed back to his post, I turned to Tiny. "I should go see my mom, let her know I'm here."

She squinted at me. "You want the security detail?"

I hesitated. Jace was the ever-present bodyguard who came with being the daughter of the queen. "Well, no, but—"

"Then skip it. We won't be gone that long. After we meet Anna, you can come back."

The thought was compelling. But so was the idea of avoiding the Golden Pickle. "If we met Anna here—"

"No." Her expression turned mutinous. "You can't avoid the place just because Gari's father owns it."

My stomach churned. "Yes, I can. Gari's usually there, and she can't stand me." I didn't like Baldwin's ex either, but I'd tried to be friendly. It never worked.

"She's probably not there. And if she is, we go in, get Anna, then leave. Okay?" Tiny gave me an encouraging smile, probably to calm me before I exploded or refused to go anywhere near the place.

I sighed. "Promise?"

"Pinky promise." We did a pinky-link, shook hands once, then set off for the other side of Linneah.

The residential area lay quiet, welcoming glows coming from treetop residences. I never tired of seeing the enormous treehouses Linneans lived in year-round. Hushed conversations drifted through the leaves as people sat outside their homes, enjoying the evening air. The buttery scent of Kunkelsteuchen rolls drifted on the breeze, and my mouth watered.

In the business area of Linneah, invisible tension filled the air. Men hurried in and out of businesses, many wearing black and gray military uniforms with Linneah's eight-pointed star on the chest. Although a few businesses had closed, most stayed open, taking advantage of the shopping frenzy.

Before I could ask Tiny what was going on—although she probably didn't know any more than I did—my favorite place in Linneah came into view.

I jammed the lid back on the sarcasm box. Gari probably wouldn't be there. Right? Right.

The Golden Pickle stood in the heart of the business district, next to a shop that made and sold helli lanterns. More restaurant than bar, it had a separate room for serving alcoholic beverages. I'd collected a handful of unpleasant meetings with Gari in the restaurant. Despite Tiny's optimism, Gari was usually there serving, cleaning up, or just hanging around. Her newest hobby was singling me out and being a jerk. She was good at it.

And I'd taken to avoiding the place like the plague.

As we drew close to the restaurant, foot traffic increased. From the open windows, laughter and music spilled into the street. Two teenage guys wrestled in the adjoining field. The group around them encouraged the wrestlers until one pinned the other. A cheer went up when they announced the winner, and two others took their place.

"Brenna and Shaynedel!" A guy with bright-red hair stepped away from the group. His hairstreak, a common feature in Linneans, glowed white in the twilight.

I grinned. "Kersen, hi!" Baldwin's best friend had become my friend, now that I knew him better.

"It is good to see you again," he said with the characteristic formal speech. I'd never heard a native Linnean use a contraction, ever.

"We're meeting Anna." Tiny raised her eyebrows. "Do you know if she's here?"

"I think she was here about an hour or so ago. I do not know if she is still here."

"What's going on?" I gestured to the group.

"Wrestling. At least among those heading out tomorrow. Baldwin probably told you about it."

I blinked once, my thoughts freezing.

"He did tell you, right?" His voice sounded far away.

"Tell me what?"

He muttered a curse under his breath. "I do not think it is my place to, ah..."

"Kersen..."

He rubbed a hand down his face. "Fine, but I think you should hear this from him. Baldwin and I were accepted for Emperor Rexson's next assignment. We leave tomorrow."

My breath whooshed out and refused to return. Baldwin and I had talked of the possibility, in the future, but he hadn't said anything about an acceptance. "For how long?"

He shrugged, his eyes apologetic. "Until Emperor Rexson says the mission is complete."

"How dangerous is it?"

"Brenna—maybe you should talk to Baldwin about this."

Anger, tears, something, pushed inside my chest. "Is he here?"

He rubbed the nape of his neck, still looking sorry. "Inside."

Reaching over, I squeezed his forearm. "Come back safe."

He nodded solemnly.

I turned and walked toward the restaurant, feeling sick.

Tiny put her hand on my shoulder. "Maybe he forgot?"

"Would you forget something like that?"

Pursing her lips, she didn't respond.

Opening the door of the Golden Pickle was like being hit by a sledgehammer of noise. Usually this place was *the* hangout for teens, the two rooms kept separate by a velvet curtain and a bouncer. Tonight there was no curtain and no bouncer. The white-painted walls were bursting with people, mostly guys who were partying like frat boys at a kegger. Loud music drifted from the back room, indicating more festivities in progress. The legal drinking age in Linneah was seventeen, the same age to join the Linnean forces. Tonight, the drink of choice was verum, a strong blue brew I'd never tried. Everyone had a glass, the bright cobalt liquid glinting like sapphires. My eyes watered from its pungent odor.

As Tiny and I inched farther into the room, Flynn and Adal stepped from the crowd. "Come to see us off, eh?" Flynn gave Tiny a flirty wink. "A kiss from you, Shaynedel, would keep me alive during our dangerous assignment."

She grinned, her cheeks pinking. "Keep dreaming, Flynn. Have you seen Baldwin?"

"You do not need that boy. You need a man like me."

"Brenna's looking for him." Tiny pointed in my direction, but Flynn didn't even blink. His deep-brown eyes stayed fixed on Tiny.

Adal rocked on his feet as a strange look crossed his face. "I—uh, I am sure he went home."

"Oh? When did he leave?" I asked.

He glanced toward the back room before inspecting the sticky floor. "You just missed him."

"That's funny," I said. "Kersen swore he was still here." I paused, but he didn't offer anything more. "He probably would've seen Baldwin leave, since he was just outside."

His gray eyes went wide. "I could be wrong. I need another drink." He pushed his way to the counter.

I poked Tiny, who was still flirting with Flynn. "I'm heading to the back room. If I'm not back in five minutes, come looking for me."

"I'll search for Anna." She linked arms with her admirer. "Help me look, Flynn."

It took several minutes to inch to the back room, my progress slowed by the press of bodies. Upon reaching my destination, I scanned the room. A band played a loud Linnean reel, and several pairs of dancers took up half the floor with their intricate steps. On the other side, clusters of people sat around battered tables, talking and laughing. I wouldn't have bothered to look closer, but a flash of blonde hair caught my eye. Gari. Ugh.

No one could ignore the girl. Not even me.

She was all blonde hair, full curves, and killer green eyes. The center of attention, she was at a table with half a dozen others. I prepared to head for the exit until I looked closer. Maybe it was the way she sat snuggled against some guy, legs draped over his.

He was tall, dark, and handsome—and mine.

Baldwin laughed at something she said as both of her hands wrapped around his bicep, their faces too close. The spilled sticky verum under my feet glued me to the floor. Hurt bloomed in my chest, and I glared holes through them both.

Something made him look up. His eyes grew wide, and his laugh slipped from his face.

I'd seen enough. I would've escaped too, if I hadn't been trapped between the wall and a guy built like a linebacker. Just as Mr. No-neck slipped past me, Gari looked up, following Baldwin's gaze.

She grinned, snaked her arms around his neck, and kissed him.

Chapter Two

Pushing through the crowd, I dashed for the door. I could cover a lot of ground when I forgot about being polite. My throat choked with tears, I stumbled outside. The hurt around my heart swelled. I hunched my shoulders, pain exploding.

In seconds, Tiny was beside me, Anna in tow.

"Brenna!" Anna gave me a big hug, unaware my world had just imploded.

"Did you find him?" Tiny asked.

I swallowed hard, a lump in my throat. If I opened my mouth, I'd ugly cry with sobs and smearing makeup. I pushed past them and jogged back to the castle as I fought tears.

"Brenna? What's wrong?" Tiny called from behind me.

"Salt it down, girl," Anna added.

But their voices only made me run faster to get away from the hurt pounding in my chest.

I had no idea whether Tiny and Anna followed me; I just knew I needed to go.

When we reached the residential area, Tiny grabbed my arm. "Brenna, slow down. What happened? Did you find Baldwin? Was Gari there? What?"

Both she and Anna gasped for breath.

The words burned my throat. "Both of them. Together." Despite my efforts, a tear slipped out.

"Shells and shimmer! That's drift talk," Anna said, her island slang making her almost impossible to understand.

Tiny shook her head. "Maybe they just happened to be standing together—"

"She was sitting on his lap. They were kissing. And he was surprised to see me."

Tiny's blue eyes grew bigger. "Unbelievable. What did he say?"

As if I would ever talk to him again. "I didn't stick around to find out."

"That storm tossed seagull needs to answer for this." Anna balled her hands into fists.

"No, absolutely not." I didn't need to subject myself to more stuff I could never unsee. I leaned against a tree, then checked its top. No treehouse, so no eavesdroppers.

Tiny's face darkened. "What a jerk."

"You can do better, Brenna, no drift about it." Anna crossed her arms.

I thought he *was* better. Why hadn't he said anything? Maybe it was my fault. I certainly didn't look like Gari. At all. She was petite, curvy, sexy. And I was, well, just me—dark hair, slender, smart mouthed, and kinda awkward.

Thoughts spun and whirled while tears fought for release. I couldn't share my pathetic feelings, so I faked it. "Absolutely. I can do better." Even with that firm declaration, my heart ached. A sudden idea occurred to me. "Why don't you guys go on to the castle? Tell my mom I'm visiting Arvandus. I'll fly back later."

"Are you sure?" Anna bit her lip.

"I'll be fine." Someday.

Tiny put her arm around my shoulders. "I don't think you should be alone."

"I won't be. I'll be visiting Arvandus." My griffin's wise words and quiet sympathy were exactly what I needed.

My act must've convinced them, because they headed toward the castle. Their figures blurred as tears filled my eyes. I hadn't seen this coming. Not at all.

After a minute of wallowing, I messaged my griffin. *Arvandus? I'm here. Can you meet me outside the residential district?*

Every time I came to Linneah, I visited Arvandus. Our bond, the vinculus, had only grown stronger, allowing us to communicate telepathically.

Raven, I will be there.

At his nickname for me, new tears sprang to my eyes. Despite the falling darkness, the glow of the Petrus Rings lit the evening. The dazzling silver-blue and gold rings spanned the night sky. Along with the moon, there was plenty of light to navigate Linneah's housing area.

The powerful whoosh of Arvandus' wings signaled his arrival. A mutant of sorts, he was an all-black panther with eagle-like wings. As he landed, he folded his massive wings, and his metallic silver wingtips glimmered in the starlight.

"Arvandus." In moments, I had my arms around his furry neck.

"Raven, it is good to see you. But you are upset. Why?"

With his words, I sniffed back tears as the story tumbled out.

There was a moment of silence before he spoke. "This is not like Baldwin. I am sorry."

I hiccupped. "You and me both."

"He is a trustworthy young man. Perhaps it is not what it looks like. Tomorrow you can talk to him, and—"

"No." It came out with more force than I intended. "Sorry. I mean, it's exactly what it looked like. Besides, he's leaving tomorrow on his first assignment—something else I didn't know about. So he can just—" My insult dissolved under another wave of tears. Sheesh.

Arvandus gave me a few moments to pull myself together. "Brenna, allow me to fly you home. Tomorrow you can make any further decisions, if needed. But a good night's sleep is invaluable. And I am here whenever you need me."

"Thanks." The events of the evening had carved my heart open. I rested my forehead against his neck, his warmth calming me before I climbed on. His takeoff, smooth and powerful, pulled at me. I tightened my thighs and buried my hands deep into his neck's ruff. The night air cooled as he climbed, and the smell of salt and wood smoke cleared cobwebs from my head.

Painted in black and silvered grays, the landscape dazzled. The sea on my right shone bright white from the moonlight. From this height, the massive trees forming the castle foundation became tall, black smudges. When Arvandus landed just inside the castle gate, I slipped from his back.

I gave his neck a final scratch. "See you tomorrow, Arvandus."

"And I you, Brenna."

"Thanks."

He turned, and with a running leap, was airborne.

Mixed emotions churned in my stomach as I contemplated entering the castle. In a dark corner, I leaned against a shuttered vendor's stall. Part of me couldn't wait to see Mom. The other part wanted to go home and hide in my bedroom until everything stopped hurting. If I left now, I could be back in Cloverdale in minutes.

The thought of Tiny's disappointed face kept me from leaving. We'd planned this surprise trip for days. She'd been acting weird, as if this trip was a matter of life and death, but I was hoping it'd be a stress reliever for her. I couldn't back out now.

The immense stone castle waited. Guards moved along the balcony, installing helli lanterns. Although I missed Mom, as soon as I caught up with her, she would sic Jace on me. It would be impossible to even go to the bathroom without a companion dogging my every step.

High above, the expansive dining room windows glowed with warm light. Mom was probably in her study or her private room, neither visible from my spot. Despite the threat of a bodyguard, I wanted my mom's hugs and the way I could tell her anything, something I desperately needed tonight.

Before I headed inside, a hooded shadow detached from the other side of the courtyard and strode toward the fountain. Flicking a hand, the individual turned off the water and stepped onto the cobblestone portal. Bending over, the person placed a small bundle on the stones before leaving and blending back into the shadows.

I hesitated. Was he coming back? Where was Reggie, the guard? A trickle of fear slid down my neck. That package would disappear any minute and end up in Cloverdale. Maybe it was supposed to. Maybe it was something that shouldn't.

I studied the shadows, waiting for the figure to appear again. Hoping he would. All was still. Creeping toward the portal, I eyed the small parcel. But before I reached the fountain's edge, a loud crack split the night. A blinding fireball lit the portal.

The massive explosion sent me airborne, debris pelting my face.

My skull hit something hard, the crack echoing in my ears, and everything went black.

Bright sunlight. Footsteps on a wooden floor. Wood smoke, cinnamon, and cloves. The gray cobblestone walls of the castle infirmary swam into view. Renke, the castle physician, listened to my heart with what looked like a stethoscope.

He smiled when I blinked a few times. "It is good to see you awake, Brenna. I will alert the queen."

Brilliant light streamed through the window, and I squinted. Too bright.

When he returned a minute later, he closed the curtains. "Any blurry vision?"

"No."

"What is the last thing you remember?"

"An explosion? I'm not sure. Was I unconscious?"

"Only for a short time," he said. "The explosion happened late last night. When the guards went to investigate, they found you. You suffered a minor concussion."

His words sparked a memory. I hadn't slept well—people kept waking me, asking my name, my birthdate, my father's name. Annoying. My head throbbed, and I closed my eyes. It didn't help. "Could I have something for the pain? My head hurts."

He turned. "Brock, get her the syrup, please."

A tall, thin man put away what looked like a medical dictionary and pulled a brown glass bottle from the shelf.

I'd celebrated a few months ago when Brock had replaced his assistant, Dirk. Since my talent was helpful with healing, I often worked in the infirmary, and things had been awkward with the Dirk. He'd never forgiven me for his injury last year and my part in it. With the bad history between us, I wasn't sad to see him go, just sad we couldn't work things out.

"Take this with some water." Brock gave me a small cup of yellow syrup. It was medicus tree sap and acted much like pain relievers from Earth.

"Thanks." I followed the sour medicine with several big gulps of water.

"Hey, you're awake." Tiny stood at the door, Anna hovering behind her. The sight of them made me feel a little better.

"She cannot have many visitors." Renke scowled. "She just woke up."

"They won't stay long, I promise." I gave him a hopeful smile. Anna and Tiny nodded.

Renke motioned them in. "Only a brief visit."

As my friends approached the bed, Tiny's features narrowed in concern. "How do you feel?"

"My head hurts. Is everyone else all right?"

"Yeah, but the portal's ruined," Anna said.

"You're kidding!"

Tiny sighed. "No, the explosion wrecked the portal opening. So now it's down for repairs."

"How long will that take?"

My best friend pursed her lips. "A portal repair? A month, at least."

"A month? Dad wanted me home by Sunday night." He couldn't ground me if I couldn't get home, right?

Tiny laughed. "Good luck with that."

"Yeah, ha ha, funny." Something pressed at my memory, a reason I wanted to go back to Pennsylvania, to be far away from here...

She sobered. "Look, there's nothing you can do. So why don't you come with me and Anna?"

"Where?"

"My home, to Ginselwyn. It'll be fun."

So why wasn't she smiling?

When my mom entered the room, all normal behavior ceased. Tiny and Anna swept into graceful curtsies, while Renke and Brock bowed low. I still wasn't used to it.

Mom smiled. "Good morning." She turned to Tiny and Anna. "Did you two sleep well in Brenna's room?"

Anna gave my mom one of her brilliant smiles, amped with a little of her shapeshifting magic. "It was shell fine, thank you."

Renke shooed them toward the door. "Now, you two must leave. Give Brenna a moment with her mother." He gave another bow to my mom. "Allow me to give you some private time as well, my queen."

"Thank you, Renke."

My friends headed for the door. Tiny gave me a forced smile. "Think about what I said?"

"Sure." As she left, I couldn't get her strained expression out of my head. Was someone in her family sick or hurt?

My mom placed a cool hand on my forehead. "How do you feel?" As she leaned forward, the metallic gold ribbon in her braided hairstreak caught the light.. A cluster of thin gold chains at her neck glistened.

I rubbed my temple. "A little tired. And the front of my head hurts."

"Did Renke give you anything for it?"

"I just took some medicus syrup." It could kick in anytime now. Please.

"Good. It will take effect soon." She paused for a moment and studied my face. "You didn't check in when you arrived last night."

A worm of guilt wiggled its way through my stomach. "I planned to right after we met Anna. But then—" I stopped. Baldwin, Gari, and the events at the Golden Pickle flashed to the front of my memory.

"You purposely met with Anna first. Then Arvandus."

I considered mentioning the situation with Baldwin. No, she wasn't in the mood to give sympathy. "Mom, I was fine. But I can't stand the security. I mean, Jace is a decent guy, but I hate being followed."

"You need to be protected."

My headache got a little worse. "From what?"

Mom pressed her lips together. "The daughter of a queen is valuable."

"When was the last time I was targeted?"

"What do you call last night?"

Paranoid much? I kept the comment to myself. "That wasn't an attack on me. That was an attack on the portal, or Linneah, or whatever you want to label it."

"How do you know? You were knocked unconscious by—"

"Because I saw it." I tried to recall the memories. My forehead throbbed in protest. "Last night, someone blew up the portal—I think—on purpose. I was in the shadows, near the vendor stalls, when this person put a package on the portal and left it there. Reggie never showed up. Is he all right?"

"He was knocked out, but he's recovering just fine."

Relief flooded me. I liked the guy. He had such a nice smile and was always friendly—

Mom interrupted my thoughts. "It could've been a lure. For you."

"I don't think the person knew I was there. And if he did, he could've attacked me when I was heading to the castle."

Mom's eyes narrowed. "Hmm. Did you see anything else?"

"Um, the person knew how to stop the fountain, but he forgot to activate it when he left. And..." Something else skirted the edge of my memory. "Oh! The package didn't disappear and go to Cloverdale like I expected. When I moved closer, it exploded. Right?" It all fuzzed together.

"As usual, you are very observant."

"Do we know who did it?"

"No, the guards are still examining the evidence. I'll share what you saw. Every little bit helps. But for now, try to relax."

"So now that we know it wasn't an attack on me, can we dismiss Jace? Please." I grasped her hand, desperate for her to understand. "Don't have me followed just because you're afraid."

Tactical error.

Mom's eyes flashed. "I will protect you with every device at my disposal. Jace stays."

Folding my arms, I pushed down the anger and tried to ignore the bass drum in my head.

She studied me for a moment. "I'm glad you're here. I will inform your father you're safe."

Um, what? The information swirled, not fitting together. "How?"

"I can send a runner via another portal." She stroked my forehead, her fingers soft on my skin. "You look exhausted, sweetie. Take a nap, and I'll visit you later."

After she left, I thought over my last twenty-four hours. My boyfriend—no, ex-boyfriend—was a lying, cheating skunk.

I was stuck here.

The portal was damaged.

And based on Tiny's actions, my best friend had a secret. I couldn't do much, but I could find out what it was.

After all, what were best friends for?

CHAPTER THREE

THE NEXT DAY AFTER lunch, I was allowed to take a short walk. I sent a mental message to Arvandus and headed for the castle steps, Jace my constant shadow. Blocky and wide, his muscles strained against his castle uniform. He'd wrenched back his medium-length brown hair into a low ponytail.

The overcast day draped the town in a dingy shroud. Far away, the section of ocean visible between the buildings reflected a gunmetal surface.

I popped a piece of fypex gum in my mouth. The natural ingredients from the fypex fern helped me focus and stay alert. Plus, I loved the vanilla-laced-with-raspberry flavor.

My griffin arrived shortly after I perched on the top step. I looked at Jace. "You don't have to stay. Arvandus is here in case anyone tries to drag me away."

He gave me an impassive look.

"I want some privacy."

"I will wait just inside the door." He turned and left.

Arvandus settled, folding his wings. "I do not know why you are unpleasant to him. He is doing his job."

I scowled. "He's a major pain. Always there, always around. Sometimes I feel like I can barely breathe."

He gave me a once over. "You must be feeling better. You have recovered your difficult personality."

I bared my teeth in a fake smile. "It's part of my charm."

He changed the subject. "Have you met Astraya?"

"No, who's that?"

"Astraya is my mate."

"What?" This was news. I was pretty sure griffins didn't marry, but how *did* they form families?

"Do not act so shocked, Raven. All things must reproduce."

"But, but—well, sheesh." My cheeks heated. The vinculus between us was for life, but this was a new wrinkle. "Does she do anything to our vinculus? Does this mean she can hear us, or comes with us on trips, or—?"

Arvandus chuckled. "We mate for life. She bears our cubs. I help her raise them. Other than that, it does not affect our relationship."

"So you don't become a family like humans?"

"I will be a father. She is my mate. The cubs grow up to live their own lives. But there are different kinds of families. I consider you part of my human family, Raven."

I patted his neck, my heart warming. "And you're part of mine."

"To return to the subject, Astraya is my mate. And she is expecting."

Ooh, cute baby griffins. I grinned. "Cool. How far along?"

"Almost three months. In another week, she will be due."

"Congratulations, Arvandus."

"Thank you. I wanted you to know because I would like to stay close to Astraya, at least until she gives birth. If you need to fly due to an emergency, I am available. Otherwise, I would prefer to stay in Linneah."

"Sure. No problem. Take all the time you need. I'd like to see the cubs when they're born. I bet they're adorable." A yawn crept up on me, and I tried to hide it behind my hand.

"I would be happy to introduce you. On a side note, I am glad you were not injured badly, but you need rest."

"I had some."

"Get more. We can visit tomorrow."

I stood up from the castle steps. "See ya, Arvandus. Thanks for the visit."

"My pleasure, Brenna." He turned and padded away.

True to form, Jace waited for me inside the castle doors.

"I'm going to my room." With another yawn, I walked toward the stairwell.

"I will escort you."

"Of course you will," I muttered under my breath.

It was a long walk with him following me.

To my delight, Tiny waited in my room. I brightened. "Hey, you. Where's Anna?" I shut the door in Jace's face.

Her smile was a ghost of its usual brightness. "She left to find Erhardt."

Her relationship with Baldwin's cousin, son and advisor to the former king, surprised me. Although I still thought she had a crush on him, they'd sometimes get together to share a meal or talk.

I plopped next to Tiny on my bed. "So why do you want me to go with you to Ginselwyn?"

"It'd be fun. And you've never been." Tiny lounged on her stomach, tracing the black flourishes stitched on my blanket.

"That's true. But it'll take forever to get there."

"We could take Arvandus."

"Not now, we can't. He's staying close to home because he's going to be a dad."

Tiny's mouth fell open. "Wow."

I grinned. "His mate Astraya is due in a week. So he wants to stay in Linneah until they're born. I just found out."

She rolled onto her back and stared at the ceiling. "Hmm. Well, I guess we could take the portal."

"Um, Sherlock, the portal's damaged."

"No, not the portal to Cloverdale. The one from Linneah to Ginselwyn."

I sat up straighter. "There's another one?"

"It's called the travel portal. The trip isn't instantaneous, but it cuts down on travel time."

"Why don't I know about this?"

"Probably because your mom keeps you on a very tight leash."

I sighed. "I know. And it's not changing anytime soon."

Her voice low, she pointed to where Jace waited on the other side of the door. "You need to give him the slip."

"Again, you're brilliant. Any idea how to do that?"

"Still thinking on it."

"Tiny?" I leaned close. "What's going on with you? For real?"

She flinched, then shrugged. "I'm fine."

My throat tightened, hurt swelling in my chest. "I was surprised Baldwin kept secrets, but now my best friend is keeping them, too."

Her eyes widened. "Brenna, I don't know how to—"

The door flew open, and Anna entered the room. "Hello, wave-keepers."

Jace stood behind her, glaring. "I could not stop her."

I grinned. "It's fine, Jace. We know she's a force of nature."

But inside I groaned a little. So close. Tiny's secret would have to wait.

After a fun visit with Tiny and Anna, I took a nap. I woke later, the yeasty smell of fresh bread wafting up from the dining room.

When I walked out my door, Jace snapped to attention. I ignored him as he followed me downstairs, where I was hoping to grab a snack. The serving staff laid out utensils and serving ware. On each table, a basket full of fragrant rolls huddled, protected by a towel. I lifted a corner and snagged one before escaping.

A walk through the castle confirmed my suspicions—my mother, Tiny, and Anna were AWOL. On a whim, I headed to the library. Maybe I could find a good book to read until supper.

The library's walls were covered with wooden bookcases, with smaller shelves at the top mounted behind etched glass panels. Big helli lanterns to my right flooded the room with light. A colorful tapestry with Linnean scrollwork hung on the opposite wall. Beside a collection of stuffed chairs and the unmanned registration desk, a waist-high case housed important books.

Terkel's Guide to Proper Etiquette, Signs and Symbols of the Jasper Territory, Dangers in the Travel Portal. The last title pulled me closer. Travel portal? Like the one Tiny mentioned? Intrigued, I picked up the book.

The castle library worked on the honor system. So I listed the date, the book I'd tucked under my arm, and signed my name. As I left the library, Jace fell into step behind me. I flipped to the foreword of the book written by some expert on portals. If there were forewords in books, I always read them, due to an unhealthy amount of OCD.

On the second floor, I almost ran over Baldwin's mother, Mariel. She grabbed my arm. "Brenna, you must go."

I offered her a genuine smile. "Hi, Mariel."

As one of the most powerful prophetesses in Linneah, she sometimes appeared bewildered. But today was a good day for her. Her eyes sparkled, her hair gleamed, and her two-toned green silk dress matched her eyes.

"Do not brood. This is part of your journey." She frowned, her eyes intent. "Do not give sadness a foothold."

"I'm working on it, Mariel. It's been a difficult visit." I wanted to add it was her son's fault but held the words inside.

"Yes, he can be stupid. It takes time for boys to become men."

There wasn't enough time in the universe for him to grow up.

"But now you are needed elsewhere. You must go. Evil is rising. Ginselwyn is dying. Help a friend, but save a nation." She leaned forward and whispered, "Remember—standing still is not an option."

Before I could respond, she was gone in a whirl of silk.

Jace's face revealed nothing. Had he heard her? Whatever it meant, if he'd heard it, my mother would know about it by this evening.

I walked back to my room. An envelope lay on the floor just inside my bedroom door. Picking it up, I traced the lettering on the front.

To Brenna, From Baldwin.

Usually those words put a smile on my face. Funny how a few minutes in a restaurant could change my view of everything.

Did I want to see what he had to say? Perhaps he'd apologize or use the old classic, "It's not what it looks like." What if he didn't apologize at all but instead said it was over? Sudden anger flooded through me, a red haze. I didn't have to listen to anything he said, ever again. Opening my desk drawer, I shoved the letter inside. So there. *Sit there and think about what you've done, you two-timing liar.*

With a knock on my door, Tiny peeked in.

"Bad news." She closed the door and dropped onto the bed. "Anna can't go with us to Ginselwyn."

"Why?"

"She's grounded again. Her mom won't let her."

That girl got grounded more than anyone else I knew. "And you think my mom will let me?"

Tiny worried her bottom lip. "I need you."

Sitting next to her, I nudged her shoulder. "What's going on? Why do you need me?"

Her shoulders drooped. "For moral support. I'm engaged."

Chapter Four

For a moment, I expected her to laugh. But she remained somber. "You—you're serious?"

"I have to go to Ginselwyn to meet my fiancé."

"Wait a second. What fiancé?"

Tiny nestled back against the pillow. Under her gauzy skirt, her aura glistened a sickly yellow. "Weldens arrange marriages. I've always said I wanted to marry for love, like normal people, and my mom agreed. But recently, my father decided it was essential for me to marry and arranged my engagement. So my parents want me to come home to meet this guy. My mom had planned to take the portal here on Sunday, visit for a day or two, then continue on to Ginselwyn to talk to my dad. Now that the portal's damaged, she'll have to fly to Reno."

I was having trouble keeping up. "What's in Reno?"

"The portal to Ginselwyn. We own a tiny piece of land with a portal on it. I've been waiting here until she arrives at Ginselwyn, hoping she can talk him out of it."

"Tiny, you can't marry. You're only sixteen."

She shrugged. "Weldens marry young. But the engagement might be enough to satisfy everyone for a year. Maybe two."

"Wow." Getting married now? My nebulous plans included a husband and kids someday in the far-away future. Funny, Baldwin had always been—I clamped down on the thought. It was over.

At another knock, Mariel entered my room. She shut the door and propped her hands on her hips. "Why are you still here?"

"Mariel, uh, my mother's not going to—"

"Come." She pulled Tiny and me from the bed. "You both need to be on your way. You have no time to lose. I told you already, evil is rising."

I gaped at her. "Evil is rising? Speaking of which, have you seen my mother when she's angry?"

"Leave a note, and I will explain. The vision claims you both must go." She pulled several necklaces from her pocket. Each chain held metal discs embossed with unique designs. Linnean money, and a lot of it. "Here." She thrust the necklaces at me.

I backed up a step, hands raised. "That's a huge pile of money."

"Yes, it is. You will need it."

"I have some money of my own."

She began dropping necklaces over my head. "The trip to Ginselwyn is expensive."

"Mariel, stop," I protested. "I can't take your money."

"You must. You may pay me back when you return, if you prefer, but it is hardly necessary. After all, we are almost family."

The pang in my heart returned. "Sorry, I don't think that's going to happen."

She gave me a mysterious smile. "The Creator has a way of surprising us."

I was done with surprises and her lying, cheating son. If Elyon wanted me and Baldwin together, it'd take a miracle.

She placed a wrapped bundle in my hands. "Food for your journey."

I still wasn't buying it. "Can I grab something from down-stairs before I leave? Because if I don't show up, Mom's going to wonder where I am."

Mariel squinted at me. "Do you question everyone like this? You will be fine. As I said, I will explain to your mother. Your friend needs help." She turned to Tiny, who stood near the doorway. "There is plenty of food for you both. Go to your room and pack your bag. Meet Brenna at the travel portal."

"Where is it?" I grabbed my bag from the corner.

Mariel pointed toward the ocean. "On the beach, near the steps."

My scrawled note to Mom blamed Mariel and was filled with apologies for failing to wait for her approval. While Mariel distracted Jace, I placed the note on my bed, threw a few things in my bag, and headed for the beach.

On the deserted shoreline, I took a moment for one more message. *Hey, Arvandus, I have to go. I'm at the travel portal, waiting for Tiny. It looks like we're both going to Ginselwyn.*

His reply was quick. *Do you need me to fly you?*

No, I'll be back soon, probably no more than a week. You stay here with Astraya. I'll miss you.

I waited, then felt his response. *And I, you. Please be careful. Although stories are exaggerated, the travel portal can be dangerous if caution is not used. Fly true, Brenna.*

Thank you. I will.

The brisk wind filled the silver-gray sea with whitecaps. I quickly laced my hair into a braid and inspected the cliff face where steps led down to the sea. Mariel had mentioned the portal's entrance was nearby.

Wind had worn the cliff's solid bulk smooth. No doorways, fissures, or slivers of light appeared. I continued to inspect the cliff, and a dim outline of a man materialized. In seconds, his image solidified a few feet in front of me.

I gasped and stepped back.

Dressed in a coarse gray cloak and brown leggings, he blinked against the wind. "Hello. Windy day, I see." He smiled, and I instinctively smiled in return. Of average height and build, his blue eyes twinkled above a cropped beard and mustache. His white, shoulder-length hair was tied back in a ponytail, his hairstreak a vivid strip of vermilion. Wrapping his gray cloak against the wind, he looked up the beach. "Ah, a Linnean guard. A rare sight here."

A quick look confirmed his statement. Two men strode down the beach in my direction. He was right—the Linnean guard rarely came to the beach unless they were ordered to. Which meant they had followed me—on Mom's orders.

I flipped up my hood to hide my face. That would buy me a few seconds. Before I could figure out my next move, the man moved closer and gestured to the cliff face. "Are you looking for the entrance?"

"Do I look that lost?"

"A bit. You need to walk straight for the cliff steps, like you are going to run into the area behind the staircase. Do not fear. It is impossible to miss."

"Thanks." I turned to leave. His hand on my arm stopped me.

"Are you traveling on your own?"

"No, I'm meeting someone." But I couldn't wait for Tiny here. The soldiers marched closer. "I'll wait for her inside."

"Please take care. It has become more dangerous in the travel portal in the last year or so."

"I thought the stories were exaggerated?"

"Oh, they are, to some degree. You will be fine if you travel with your friend."

"Thanks again."

He smiled, the gesture warming me even while he backed away. "It is my pleasure. Travel safe, Brenna."

Hurrying toward the underside of the stone staircase, my steps faltered. I'd never told him my name.

I turned. No time for questions. He hurried toward the oncoming soldiers. "Pardon me, good fellows." His voice carried above the roar of the surf. "I am here to repair the portal. Could you escort me to Queen Sarah?"

Taking the opportunity to escape, I approached the cliff face. A pleasant haze enveloped me, followed by a feeling of suction. The next moment, I stumbled into a dim room. I rolled my shoulders, trying to dispel the feeling of being squeezed through a toothpaste tube.

The travel portal entrance resembled a welcome center. Gray pavement led to three tunnels, each labeled with a destination. One read *Matana Island,* still another *Wildamek,* and the last, *Restrooms.* Against the wall, a bored-looking attendant sat at an information desk and read a book. Where should I wait for Tiny? If I went to the bathroom, I might miss her. A small bench placed against the wall near the information desk seemed like a safe place to wait.

I settled on the bench, aware of the attendant who kept shooting me curious glances.

After more than several minutes of his staring, I looked up. "Can I help you with something?"

"What do you mean?"

"I mean, you've been staring at me for a while now, and it's rude."

He sniffed, his thin nose wrinkling like he smelled something bad. "Speaking of rude..."

"Yes, I was, and you are. If I can help you, I'd be glad to. Just please stop staring."

"I thought you were the Fulfiller of the First Prophecy, but she would never be as rude as you are."

This wasn't the first time I'd faced someone's dashed expectations. "That is true." I tucked my red hairstreak behind my ear and slipped into the more formal Linnean speech. "She is very nice and gets along with everyone. Very pretty, too."

"I have heard such lovely things about her, probably due to her royal upbringing." He gave me a pointed look before he picked up his book. "I will offer a word of advice, although I am not sure why I should help you. If you loiter, you will draw unwanted attention. Your best choice is to keep moving."

Jiggling both legs, I tried to ignore my churning stomach. "But I was going to meet someone here."

"That is unwise. Many people meet at the trading center beyond Wildamek."

Standing, I peered down the tunnel labelled *Wildamek*. If I walked slowly, Tiny could catch up. If not, then the trading center waited. Hefting my bag onto my shoulder, I waved to the attendant. "I will do that. Thank you for the information."

He returned to his book.

After a quick restroom trip which I couldn't avoid, I adjusted my bag, then headed down the tunnel. How long would it take to reach Ginselwyn? No idea.

Cobblestone soon transitioned to a stone with thick veins of gold and silver. Helli lanterns were mounted high in polished silver brackets every couple of yards, offering reassurance. The stone's veining shimmered in the light. People hurried in both directions, offering reserved smiles when our eyes met. The tunnel's high ceilings and wide pathways made danger improbable. Too obvious and too much light.

I wish I'd had time to read the book I'd taken from the library, because all I had were warnings from other people. After five minutes, I stopped at the sign reading *Wildamek Exit. Hamlin Bay Ahead.* The tunnel to Linneah's neighboring city veered to the left before disappearing into black nothingness. After flying over Wildamek last year, I had no desire to visit its steep mountains and dark forests.

Opening my bag, I found a granola bar from last month. I nibbled on the stale bar and waited for a few minutes. Tiny should've caught up by now. Anxiety urged me to turn around and head back to the information desk.

Staying still is not an option. Mariel's words echoed in my memory. I had to keep moving, even if at a crawl.

My footsteps echoed off the empty tunnel. After ten minutes of walking, the conditions in the tunnel deteriorated. The helli lanterns shrunk to smaller models, spaced at wider intervals. Some lanterns were missing, their rusted shells hanging empty. Flimsy wooden boards covered holes in the beat-up walls, and rusted mesh patches shielded openings curving from the main tunnel. Deep ruts in the path made me trip, and a disgusting, smelly liquid trickled in the gutter. Where was Tiny? And where was that trading center? Dread climbed my stomach walls.

My footsteps still reverberated in the tunnel, but they sounded different, louder. Hair lifted on the back of my neck. I couldn't do this anymore. I'd go back, wait for Tiny, bother the welcome desk attendant if I had to. Taking a deep breath, I turned.

Four hooded figures in brown robes advanced. I had no time to run.

When they came close enough, I challenged them. "What do you want?"

One of them stepped forward and slid a knife from his sleeve, along with a bag. "Put your money in the bag, and you will not be hurt."

The voice was young, and the hood obscured the upper part of his face. The bottom half was tattooed with dotted lines that disappeared under his hood, the classic sign of a Shadow Power addict. When I hesitated, he snapped his fingers. The other three moved closer, their features coming into focus under their hoods. Three more men with dotted lines covering their faces, beady eyes, and the sharp smell of rotting spices. Another hallmark of Shadow Power. One had a crooked nose. Another had a scar carved across a cheek. The third twisted a rope through his hands.

"I don't have any money."

The leader's mouth curled into a smirk. The knife flashed, slicing my cloak open. I jumped back. The necklaces jingled, metal glinting in the shadows. "Liar."

A warm trickle slid down my throat. I reached up, and my fingers came away smeared with blood. Fear clutched my stomach and twisted. "That's mine. I need it for my trip."

The leader laughed, and it sounded familiar. "It is not yours anymore. Put it in the bag."

I produced a ball of fire the size of a tennis ball. A warning. "No."

Scarface and Nose Job took a step back.

The leader sheathed the knife. "You have become powerful in only a year."

"Who are you?"

Producing a handful of what looked like pale-blue sand from his pocket, he shrugged. "It does not matter." Before I could react, he blew the sand in my face.

I couldn't back up fast enough.

It whirled, engulfing me. I tried not to breathe. My fireball sputtered, dying a quick death. The tunnel walls undulated. Despite my circumstances, I grinned blissfully when the drug hit my system.

As my legs collapsed, the leader caught me. Faces shuffled and curved like a kaleidoscope. He turned to the man holding the rope. "Tie her up and follow me."

Rope Guy snapped the thick cord and stalked toward me.

Chapter Five

I squirmed on my mattress of rocks. My shoulders ached, and I strained at the rope binding my wrists. Opening my eyes didn't help. The blurry walls rippled like a hula dancer's hips.

Closing my eyes, I took a slow, deep breath. No panicking allowed. I did a quick mental inventory. Hard stone floor. Arms tied. No gag. No serious injuries. I slit open my eyes, relieved the stone walls remained still. A brick fire pit sat in the center of a large room, small flames throwing out meager heat. Although I lay near the fire, damp air iced my arms and legs. My captors sat at a large table near the far wall, breaking my necklaces into pieces and dividing the coins.

Nose Job leaned back in his chair. "We need more. There are four of us."

"Shut it, Iko." When the leader turned, I almost choked. It wasn't a man, but a woman I knew, someone I hadn't seen in months.

Rosamunde.

The last I'd seen her, she'd run away from me and Baldwin and *toward* the army invading Linneah. Traitor.

She paced next to the table. "We will have to hit a few more marks."

Scarface grinned. "We could hold the pupella for ransom."

I winced at the Linnean curse. If I'd used that word, my mom would ground me. For a year.

Rosamunde considered. "Hmm. We need to be sure she has a wealthy family. No more mistakes."

She didn't recognize me?

Scarface leaned toward Rosamunde. "Did you see her clothes? They are expensive."

She nodded. "It is an idea worth considering. Do not rough her up, then. Treat her gently."

Nose Job's voice lowered to a growl. "We are already doing that with the first one."

Rosamunde's voice dropped the temperature in the room by several degrees. "Yes, and it will continue until further notice. Unless you fine gentlemen would like to make a living somewhere else?"

The men shot each other looks but said nothing.

When Rosa began walking toward me, I slammed my eyes shut.

She stopped near my feet. "How are we today?"

I pretended to be asleep. There was no way she could've seen my eyes slitted open from across the room.

Someone behind me spoke, his voice raspy. "Water?"

"Iko, get our guest some water." Her voice lowered. "Say nothing about our other guest, and we will release you early. Understand?" She grasped my arm. I held my breath. "And you may as well sit up. You jumped when he spoke, so I know you are awake."

Stupid, stupid, stupid.

I struggled to a sitting position while she talked, her voice mellow and warm like I remembered, but still low.

"You will not answer to Brenna for the duration of your time here. You are now Jamie. If you are smart, you will go along with what I say."

Nose Job approached with a glass. She held it so the young Kell next to me could take several swallows. The Kell's features were angular, his cheekbones sculpted ridges. When he blinked, the typical twin set of eyelids fluttered, the first set closing vertically. His red shirt with the Linnean star and brown pants, though ripped, identified him as a castle employee. He was tied up like me, and his bloodshot eyes stood out in his pale face.

Rosa walked back to the table with the empty glass and began to talk with the men in low tones. Their voices ebbed and flowed, a murmur of indistinguishable sound.

My shoulders burned from being bound. Concentrating to generate some heat, I stretched. The fibers warmed, and the rope gave a little. It'd take time, but it would break—eventually.

I turned to find my fellow prisoner studying me.

"Hey, how's it going?" That was me, a sparkling, witty conversationalist.

"You are Brenna the Firebrand, Fulfiller of the First Prophecy."

"According to her, I'm Jamie."

"Yes, I heard. I'm Gareth, runner for Queen Sarah. You're her daughter."

A memory of a previous conversation flickered. "Did you take a message to my dad, Harrison James?"

"Yes, I did. And then I delivered another in Kelda Hills but was captured on my way back. I thought the travel portal would provide a faster trip home."

"I guess we're both unlucky. What did she mean about releasing you early?"

"They're holding me for ransom, but they won't get much. My wife is pregnant with our first child, and my sick mother lives with us."

"Does Rosa know this?" The woman I knew would never be that unfeeling.

"Who's Rosa?"

"The leader." I gestured with my head toward the table. When I wiggled my hands again, my wrists stung.

"Here in the travel portal, she's known as the Scorpion."

Wow. I hadn't seen that one coming. "What does she do, aside from robbing people?"

"Whatever she wants. She's a pirate and a well-known crime leader. The Scorpion controls most underground activity."

Rosa stood, stalling our conversation. She handed a small package to each man. "That is all. You may have your daily share now, but do not take it here."

Each man took a package and headed for the door. Scarface turned back to Rosa, his face suspicious. "What about the prisoners?"

"They are both tied. If you did your job, I can handle them."

Once the men left, she pulled a chair over and sat facing us. "Now that we are alone, we can talk freely. The drug will keep them occupied for a few hours, but both of you have presented me with an interesting problem."

It was my first unobstructed close-up of Rosamunde. Her once-glossy hair hung like brown straw, and her eyes lacked sparkle. The dotted tattoos on her face aged her.

"I have already presented my demands to your family, Gareth. And, Jamie, I believe I can get double for your safe return."

"You can call me Brenna. Nobody else is here." Before I could continue, her foot lashed out. It caught me in the chest and sent me crashing into the wall.

For a second, my lungs stopped working. My head pounded. I was going to die.

She spoke, her voice hard and brittle as glass. "That is not acceptable. For as long as you are here, you are Jamie."

Absolutely. Whatever. I concentrated on dragging in precious oxygen.

After several breaths, I maneuvered into a sitting position. Tough to do with bound arms. I probably looked like a beached whale. "Maybe you could let Gareth go?"

Her musical laugh wrapped around us. "And why would I do that?"

"His family doesn't have any money."

"Yes, I discovered that."

I scooted closer to Gareth and the pale warmth of the fire. "You could let him go. Ask double for me."

"If I let Gareth go, I will have to ask triple for you."

"You could." My hands rasped free of the binding. I resisted the urge to roll my shoulders. "But Linneah does not give in to terrorist's demands."

"Please. The daughter of the queen? You will pull in a nice amount, especially if there is evidence of torture."

My blood froze.

"But I would like to keep things civil. So to start, I will present my terms to the esteemed Queen Sarah. If all goes well, she will meet my demands, and we will let you go. If not, then I will proceed to the next step."

"Torture?" I squeaked the word out.

"I dislike it, but sometimes, there is no other way."

I couldn't figure her out, and the words slipped out of my mouth before I could stop them. "Rosa, what happened to you?"

When she gave me a strange look, I continued.

"You had a powerful position, friends, respect. I don't understand why you threw it all away."

She leaned toward me, her face stretching into a snarl. "I have a powerful position, money, and respect now. Plus, I am my own commander. Nobody will ever use me. Ever again." With a violent shove, she pushed the chair away. It fell over, clattering onto the stone floor. "Story time is over."

Stalking back to the table, she picked up a package like the ones she'd given the men. She ripped it open and poured the contents onto the table before grabbing a few weird instruments from a cabinet.

"Shadow Power." Gareth kept his voice low. "She's making rollers."

As Rosa began assembling Shadow Power cigarettes, she seemed to forget us. Despite our precarious situation, a risky plan began to form.

I turned to Gareth. "Give me your hands." While her back was to us, I forced heat into his bindings. After a few minutes, the rope fell off.

"Are you planning an escape?"

Bright boy, that Gareth.

"Shh, yes. Don't move too much. We don't want her to know your hands are free. If things don't go well, don't wait for me. The first opportunity you get to run, do so."

He paused. "That's not acceptable."

"What?"

"As a man of honor, I should make sure you are safe first. It's my duty."

Aw, how sweet. And stupid. "No, your duty is to get home to your wife and unborn baby."

"I will not run and leave you behind like a coward. My gift could prove useful."

I sighed. "Let me guess. You're a runner, so your gift is speed?"

His lips twitched, his eyes twinkling.

Rosa turned to look at us. But our hands were behind our backs, and apparently she saw nothing unusual. When she turned back around, Gareth continued.

"I'm an amplifier, also known as an Ampbrand."

I'd never heard of that. "What can you do?"

"On my own, not very much. But I can amplify your talent. Together, we could start a large fire."

"There's no fuel. Everything in here is made of stone or metal."

"Not everything."

I glanced around. The wooden table and chairs. The counter and cabinets along the wall. But a bonfire could choke us, trap us in a burning grave, possibly explode. I closed my eyes. He had a young, pregnant wife waiting for him, and there were so many ways this could go wrong.

He nudged me with his shoulder. "You might remember the drug strengthens them."

As a Wisdom Trainer, Rosa was smart. And as a Shadow Power user, she was powerful. We had to strike before she lit a cigarette. "Get as close to the door as you can without her noticing."

"I'll need to touch you to amplify your talent."

"Don't worry. I'll be right behind you."

We stood and crept to the far corner before I slipped in front of him. While I gathered my talent, he placed a hand on my shoulder. Raw power shuddered through my arms, and I released the amped fireball. With a crackle, the flames caught and raced the length of the scarred wood. Rosamunde jumped to avoid the flames, and her eyes widened as she saw us.

"No!" she screamed. She tried to beat out the flames heading for the drugs. When that failed, she turned on us, her expression ugly.

She'd wanted both the drugs and us. She'd lost the first.

I sent a flamer beam toward her. "Run," I told Gareth, his hand still warm on my shoulder. A usual flamer beam stung but left no marks. This one hit her leg and left a crater. I gasped. With a curse, she fell, her injury blistering.

Gareth reached the door and pulled. Then yanked with both hands. "Locked."

The flames crackled, devouring the wood, drugs engulfed in flames. Rising smoke scented the air with the typical Shadow Power aroma: bad spices. My stomach flipped. We needed out.

I ran toward him, reaching for his arm. When we touched, I released another fireball at the wooden door. The deafening explosion created an opening, the edges of the wooden hole burning. Gareth slipped through.

Before I could clear the door, a brutal jerk on my braid stopped me.

"Where are you going, pupella?" Rosa seized my arms, her grip iron hard as she dragged me back into the room. "You ruin my supply and then leave? You will pay."

I struggled, the madness in her eyes scaring me more than her death grip.

"I could slit your throat and be done with it, but you are money. So I will tie you back up, and when the men get back, I will give them some play time."

Terror icing my skin, I struggled harder. I had no weapon. With the way she was holding my arms, I couldn't use my talent. Desperate, I shot a fireball anyway, which sputtered and died on the floor. Pungent smoke filled the room. The unforgettable scent took me back to every unpleasant encounter I'd endured with Talus last year.

Rosa laughed. "You thought you could escape. A poor decision on your part. You will—" Her eyes rolled back, and she fell.

Gareth stood behind her, holding a rock slab. "Come. Before her men return."

I scanned the room for my bag, but it had disappeared. Linking hands, Gareth and I rushed from the room. We exited into a dark tunnel, but it didn't look like the one I remembered. A pinpoint of light at the end glowed like a beacon.

"Where are we?"

He shook his head. "I don't know. I was knocked unconscious when I was kidnapped."

We set a quick pace, hurrying toward what I hoped was an escape to the main tunnel. Thankfully, it remained empty in our rush for freedom. I was hyper-focused on remaining alive and far away from Rosamunde.

At the end of the tunnel, we skidded to a stop. A flimsy screen blocked our exit, but it swung open at Gareth's push. We stumbled into the main access tunnel. This time it teemed with people hurrying toward the city.

I gulped deep breaths. "What's with all the people?"

"Not sure. I don't know how long they held us. However, we cannot stay here. We need to move far away in case she pursues us."

"Let me guess. You were heading for Linneah?"

"Yes, and you should head that way, too. Where's your security?"

"My friend Tiny was going to meet me. We were heading toward her hometown."

Gareth's eyes narrowed. "Shaynedel Lee from Ginselwyn? That's a long trip. Your mother authorized this?"

No. Not at all. I shrugged, hoping I didn't look too guilty.

He crossed his arms.

Although I wanted to head in the opposite direction, I couldn't go any farther on my own. "I'll head toward Linneah with you."

"That's an excellent idea. Why?"

"Tiny's probably coming this way. And the Scorpion and her men wouldn't expect me to go the opposite way I was originally heading."

Gareth pursed his lips. "Those are good reasons."

I pulled on his shirt. "Let's put some distance between her and us."

He followed me, his expression still thoughtful. "Why are you and Shaynedel separated?"

Sighing, I tried to imagine where Tiny might be. "No idea. She was supposed to meet me at the portal entrance. When she didn't show, I couldn't wait any longer. I had to—" I stopped. I had to get away before my mom stopped me.

"Why?"

"Sorry?"

"Why were you unable to wait any longer?"

The soldiers, my mother. I couldn't tell him any of it. If I did, he'd haul me to the Queen's chambers faster than I could say trouble. "Shaynedel has to get to Ginselwyn right away. Mariel the prophetess said it was important I go with her. She gave me money, food, and told me to hurry to the travel portal. I assumed my friend was right behind me." More or less.

"Mariel's crazy."

"Excuse me?"

"Once, she was very wise. Not so anymore."

I grew the tiniest bit defensive. "She's the castle's best prophetess."

"The visions have taken their toll. I'm only stating common opinion."

"Just because it's common doesn't mean it's right."

"True." Gareth said nothing more.

My stomach sank. Did I listen to Mariel for the wrong reasons? Maybe I wasn't supposed to be here at all. But leaving the heartache named Baldwin had been my first priority. When Mariel had mentioned the vision, it was the perfect opportunity to get away and support Tiny. I couldn't even imagine what an arranged marriage would be like, and I'd want my friends around to encourage me, too.

We continued walking toward Linneah, our progress slowed by the clusters of people going in the other direction. Many of them wore the common clothes of laborers, tan pants and off-black tunics.

The farther we walked, the more I worried. She should've been here, somewhere.

After passing the exit for Hamlin Bay, I continued to search for a white-blonde head. More nail-biting minutes passed. No Tiny.

"Gareth?" I moved closer to him so I didn't have to yell.

"Yes?"

"Where's the trading center?"

He slowed to a stop. "Right here, down this corridor." He pointed to his right, where a passageway branched off into the gloom. The sign read *Half-Mile Down Trading Center.*

My scalp prickled. The corridor carried a funky, musty smell, and shadows cluttered the passageway. "I have to see if Tiny's here. Can you go with me?"

He gave me a smile. "Absolutely."

Our walk through the murky half-light sent my pulse skittering. Despite the tunnel's shabby appearance, a weak but welcome light glowed from the door at the end.

Chapter Six

THE FLIMSY WOODEN DOOR creaked open and then slammed shut, rattling the grimy glass pane. A broad fireplace with a roaring fire near the bar lit the room, leaving dark corners. Occupants in dim nooks or booths nursed a drink or ate a meal. The filthy floor pulled at my boot soles. Yuck.

Gareth nudged me farther into the room and spoke close to my ear. "Confidence. Don't hunch your shoulders. You look like an easy mark. Head for the counter."

Right. I faked my best swagger up to the counter and slid onto a stool. No mirror hung on the opposite wall, just a corkboard with yellowed notices pinned to it. Inadequate light eked from the wall sconces high above, and bottles filled with different-colored liquids lined the counter.

Gareth slipped onto a stool next to me and gestured to the bartender, a Camlo with an eyebrow pierced with two gold hoops. "Two fruit sips."

The muscular man turned to fill our order, his hulking body a mountain. When he placed our fruit sips on the counter, his dark eyes narrowed.

Dropping my gaze, I squirmed in my seat.

"Someone left a message for you." He slid a folded piece of paper across the counter, its glob of wax unbroken.

I turned to Gareth as I ripped it open. "It's probably from Tiny."

But my friend's loopy script was absent, and in its place was a strong scrawl.

Brenna James, I have been tracking your progress since you left your hometown. A young girl on her own is vulnerable. My men are patrolling the portal, looking for troublemakers. Your lovely mother will worry should you encounter misfortune. You should return to the safety of your family in Linneah.

Until next time, R

My hands shook as I pocketed the note. Why was he following me? And why did he want me to go home?

Gareth took a sip of his drink. "So where's Tiny?"

My mouth suddenly dry, I took a drink of the fruit sip. Not bad, more like watery punch. "It wasn't from Tiny. It was a warning from Rune. He thinks I should go home."

"Why is Rune concerned about your welfare?"

"He's not. It's a threat, so I'm ignoring it. And you should, too. Let's focus on finding Tiny right now." Worry swirled through my stomach. Rune's bullying tactics wouldn't scare me. Right. I took another sip of my drink.

"But if he's sending you threats—"

"Can we talk about this later?"

Gareth dropped the subject. "Do you see your friend?"

"I don't see much of anything in here." I chanced another quick look. "If she's hiding in a booth somewhere, I won't know it."

He grabbed a flyer from the counter and read aloud, "Starfall Rules and Regulations."

"What's Starfall?"

"It's the reason for all the people in the tunnel. Many of them will set up booths to sell wares and equipment to the gatherers."

I drained my glass and set it aside. "I have no idea what you're talking about."

"Give me a moment." He turned to the bartender. "Excuse me, friend, what day is today?"

The bartender's gold hoops jerked as he leaned over the counter and glared at Gareth. "First of all, I got friends. You don't look like one of 'em. And second, why do you care what today is?" His dark skin gleamed in the low light.

"TPC."

"Ah." The bartender's gruff demeanor softened. "Tuesday. But I still ain't your friend."

"Of course." Gareth relaxed as the bartender headed to the other end of the bar. "TPC stands for Travel Portal Crawl. It happens when you stay in the travel portal too long. You lose track of days."

"How long does that take?"

"We're in no danger of it. It would take a few seasons at least." He gestured to the flyer. "Starfall's in five days. Every traveler is heading to Kelda Hills."

"For the last time, what's Starfall?"

"It's a natural but rare astral event. Bella's Comet orbits Eventyr, our planet. The comet crashes through the Petrus Rings every one hundred times. When it does, it dislodges particles in the rings, and they fall through the atmosphere and land near Kelda Hills."

As Gareth spoke, he grabbed a pencil and drew a rough map on the back of the flyer. Little rolling dunes for Kelda Hills, broad flat lines for Aviva Desert. He added bigger peaks on the left side of the paper and labelled them the Steen Mountain Range, with the city of Syeira at the top left of the map.

"People get together to watch Starfall?" Meteor showers on Earth came to mind.

"Some do. Braver souls gather the stars. And still others travel to the desert to sell equipment to the gatherers."

Leaning forward, I propped my elbows on the counter. "Why would anyone collect chunks of space debris?"

"Because they're extremely valuable. As those 'chunks' travel through the atmosphere, they're sculpted into beautiful gems that fetch a handy sum. Resourceful gatherers can become rich off one Starfall."

"'Scuse, lady." A tug on my tunic's hem drew me from the conversation. A boy, about eight or nine, stood at my side, chewing on his lip. His ragged clothes were smeared with dark stains.

"Yes?"

He scrutinized me, his dark eyes unreadable. "Someone wants ta talk ta you in the back room."

"Who?"

"Don't know. Gave me a coin, told me ta find the black Linnean lady."

Gareth touched my forearm. "Not safe, you know."

I eyed the back room. No light seeped from its recesses. "I am not black."

The boy smirked. "Hair is. Dark as pitch, it is. Or Bragnaborn oil."

You could make oil from those cute little parasites? Ew. "Was it a man?"

The boy tilted his head, considering. "Only an old lady." He skittered away, into a corner's gloomy shadow.

"It couldn't be Rosa, the Scorpion," I mused aloud.

Gareth shook his head. "Meeting a stranger doesn't seem like a good idea."

"But what if it's a message from Tiny? She might need help or be in trouble. Or maybe she's decided not to travel, and that's why I can't find her."

Gareth sighed. "We'll go together. I'll have my hand on your shoulder when we enter the room to amplify your talent if needed."

We headed for the back, Gareth right behind me. The closer we moved to the back, the darker its alcoves became. My gut tightened. This felt all wrong, but I couldn't leave without meeting this person.

The main room narrowed into a dim hallway, which led to the back room. I edged into it and paused, allowing my eyes to adjust. Dark olive walls made the room appear smaller, and red helli lanterns cast a rosy hue on everything. Wooden flooring finished off the space, and thankfully, it looked cleaner than the main room.

Weaponry hung on the wall as decoration—glittering knives, elaborate shields, a few double-bladed axes. The vibe screamed neo-torture chamber, minus the rack. Several booths and square tables hugged the walls, as if afraid to venture too far into the center. At a booth near the back stood a dark-robed figure. Shorter than me, and a hunchback. Completely covered. My stomach seized up, and I stopped short.

In a low voice, Gareth said what I was thinking. "That doesn't look like Shaynedel."

The robed figure gestured. "Come. Sit."

I forced my feet to move closer. "I'll stand, thanks."

"Sit." Hard. Commanding.

"Okay." I pulled Gareth into the booth with me.

Dark curtains hung suspended from the ceiling. The figure pulled one around the booth, giving us complete privacy. Sitting down, she flipped back the hood, revealing white-blonde hair. And smiled.

Relief flooded me. "Tiny! Where have you been?"

Gareth relaxed.

Tiny pointed to herself. "Me? I've been waiting for hours."

Only hours? It felt like it had been a week. Gareth and I shared a look. "We had a few unexpected delays."

My friend leaned forward. "The guy at the desk said you'd left hours before. Why didn't you wait for me at the entrance?"

"That guy said I shouldn't, that it was dangerous. Apparently, it made me a target for bad people."

She pointed at Gareth. "Are you 'bad people'?"

"Gareth, meet Shaynedel Lee, also known as Tiny. Tiny, meet Gareth, a runner for Linneah and fellow prisoner."

"Fellow prisoner?"

"I ran into an old friend, Rosamunde. Also now known as the Scorpion. She found me while I was waiting for you."

Eyes wide, Tiny gasped. "I'm so sorry."

"It's all good." Kind of. If I ignored being bound and the threat of torture.

Tiny wouldn't meet my eyes. "Your mom caught up with me. It was at least an hour before I could leave."

I winced. And that's exactly why I'd left early.

She continued. "Yeah, that was fun. She's not happy with you. What did you say in that letter anyway?"

"That I was sorry, but Mariel was making me go with you to Ginselwyn." With a lot more *I'm sorry's,* but I didn't mention that part.

Tiny leaned forward. "You're lucky. A message from Matana Island distracted her, then a guard arrived with the guy who's supposed to repair the portal. She was going to send Jace with me, but I left when she wasn't paying attention."

Mom wouldn't be happy about that either.

Tiny settled in her seat. "So was Rosamunde happy to see you?"

"Not exactly." I filled her in, then finished with, "Gareth was my rescuer. If it hadn't been for his Amp power and his handiness with rocks, I'd be dead. Our plan is to put as much distance between us and our captors as possible." I eyed her. "How did you know we were here?"

Her eyes were wide. "I saw you come in. That's why I bribed the boy and headed for the back."

"Why all the secrecy?"

"I didn't want people to see a female Welden alone. It didn't feel safe."

Gareth spoke up. "That was wise. And because of that, I will escort both of you ladies home."

Unbelievable. "But I thought—"

A muscle ticked in Gareth's jaw. "You thought what? That traveling alone or even with a friend was an intelligent choice? We were almost killed."

I raised my chin. "But we weren't."

"Your mother is not in favor of this trip."

"My mother is not in favor of anything that allows me freedom." Anger grew in my chest. "I've had it with everyone trying to control me. My mother, Jace, you. I'm done. I'm going with Tiny to Ginselwyn. Period."

Gareth rubbed his forehead. "But why?"

"Because." I couldn't go back. I. Just. Couldn't.

Tiny waved a hand. "Go ahead. You can tell him."

For a second, I thought she wanted me to tell Gareth about Baldwin. Clearer thinking won. "She's meeting her fiancé for the first time. This is an arranged marriage, and she's never met him. I want to be there to support her. The fact that Mariel thinks I should go is important, regardless of your opinion."

Tiny wrinkled her brow. "His opinion? What do you mean?"

I had to tamp down another rush of defensiveness. "He thinks she's certifiable."

Gareth shook his head. "I didn't say that."

"Excuse me," I amended. "He said she was crazy."

Tiny gave him a reproachful look. "That is *so* not nice." She turned to me. "Where's your bag?"

I grimaced. "My bag, my cloak, the money—they're gone. So you'll have to pay our tab."

"You ran up a tab? Thanks."

Gareth gave her a sheepish look. "Just two fruit sips. Sorry."

Tiny pulled a backpack out from under her cloak. "I don't have that much. And—" A horrified expression transformed her face. "You needed that money."

"Well, it would've been nice. But I can make do until we reach Ginselwyn. Didn't you bring some food with you?"

Gareth's voice was firm. "You are not going to Ginselwyn."

Tiny ignored him. "I don't care about the food." Pulling a silver money chain from the bottom of the bag, she pulled off a few coins. "You needed that money."

"So you said. Why?"

Sighing, she put the bag back under her cloak. "It was your entrance money. Every unattached female has to pay an entrance fee to get into Ginselwyn."

Her words just didn't make sense. "A fee?"

Gareth leaned back. "That's true. Women are viewed as property, and if they don't have an owner—"

"An owner? We're not pets!"

He held up his hands. "It's their view, not mine. Like I was saying, if the woman doesn't have a husband or guardian, she must pay a considerable entrance fee."

Tiny dropped her head into her palm. "We have to go back. There's no other way."

Two loud male voices carried from the hallway and penetrated the curtain. "If we find them both, we will get double. You remember what she said."

"What about the notices?"

"Let's try our luck first. I have a good feeling about this."

A sour taste filled my mouth. The blood drained from Gareth's face.

Tiny threw up her hood. "Brenna, under the table. Gareth, grab my hand and give me a little boost."

While Gareth grasped Tiny's hand, I scrambled under the table. Weldens didn't have legs, just a lighted aura from their thighs down. The muted glow seeping from under Tiny's cloak exposed everything in disgusting detail. Bits of moldy unidentifiable scraps lay along the wall, and an immense hairy spider skittered past my boots.

I muffled a squeak, scrambled for safety, and almost face-planted in my effort to get away. Before I could find a place free of hairy arachnids, Tiny's other hand snagged the back of my tunic, pinning me in place. I crouched in a pool of indeterminate liquid, heat from her aura seeping into my shoulders.

The sound of the curtain being ripped aside grated in the small room. "Well, well, isn't this cozy?" Two pairs of boots stood next to the table. Chills wracked my body. I knew those voices.

"I was reading his palm." Seven or eight decades had seeped into Tiny's voice. "You must wait your turn."

"Iko, neither of them are Linnean or Kell. And she's old."

"Well, uh, hmm."

Under the table, I frowned. Gareth was a Kell. Anyone could see his double-lidded eyes and high cheekbones. Both men were dumber than a bucket of hair.

"Privacy." Tiny's voice screeched through the room. "I must have it. Losing the vision, I am."

Yoda, she was.

Scarface growled. "Shut it, woman, or you'll lose more'n that."

Gareth was shoved farther into the booth. I pressed my back against the bottom of the booth when one of the men's worn boots slid into the cramped quarters. "I'm next."

Underneath the creak, Tiny's voice firmed. "Privacy, I said."

My heart hammered.

"You, outside the curtain," Tiny demanded.

The other man stepped back, and the curtain swished shut, enclosing the four of us in a tense cocoon.

"Let go of his hand," Iko said. "My turn to get some answers."

"We are not done," Tiny protested. "He hasn't heard what his future holds."

"I'm not waitin' anymore. We're looking for a missin' couple. It's an emergency." The man banged the table, a sonic boom slamming my eardrums. Dumb *and* poor social skills.

She sighed, the sound far older than her years. With a cough and a flounce, she shoved me toward the wall. I executed some fantastic gymnastic skills to avoid Iko's boots. What size were they? Twenty?

Suspicion snaked through the other man's voice. Scarface. "What's going on in there?"

"Close your eyes and give me your hand," Tiny demanded.

Silence reigned while I waited to see if my last moments would be under a booth in a trading post. My parents would miss me. Would Baldwin? I closed my eyes against the ache and pushed the thought away.

Tiny's voice was full of manufactured wonder. "Ah. In all my years, I've never seen strength such as yours."

Iko grunted. "Don't care about it. Like I said, two people are missin'. We need to find 'em, and we think they headed east."

"That'll be fifty zoharet nomas."

Coins clinked on the table.

Tiny allowed a moment of silence. "I see them, vague though they are. They're moving slowly, heading through Wildamek toward Linneah. The female's limping, injured."

"I knew it." Iko stomped his boots in triumph, and I curled into the corner so I didn't get squished. His boots slid out of sight as he stood, the privacy curtain swishing open.

Scarface immediately started talking. "We'll take the portal to Wildamek. They shouldn't be too far ahead if she's hurt. Poor thing." Scarface's voice dripped with fake sympathy.

Tiny sighed. "Be gone. This man has waited long enough."

Gareth slid back into his place as the two men hurried down the hallway, their voices growing fainter. After a count of five, I peeked above the seat on Tiny's side.

She held a man's hand, her form barely discernible in her cloak. In Gareth's place sat a large, dark-skinned Camlo. His bald head gleamed in the pale light.

I gasped. "Where's Gareth?"

CHAPTER SEVEN

TINY DROPPED THE MAN'S hand and wilted against the booth. "They're gone."

The man's bald head sprouted hair, and his skin lightened. His features stretched and shifted until Gareth sat across from her.

My mouth fell open. "What just happened?"

He stood and pulled the privacy curtain. "Rosamunde's men."

"Not them, you."

"It was me." Tiny's voice wobbled. "With his enhancement, I stretched my illusion to include him. The men saw only what I wanted them to see."

I shook my head. "I don't get it. What illusion?"

"My talent. I use it to conceal my aura." She pushed back her bangs with a shaky hand.

Wow. After crawling from under the table, I dusted off my pants. Or tried to. "I didn't know you could do that."

"Well, I have to be careful not to overdo it."

Gareth leaned across the table. "We need to go. If they asked questions at the bar, the bartender may come looking for us."

"So we're just going to waltz past him?"

Gareth pursed his lips before Tiny raised a hand. "I can do it. I'll hide the three of us. But I'll definitely need your Amp talent, and everyone has to stay in contact with me."

I studied her closely. "Are you sure?" She'd been trembling just seconds ago.

"Do you have a better idea?"

I scanned the room, but no other exit existed. "All right, but don't go overboard. Just darken my skin. That way I'll look like a Camlo."

Gareth and Tiny shook their heads at the same time, but Gareth spoke first. "Camlos—all Camlos—are bald."

Tiny slid out of the booth. "I can stay as I am. Nobody's looking for me. And we'll keep Gareth as a Camlo, and you, girlfriend, are going to be a Kell. It'll change your looks the most." She adjusted her pack and cloak and gave Gareth a grin. "A little boost, please?"

"Just a second." I peeked into the other room. Rosamunde's men were gone.

When I returned, Tiny dropped a few coins on the table, then linked arms with me and Gareth. "Okay, boys and girls, it's showtime."

After a few seconds, I looked at Tiny. "Are you doing anything yet?"

Gareth grinned. "You're a very attractive Kell, Brenna."

I touched my cheek, but nothing felt different. So weird.

Tiny tugged us both toward the main room. "Let's go."

We proceeded through the main room, a few patrons shooting a look at our odd trio heading for the exit.

When we reached the wooden door, I breathed easier. Just a few more steps...

"Hey! You trying to skip out on your tab?"

The mountain of a bartender stood at the end of the counter, arms crossed.

Tiny turned and peered from under her hood. "Payment's on our table, young man."

He squinted, the gold hoops glittering. "Stay right there. We'll see." And he hustled toward the back room.

"Now!" Gareth urged.

As we exited the room, he released Tiny's hand. The low tones of two men talking near the end of the hallway drifted to where we stood. I knew those voices. Gareth was almost back to normal, but I grabbed his arm.

"Hold Tiny's hand. Rosamunde's men are in the hallway."

His mouth dropped open, but he clutched Tiny's hand again. His face darkened. The male Camlo was back. "Thank you," he whispered.

After a few seconds, the two men hurried into the main corridor, disappearing from our sight.

Tension released its death grip on my neck. "It's safe now."

Gareth dropped Tiny's hand, his features returning to normal. When I removed my hand from Tiny's elbow, she sagged against the wall.

I reached for her. "Are you okay?"

She waved a hand, her eyes still closed. "Fine. Just resting."

Shooting Gareth a look, I slid an arm around her shoulders. "Tiny, we need to move."

"Mm-hmm. Just a sec." Her head drooped.

Gareth caught her just as she toppled. "If you take her bag, I can carry her."

With a little maneuvering, the three of us entered the main tunnel.

If I could find a place where Tiny could rest...

I gave Gareth my best confident smile. "At the next stop, Tiny can recover. Then we'll head to Ginselwyn."

"No." He set his chin at a determined angle. Baldwin looked like that when he made a decision. "We will all travel to Linneah."

"First, Rune suggested I go home. Not doing that. Second, Tiny has to go to Ginselwyn, and I'm going with her."

Gareth grimaced but finally huffed out a breath. "With Rosamunde's men looking for us, it's too dangerous."

Terrific excuse. I'd go with it. "If we travel separately, we'll be safe. But the two of us shouldn't be seen together."

His lips firmed. "I don't like this."

I patted his arm. "Gareth, thank you so much. If it hadn't been for you, I'd be dead. But you need to get home to your wife and baby. They won't need to pay the ransom. And you can tell my mom I'm good and I love her. Tiny and I will be fine."

He stood there, considering, his eyes on Tiny. "She cannot travel the way she is."

"She just needs a quick nap."

"The closest stop is Hamlin Bay, but with Rosamunde's men searching for us..." He sighed, his shoulders slumping. "Follow me. I know a place."

Tiny dozed peacefully in his arms. As we passed the Hamlin Bay exit, I gave in to the urge to look behind us. No one gave us any extra attention, but I still felt jittery and nervous. Stopping along the side of the tunnel, Gareth placed Tiny on a spot clear of debris. In the tunnel wall, a six-foot square screen covered a hole.

He gestured to the wire-covered opening. "This opens. Both of you crawl in, close it behind you, and stay there until Shaynedel has recovered. It's safer than staying in the travel portal. If you crawl back far enough, no one will know you're there." His face had uncertainty written all over it.

"Where does it go?"

"I don't know. It's unfinished. Don't attempt to use it."

"Thank you, Gareth. You're a hero."

A blush came and went on his face. "No, a hero would take you home."

"A hero acts bravely, keeps people safe. You're doing that." I shook Tiny's shoulder. "Tiny, come on."

Her bright-blue eyes blinked open. "Hmm?"

"We need to hide in a tunnel. Just for a little bit, so you can take a nap."

A blissful smile covered her face. "I like naps."

"I know you do. Let's go." I tugged her up like a toddler while Gareth moved the wire screen.

"I'll stand here for a moment to shield you, then I'll leave for Linneah."

I gave him a quick hug. "Stay away from the Scorpion and her men."

"Of course." He flashed me a quick smile. "I have an important message for the queen from her rebellious but loving daughter."

I ducked into the tunnel, then turned. Tiny stood, a slight wobble betraying her exhaustion. Reaching for her hand, I pulled her through the opening.

She stumbled in, her voice childlike. "What're we doing?"

"Taking a nap, remember?"

After Gareth waved goodbye and replaced the screen, Tiny and I moved away from the opening. Looking back, I gauged our distance. About two hundred feet. A shifting gloom surrounded us. Pulling up her hood, Tiny lay down in the small space. Her aura glowed beacon bright until I arranged her cloak to cover her bottom half.

"What's going on here?" An unfamiliar voice carried back to our hiding place.

I peeked to see what was going on. Someone marched up to Gareth. Covering most of my face with my hair, I pressed myself against the cold tunnel walls. Tiny slept on.

"I lost a message, my lord. I've been checking openings on my path."

"Unacceptable. This is an unauthorized breach and tampering with a deactivated portal opening."

"I'm terribly sorry. It was an important message for Queen Sarah of Linneah." Gareth dropped the name like a bomb.

A beat of silence, then, "Hurry on your way, and do not let it happen again."

"Thank you very much." After a moment of hesitation, Gareth left.

The officer looked down the tunnel, an indiscernible black outline. I sat still, silent, and prayed Tiny would continue to sleep. After an eternal moment, he stepped back. The shuffle of his feet echoed in our hiding place as he walked away.

My breath escaped in a rush, although my heart still raced. I got up and walked a little farther down the tunnel. How far did this passage extend? I created a small flame. The smooth walls of the tunnel sprang to life.

Intricate silver bracings every few feet supported light-brown stone walls. The gutters on both sides held dry leaves. My curiosity spiked. Strange for an unused tunnel. My firelight glowed off a silver sheen ahead. I approached a wall of...something. Although not transparent, light leaked through. The wall created a dead end, blocking further exploration. I dragged a finger across the cold, smooth surface. Slick, with a slight give, it reminded me of rubbery glass. What was this stuff? I walked back to Tiny. Why install a barrier to block a deactivated portal opening? What was on the other side?

Tiny slept on, her breathing soft and even. Maybe I should take a nap too. Who knew when I'd get the chance to sleep again? But what if there were huge bats, or snakes, or large, fanged beetles hiding in the ceiling that would savagely attack while we slept—I squeezed my eyes shut, blocking the thoughts. I'd explored as much of the tunnel as I could. It was safe and clean. I needed a nap.

When Tiny awoke, we could decide what to do next.

I woke with a start and a crick in my neck. Sitting up, I stretched and rubbed at the ache sitting at the base of my skull.

Next to me, Tiny ate, her aura peeking from the edges of her cloak. The scent of honeyed, ripe peach hung in the air. Rainfruit—my favorite.

"Want some?" She nudged my hand before dropping a large piece into my hand.

I took a bite of the slippery fruit, its sweet juices sparkling on my tongue. After devouring it, I wiped my hand on my pants and leaned against the tunnel's cold wall. "How do you feel?"

"Much better. It's been a while since I overdid it like that."

"I didn't know you could do that. It's almost like Anna's shapeshifting."

She shook her head. "No, that's a separate skill. This is an illusion. And I can't hold one that big for long. But it did the job, thanks to Gareth." She looked at the shadows enveloping us. "Where are we?"

"According to the officer that almost caught Gareth, we're in a deactivated portal opening. Gareth said we should hide here until you recovered. I explored it a little while you slept. I'm not sure it's deactivated, but it dead ends ahead." I kept my voice to a whisper to prevent our conversation from carrying.

"Where is he?"

"Probably to Linneah by now. With those guys looking for a female Linnean and male Kell? It'd be stupid to stay together."

Tiny nudged my shoulder. "Speaking of which, we should get going. The longer we're away from Linneah, the angrier your mom's going to be."

"No, we're heading to Ginselwyn, remember?"

Tiny picked at the seam of her cloak. "I don't have enough money for you. You wouldn't be allowed in."

"That's a weird law you guys have, you know? It's not like I eat too much or anything."

"That's not it. Remember learning in history class about the women's rights movement?"

I nodded.

She shrugged. "Yeah, the memo never reached Ginselwyn. Women are property, things to own. They stay quiet and support-ive, and hopefully, make good wives."

"So wrong."

"I know. But now here I am, with the same thing happening to me that's happened to every Ginselwyn female before me." She exhaled a shaky sigh.

There had to be another way. "What about your mom? She seems pretty strong. I can't see her as a quiet, submissive wife."

"In Pennsylvania and behind closed doors, she's permitted to state opinions and be somewhat independent. In front of the Ginselwyn public, forget it. My dad makes sure we keep up ap-pearances. Mom's my only ally in trying to escape this arranged marriage."

Hope sparked within me. "So it's not a done deal? There's still a chance you could marry someone you love?"

Tiny bit her lip. "I guess."

My heart lightened, excitement filling my veins. "Then there's time. Maybe when we arrive, your mom will have talked with your dad."

She threw her hands up, her voice strident. "You can't go, so it doesn't matter!"

"Shh! I've got an idea." I hadn't worked everything out, but I wasn't worried. Anything was better than returning home.

Tiny pouted and crossed her arms. "What kind of idea? Is this one of those weird ones where it seems like a good plan and then everything falls apart? Because I hate those."

I sniffed. "That hasn't happened in a long time."

Smirking, she closed her bag. "Yeah, because I've talked you out of them."

True. "Well, no one should have to face what you're facing alone. So I'm going with you. Have you ever seen a Starfall?"

"I know what it is, but I've never seen it. Why?" She hurried toward the mesh opening and peered out. "Too many people. It must be early evening."

"Wait until the tunnel clears, then we'll leave."

We moved back to our position deep in the tunnel and sat. As she covered her aura with her cloak, I gestured to it. "I've got a question for you. Why do you have an aura but your younger sisters don't?"

She smiled. "Weldens get their aura when they come into their talent. Like the Linneans' hairstreak, it usually happens in the teen years. Both Stellara and Silver are too young. Now I've got a question for you. Why'd you mention Starfall?"

I lifted my chin. "I'm going to do it."

Tiny's mouth dropped open. "I've heard it's dangerous."

"Yeah, well, life is dangerous." Her expression didn't change. I sighed. "If we go to Kelda Hills, we can get more information. I think Gareth said it would happen in five days, and we're down to four now."

"It doesn't matter what I say, you're going to do it anyway, aren't you?"

Absolutely. I needed to keep running. Once I stopped, memories would overwhelm me. Even now, sitting still, they hovered, waiting to crowd my mind and reduce me to a weeping wreck.

We talked and snacked on rainfruit until the tunnel cleared. Tiny pushed off the mesh, we both climbed out, and then we quickly placed the screen back over the hole. We hurried down the passage at almost a run to be away from our hiding place.

Several hours later, we'd left the Lennor and Aviva Desert Oasis exits behind. As we drew closer to the exit for Kelda Hills, the number of travelers increased. At a wide doorway, a lane forked away from the main tunnel. Helli lights hung on either side of a sign reading *Kelda Hills*.

I forced a bright smile. "This is our stop."

Tiny chewed on her lower lip, her blue eyes worried. "I hope we can find somewhere to stay."

"Do you have enough money for a room?"

"Yes, but not much else."

"I'll pay you back when we get home."

"Don't worry about it."

There were plenty of other problems to worry about. Despite my claim of a plan, it was more of a murky idea, not a detailed diagram with steps one through three. This operation ran on intuition and gut feelings.

The mass of people swept us into the flow heading down the path. Some people carried lanterns or helli lights. Conversation swirled, faint accents of each race overlapping. While we walked, the conversation of two Kells passing us filtered through the noise. I still wasn't used to the two sets of eyelids, although the time with Gareth had helped. They both wore tan pants and shirts made of a rough beige cloth.

The first Kell blinked furiously, his eyelids fluttering. "Do you have the map?"

"Don't need it. Just follow everyone."

The first Kell's brow wrinkled. "We'll need to set up."

"Not this early. Besides, setup is in the morning. If we haven't done it by lunch, we'll have to wait until the next day. So I made arrangements at Starfall Inn." The blond's muscles bulged when he rearranged his full pack.

"What about Goldie's?"

He snorted. "Overpriced and not as nice."

Good news—there was more than one place to stay. If we followed the crowd, we'd find our way.

The air grew close as we walked the lane of packed dirt. The rough corridor had been carved from porous rock. Brown, maroon, and cream stones studded the walls. With so many people in the enclosed area, a dozen scents jostled for space. Body odor, garlic, verum—an acrid whiff of Shadow Power, too.

As the tunnel ended, a squeezing sensation came over me. With one extra step, the pressure vanished. I rolled my shoulders, trying to dispel the feeling. A wide dirt path lined with rocks and boulders stretched before us in the moonlight. Beyond, massive boulders formed a makeshift railing before the sides fell away in a sheer drop. Far below, sand, scrub brush, and an occasional pine tree decorated the landscape. The distant, jagged silhouettes of mountains stabbed their maroon outlines against the darker sky.

Tiny and I followed the crowd until we neared a bridge. The couple in front of us stepped forward, but Tiny yanked me off the path next to the sign reading *One Maiden Chasm*. The old man behind us stepped around us and shuffled toward the bridge.

Her ice-cold fingers gripped my wrist. "We need to find another way across."

I eyed the bridge. "I think this is it."

"No." Her eyes grew wider, white discs in her pale face. "I can't."

"Why not?"

"Gephyrophobia."

"Bless you."

She gave me a withering glare. "I'm afraid of bridges."

"Oh. Since when?"

"Since forever. I just don't go around saying, 'Hi. I'm Tiny, and I'm afraid of bridges.'"

My mind scrambled for a way to help her, to help us, get to the other side. "I'll hold your hand on the way across. Just a few seconds, and you'll be done. You can do it."

A long moment passed. "Okay." She closed her eyes, then blew out a shuddering breath. "I can do this."

She moved tentatively onto the wooden slats. Behind her, a guy my age muttered under his breath.

I glared at him. "Go around if we're moving too slow for you."

He did, and the flow of the rushing crowd followed his path. Tiny and I became two slow-moving pebbles in a hurried stream of people.

Built of rough-cut lumber, the bridge was tethered with rope to the stone cliff high above our heads. We picked our way across the two-by-fours loosely joined side by side. Except where they were missing. A breeze gusted through the gaping holes. My foot caught on a splintered board, and I grabbed at the railing—one utilitarian metal bar linked to the bridge by the occasional post. The wind picked up, swirling the scent of sage while the bridge rocked. Tiny swallowed hard but kept moving.

In a hurry, three men pushed past us. Tiny slipped and pitched toward the railing. Her small hands flailed. I gasped and grabbed for her but found only air. Her aura slipped through the opening, and for one heart-stopping moment, she dangled over nothing. Slamming her eyes shut, she wrapped both arms around a post and held on.

CHAPTER EIGHT

I GRABBED HER CLOAK, winding it around my hand so she wouldn't slip from my grasp. "I've got you. It's all okay."

She whimpered, shaking her head.

"Tiny? I've got a death grip on your cloak. You're not going to fall. C'mon."

Trembling, she grabbed my other hand and pulled herself up, still clutching the railing and shaking her head.

"No! You're bigger than this stupid bridge. You can do this." Her eyes sought and found mine in the moonlit darkness.

I squeezed her hand. "Say, 'I can do this.' I know you can."

A heavyset woman bustled up behind us, carrying a large pack. "Move along, birdie. People are getting upset."

I glared at the woman, my anger a whip. "They'll have to wait. She's doing the best she can."

With one look at Tiny's frozen face, she patted her shoulder. "The bridge used to scare me close to death too, dovey. The trick is to focus straight ahead. It may not feel secure, but it's been here a couple thousand times. You can trust it. I'll follow right behind you."

Tiny's gaze fastened ahead in a dead stare. Her aura quivering, she whispered prayers under her breath. Despite my firm grip, her frozen hand trembled.

I gave it another squeeze. "You can do this, girlfriend. You're almost there."

The woman lumbered behind, a sturdy guardian angel.

With several feet left, Tiny lunged for solid ground. When she reached dirt, she collapsed and buried her face in her hands.

I knelt next to her and gave her shaking shoulders a squeeze. "It's over. I knew you could do it."

The woman stopped next to us. "Good for you." She squeezed Tiny's shoulder too, then looked around. "Are you two chickies traveling by yourselves?"

Tiny still had her face buried in her hands. With Rune's warning swirling in my mind, I shrugged, refusing to answer the question. What if this woman was one of his spies?

The woman held up her thick, pudgy hands in a nonthreatening move. "My name's Shiraz. I won't do you any harm. But this land isn't kind to lone travelers. Would you like to journey with me, at least as far as your lodging?"

My suspicions wouldn't be appeased that easily. "Are you alone?"

"Well, yes." She smiled, dimples appearing in her full cheeks. "So you're doing me a favor by traveling with me as well."

After a long moment, Tiny wiped tears from her face. "We can do that. Maybe you can tell us the best place to stay."

She blinked. "You haven't made plans?"

Tiny gave me a wordless glare, her eyes double knife points.

I tried not to squirm. "No, this was a spontaneous trip." How was I supposed to know I needed reservations? It's not like I could book a place online.

Shiraz shook her head. "Like Elyon's Son, you won't find any room. You'll be lucky to find a barn with space, and even then, you'll be sharing with strangers."

"Would you give us a minute?" Tiny pulled me a short distance away, her voice a furious whisper. "Now what do we do? Huh? Tell me you have a fantastic plan tucked in your back pocket. Because if not, we might as well head back to Linneah."

I shook my head, desperate. "I can't go back. Not now." We were so close to Ginselwyn, one stop away. Right now, any place that didn't look like Linneah, that didn't hold a special memory, was a good thing.

Tiny nudged me with her elbow. "I'll go back with you and stay a few days before I leave again. Your mom will be so thrilled you're home safe, she won't ground you forever."

She didn't understand. "It's not about Mom. I just can't be there right now. I don't need to be reminded—" My eyes burned, and my throat closed off, damming the words inside.

Tiny winced. "Sorry. I forgot about the jerk."

"Not your fault. Your invitation came at the perfect time. If I keep busy, it doesn't hurt so much." I didn't mention Rune's advice that I return home. Definitely made me even more reluctant.

"But where will we stay? We have to room somewhere."

A quiet second went by, then another, while I tried to invent a solution.

Shiraz stopped next to us, her round face pale under her dark cap of hair. "Sorry to interrupt, but I was thinking on your problem. A friend of mine might agree to let you stay in her extra room for a small fee."

I resisted the urge to give her a relieved hug. "Any help you can offer is great."

"Come along, then." She gave us a cheerful smile and took the lead.

Ahead, the path widened into a main road. A red and yellow banner hung overhead, welcoming visitors to *Starfall's Fiftieth Anniversary Celebration!* In a shallow depression, the road led to a broad swath of dwellings, all carved from the same brown stone. Conical buildings with carved entryways, some tall, others squat and wide, and still others formed like mushrooms, lay in clusters, while the main road threaded through their midst.

Shiraz hefted her pack higher. "It's a bit of a hike. Abira lives with a beautiful view of the desert."

Glittering among the stars, Bella's Comet glowed in the midnight-blue sky as the Petrus Rings' blue and gold bands stretched overhead. A cool breeze smelling of cactus flower scented the air and brushed the night sky with shifting clouds.

When we reached the first intersection, two signs were posted. One read *Goldie's* with an arrow to the right. The other read *Starlight Inn, straight ahead.* Two-thirds of the crowd took the right fork, while the remaining third stayed on the main road. Following Shiraz, we turned left in silence. The road climbed higher, the rolling hills offering not much besides stubby grass, sand, and an occasional tree.

Once the path leveled off to a more gradual slope, Shiraz dropped back to walk with us. "Only about a quarter of a mile more." She smiled, her teeth a gleam of white. "Before I introduce you to one of my closest friends, I'm curious why you decided to journey to Kelda Hills."

Tiny pressed her lips together and stared straight ahead. Great. I was on my own.

"Well, I've never seen a Starfall."

"You're a spectator, then."

"Uh, no. A participant."

Shiraz's eyebrows climbed her wide forehead, her eyes studying my expression. "You know, this isn't hide and seek. It's dangerous."

"Have you participated in one?"

She waved my comment away. "It's an event for the more youthful, adventurous ones. My friend, Abira, took part in the last one."

"Do you think she could give me some tips? This is our only option to get us, well me, into Ginselwyn."

"You can't go home?"

"No."

While Shiraz waited, I remained silent. I wasn't spilling all my secrets to a stranger, no matter how friendly she seemed.

Finally, she turned to Tiny. "Are you headed home to family in Ginselwyn?"

"Yes." But her brow furrowed.

"Most people enjoy family visits. I'm sorry you're not looking forward to it."

"No, my family's great. I just—" She sighed. "This trip's been difficult and probably won't improve much."

I patted her shoulder, guilt swamping me. Why couldn't I do more than just screw things up? If I hadn't lost my bag, we would've been in her hometown by now.

"Well, that's a shame. Perhaps things will turn for the better once you arrive."

Tiny remained silent, offering a grim smile in reply. I could almost read her thoughts. *Yeah, not betting on it.*

A cluster of lit houses came into view, huddled against the rolling hills. A larger cottage stood several yards away from the others, bushes and tall pines surrounding it. Extra rooms mushroomed from the back, afterthoughts in construction.

Her gait like a lumbering bear, Shiraz quickened her pace and hurried toward the porch. Breathless, I lagged behind. There was no air here in the hills. I stepped onto the porch as the sapphire-blue door swung open.

A woman with long white hair walked onto the porch, holding out her arms. "Shiraz!"

"Abira!"

The two hugged, their faces wreathed in smiles. Abira pulled back, her hands on Shiraz's arms. "It's been too long. You're staying for the whole week, yes?"

"I can stay until after Starfall. Then I'll head into town to visit my brother."

"Four days isn't nearly enough time. I only see you once a year during the holiday." Abira's sharp eyes focused on Tiny and me. "Who's this?"

"Oh, yes, I found these turtledoves traveling toward Kelda Hills. They've nowhere to stay, so I invited them to stay with us."

Abira's eyes went flinty. "You want me to room complete strangers in my house?"

Shiraz's smile froze, and she turned to both of us. "Excuse us a minute." With a firm hand, she led Abira a short distance away. Bursts of words exploded in the darkness.

"Can't believe..."

"...charity?"

"...likely trouble..."

Tiny's quiet voice broke my study of the arguing women. "Doors are closing fast, Brenna. If this doesn't pan out, we're heading straight for Linneah."

"But—"

She didn't give an inch. "No buts. I'm not sure this plan of yours will work."

Well, that was two of us.

Tiny continued. "Whenever we force stuff, bad things happen."

Hurt and guilt burned in my chest. I looked away. "Sorry. Next time I'll avoid getting mugged and kidnapped."

Her voice softened. "Hey, I didn't mean it like that. I just meant, well, maybe I'm supposed to face this whole thing on my own. When I marry this guy—"

"*If* you get married."

She waved my comment away. "I'll build a family in Ginsel-wyn. And you'll be living your life somewhere else."

The thought of being separated from Tiny was another blow. First, my mom. Then Baldwin. Now Tiny. Why was I always left behind?

I had to force my voice out, the sound rusty. "But we'll always be friends, right?"

Tiny's grin gleamed in the dark. "Of course. You can come visit."

"Good. I'd love that." But it wouldn't be the same. And we both knew it.

Abira turned toward us, her sharp gaze missing nothing, and motioned us forward. "Everyone, inside."

I followed the women into the cottage, Tiny trailing behind.

Inside, a low fire burned in the hearth, lending the room a cozy warmth. A rug in tones of blue covered most of the wooden floor. Lining one wall was a massive bookcase with a desk and matching chair, while the other wall held a fireplace. After turning up the glow on a large helli lantern, Abira set it in the middle of the desk and faced us, her eyes nailing us to the floor.

"All right. Let me see if I have this figured out. You two get a foolish idea to leave your safe home and toddle off to Ginselwyn via the travel portal. Along the way, you discover it's harder than you thought, you didn't plan well, and you don't have enough money to get into the city. So you figure Starfall is a quick and easy way to get some money. Then you turn on the puppy eyes, hoping for sympathy from a soft heart. You find Shiraz, and now you're here. Is that about right?" She crossed her arms, the light from the lantern casting shadows on the planes of her face.

The heavyset woman scowled at the title. "Excuse me?"

Abira patted her friend's shoulder. "I'm sorry, my dear, but you are a softie." Then she turned to us with pursed lips.

Heat flashed in my cheeks as anger spiked. She didn't know anything about what we'd gone through. I opened my mouth, caustic words burning for release, when Tiny spoke.

"Not quite. First of all, Ginselwyn is my home. I asked Brenna to come with me. I'm supposed to meet my fiancé, whom I've never met, and I wanted her support. We had food, a plan, and she had plenty of extra money to get in. But I was delayed, and then she was kidnapped and robbed by the Scorpion. Despite all this, she's determined to get into Ginselwyn so I don't have to go alone. We don't think Starfall's easy, but right now it's our only option. And if you don't feel comfortable taking us in, that's fine. We'll go with Plan B."

Abira cocked one eyebrow. "What's that?"

Tiny grimaced. "We haven't discussed it yet."

I let my breath leak out, thankful I hadn't opened my big mouth and ruined it. The dwindling anger swirled through my bloodstream, slowly dissipating in the wake of Tiny's confession.

"You poor little chickadees! I had no idea what you'd been through." Shiraz snatched us close for a group hug. The faint scent of gingersnap cookies enveloped me.

Her eyes softening a bit in the low light, Abira took in the show of emotion. "It's late, so there'll be no payment tonight. Tomorrow, you'll have to work if you want to stay. There are no free things in this life, including room and board here."

Shiraz frowned. "Abira."

"These are the rules."

"Sounds fine," Tiny said.

Relief cascaded through me, tripled by exhaustion. The little nap in the deactivated portal entry had been hours ago, and I felt every one of them.

With a quick jerk of her head, she led us through a hallway to my right. "It's past your bedtime and mine. Your room's back here. You'll have to share."

After opening the door, she turned and studied us. "The bathroom's across the hall. Linens are in the drawer under the bed. Bedtime is now. No noise, or tomorrow you can find a new place to bed down." She left, the door closing behind her with a click.

I knelt to take off my shoes. If I just leaned over and put my head on the floor, I'd fall asleep.

Tiny dropped onto the bed. "Someone has anger management problems."

"Yeah, mad at the world, and today it was our turn."

A squeak of wooden boards in the hallway killed our conversation for a few tense seconds.

Tiny released the clip in her hair and massaged her scalp. "We'd better keep it down. I don't want to sleep in a barn. At least she's letting us stay here."

In silence, Tiny changed into a cotton nightshirt. Under the bed, storage drawers lined up like soldiers. Using a flashlight Tiny had in her bag, I found a set of sheets and two blankets and made the bed while Tiny changed. No bag, and therefore no jammies.

I crawled under the covers.

A framed print hung on the opposite wall above a cold fireplace. I squinted and focused the flashlight on it. It looked like a stamp, black lines and cutouts curled into the shape of a flame. Pretty cool.

In minutes, Tiny's deep, slow breaths indicated she'd fallen asleep. My nose tingled from the chilly air. Too bad nobody made nose mittens.

I woke to the dim half-light. Dawn slipped through the space between blue curtains.

Tiny lay asleep. I slid from the bed and grabbed a blanket, the bedroom still freezing. Tiptoeing to the door, I eased it open, then closed it behind me before walking into the living room. The house remained silent, waiting for a new day. The chilly living room set my teeth on edge.

I couldn't stand it any longer. I'd been cold all night.

Moving toward the wood stacked in a corner bin, I pulled out a few logs and arranged them in the wrought iron grate. A search in a nearby basket of small sticks and grass supplied tinder. After arranging the materials, I leaned forward and released three small balls of fire into its center. The wood ignited with a pleasant hiss, a curl of smoke disappearing up the chimney.

"How'd you do that?"

I whirled around, my feet sliding on the worn floor. I caught myself on the couch to prevent a face-plant. Abira leaned against the wall, studying me. The early morning light played across her clear gray eyes and high cheekbones. Her long white hair hung loose, framing a surprisingly unlined face. A strong chin hinted at the stubborn streak I'd seen last night. And judging by the impatient look on her face, I'd spent too much time thinking.

"Uh, I started a fire."

"I didn't ask what you did. I asked how."

"I'm a Firebrand. It's the ability—"

"I'm well aware of what a Firebrand does." Sitting on the couch, she watched the fire dance with a puckered brow.

I sat still, afraid to move. At this point, she wasn't yelling or glaring at me, and I was warming up. Life was good.

After a moment or two, she jutted her chin toward the fire. "Nice work. What else can you do?"

"Yard work, cooking, cleaning. What do you need done?"

Huffing out a breath, she rolled her eyes. For that split second, she reminded me of Tiny. "That's not what I meant. Follow me."

Rising from the couch, she snagged a large square of folded fabric by the door and walked outside.

Chapter Nine

On the porch, she shook out the thick, knitted fabric and wrapped it around her shoulders. The sun peeked over the horizon, but a chill still clung to shaded areas.

Hiking up my blanket so it didn't drag, I wrapped the extra fabric around my chilly hands. Abira headed for her backyard, a small patch of green grass ringed by lanky pines, scruffy bushes, and crumbled dirt. I followed, keeping my distance in case she became annoyed again.

She stopped at a wide patch of bare earth. Turning, she gestured to my hands. "Take them out of the blanket. How can you produce fire with them tucked away?"

"Just trying to keep warm." I slid my hands out of their hiding space, my fingers growing cold.

"Now, show me what you can do with your gift." She wrapped her fingers into her knitted scarf. At least one of us would be comfortable.

"I can produce a flamer beam, but you won't be able to see it. I can also do a firewall, but I don't want to ignite anything. And I can do a few other things." I laid aside the blanket and produced a few sparks, a single flame, and a larger fireball.

She narrowed her eyes. "Just production? That's it?"

"No. Healing too. I help in the infirmary sometimes."

She tilted her head, still squinting. "And you're happy with that?"

"Well, yeah. Helping people makes me happy. Shouldn't it?"

"No, I meant, are you happy with your limitations?"

For a brief second, her words didn't register. When they did, my mouth took over. "Limitations? I can do quite a bit!"

"No, you can't. Your ability puts you at a Level Two. If that."

"What, there's like a rating system for Firebrands?" My chin shot up. "How do you know? Are you an expert or something?"

Pushing up her sleeves, she held out her hand, palm up. A fireball the size of a golf ball appeared, the flames curling into itself, a burning ball of power. It expanded, flames licking out like solar flares. It stopped at a six-inch diameter before it shrank, then grew again to the size of a beach ball. Its flames flickered yellow before morphing to dark mustard, to apricot, to sapphire blue. With a flick of her fingers, the ball transformed into the shape of a bird, its wings flapping. After several seconds, she grabbed the fiery creation and collapsed it, flames disappearing.

I closed my gaping mouth. "You're a Firebrand?"

"Yes, Level Five."

She was a Level Five Firebrand. Sheesh. I didn't even know there were levels. "What does that mean?"

"It means I've mastered the advanced abilities of the talent beyond defense and healing. But there's always more to learn." She walked to a small garden and knelt. After pulling a few weeds, she spoke, her voice pitched low and steady. "I heard a Firebrand was instrumental in Linneah's victory over Rune's forces. Do you know this person?"

I wasn't comfortable with where this was going. "Why?"

"Because I think you are that person."

I gave a careless shrug. "What if I am?"

"It means you're the queen's daughter."

Of course. More times than I cared to count, I'd been used to get closer to the queen. I squelched the disappointment rising inside and schooled my expression into disinterest. "Well, the queen's daughter was involved in Linneah's victory. At least that's what everyone says."

Abira shot me a speculative glance but dropped the discussion. "Who taught you?"

"My griffin Arvandus. I needed to train quickly and managed to learn the basics. Destruction and healing, all with fire."

She pulled another weed. "Level Two learning."

I stiffened. "Not all of us get to learn from a master. Most of us make do with what we have." Maybe I could've gotten better. Marziah trained Firebrands at the castle on Fridays. But with schoolwork, it was impossible to make it to Linneah every Friday. And I couldn't practice at home. What if someone saw me create a fireball out of thin air?

"If you had the opportunity to improve your skills, would you take it?"

I shrugged. "Sure. Someone once told me I could do more." Talus's words from months ago still haunted me. *Did you know there is so much more you could learn to do with your ability?* I knelt next to her and pulled some weeds.

"Ugh. Stop. You just pulled my golden garlic. Look for the stems with three leaves, instead of two, and pull those." She leaned back on her haunches. "That person was correct. And I'd be willing to teach you."

My heart leaped to my throat at the unbelievable opportunity. "Why?"

"You show promise. With self-control and determination, your gift could be a powerful thing."

"Uh, I don't have a lot of self-control. With my ADHD, it's kind of nonexistent."

Abira shook her head. "No excuses. I've not heard of Ay-dee-atche-dee, but everyone's able to foster self-control. Maybe this thing makes it harder, but it's still possible."

I gave a skeptical snort and added to the pile of weeds growing between us. "Why the offer? You don't like Tiny or me that much."

She gave me a startled look. "Not true. I don't know you or your friend well enough to form an opinion. But the opportunity to expand your gift would benefit yourself and the Jasper Territory. The territory needs powerful talents, because Rune will come again. He's waiting, plotting. And when he attacks, we'll need allies, power, and Elyon's grace."

That *sounded* good, but still... "Let's say I accept. How can I train with you and go with Tiny to Ginselwyn too?"

Abira rubbed her hands, her fingers stained with dirt. "Hmm. We could begin your training, prepare you for Starfall, then after your trip to Ginselwyn, you could come back, and we'll finish what we've begun."

"For how long? My parents will want to know where I am." And punish me for the next decade.

"I'll send a foslykos, ask for their permission."

The opportunity was too great to ignore. And Abira was right—Rune wasn't done. He wasn't the type to let go of something he wanted. And he wanted the Jasper Territory.

That settled it. "I'd like to learn more."

A pleased smile crossed the older woman's face. "We can start this afternoon. And this evening, we'll make a list of needed items for Starfall." She stopped, her expression pensive. "Are you sure you want to do it? Starfall makes people greedy."

"Absolutely." If I wanted to get into Ginselwyn, I had to. I couldn't let Tiny down—again.

"All right, then." She gestured to the substantial pile of weeds. "Throw those under the pines, then come on in. We'll see how you do at cooking breakfast."

I cooked up a decent pile of scrambled eggs, mostly without shells. While Shiraz and Tiny cleaned up afterwards, Abira and I went outside and sat in the shade of the back porch. The mid-morning sun baked the landscape—sandy earth, celery-green plants, and red and brown mountains shimmering in the distance. A dry wind carrying the faint scent of desert flowers drifted past. Pine needles rustled, then fell still.

Abira's gaze was direct. "If I'm to train you, you must tell me who you are."

I stifled a sigh. I hadn't escaped her probing, just postponed it. "I'm Brenna James. Firebrand. Fulfiller of the First Prophecy."

"And Queen Sarah of Linneah's daughter."

I settled back against the seat. "Yeah. That too."

"I thought so. Thank you for your honesty. My name is Abira Edan. Will I receive a royal reprimand if you stay here?"

"No, she'll be relieved I'm safe." And with other adults. If I knew Mom, she'd rather have me home in Pennsylvania, but with Linneah's broken portal, that wasn't going to happen anytime soon.

"Does she need a message letting her know you're safe?"

"I sent one with a Linnean runner a day ago. But if you want to send another, go ahead."

"I'll do that. Let's discuss what you'll be learning."

Yawn. Boring. But if she wanted to talk, I'd try to take it in. "Sure."

Her smile transformed her face. "Just a joke. You'll learn better by doing. Follow me."

Great. A comedian.

Standing, she offered me a hand up, and I followed her to the front of the house. "Wait here. I'll be right back."

She left. I shaded my eyes and began to sweat. The stubby pine to my right offered shade, so I walked over to stand in the cooler shadow. The sun shone bright in a robin's egg-blue sky. No neighbors worked outside to break the quiet, and under the porch roof, the front door glowed azure against brown stone. In several hours, the front porch would receive the sweltering afternoon heat.

When Abira returned, she carried a pan of hot water. Curls of steam drifted off the water's surface. "Now, watch carefully." She dipped her hands into the scalding water, her eyes steady and focused. For a few seconds she remained still, then pulled her hands away. Steam rose from her fingers until she released a small fireball. It landed on the dirt with a fading sizzle before dying out. She touched my arm with a cool hand. "Feel the water."

I slipped a finger in and found the previously hot water tepid.

"Removal of heat from water. A Firebrand must focus on becoming open for the heat to be pulled into the body, then released into the atmosphere. The last part is easier, because it wants to be released. Allow me to heat the water again, then you can try."

After creating a fireball, she held it near the water. In seconds, the water began to boil.

"Your turn." She gestured to the pan. "Focus on pulling the heat into your palms."

Intense heat radiated from the pan, but there was no chance of injury. In the past year, I'd discovered my gift made it impossible for me to get burned. I slid my palms into the water and closed my eyes. Nothing happened.

I waited a moment, then pulled my hands out. "I don't feel anything."

She thought for a moment, lips pursed. "Rather than focusing like you do for healing, open yourself up. It's a relaxed concentration. You aren't doing this in your own power. Use the gift Elyon has given you. Empty negativity and tension and allow yourself to be free and vulnerable."

After heating the water again, she waited, the pan of water simmering between us. I tried not to think of anything, which was impossible. Mental noise filled my head all the time. Instead, I slipped my hands into the water and imagined a huge web. When I inhaled, I visualized gathering the heat into the net. A jittery buzz like insects swarming swept up my arms, pooling in my shoulders.

"Now, pull your hands out and release the heat."

As I pulled my hands out, a tickle on my calf distracted me. There, on my foot and picking its way toward my calf, crawled a glowing white scorpion.

I squawked, slapping at it several times. It finally tumbled to the ground, burned to a crisp.

"Brenna, release the heat!"

"Huh?" Too late. A rush of wet heat swamped my torso. Shaking, I bent over, my stomach flipping. I swallowed hard against the return of breakfast.

Placing her hands on my shoulders, Abira waited. The heat and nausea dissipated, leaving me sweating and weak. She flicked her fingers, flames dancing off the tips before winking out. "You have to release the buildup, Brenna. If you don't, it can damage your system. Over time, it will warp your gift."

Right. I was melting, the full sun overhead a blast furnace.

Her concerned eyes scrutinized me. "Go inside and drink several glasses of water. Now."

I tottered off, too hot and exhausted to argue.

Tiny met me inside the cool living room. "Your face is fire-engine red. Are you okay?"

"Debatable." I staggered into the kitchen, poured a glass of water, and downed it in several swallows. After drinking another full glass, I grabbed a big pan from the cupboard. Filling it with lukewarm water, I hurried into the front yard and then dumped the water over my head. I could've sworn the water sizzled as it evaporated off my skin.

Abira walked toward me. "Feel better?"

"Close enough."

"Let's try again."

She made the water boil, and I dipped my fingertips in. I breathed out, then in. Like the pull of a magnet, heat gathered in my fingers, miniature rods of dynamite waiting to blow. I withdrew them and released a fireball that dropped to the dirt and fizzled out. Done correctly, releasing the collected heat was as easy as breathing.

"Much better." She touched the water with another fireball until it boiled. "Try again."

And that's what I did for the rest of the afternoon. After a quick afternoon snack, I practiced Gather Heat and Release. Again. And again. Tedious, but by suppertime, I'd improved and could gather larger amounts.

Shiraz stuck her head out the back door. "Supper's ready. And a delicious dessert."

My stomach grumbled in response.

Abira picked up the pan of water and poured it over her garden. "We're done for today."

She could say that again. I stood, my unsteady legs wobbling.

The stew melted in my mouth, full of roasted meat, root vegetables, and a savory broth. Fluffy, herbed dumplings were perfect for sopping up leftover gravy. Tiny contributed a pupkissberry pie for dessert, which held the sweet flavors of sun-ripened berries and almonds.

I pulled a forkful of whipped cream off my slice of pie. "This is so good. You're turning into a regular Betty Crocker."

Her smile dimmed. "I'll have to be if I'm getting married."

The stew grew leaden in my stomach, reminding me this was no vacation. I turned to Shiraz. "Supper was delicious. Thank you."

The heavyset woman beamed.

Shiraz and Tiny left for the living room while I helped Abira clean up. After the plates were washed and dried, she pulled out a kitchen chair. "Have a seat."

I dropped into the chair, tired and ready for bed. That was new. Most nights I had no trouble staying up for the crazy-late shows on television.

"We need to discuss what you need for Starfall." She sat next to me, her gray eyes serious. "If you're to be safe and successful, you need to plan well. Shiraz and I will give you safety tips and good locations. But a lot of this is luck. And you can never be too careful. As I mentioned previously, greedy people are dangerous. Theft is common. So are muggings."

Great.

She raised an eyebrow. "Are you planning to include Tiny?"

"No. I lost the money." This was my mess.

"You were mugged."

"Still." I shrugged. "My problem."

She shifted, the chair creaking a bit. "You'll need a bag, a pocketed jacket, a scarf, and a reinforced hat."

"Reinforced?"

"The hat is constructed with a metal top and covered with fabric to protect the head from falling stars."

I leaned forward. "And the scarf?"

"To disguise your gender." Abira jotted the items on paper, her precise writing neat and even. "I told you, this is dangerous. Anything you can do to make yourself appear strong and formidable should be done. It will make others think twice before choosing you as a target."

Shiraz and Tiny drifted into the kitchen, each settling into a chair.

The heavyset woman looked over the list before tapping it with a sturdy finger. "I think I packed a pocketed jacket. Do you have a hat?"

Abira shook her head. "No, but we can pick one up at the market tomorrow."

I gritted my teeth. "I don't have any money." As usual. Everything needed to be bought, which put me at a distinct disadvantage. "I don't need a hat. I'll just be careful."

Abira waved away my comment. "Don't be stupid. A falling star could hit you without a sound. You'd be injured or most likely killed. Not all of them make noise."

My eyes widened. "They make sounds?"

"Some of them. A high-pitched, hollow whistling that gets louder as it approaches."

Shiraz scanned the list before adding, "Abira's right. You'll have no time to prepare, and some are quiet. Even with a hat, a star can injure you. Without it, it'll kill you."

Abira picked up the list, folded it in half, and tucked it into her shirt's pocket. "We'll pick one up tomorrow, and if you get a star, you can pay me back." She stood. "Tomorrow we'll talk about location. That's just as important as tools. For now, you need sleep."

I stood, my head buzzing with information and apprehension. "See you in the morning."

Tiny followed me into the bedroom, unusually quiet. While she changed into pajamas, I built a fire in the fireplace with the stack of wood that had miraculously appeared sometime today. The flames danced and snapped, filling the room with a comfy warmth.

Tiny's low voice came from the bed. "Maybe you shouldn't do Starfall."

I turned. "Thanks for the vote of confidence."

From the nest of blankets, her blue eyes reflected firelight. "That's not what I meant."

"What do you mean?"

"What if you get attacked? Or mugged? Or killed?" Her voice climbed higher.

"I'll be fine." Although what-ifs lingered, I refused to think about returning to Linneah. This goal was the only thing keeping me from turning into a pathetic, sniveling mess. My broken heart hadn't registered the loss yet. But once I stopped moving...I didn't want to think about it.

"Or we could just go back now."

"No. Absolutely not." I walked to the bed and climbed under the blanket. "What's going on with you?"

Tears filled her eyes before she burrowed further under the covers. "Nothing. This just seems so dangerous. I want you to be okay."

"I am. But you're not." I nudged her. "Come on, spill."

She threw off the covers and sat up, swiping at her face. Words tumbled out. "I don't want to go home. I want to stay in Pennsylvania or Linneah, anywhere where my fiancé isn't. I'm not ready to get married. I want to go to school dances and prom and college and date and fall in love. I want someone to love me for me. Not because it's been arranged, but because I'm me."

I put my arm around her shoulders. "I think Flynn likes you."

She sniffed. "Flynn likes females. Period."

I breathed out a laugh. "No, I don't think that's it. But even if you're right, there's someone out there for you, Tiny. What if your fiancé's gorgeous with a good heart?"

Like Baldwin used to be. The thought slammed into me, leaving me breathless. My heart ached, hollow. I shoved the thought aside and focused on Tiny.

She gave me a sad smile, the wet sheen in her eyes glistening in the firelight. "Too good to be true. They're usually thirty years older with bad teeth and worse attitudes."

I gave one more squeeze and dropped my arm. "Let's hope for a miracle, then."

"Yeah, sure." She lay down and pulled the covers up. "I'll do that."

I shifted onto my side, exhaustion weighing down my eyelids. Tiny's sad smile pulled at my heart, and hopelessness filled me.

I whispered a desperate prayer for her. Everyone deserved the chance to fall in love.

An unfamiliar sound woke me from a dark dream. Brushing away the creeping chill on my neck, I frowned and sat up, scanning the shadowy room. A nearby creak split the night's silence, and I stiffened. Unfamiliar house = strange noises.

Another squeak accompanied by a muffled footstep propelled me from bed. I hesitated at the doorframe. It was probably just Abira. With a deep breath, I nudged open the door and edged into the hallway. At the soft click of the front door, my breath stalled. Had someone just entered or just left? I peeked into the dim main room, nerves jittering under my skin. All was still.

A few seconds of silence passed, and I waffled between cowardice and curiosity. My nosiness won. I peered out the window, but only shadows waited. Tiptoeing to the door, I eased it open. A quick check revealed an empty porch. I stepped out. The warm breeze brushed my cheeks, easing my tense shoulder muscles. Nothing evil lurked beyond the house, and as my eyes adjusted to the dark, malevolent shadows disappeared.

So strange—I'd heard footsteps. Maybe Abira or Shiraz had gone for a walk. As I turned to head back inside, my foot caught on a piece of paper. I picked it up and carried it into the living room, locking the door behind me. After turning up the nearby helli light, I held the paper closer. The notecard was embossed with a familiar serpent on the front.

My stomach flipped. The image looked like the creature Baldwin and I had fought last year. The same serpent Taurin had used when he marched toward the battle with Linneah. I flipped it open, scanning the powerful scrawl.

I had planned a nostalgic visit after my business in Kelda Hills was concluded. Unfortunately, that will be impossible. I will arrange a visit when I become emperor—it won't be long. I see you've met the palace brat. Her present will be used well.

Until we meet again, R.

My hands shook, the paper fluttering like moth wings. Rune had been here. Here. Had he watched me sleep? My breath caught, trapped in my throat. At a squeak of floorboards, I looked up.

Abira appeared in the hallway, rubbing her eyes. "You're up late. I thought you were tired."

Despite the fear and tears blurring my vision, I handed her the note. "Someone was here. They left this."

Her face hardened when she saw the serpent. After scanning the card, she tossed it on the table. "I'm assuming you're the palace brat. What did you give him?"

I shook my head. "Nothing." My fingers brushed my collarbone. Bare. Shock hollowed out my stomach. "My jasper! It's missing."

Her nostrils flared. "Why would he...?" She shook her head. "That doesn't make sense. It probably fell off while you slept."

I rubbed my arms, trying to dispel the creepy helplessness coating my skin.

She gently squeezed my shoulder before gesturing to the bedroom. "It's late. You can look for it in the morning."

I headed back to bed, cradling the fragile hope in my heart. It was probably tangled in the sheets or under my pillow.

As I crawled into bed, I puzzled over the note's contents. How did Rune know Abira?

CHAPTER TEN

THE NEXT MORNING, DELICIOUS, savory scents pulled me from dreamland. In the bright light of day, the events of the previous night seemed like a bad dream. I touched my exposed neck—nope, no dream.

Tiny stood in front of the mirror, dressed and arranging her fine blonde tresses into an intricate braid. "Shiraz said they want to leave for the market in the next half hour."

"What about breakfast?"

She grinned. "I already ate. Cheesy scrambled eggs and sausage. I don't think there's any left."

I rolled out of bed, dressed in the same clothes I'd been wearing for the past three days. At this point, they should come when I whistled.

While I made the bed, I searched for my jasper—on the floor, tucked in the pillowcase, at the bottom of the bed. Despair and vulnerability mingled when my search came up empty. If Rune had taken my jasper, why? I trudged into the kitchen, and Abira stood at the sink, washing dishes.

Shiraz flashed me a sunny smile, her round cheeks rosy. "Good morning, chickie."

"Morning. Something smells good."

Abira gave me a quick glance. "There's not much left."

Wow, grumpy. Maybe she was still thinking about our late-night visitor.

Shiraz pushed a plate of sliced bread studded with nuts in my direction. "We're heading to the market. Abira's in a snit, so if you want to come, you'll have to hurry and eat breakfast."

Abira sniffed. "I am not in a snit."

Shiraz offered her an angelic smile.

After scarfing a leftover sausage patty and a few slices of nut bread, I left with everyone else. No way was I staying at the house. I'd overheard the women discussing the market the day before. Apparently, it was epic, Kelda Hills' version of a superstore.

We traveled the road we'd taken on our way in. The morning sun blasted bright, climbing high in the sky. After a few minutes on the dusty thoroughfare, sweat dripped between my shoulder blades.

Tiny wiped her brow with her forearm. "Even though I don't have any spending money, I can't wait to see what's there."

I grunted. "Anything's better than staying at the house and playing with heat and flames."

"I saw you working with it yesterday before supper. Pretty cool."

"Yeah, but it's a wicked amount of practice."

She smiled. "It'll make you wicked good."

The trail meandered over rolling brown earth with precious little greenery. Along the way, people worked outside their houses, toiling in garden plots. White globes the size of basketballs were stuck in the ground at the corner of each plot. "Shiraz?"

The woman turned.

I pointed to one. "What's the white thing in everyone's yard?"

"It's a watering system for their garden."

I tilted my head. "Abira doesn't have one."

Abira flipped her hair over a shoulder. "I don't need one."

Shiraz shook her head and spoke in an undertone. "She's saving for one."

Yet she was housing two unexpected guests and buying me stuff. Guilt clogged my throat. It was yet another reason to get a star. As if I needed one more reason. I quietly filled Tiny in on the events of the previous night.

Her eyes grew wide. "Why would he take it? He can't use it or anything."

"That we know of. I don't know. I feel kinda sick, knowing he stood there and watched us sleep."

She shuddered. "I'm checking Abira's locks from now on before bed."

Would that help? Rune always seemed to have a new trick up his sleeve.

The brown stone and clay houses gave way to a more rolling landscape. A herd of hillside animals, something like goats, picked over the rocky mound and munched on whatever vegetation they found.

As we drew closer to Kelda Hills, cone-topped houses came into view. In the bright morning light, the hillsides revealed a surprise. People had carved doorways and windows into the tan cliff faces. A line of wash hung in one opening, and pots of flowers graced a window. Stone stairs from the ground led to higher levels, sometimes three and four stories high.

Kelda Hills proper included cone-topped houses, rock-face dwellings, and a few typical buildings. The whole effect offered a jumbled fairyland scene lining a large town square.

The two women walked ahead, the low murmur of conversation rising and falling. Tiny and I followed, gawking like tourists. The smell of grilled beef wafted on the breeze.

Tiny put a hand on her stomach. "Oh, it's just like popcorn. You don't have to be hungry, but the smell makes you want a nice, juicy burger."

Shiraz turned, her normally smiling eyes grave. "When we get to the market, birdies, stay close. Newcomers can easily get lost in the crush."

We walked closer as we took it all in. Three sides of the square held the outdoor market. Food vendors occupied one side, their brightly colored signs declaring their specialties. Rason burgers, spiced-fruit kebabs, and herbed veggie pockets mingled with other delicious aromas, scenting the air like a buffet. My stomach gave a happy lurch when I spotted a sign for Kunkelsteuchen.

Necessities filled another side of the square. We walked past people selling eggs, soap, pots and pans, thread, helli lanterns, knives, clothing, and a myriad of other objects. The colors dazzled, scents mingled in the warm air, and voices called for customers until it all coalesced into a whirling blur.

When we walked to the next section, an invisible tension rode the air. The vendors were louder, but fewer customers perused the stalls. Abira and Shiraz slowed, scanning merchandise. A few stalls were held together with shaky timbers and prayers, sellers hawking everything from pails and pouches to hand-drawn cards with "Starfall!" emblazoned on the front.

A seller with an eyepatch and a gold tooth grabbed my elbow in a painful grip. "Carry the luck of the stars with you." He held out a glass cube, holding a pitiful amount of questionable dust.

I yanked my arm free. "No, thanks."

"Only one zoharet noma for true star bits!" He crowded in again, pungent body odor filling my personal bubble.

Abira stepped in. "Sell elsewhere." One look from her gray eyes, and the man scuttled back to his booth. She turned to me. "You must be firm. Greed makes them desperate."

I rubbed my still-sore elbow as we continued, looking at tools, necessities, and kitschy merchandise. On the other side of the path, an elegant stall selling spiegel globes caught my attention. Regular spiegel globes were clear and allowed the viewer to see another person, yet the clear glass surface of these had been swirled with colors, creating a watercolor effect. I drifted closer, and the seller looked up with a friendly smile.

"Hello, interested in unique hand-blown spiegel globes? Perfect for checking on loved ones. Made by skilled artisans in Kelda Hills."

"They're beautiful."

"And functional, too. Have you used one before?"

The memories of Talus's initiation eight months ago flashed through my mind. "It's been a while."

"Go ahead and try it. Free, no pressure to buy." She offered me another smile.

I picked up the closest one, its surface swirled with blues and greens. Who was I most interested in seeing? My heart whispered a name, but I pushed it away. I didn't need to see the deceitful jerk. He'd probably never even given me a second thought.

Despite my head's arguments, my heart won. I focused on the globe as it warmed in my hand and turned soft pink. The center cleared, and Baldwin's face filled the globe. My globe displayed the curved surface of another globe in his hand. His green eyes were dull. But as they met mine, surprised joy spread across his face. He reached out his hand and mouthed, *Brenna*.

With a squeak, I let the globe go dark. He could see me? How? With a shaking hand, I handed the globe back to the seller. "Is this a regular globe or one that displays fantasies?"

The smile slipped from her face. "Well, they are handcrafted. But it functions just like a normal globe. Milady? Is everything all right?"

I stammered a nonsensical reply and drifted back into the crowd. What had just happened? My heart pounded, beating out a painful rhythm. Something tickled my cheek, and I reached up, my hand coming away wet. Great.

Tiny approached me. Her eyes widened when she saw my face. "Hey, why're you crying?"

Using my sleeve to stem the tears, I ushered her to a large tent displaying kitchen items.

She turned to me, her brow furrowed. "What's wrong?"

I pulled in a shuddering breath. "Those spiegel globes? I saw Baldwin."

"That skunk. Was he with Gari again?"

"No. I mean, he saw me—we saw each other. He had a spiegel globe, too. And we could see each other, like Facetime. And he—" And that was where I lost it. Even as my heart hurt, anger flared. I hated crying, especially in public. "He looked sad."

"Of course he did. He lost you. Did he apologize?"

"I couldn't hear anything. But I saw him say my name, and he smiled." My heart squeezed at the memory. I gave her a watery smile.

She rolled her eyes. "Do *not* let him get away with this. He needs to apologize, explain, and top it off with some groveling."

Although she was right, my head and heart were back at the moment I saw his smile.

She leaned close to my ear. "Pull yourself together, unless you want questions. Shiraz is headed this way."

Wiping my face, I took a deep breath and blew it out slowly.

Her voice came from behind me. "Checking out kitchen wares?"

Tiny covered for me, picking up the closest item. "Look, a melon baller. I've never seen one so, uh, round."

Shiraz chuckled. "Does your melon baller make another shape, then? I'd like to see it. Anyway, we found a booth selling hats. Come along."

We followed her through the crowd. When we reached Abira, she turned and held out a gray hat. "They also have dark green or black. Which would you like?"

Covered in sturdy fabric, the hat's tough inner layer reminded me of a hardhat. A small brim circled the crown. I placed it on my head, where it wobbled. "It'll work, I guess. A little big."

She pulled a black one without a brim from the collection. The hard, formed crown wasn't noticeable since it lay hidden in slouching fabric like a beanie.

I slid it on. "This one's comfortable."

Shiraz studied me and rubbed her chin. "It looks big."

"I'll tuck my hair up in it."

Abira offered me a half-smile. "You certainly have a lot of it. Is the black color acceptable?"

I nodded, thankful she was willing to pay for it. Of course, that meant I owed her even more. I had to find a star, not only to get to Ginselwyn, but also to pay Abira back. After picking up eggs, yarn, and some fypex gum I requested, Abira finished our trip by purchasing Kunkelsteuchen pastries for us to eat on our walk home.

The vendor handed over the light balls of dough, their warmth soaking through the paper napkin. I smiled at Tiny and took a bite, the cinnamon and sugar topping melting on my tongue in a burst of crystalline sweetness.

Abira dropped back to walk with us. "I also picked up a few sets of clothes for you in the market. I guessed your size, but most of it is adjustable."

I ate another bite of pastry. "Thank you. I'll pay you back, I promise."

She shrugged. "It doesn't matter. You need clothes. You can't keep wearing the same ones, and you needed a sturdy black shirt and pants for Starfall. We'll have another lesson when we get home. You need to keep practicing."

I scowled. "I practiced yesterday."

Abira waved away my comment. "Not enough. You need to stretch and practice your talent every day, like learning to play an instrument."

She was silent for the rest of the walk.

When we arrived at the house, she thrust a package at me. "Change and meet me in the backyard. If I'm not there, start practicing."

Accepting the package, I stifled a groan. Maybe if I hurried, I could get there first and pick a shady spot.

Once in the bedroom, I unwrapped the clothes. A few sets? More like a whole new wardrobe. There were three pairs of pants, three shirts, four tank tops, a jacket, a skirt, and several pairs of underwear. I changed, but then I couldn't find a hairbrush. Finally, I located a comb to fix my tangled mane. By the time I made it to the backyard, Abira was there, impatiently waiting with a pan of water.

"Sorry." *ADHD's time blindness strikes again.* I was always apologizing for the way minutes and seconds slipped away from me.

"Let's begin. Practice with gathering and releasing."

I did that for an hour with two dousings because I didn't release soon enough. A dousing was the quickest way to keep from overheating. After a lunch break, I continued practicing. Late afternoon found me slumped under a tree, damp, exhausted, and sticky with sweat.

While I rested, Abira picked vegetables from her garden before settling next to me. "You're doing well. Tomorrow we'll go over gathering heat from the earth. But continue to practice—old and new skills. If you want to succeed, you can never quit."

With a small moan, I lay down, letting the shaded spot of earth cool my skin.

She became quiet, and my mind drifted. I jumped when she spoke again. "Those from the old ways, back when there were guilds for each talent, had a tradition that celebrated learning new skills."

She pushed up her sleeve. On her upper arm was a scrolled tattoo, five elegant rolling outlines of flames coming together to form one giant flame. It was an exact replica of the print in her spare bedroom.

"For each level you attain, you receive a piece of the design. You already could receive two of the pieces. If you work hard, the third could be yours too."

I sat up. "You mean, get a tattoo like that?"

Her eyes were steady. "Yes."

I raised an eyebrow. "Does it hurt?"

"Hmm. A little. But it's over quickly. And if we used secatic oil on your skin before starting, it would sting less."

I tugged on a blade of dry grass, my stomach fluttering. "Can I think about it?"

She stood and dusted off her pants. "Sure. Take a shower and change. Supper will be in an hour."

As she walked into the cottage, I thought about her offer. My mom would kill me if I got a tattoo. But it wasn't a meaningless design. And I'd strive to finish my training so the flame would be complete.

I walked into the house, still thinking, and dropped my dirty clothes on the bathroom floor. Jumping into the stall, I pulled the cord, allowing some of the stored water to wet my skin. I missed showers at the castle. There the water was warmer and more plentiful. Here, at the edge of the desert, we had to conserve.

After a quick shampoo, soap, and rinse, I dried off and slipped into a set of dry clothes. The shirt's sturdy cloth rasped against my skin, but I loved all the pockets. And the pants were constructed like comfortable jeans with a drawstring waist. I took a few minutes to wash my dirty clothes out, hanging them to dry on nearby hooks.

I padded into the yellow kitchen, where roasting meat and freshly baked bread scented the air. Rather than snatch a roll from the table, I poured myself a glass of water. Playing with fire meant I was wicked thirsty all the time.

Shiraz stood at the counter, chopping veggies. Tiny washed large green leaves before patting them dry and stacking them on a plate.

Abira walked in and pulled a stack of plates from the cabinet. She handed them to me. "Set the table, then meet me in the living room."

Moments later, I dropped onto the sofa, exhausted from the simple task. It must have shown because she grinned from the other end of the couch.

"You'll sleep well tonight. Over time, you'll build stamina. Learning new tasks can cause extreme fatigue, especially if you're doing it correctly."

My learning must be perfect, because I felt like I'd sleep for a week.

She tapped a pad of paper on her lap. "Take a look at this. I've drawn a map for you."

I slid over to get a better look. "Is that your house?" I pointed to a little blue square near the right edge of the paper.

"Yes, and the rest of this space is Kelda Hills, which turns into Aviva Desert. Here's where Starfall occurs." She circled a large area near the northern mountains.

I closed my eyes for a second, fatigue making things seem so much worse. "I'm going to have to hike in and camp there." Anxiety and weariness swirled, filling my stomach. I couldn't do it. I. Just. Couldn't.

"Although Starfall occurs over a wide stretch of land, it's too far away to make the trip in a day. By the time we reached it, the event would be almost over."

Knowing I wouldn't be alone made me feel better. "When do we leave?"

"Thursday evening. We can all go, if you'd like, or just me or Shiraz."

"I don't know what to expect, so you decide." Although if I failed, I really didn't want an audience.

"Then it'll just be the two of us. Shiraz doesn't care for crowds and noise." She sketched some mountains on her map, shading the sides and adding trees. "Along this side, there are some caves and overhangs that will be protection enough. I know a few places where we can set up."

I stifled a yawn.

Her mouth quirked in a half-smile. "We'll talk more tomorrow."

Chapter Eleven

The next day after lunch, Abira led me to the backyard for a demonstration of heat removal from the earth. She plunged her fingers into the sandy soil before withdrawing her hands and discharging the heat in a large flame.

She pointed to me. "Your turn. Just like with water, only this is dirt."

After a few tries, I managed a retrieval. Grinning, I refrained from doing a happy dance.

"Good job. Use different areas of the soil to withdraw the heat. There's plenty from the sun. Keep going."

While I practiced, she sat in a tree's shade and watched.

I sank my hands into the sand for the eighth time and began to pull in heat. The grains of sand vibrated, tickling my fingers. At the low rumble underground, I pulled away. "What was that?"

"What?"

"It was like a rumble, or a vibration, under the—"

She shot to her feet. "Uh-oh. Move."

I stood from my crouched position. "But why? What's—"

The sand swelled into a mound near my feet before splitting open. I stumbled back. From the fissure poured dozens of glowing, white scorpions.

"Swarm! Head for the house!" Abira ran for the back door.

They reached me before I could will my feet to move. In desperation, I shot fireballs at them. Despite frying a few, the flames only agitated the ones left behind.

Her yell slashed through my panic. "Stop playing around and get in here!"

Whirling around, I dashed for the house and slammed the door on the rising tide of white scorpions. Their tails striking the wooden door freaked me out.

"What's wrong with them? What are they?"

"They're Spierwhit Scorpions, and they live in the hottest parts of the desert. When you started retrieving, they tried to protect their home."

Maybe she should've mentioned that *before* we pulled heat from the sand?

After a brief break, Abira suggested we go back outside. I peeked out the window. "Are they still out there?"

She peeked too. "They've probably moved to a warmer location. The venom in their sting will knock a grown man unconscious for a full day." She smiled. "Since I prefer they not nest on my property, I pull heat from the soil here often."

I spent the next hour trying to forget the nightmarish image seared into my brain while I pulled heat from the backyard. But at least they were gone, right?

I hoped.

After supper, Abira gave me a bag and instructed me to pack. I hurried to the bedroom and gathered the list of supplies she'd written for me. Change of clothes (the black ones), scarf, water, blanket, jacket, and snacks all got stowed in the large knapsack. I lifted it to my shoulder, turned, and found Tiny watching from the doorway.

I smiled. "Wish me luck."

She eyed my bag. "Why are you leaving so early?"

"Abira said if we don't, most of the safe spots will be taken. Overhangs, caves, that sort of thing."

"You don't have to do this." I barely heard her.

"Yeah, I do." We'd had this conversation a million times already. I wasn't going back to Linneah. Period.

Her face grew dark, her brow furrowed. "Don't do anything stupid."

I sighed. "I love you, too."

After a quick hug, she pulled back. "If you don't get a star, it's not the end of the world. We'll figure something out."

Without a star, there was nothing to figure out. We'd go home.

As usual, Abira waited for me at the door with her own bag slung across her shoulders. We said goodbye to Shiraz with a promise to return by Saturday afternoon. Closing the front door behind her, Abira grabbed a six-foot walking stick from the porch. The sky glowed peach, the sun descending behind the mountains. Bella's Comet was the showstopper, a bright orb, its tail glittering streamers of light, while the Petrus Rings sparkled.

We walked to the main path away from town and headed north. At the top of a small rise, the land dropped away into a series of small rounded hills.

She pointed to a hazy shape on the horizon. "That's our first destination."

"First?"

"Yes. We won't make it to the Starfall fields tonight. We'll stay at that inn and leave before dawn. That'll put us at the fields before noon."

I closed my eyes for a second. How much did I owe her now? The clothes, the hat, and now the price of an overnight stay. "I can't afford this. I might not even get a star. Then I'll owe you all that money."

"You worry too much. We don't know what's going to happen at the fields."

Right.

She whistled while she hiked, apparently thrilled to be out of the house. Me, not so much. After thirty minutes, I dripped with sweat, despite the dropping temperature.

She pulled on the cloak she'd been carrying. "You might want to put on another layer."

After pulling the jacket from my bag and struggling into it, I spoke. "I think I'd like to get the tattoo."

Even as she cautioned me, her voice sounded pleased. "You don't get it all at once, you remember."

"Yeah, I know. But it's who I am. And if your predictions about Rune are right, we all need to be at the top of our game."

Her eyes became chips of ice. "You think this is a game?"

"No! It's a saying, meaning you have to be the best, the winner." Sheesh.

The explanation took the high color off her cheeks. "Oh, well. That's true." She was quiet for a moment. "There hasn't been much news regarding Rune. It worries me."

I knew what she meant. Rune hadn't retired to a quiet little town to play golf. His suspicious note for me at the trading center still made me nervous. "He sent me a note, encouraging me to go back to Linneah."

"When?"

"In the travel portal. Somehow he knew I'd be at the trading center."

Abira's brow furrowed. "Maybe Declan will have more information."

"Who's that?"

"The owner of the inn. And my brother." She smiled. "So don't worry about owing me."

When it grew too dark to see, Abira and I took turns using our gift to light the way with flames. Although it worked, I missed Tiny's flashlight.

I missed Tiny, period. She'd been so withdrawn since she'd dropped the bombshell about having a fiancé.

We arrived at the inn late, tired and thirsty. The two-story building had been sculpted from rock, its windows irregularly carved openings.

Nobody waited at the front desk. Abira shook her head. "At the busiest time of the year? Declan needs a clerk here at all times, even this late."

I followed her through swinging doors into a large room with a bar, where customers' voices mingled with music. Colorful paintings hung on cream-colored walls, which were hard to see with all the smoke in the air from patrons enjoying an evening pipe or cigarette. A well-built Welden stood behind the counter, mirrored-glass cabinets behind him, pouring drinks for customers perched on stools. His aura lit up the area behind the counter and reflected in the mirrored glass.

When he saw Abira, he broke into a toothy grin. "Haven't seen you for several seasons."

Abira returned his smile. "I've been keeping busy."

He gestured to the stools. "Have a seat. What do you want?"

She looked at me. "Well?"

I swallowed against the grit coating my throat. "Could I have a fruit sip?"

She held up two fingers. "Two fruit sips, Johnson."

He turned to prepare the drinks, his shoulders blocking my view.

Despite the bar atmosphere, it was clean, neat, and I wasn't afraid to eat here. I'd give it three out of five stars. My mind went back to the trading post. Could you give negative stars?

The bartender placed my drink in front of me. "And who might you be?"

"Brenna. Nice to meet you." I pulled out the decorative toothpick and bit off a piece of skewered fruit. Its juice, sweet and refreshing, slid down my parched throat. A decorated fruit sip? Maybe this place deserved an extra star.

Abira took a swallow of her drink. "So where's Declan?"

Johnson smirked. "Out in the kennel."

"He doesn't have a kennel."

"He does now. Just finished construction last week. The guy who was at the front desk is now in charge of the fo-lis." Johnson chuckled before leaving to serve another customer.

She shifted in her seat. "After we finish our drinks, I'll see if we can get a room."

I wanted to see the fo-lis, but I needed a bed. And a full night's sleep. Unfortunately, I had a feeling I'd only get one of the two since we planned to leave early.

Despite the late hour, customers trickled in and out. A dice game took place in one corner; a musician softly played a guitar in another. Most of the customers looked like travelers in their cloaks, bags at their sides. They'd have to be—this place was in the middle of nowhere.

I took the last sip of my drink. Abira suddenly stood, smiling at a man making his way toward us, then threw her arms around him. "So good to see you."

He returned her hug before pulling away. "You, too. This is a nice surprise. But why during Starfall season?"

She pointed at me. "She's a participant, and I'm escorting her to the fields. Brenna, meet my brother Declan."

Her brother had the same sharp features. His white hair, though shorter than his sister's, had been pulled into a ponytail. He shook my hand. "Nice to meet a friend of Abira's."

I studied them both. "Are you two twins?"

He tilted his head. "Yes, although I was born first."

Abira snorted and picked up her bag from the floor. "Do you have a spare room?"

"You're teasing, right?"

Abira frowned. "We could bed down in the barn."

He set his jaw. "Absolutely not. You'll take the bed in the loft."

"We'll pay you—"

"Don't say another word."

"Declan—"

His eyes grew flinty. "You're family. You don't charge family."

They continued to argue, fast volleys back and forth. When Abira *finally* consented, we followed him through the maze of the inn until he stopped at a door.

Declan unlocked it and ushered us in. "Welcome to my home."

Only half the size of the bar, the cozy living room held two stuffed chairs, a large helli lantern, a footstool, and a tall bookcase overflowing with books. Smaller rooms sprouted from this hub. Each room gave a clue of its use—the edge of a stove visible in that doorway, a bathroom vanity peeking around another, and the last entryway framing a quilt crumpled on the floor. An open stairway against the far wall led to a bed occupying an open space above the living room.

"It's not much, but it's a place to sleep. If I had known you were coming..."

Abira placed her bag near the stairs, and I followed her lead. She put a hand on his arm. "It's exactly what we need. But we need something else, as well."

She took a seat. Declan began to sit in the other chair, then offered it to me.

"No, I'm good, thanks." I waved away his offer and sat next to my bag on the stairs.

Abira leaned forward, her voice low. "Have you heard any rumors about Rune?"

He grimaced. "A lot of information is floating around, not all of it true."

It sounded like the internet.

She tilted her head. "What have you heard?"

"Some Weldens came through last week claiming they saw him in Ginselwyn. Although Ginselwyn is not a vacation spot. Not with the water shortage."

I cut in. "Water shortage?" Tiny hadn't mentioned a drought. Did she know?

Declan propped his legs on the nearby footstool. "The Calder River's level has dropped. Nobody knows why."

Abira's brow puckered. "Brenna and a friend are headed there in a day or two. After Starfall."

"I wouldn't worry. They'll get it straightened out. So, Brenna, you're interested in trying Starfall? Pretty exciting time, what with the soldiers and all."

"Yeah, I've—what soldiers?"

"A large detachment of Emperor Rexson's men is helping with the crime that sometimes accompanies Starfall. They're stationed around the perimeter. A group of Kells saw them arrive two days ago."

My heart gave a lurch. Was Baldwin here? I shook my head to clear my thoughts. Emperor Rexson's men came from all over—Lennor, Wildamek, Ginselwyn. The chance Baldwin would be in that group was a long shot. I wasn't sure whether I was happy about that or disappointed.

Abira smiled. "That's good news. There'll be a lot less thievery and attacks if the soldiers are here."

"That's the hope. The last Starfall was a disaster. Something had to be done." Pushing back his chair, he slapped his legs and stood. "Well, I wish you luck, Brenna. Not everyone gets a star, but the search is part of the fun. Just don't get lost in the dark. Bad things happen to those who get lost."

Thanks, Mr. Sunshine.

Abira lifted her bag from the stairs and slung it over a shoulder. "Declan! She'll be fine. Firebrands never lose their way."

"When are you leaving?" he asked.

"Before the sun rises."

He walked toward the door. "The bar doesn't open until hours later, so I'll have breakfast ready for you both."

"Thank you. Goodnight."

With a soft "goodnight," he left the apartment, locking the door behind him.

Fatigue swamped me, and I trudged after Abira up the stairs. In minutes, I snuggled between the covers and headed for dreamland.

I opened my eyes. Darkness. A soft murmur of voices wafted up to the loft. Abira's space next to me lay bare, an indentation the only sign she'd slept there. Leaning over her edge of the bed, I found her packed bag resting near the footboard. Breakfast was probably ready. Letting out a small groan, I rolled over. Why couldn't I have four more hours of sleep?

I finally pulled myself out of bed and dressed quickly.

Breakfast, a simple affair, included toast with spreads, a strange red porridge, some cold sliced meat, and juice. In a half-hour, we'd finished and began putting the foodstuffs away.

Abira popped the last bite of toast in her mouth. "We need to be going. Thank you so much, Declan. It was good to see you."

He gave her a hug. "Come sooner and stay longer next time. And Brenna, it was good to meet you. Good luck at Starfall."

"Thanks."

He walked us to the front door. "Next time I'll show you my new business venture."

Abira gave him a half-smile. "Animal trainer?"

His face fell. "It was supposed to be a surprise. Who told you?"

"Johnson did, last night."

He grinned, the action making him look younger. "I'll be raising both breeds. The colored and the invisible."

I gasped. "There are invisible light wolves?"

"Yes, there are two kinds of foslykos. One glows with colored light. The other is mostly invisible. Usually used for highly sensitive messages."

Despite my hopeful look, Abira shook her head. "Next time."

I grumbled a little but followed her anyway.

Declan waved from the front door as we set off.

Chapter Twelve

During the next few hours, the landscape transformed from a shadowed, gloomy plain to a sun-scorched bowl of beige. After reaching the summit of yet another sand and shrub dune, I stopped and dug in my bag for my canteen.

Abira drank as well, then pointed to a line of irregular mounds in the distance. "That's the beginning of the Starfall fields. We'll head for the west side."

I wasn't impressed. "It looks kinda small."

Amusement colored her response. "That's because it's so far away."

Judging from the rumbling in my stomach, it was lunchtime when we reached the fields. The small town had ballooned into a small city with markets and street hawkers selling everything from cheesy souvenirs to useful tools, hats, and pouches. A boxy restaurant spilled its clients into an impromptu eating area outside, while a nearby bar served a steady stream of customers.

I followed Abira through the crowds to a food vendor selling balls of dough with a seasoned meat filling. She bought two for each of us, and we ate our lunch as we hiked toward the west side of town.

The crowds thinned the farther we walked, although the roads remained busy. At the bottom of the hills, families and lone individuals relaxed near freestanding lean-tos set back from the main road. The flimsy structures wobbled in the breeze, the stiff material across the top lifting before flapping back down.

"What's the deal with the tents?"

She glanced in the direction I was looking. "Some people view Starfall like a reunion, a time to see family or friends. Still others are desperate for a good spot and will come early."

These people were braver than I was. "Will they be safe?"

"Hmm, hard to say. Let's hope so."

The road curved around the perimeter of the fields before turning northwest and disappearing over the horizon.

Abira left the road and trudged through the sand toward a rock wall. "Here's our destination."

I stopped. "How is a wall going to keep us safe?"

"Watch and learn, spitfire."

"Spitfire?" I gave her a glare.

She smirked, her gray eyes lighting up. "You're a young Firebrand, so yes, spitfire. It suits you."

I wasn't so sure about that...

At the wall, she drew her fingers along its rough surface, tracing brown veins mixed among gray. "Here, help me push."

I walked over and placed my hands flat next to hers.

"At the count of three...one, two, three."

When we pushed, the rock shifted, then slid backward, revealing a four-foot opening. The rock thumped to a stop, and she dusted off her hands with a pleased smile.

I stepped high into the carved hollow, remaining a little stooped so I didn't hit my head. "This is so cool. Hey, there's a hole in the floor back here."

"It leads to a bigger underground cavern."

"Why has nobody else found this place?"

Abira shrugged. "It's not very noticeable from the road. And Starfall is rare enough that perhaps people forget, die, whatever. The space has always been available when I needed it." She gestured for me to join her at the front. "See this mound of earth to your right?"

When I nodded, she continued. "The stars fall from the sky at a slant from your upper right to your lower left. That mound will give you some cover, should you need it. Once the stars start falling, there'll be moments where you can't move without getting hit. Then you'll have a period where nothing's happening. Listen and listen well. Some stars, as they come in, give off a high-pitched whistle, like a lonely wind through the trees. That means take cover."

My stomach clenched. Now that I was finally here, reality hit hard. Waiting was the worst part. I tuned in, realizing Abira was still talking.

"—so take a nap. We'll have a late supper, you can change, and then we'll wait. Every Starfall comes at about the same time, after midnight."

I rubbed my hands over my goose-pimpled arms. "I'm kind of nervous."

"Good. People who aren't make stupid mistakes. Get some sleep."

Carrying my bag to the back of the tunnel, I pulled out my blanket. After laying it out, I situated my bag as a pillow. When I lay down, I studied the ceiling, my ears tuned to every sound. Too keyed up. With some deep breathing, my thoughts steadied. Maybe Baldwin was around here somewhere. My heart lurched, then twisted. Did I want to find him? It didn't matter. The fields were a zoo. But even knowing he might be close was a bittersweet ache.

I ground my teeth and turned over. I hated those television shows where the sappy heroine moped for days and ate ice cream when she lost her guy. So how had I become that girl? Well, minus the ice cream.

A small part of my brain reminded me we hadn't talked. I hadn't read his letter. Closing my eyes, I redirected my thoughts. How was Arvandus doing? Did he miss me? Did Baldwin? My eyes grew heavy, and I drifted off.

Abira shook me awake. "Time for supper."

Our meal was nuts, peeled fruit, flatbread, and jerky, all washed down with lukewarm water. I sat at the entrance of our cave and let my legs hang over the edge. Darkness fell quickly, shadowing hollows and rolling hills. Near the lean-tos and along the road, men gathered. I squinted, trying to figure out what was going on.

"You'd better change your clothes. The temperature's dropping, and we'll have to make sure your disguise works."

I sighed. "Is that necessary?"

She gestured to the people. "Do you see any women or girls ready to gather stars?"

"Um, no?"

"That's right, because they're smart. But you're stubborn and don't listen to reason. So the best thing we can do is make you inconspicuous."

At my glare, she gave me a steady look.

"Go get changed."

Changing into my black pants and shirt took two minutes. The rest of the time I struggled to get my hair into the hat. Ten minutes and dozens of bobby pins later, I walked up to Abira. "My hair has revolted."

"Let me see."

I pulled off the hat. She chuckled. "Saints and sinners. Let me see what I can do."

She pulled out the pins, brushed my hair, and then gathered it into a twist, pinning it in a few crucial but secure places. "There. Put on the hat and let's see how you look."

I tugged on the hat, carefully pulling it over my pinned hair. "You'll have to teach me how you did that."

Abira studied me. "Well, I'd never believe you were male, but with the scarf, you might pull it off. Don't talk, but if you must, keep your voice low." She took the scarf looped around my neck and arranged it to cover my mouth and nose. "Yes, better."

I jerked as voices drew close to our cave.

"Anyone here?" a male voice called.

My heart leaped. That voice. It couldn't be.

Abira produced a small flame to better see the visitor. I nearly swallowed my tongue when Baldwin's face came into view. "Hello, my lady. My lord." He waved in my direction. "I am Baldwin Marek, a soldier with Emperor Rexson's forces."

"Can we help you?" Abira asked.

"Allow one of us to assist you if you encounter problems. We are here to keep the peace and ensure the safety of participants and spectators."

Baldwin wore the uniform of the Royal Linnean Forces, the eight-pointed star stitched on his chest. The cut of his black and gray coat emphasized his broad shoulders, and his black pants accentuated his height.

I wanted to pull off my scarf and give him a hello kiss he'd never forget.

I recoiled at the thought. No, I didn't. What was wrong with me? Gari had been all over him, and I'd never be able to forget it.

"Thank you. I'm Abira, and this is B—"

"Bob." I jerked my chin and offered a two-fingered wave. "Hey, how's it going?"

His brow wrinkled.

Mental facepalm. Nobody talked like that here. I was a lousy dude.

Abira gave him a smile. "It's reassuring to have a Linnean soldier for protection."

He returned it with a sparkling-white smile of his own. "I will do perimeter checks in your area for the duration of my shift."

"Thank you." She gestured for him to come closer. "Have you eaten? We have extra nuts and Bora fruit."

What? No. He had to go far, far away.

He smiled his thanks. "Thank you, but I am fine. I will eat after my shift."

"After your shift? Nonsense. Br—Bob, can you get Baldwin some Bora fruit?"

I sauntered over to her bag, trying to imitate how guys walked. I must've missed the mark because Baldwin frowned and tilted his head.

When I handed him the fruit, his fingers brushed mine. I yanked my trembling hands away.

"Thank you." He popped a piece in his mouth.

I retreated to the back of the hollowed space, unable to pull my eyes from him.

After he finished the fruit and left, I pulled the scarf under my chin and took deep breaths.

Abira walked toward me, her eyes full of speculation. "Why did you call yourself Bob? He's here to protect us. Why didn't give him your real name?"

"You said I should stay hidden."

"But he's a Linnean guard."

"Soldier, not a guard. This is his first deployment."

Her eyebrows climbed her forehead. "And you know that how?"

"Um." Sheesh. "He's someone I know."

"How well?"

"None of your business!"

She eyed me, a slight smile on her face. "So he's your boyfriend then."

I looked at the floor. "Used to be." Swallowing against gathering tears, I hitched up a shoulder. "Don't know." A single rogue tear escaped down my cheek.

She rested a comforting hand on my shoulder. "Brenna? What's wrong?"

"I came through the portal to surprise him last weekend. I caught him with his old girlfriend. She was all over him." Why couldn't I get rid of that image?

She squeezed my shoulder, her eyes compassionate. "What did he say?"

"Nothing. I ran out of the restaurant, and he left the next morning for his assignment."

"You two should talk about it."

"Yeah, definitely not. You tell him I'm here, and I'll never get to participate. So for now, I'm Bob." I yanked the scarf back up over my nose.

Pursing her lips, she sighed. "Let's sit at the opening. It's a nice night."

We relaxed next to each other as Bella's Comet moved slowly in the night sky, the Petrus Rings' silver-blue and gold bands sparkling. Several dark clouds played tag with an almost-full moon.

After a few minutes, Baldwin walked by. He paused and strolled over to where we sat. My stomach flipped, and my shoulder muscles turned to steel. What now?

"It is a beautiful night," he said.

"It certainly is." Abira glanced at the sky. "I'm sure you're glad it's not raining."

"You too. Gathering stars in the rain would not be fun."

"Oh, I'm not gathering tonight. Bob is."

His steady gaze pinned me in place. I resisted the urge to squirm. "I wish you good fortune, then."

I gave a quick nod and looked out into the night, pretending permanent interest in the dark landscape. This had to be the worst kind of torture—pretending to be a guy with your gorgeous ex-boyfriend right in front of you. Sadness, frustration, anger—all of them fused into a hot mess in my chest.

Baldwin studied the shadowy surroundings. "Where are you from, Abira?"

"I was born and raised in Kelda Hills."

"What about you, Bob?"

My brain scrambled for an answer that wasn't a lie.

After a beat of silence, Abira helped me out. "Bob's on his way to Ginselwyn after Starfall to help a friend."

Which didn't answer his question, but he didn't push for more.

Rubbing her arms, Abira gave a small shiver. "The temperature's dropping. I need my jacket."

She stood, walked over to her bag, and began to search inside.

Silence slipped between Baldwin and me, thickening in the darkness.

He leaned against the rock. "You know, you remind me of someone back home."

I sliced him a sideways glance, but his eyes remained on the shadowed countryside. *Say something, but not too much.* "Yeah?"

His teeth flashed in the darkness. "Maybe it is your eyes. They are the same color blue."

"Maybe."

Silence settled again. Awkward.

"We had a disagreement before I left. We should have talked about the unfortunate situation."

Captain Understatement thought another girl kissing him was an unfortunate situation? Or was it my catching him?

I decided to take a risk. "Woman problems?"

To my surprise, he grimaced. "Yeah. We need to talk. She is pretty stubborn, but maybe she will understand."

My thoughts whirled. *We need to talk* was code for *this relationship is over.* Oily dread coated my stomach. "Good luck." I forced the words through clenched teeth.

He chuckled. "Thanks. Do you have a special girl somewhere?"

I shook my head. "Too busy."

Baldwin's smile grew slowly, the action heartbreakingly beautiful. "Too busy for love? When you are in love with the right girl, you make time."

My breath stalled in my throat. Was Gari the right girl? Or me?

Turning around, he headed back to his post. "Have a good evening, Bob."

My heart, a dead weight in my chest, trapped me on the edge of the rock. Heavy clouds shifted, blocking the moon and the beautiful view of Bella's Comet.

Why in all of Linneah did he have to be here?

Chapter Thirteen

Abira's voice from my right startled me. "Is everything all right?"

"No." I fought the swirl of anger and hurt in my chest. "He's going to break up with me."

Sitting down, she frowned. "How do you know?"

"He said we had to talk. Everyone knows that means it's over."

She waved the comment away. "Don't assume anything."

My mind spun in the silence, while a breeze wafted the scent of sage into the cave. "I saw him at the market, in a spiegel globe."

"The painted ones? I know the seller. They're a good investment, if you're looking for that sort of thing."

"He saw me too, when I looked into the glass." I searched her gray eyes. "How does that work?"

She raised an eyebrow. "Don't be so sure the relationship is over. It only works if the other person's looking for you in a globe as well."

At a muffled thump from the field, a cry went up from the crowd.

Abira shifted. "It's starting. Remember, stars go in the snapped pockets so they don't fall out."

At this point, Starfall was the last thing I wanted to do. But what I'd been waiting for was here and now. I tucked my confused thoughts away and turned to Abira. "Wish me luck."

"May Elyon bless your search, keep you safe, and guide you home."

"Uh, thanks." I liked that one better anyway.

Searching my pockets, I found a stick of fypex gum. If I ever needed to focus, it was now. I shoved it into my mouth and left the safety of the rock.

Hurrying to the mound of earth was like taking a walk during a fireworks display. Bright streamers of white light lit the heavens, stars falling at a slant from my right. Faint whistling filled the sky, and most of the gatherers looked over their shoulders. Blinding ribbons of light fell, and a jolting thump near my hiding place made me jump. I dashed out of cover to find the star. At a sudden push from behind, I fell, scraping my hands. Before I could get my feet under me, the guy scooped up the star and dashed off toward another prize.

Grumbling, I wiped my stinging hands on my pants while checking the sky. The groups of people and families set back from the road seemed to be out of harm's way as the stars landed in the middle of the fields. I jerked again at another solid strike to my left. Before I could move, another man grabbed the star and loped away. As the glittering stars fell, their high, faint whistles made the hair on my neck stand on end. This was way more dangerous than I'd expected—like a carnival whack-a-mole in the dark, and I was the mole.

To my left, a ribbon of light slammed into the dirt. I raced over, but a teen boy materialized from the shadows, picked it up, and ran off.

I made several more attempts, running from the safety of my earth shelter. I missed the first two by being too slow. The third I couldn't find. I produced a small flame to search the ground, but the whistling in the sky and my vulnerable position made me dash for cover. When another began its descent, I quickly estimated and sprinted for the expected landing spot. It landed a couple of feet in front of me, and I grabbed it, the heat intense on my scraped palm.

A guy grabbed my wrist. "Give it up." The odor of verum wafted over me.

"Get off." Producing a large flame, I jerked my arm from his grasp. "Or I'll light you up." Not really, but it was a good bluff.

With a growl, he grabbed my wrist again and twisted.

I screamed, dropping my find. His teeth gleamed in the dark. Flinging my hand away, he picked up my star and dashed away.

Out in the fields, a fight started. Two dark figures grappled, arms swinging, curses thickening the shadows. Moonlight flashed silver on a blade before two Linnean soldiers intervened, separating the combatants and leading away the knife wielder.

Gently rotating my wrist, I ran back to my mound of earth. At least it wasn't broken. The sky flashed, and stars continued to fall. How could I get a star if they kept getting taken? Maybe I wasn't being tough enough. Well, duh. I rubbed my aching wrist. This wasn't an Easter egg hunt, and the gatherers weren't little kids.

"Bob!" I turned. Baldwin stalked toward me. "Are you injured? Did that man assault you?"

Assault me? I suppressed a snicker. "No. Just reevaluating."

He studied me in the dark, his head cocked. "If you are sure."

"Yes, thank you." With a quick wave, I checked the sky and hurried back toward the field. I growled low in my throat, psyching myself up. Warrior Time.

When the next star landed a few feet away, I lunged for it. Mine. Another person grabbed it at the same time, but I yanked it away. Triumph filled me until I saw my opponent. It was a little boy. His dark eyes filled with defeat, and he turned away. Guilt swamped me.

"Hey."

He turned back, and I handed him the star. His star.

Eyes wide, a disbelieving smile filled his face. "Thanks, milord!" He ran off into the field, his night complete.

My shoulders sagged. It was the right thing to do, but I'd just sealed my broke status. I'd have to go back to Linneah. Tiny would meet her fiancé alone, and I'd be grounded for life. Worst night ever.

With the hollow whistles filling the sky, I checked above. A couple large, blazing lights to my right and coming in fast. The stars landed a few steps away. With desperation filling my chest, I dove for the prize. In the darkness, I scrabbled on my hands and knees, taking no time to create a flame. My hands closed around a small rock, its heat penetrating. Breathing out an incredulous laugh, I didn't bother to check. Its warmth identified it as a star. Stuffing it into my pocket, I snapped the flap closed and hurried toward the earth mound.

High-pitched whistles pierced through my excitement. I began to turn. A searing blast punched my shoulder blade, pinning me to the ground and robbing my breath. Before I could get up, my head exploded.

Arvandus! Help!

In seconds, Abira's hands grazed my cheek. "Don't move. Where are you hurt?"

I groaned, pain making it hard to think. "My head, behind my ear. My shoulder blade."

"Here?"

I screamed, her touch feeling like fire on bare, raw nerves.

Baldwin's voice drifted above my head. "Abira, my lady. What happened to Bob?"

"He was hit, a star on his shoulder and his head. But sh—" She cleared her throat. "*He* hasn't lost consciousness."

"Bob?" His face filled my vision. "Do you have feeling in your arms and legs?"

My vision fuzzing, I blinked a few times. "Yes."

"Good." He stood. "I can carry him to a litter available for the injured."

"No, move him back to our spot. I can heal him."

"Um, my lady, I must disagree. He needs to see a doctor."

"I'm a Firebrand. I can heal him better than any doctor." Abira immediately moved to my head and picked me up under my arms.

I cried out, pain streaking from my shoulder blade to my back. "Stop, stop. Please." My tears soaked the scarf covering my face.

Abira put me down, her face pinched in the moonlight.

"My lady, allow me. I can move him quicker, and we need to vacate the field. It is not safe."

"Of course." Abira moved aside while Baldwin scooped me up.

His scent, oranges and worn leather, drifted over me. His muscular arms held me close, and I bit my lip until I tasted blood. The pressure of his hands on my back was almost unbearable, although his touch was gentle. Taking a deep breath, I flopped my head onto his shoulder. Would a dude do that if injured? I moaned. Didn't know, didn't care.

In moments, he strode into the cave and placed me on my blanket on my side.

Abira knelt near my head. "Thank you, Baldwin, for your help."

"What else can I do?" He hovered near her shoulder.

"Nothing, only privacy. If I need any more assistance, I will let you know." She gave him her back, blocking my view of his furrowed brow.

After he left the cave, she pulled off my hat and probed the wound on my head. Tears slipped down my cheeks, drenching the blanket. So. Much. Pain.

Suddenly, a warming sensation swept through me, shuddering my limbs once. I relaxed as soothing heat sank deep. Above me, Abira muttered as she gently probed my scalp.

With a sudden ripping sound, cool air touched my back. "Hey!" My shoulder throbbed.

"Lie still. I need to reach your wound."

Rolling me onto my stomach, her fingers danced across my skin before moving to my shoulder. My muscles loosened, melting like warm butter. Her murmured words as she healed me were requests to Elyon for recovery, strength, and wisdom since I'd made a stupid mistake. The healing felt so good, I let the insult pass.

She finally sat back. "How do you feel?"

"Exhausted."

"Your head wound should feel better. Your shoulder is deeply bruised, but you'll heal fully in a day or two. Unfortunately, we can't stay here. I need you to sit up."

Offering me a hand, she pulled me into a sitting position. The pain in my head had lessened, but my shoulder still throbbed. I held out a hand as the room tilted. "Whoa."

"Can you walk to the closest inn?"

"I don't know." The room listed whenever I moved my head. "Let's try."

I stood but grabbed her arm and squeezed my eyes shut. "I can't."

"Fine. Let's rest here for an hour or so."

After an hour, Abira went looking for Baldwin, but the soldier who brought a horse and wagon for our short trip was his replacement. I stifled my disappointment. I didn't need to see him again. As the young soldier transported us to the inn, my heart ached, knowing before long Baldwin would give me the *it's not you, it's me* speech.

Dismay filled me—there was no way we'd get a room, not during Starfall. But luck was on our side. Abira booked a tiny room someone had just vacated. It was way better than a barn.

Although I had every intention of getting myself ready for bed, the last thing I remembered was Abira helping me take off my boots.

Voices in the hallway woke me the next morning. Moaning, I cracked my eyes open. I lay tucked in a narrow bed. The sheets snug around my chin smelled of cloves, cinnamon, and lemon, a common disinfectant. In the windowless room's small hearth crackled a fire, its warmth welcome despite my thick blanket. The wooden walls glowed with a well-polished sheen.

When I tried to sit up, pain impaled my shoulder, and I dropped back into bed with a whimper.

I took several deep, slow breaths. Scraping sounded from the other side of the door. As it opened, I feigned sleep, keeping my eyes slit. My social skills, never stellar, were nonoperational. If it was a stranger, I wasn't interested. A blond male peeked in, his broad shoulders and golden aura filling the doorframe.

Except for him. I could definitely be interested in him.

He turned to a person behind him. "Shh, she's still asleep."

"Well, she needs to get up. Shiraz said to wake her every couple of hours." Tiny's voice.

"She looks so peaceful."

"Yeah, sleep does that to people. Get out of the way." Muted footsteps came closer to the bed. Then Tiny's hand on my wrist. "Brenna? Time to get up."

I rubbed my eyes, wondering who the gorgeous blond guy was. Unfortunately, I had to wake up to find out.

"We let you sleep longer than we should've." She glared at the guy. "But I need to ask you some questions. Do you know your name?"

"Someone already asked me that. Before." A vague memory played at the edge of my mind—people waking me, asking questions, then precious sleep.

"Yes, I know. We need to ask you again. What's your name?"

"Brenna James."

"Good. Do you know your address?"

"The Linnean castle. Or 5 Reservoir Lane, Cloverdale, Pennsylvania."

"Do you know who I am?"

I sighed. "Yes. You're Cinderella."

Her blue eyes widened. "Oh, no."

I managed a weak grin. "Just kidding, Tiny. I didn't lose consciousness." Unfortunately. The pain only made me wish I had.

"Hey, I'm just following orders. By the way, this weird guy is my brother."

He stepped forward, his gorgeous smile slightly crooked. "I'm pleased to finally meet you, Brenna. I'm Storm."

Wow. Tiny's brother was seriously hot with a killer smile. If I could just avoid the awkwardness that always hit with cute guys... "Nice to meet you, too. As well. I mean also." Stop. Talking.

He grinned, shook my hand, and then continued to hold it while settling into the chair next to my bed.

I waited for him to drop my hand and look at me strangely. Nothing. I gave him a look out of the corner of my eye. Yep, still there. Maybe he was deaf.

Tiny sat on the bed's edge before leaning over to Storm. "Hey doof, let go of her hand."

He grinned wider but let go. "Sorry, but I feel like I know you already. Shaynedel has told us so much about you."

Ah, that was it. I was just his little sister's incoherent best friend. I hadn't met all of Tiny's large family, except her younger sisters who went to Cloverdale Elementary. She'd told me her three older siblings stayed in Ginselwyn because they were done with school.

"Can you sit up?" Tiny asked.

I grimaced. "I tried earlier, but my shoulder protested."

She gestured to Storm. "Let's help her."

Even with both of them, I closed my eyes against the wash of pain spreading through my shoulder. Stifling a moan, I leaned against the pillow.

Tiny winced. "I'm so sorry."

I attempted a smile. Didn't work. "Not your fault."

"I'm going to get Shiraz. Maybe she can give you some more medicine."

After she left, Storm studied me with his bright-blue eyes, so much like Tiny's.

"So do you come here often?" I closed my eyes. Oh. My. Word. Why did all this dumb stuff come out of my mouth?

He chuckled, the baritone setting off fizzy sparkles in my stomach. "I've actually never been to any Kelda Hills establishment. So this is a first for me."

"I meant, why are you here and not in Ginselwyn? Not that I don't appreciate it, I do, but I don't know you. But you know Tiny, and she's here, so—" I pressed my lips together to stem the flow of stupid.

"My parents received a fo-li from Abira, asking for an escort to Ginselwyn for the two of you. Right after you left, I arrived in Kelda Hills. Then when Shiraz heard you were injured via another fo-li from Abira, we came to the starfield to find you. I'm glad you weren't injured badly."

"I can't believe I got a star."

He cleared his throat. "Actually, two. Abira picked up one of the stars that struck you. You're exceptionally wealthy now."

I blinked at that information, then stared at him curiously. "How much does it take to get into Ginselwyn?"

He shook his head. "I can pay for your entrance."

"Don't try it, Storm." Smiling, Tiny entered the room and pointed a finger at him. "You've got to tell her what it means if you pay for her entrance."

He blushed but gave me a mischievous smile. "It only means I'm your guardian during your stay." He held up his hands and gave me a wink. "I'll be a perfect gentleman."

I bit my lip to hide my smile. What a charmer. "Thanks, but I'd like to pay my own way."

"One star is more than enough. Cash it in before we leave, and you'll have no problem entering Ginselwyn." He leaned closer. "But I'd like to ask a favor."

I waited.

"If you need a guardian while visiting—and unattached, beautiful women sometimes do—I'd ask if you'll consider my protection."

My mouth fell open. "You're kidding. Protection?"

Tiny sighed. "Sometimes it's needed. You're cute, crazy rich, the daughter of the Queen of Linneah, and without a chaperone. It might be a good idea. I was planning to ask one of my brothers."

Good grief, what was Ginselwyn like? "All right, thanks."

He smiled, squeezing my hand before standing. "I need to send a fo-li to our family. They should be informed of our arrival."

He walked out of the room, and I closed my eyes, letting financial concerns drift away. I could pay for this hotel, reimburse Abira, and get into Ginselwyn without worry. I opened my eyes and looked at Tiny. "I did it. I got the money."

She scowled. "And almost got killed in the process."

"No, just injured."

Tiny threw her hands up. "Falling stars killed two people last night. You were lucky. You escaped with a headache and a shoulder wound."

"True. Although if I don't move, it doesn't hurt so much."

She grimaced. "You'll have to move to get to Ginselwyn, although it's not far. Shiraz said she'll bring up medicine and food."

At the thought of food, my mouth watered.

When she settled in the chair, I turned to her. "Hey, can I ask what's up with your brother?"

"What do you mean?"

"Um, he's nice and all, but he's, um, attentive."

Tiny tilted her head. "You know, he's always been the flirt in the family. But I've never seen him like this. He's crazy about you."

"That's nice." And creepy. "He doesn't know me."

"Well, he kinda does. When I go home, I've always talked about us and what happens at school. When you were involved in the battle last year, I told my family. He was super impressed. And he also knows the insane stuff you went through to come with me on this trip. But then when he arrived here and saw you?" She shook her head. "It was love at first sight."

"No such thing, Tiny."

"I saw his face. He said, and I'm not making this up, 'a maiden more beautiful than a rose.'"

I let out an unmaidenly snort of laughter. "Really?"

"Yeah." She giggled. "What if you two paired and eventually got married? You'd be my sister-in-law!"

"I can't think of anyone else I'd like to be related to." I grinned back at her, but what was the chance of that? Her brother was cute, yes, but I didn't need or want a replacement boyfriend.

When Shiraz showed up, Tiny left with a promise to visit later. After a dose of medicine, Shiraz placed a large platter of food on my lap. The scent of unfamiliar herbs drifted up from a cut of meat smothered in gravy. A thick slice of cheese bread slathered with fruit spread was off to the side, as well as a small cup of chopped rainfruit. I wolfed it all down and accepted a second piece of bread.

After the meal, I closed my eyes, my thoughts settling on Storm. His instant attraction was kind of ridiculous. Who actually believed in love at first sight? Maybe lust or attraction, but love? There was a flicker of interest on my part, but I didn't know him. If he thought I was going to fall into his arms just because he was charming and had muscular shoulders, and those bright blue eyes, and oh yeah, that crooked smile...

I sighed. Why did guys always have to mess things up?

Chapter Fourteen

The next morning, my pain had almost disappeared. Abira questioned me about leaving, and I'd agreed. We needed to get back to her house and then be on our way to Ginselwyn—we'd been gone long enough. So Abira cashed out all but a couple slivers of my stars and rented four horses. They stood tied to the shaded entryway and saddled for the journey.

As I joined the others on the porch, Storm took my hand. "I'd like to ride with Brenna, due to her injury."

I gave him a sideways look but climbed on in front of him. Everyone talked while we rode, but I remained silent, relaxing and enjoying the lack of pain.

After several hours, we stopped at a stand of cedrus trees to have a snack and let the horses rest. Storm helped me down and handed me a canteen. "Are you looking forward to visiting Ginselwyn?"

"I'll be honest—I'm a little nervous. Women are given more freedom in Linneah and Pennsylvania than in your hometown. We don't usually need protection when we go about our daily lives." I took a deep drink and handed it back.

We settled in the evergreens' shade, and he gave me a warm smile. "You don't need to be afraid. Be assured, I will protect you. But how is Pennsylvania different?"

"Well, arranged marriages are unusual. And we don't need guardians."

He handed me a small bag of dried berries out of his pack. "What about your appointed leaders?"

My fingers brushed his, and I jerked away. "Yeah, sometimes. But not your average citizens."

He gave me an appreciative smile. "Average is not a word I'd apply to you."

I blushed, and he continued.

"Shaynedel has mentioned similar differences. And I used to worry when she'd come home to visit. But now that she's engaged, I'm certain she'll be well cared for."

He popped a piece of dried fruit into his mouth.

Well cared for. The words crawled under my skin, irritating like a wool sweater. It was like he was speaking a different language. Snacks forgotten, I watched him closely. "Have you met her fiancé?"

A lock of golden hair fell over his forehead. "Yes, a good man, I think. The family will get to know him better over the next week."

"Storm, what if Tiny doesn't love him?"

With a wink, he leaned forward. "Love grows as two people learn about each other."

Suddenly, I wasn't sure if he was talking about Tiny and her fiancé or us. I looked away from the warm look in his eyes, my cheeks hot, and ate another handful of berries so I didn't have to answer.

After a few moments, we climbed back on our horses and headed toward Abira's home. The return trip was uneventful, and we trotted into Kelda Hills as the sun set, painting the sky with streaks of pink, orange, and purple.

Storm agreed to take the horses to the drop-off stable in town. After a quick supper of sliced meats, cheeses, and breads thrown together by Shiraz, Abira joined me in the living room. She laid a comforting hand on my shoulder. "What's wrong?"

I'd already curled up on the couch. "Nothing. Just tired."

She put another log on the fire crackling in the hearth. "It was a pretty exciting Starfall. I guess that means you're leaving soon."

I shrugged. "Storm hasn't said when. And I've decided I want the Firebrand mark before I leave."

"I see."

I'd been thinking about it off and on while we were at the starfields. Continuing my training made the most sense.

She sat next to me. "We'll have the marking and celebration ceremony tomorrow afternoon then. Are you sure about this? It's a commitment, and there may be sacrifices required."

Unable to meet her eyes, I looked away. What kind of sacrifices?

"Brenna, this is an important decision. You must be sure this is the path for you." She patted my hand. "Take some time to search your heart."

I spent the next hour pondering my choices. My thoughts whirled. What else would I do? Finish high school and then what? College? Probably. But a future without Linneah seemed empty and almost pointless. I wouldn't be able to use my gift on Earth. But a future fighting a man trying to take over the Jasper Territory? That was worth preparing for.

What about Baldwin? my mind whispered.

He'd always figured in my plans. Even though I was angry at him, a small part of me had hoped for reconciliation. No more, not after our conversation at Starfall. Although I'd stay in the Jasper Territory and fight Rune, I wouldn't do it in Linneah. Watching Baldwin and Gari build a life together would kill me.

Before bed, I walked into the kitchen. Abira poured a cup of tea, her simple cotton nightgown brushing the tops of her bare feet.

A light gray knit shawl draped around her shoulders. Mint tickled my nose.

When she turned, I met her steady gaze with one of my own. "I want the Firebrand mark."

Taking a sip of tea, she was silent for a moment. "Tomorrow, then. Get some sleep."

The next morning after breakfast, I spent more time thinking, per Abira's request. She seemed determined to make sure this was what I was supposed to do, but I knew deep in my heart: it was. Elyon wanted me here, learning to use the gift He'd given me.

In the bedroom, I gathered my few possessions and packed them. I stowed my bag next to the bed, then lay down and stared at the ceiling. Despite my certainty, I was still nervous about the ceremony. The women had scheduled it right before noon, followed by a celebratory-slash-going-away lunch.

Raven? Where are you?

I bolted up in bed, stunned to hear my griffin's voice. *Arvandus? Where are you?*

Flying over the Aviva Desert. Tell me where you are.

I'm in Kelda Hills, on the western outskirts of the city. I'm living with a woman named Abira Edan. She lives in the hills.

I will find you.

Shaking my head, I walked outside to wait on the porch. Arvandus was coming, although I wasn't sure why. Suddenly, I remembered calling for him after getting hit at Starfall. He must've heard me. Guilt flooded my throat. He'd left Astraya to come here, and I didn't need him. Not that I didn't want to see him—I did. But I wasn't dying.

Storm joined me on the porch. "Do you normally like to sit outside when it's this hot?" Grinning, he sat in the chair next to mine.

"My griffin's coming. He just messaged me."

His eyebrows rose. "Shaynedel told me they're magnificent creatures."

I scanned the sky. "Yes, and he's probably one of my best friends, although don't tell him that. He'd get a big head. Would you like to meet him?"

"I'd love to meet anyone you're close to."

And there was the awkwardness again. "Storm?"

He turned toward me, his blue eyes bright.

I swallowed a sigh. "You seem like a great guy. But I don't know you. And the way you're acting—like we've known each other forever and are the closest of friends—makes me uncomfortable."

His blue eyes clouded with hurt, and I mentally winced. Maybe I should kick a puppy while I was at it.

Touching his forearm, I gave him a smile. "I'd like to be friends. But it takes me a while to get to know someone until I'm comfortable with them."

He grimaced. "I'm sorry. I never meant to make you self-conscious."

"I know. You just came on pretty strong when we first met, and I'm not there yet." I wasn't explaining myself very well, but he seemed to understand anyway.

His eyes darkened. "Just so you understand, though, I don't want to be only friends."

My cheeks grew warm. Wow. He got points for bravery and directness. Still, a part of me wasn't a fan of his Insta-Love, and he needed to know. "I understand, but that's all I can offer right now."

He looked down, his fingers rubbing a callous on his palm. "Do you have someone special?"

I jerked but covered it with a shrug. "It's complicated. I did, but he made a huge mistake. Now I can't trust him."

His blue eyes shone with a shrewd light. "Trust is important. You need it for a solid relationship."

A large form flying in the sky caught my attention. *Arvandus? I think I see you. Tip your wings.* He did, his silver wingtips glinting in the sun. *Yes! I'm waving from the porch, the house with the blue door and roof.*

The griffin circled once, coming in lower. I ran out to the yard, stubby grass rustling under my boots.

Arvandus landed near the road and padded toward me.

I hurried to him, meeting him at the yard's edge with a hug. "It's so good to see you."

"You called for me. You were hurt, yes?" His wingtips threw silver sparks, letting me know he was distressed, angry, or worried.

I couldn't help but feel guilty all over again. "I participated in Starfall and got hit with two falling stars."

Arvandus growled, the sparks from his wings growing more numerous. "Why would you do something so dangerous?"

"It's a long story."

"I have time."

I gestured toward the porch. "Come sit in the shade. I'll get you some water, let everyone know you're here, and then tell you what happened."

When we reached the porch, Storm stood, his face pale. I grinned. Arvandus made a big first impression.

"Arvandus, this is Storm, Tiny's older brother. He helped us get here from Starfall safely."

Storm gave a small bow. "It's a pleasure to meet you, Arvandus."

My griffin inclined his head, his gold eyes keen, before he sat on the porch near my chair.

"I'll be right back." I left the two of them studying each other like rival gang members. Hopefully, they'd both be alive when I returned.

Inside, I filled two glasses and a large bowl with water, then placed everything on a tray. Abira walked in and glanced at the tray. "Do we have company, or are you that thirsty?"

I grinned. "Ha. Funny. My griffin, Arvandus, is here. He heard me call for him at Starfall."

She relaxed. "Ah, you used your vinculus."

I shrugged, jostling the tray a little. "Yeah, but I didn't mean to. When I got hurt, it just happened."

Abira waved away my excuse. "It's good he's here. Storm's a little too interested in you."

Tiny walked in to hear the last sentence. "Of course he is. He's in love."

A tiny bubble of irritation rose in my chest. "You keep saying that, but love doesn't just *boom*, happen like that. You have to know someone before you can truly love them." I didn't know much about love, but I knew it wasn't instantaneous. At least, not for me.

Tiny shrugged. "He thinks he is. And is that so bad?"

I couldn't prevent my scowl. "Yes, it's very bad, because I can't give him that right now. He's a great guy, but I'm not ready for a new boyfriend."

Her glare matched mine. "He's better than the last skunk you dated."

Annoyed, I grabbed the tray and stomped out of the kitchen. Tiny was biased, but I refused to be bullied into a relationship.

I walked back onto the porch. Storm and Arvandus had apparently called a truce instead of killing each other.

Storm spoke. "It's exciting you're here for the Firebrand ceremony."

Arvandus tilted his head. "What exactly is that?"

"Brenna's getting the Firebrand mark."

His furry head shot up, a feral look gleaming in his eyes. Silver sparks flashed. "A mark, Raven?"

Whoa. An angry Arvandus wasn't something I saw often. "Yeah. Why are you upset?"

His ears flattened. "I do not know this woman, but I know about the gift marks given by guild masters."

"What about them?"

Arvandus's tail swished back and forth. "Three hundred times ago, there were guilds for each talent. Marks were given as the students attained each level. Over time, tensions grew between the guilds, and some instructors nurtured the combative environment."

"Why would they do that?"

"In the hope students would strive to excel at their gifts. Although they did, their plan backfired, and the territory was plunged into the Fifty-Time Guild War. Thousands of talents died. As a result, the guilds dissolved. So I question why this stranger wants to give you a gift mark. Where do I find her?"

"She's inside, in the kitchen." I stood and opened the door. "Good luck getting through the door."

He gave me an unsettling glare.

O-kay. "I'll get her. You two can talk in the backyard."

In the kitchen, Abira had just finished setting the table. I pulled her aside.

"My griffin is not happy about the Firebrand mark. Or my injury. Or much of anything at this point. Could you talk to him in the backyard? Maybe even make him happy?"

She chuckled. "I'll see what I can do. But griffins do what they want."

I wandered back to the porch to hang out with Storm. A small kernel of worry settled in the back of my mind. What if Arvandus convinced Abira I shouldn't do this?

"I'm sorry." Storm's voice pulled my attention from my worry. "I shouldn't have said anything."

"No, it's fine. I think it'll be all right once they talk. I need the training, though. There's so much more I need to learn."

"Mastery of a talent can take many times. Many don't use their gifts to their maximum potential."

"What's your talent?"

He leaned forward and braced his elbows on his knees, his jasper swinging forward from his shirt collar. The deep-blue stone glittered in the sunlight.

I rubbed my bare neck. I missed my jasper. Maybe I had lost it. I could hope, right? Or did Rune have it? I pushed away the thought, hoping the hollow pit in my stomach would close.

Storm studied the desert scenery. "I'm an Illusionbrand. My entire family is, actually. We all have different versions of the same gift."

My curiosity piqued, my ADHD instantly pushed aside thoughts of my jasper. "Different versions? How does that work?"

"Do you trust me?"

I gave him a sideways glance. "Sure." I think.

"Look at the front yard."

I did, taking in the dry grass, stubby pines, and sandy earth stretching into the distance—and gasped as it morphed into a landscape of green grass dotted with shield trees. The Linnean castle stood next to the fountain portal, the cascade of water a glittering curtain. The Argent Ocean gleamed silver in the distance. A twinge of homesickness pierced my heart.

"Linneah. It's beautiful."

The image shimmered before dissolving. Storm took a deep breath and blew it out slowly. "Thanks. My older brother Sloane and Shaynedel can alter their form quite well."

"Yeah, I saw Tiny's in action at the travel portal trading center."

His eyes widened. "Half-Mile Down? That's rough territory."

"No kidding. She did this great old-lady-fortune-teller thing."

He smiled as if familiar with her transformation. "My older sister and mother can do illusions with environments, for example making a house appear more comfortable or cleaner than it is. My father is one of the most powerful Illusionbrands in Ginselwyn. He has kept most of the residents happy, despite the water shortage."

I squinted. Their father must be a pretty important guy. Still... "It sounds a little like mind control." I immediately snapped my mouth shut. No filter again. I waited for Storm's explosion.

"Well, in some ways, yes. It keeps the public from rioting. Although they know there's a problem, he reassures them things are firmly in control and not to worry. He fosters a feeling of safety within the community. An Illusionbrand's only weakness is being easily deceived by another's illusion."

"That's weird. You'd think you'd be more aware of it."

He shrugged. "It's a drawback to the gift."

Abira joined us on the porch. "Your griffin is a good friend. He was worried when he heard of your plans."

I jumped to my feet. "Am I still training with you? Or did he change your mind?"

"No, I reassured him. I think we understand each other now."

Relief filled me, loosening my muscles. "Where is he?"

Abira nodded toward the house. "Shiraz is quite taken with him. She immediately gave him some water and began preparing a snack." Abira turned to head inside. "We'll begin the ceremony shortly. Meet us in the backyard."

The tent in the backyard was a wide swath of white fabric held up by poles, but it kept the sun off our heads. Under it, a gray blanket had been spread out with a few pillows. An enormous bowl of water rested nearby.

Abira stood under the tent, wearing a loose white tunic and white pants. Despite the garments' casual cut, it looked professional. She leaned close. "Do you have a sleeveless top on under your shirt?"

I frowned. "Yes. Why?"

"Take off the shirt. It's required for the test."

I just stared at her. "Test? What test?"

Chapter Fifteen

Abira turned away. "Everyone, gather around. We'll have the ceremony and then follow it with a delicious lunch and pupkissberry pie for dessert."

Although pupkissberry was a favorite, my stomach had morphed into a leaden knot. Grimacing, I peeled off my shirt and dropped it on the blanket.

Tiny sidled up behind me and squeezed my hand. "Good luck."

I swallowed, my mouth suddenly dry. "Yeah, I just heard there was a test. What's that about?"

She tilted her head. "Didn't she tell you? You have to demonstrate your abilities."

I turned to Abira. "Don't you think you should've mentioned that?"

She shook her head. "You either know it or you don't. You've practiced. I believe you're ready."

Glad one of us did.

Relax, Raven. Elyon made you for this.

My griffin sat at the edge of the blanket. I gave him a smile. *Thanks, Arvandus. Just a little nervous.*

Storm, Tiny, and Shiraz sat on the ground. Nerves shimmied under my skin at the small crowd, although a part of me wished Mom and Dad were here, too.

Abira perched on the only chair. "Thank you all for attending. Today, Brenna James chooses to test to a Level Three Firebrand. If successful, the demonstration will be followed by the taking of the mark. That part of the ceremony is optional for the audience. Let us begin."

She pointed beyond the tent to a circle of dirt the size of an above-ground swimming pool. "Please stand there and demonstrate Level One: creation of fire."

I walked over to the area, the sun beginning to bake my bare shoulders. Holding open a hand, I brought forth a flame the size of a cell phone. No problem.

"Hold that," she called, "and expand it."

What? I scowled. Hadn't practiced expansion much. I'd create a small, medium, or large flame. I concentrated on the glowing flame, sweat breaking out on my forehead. The fire grew, eventually curling in on itself until it resembled a glowing volleyball.

"Very good. Level One complete." She gave me a pleased smile.

Everyone clapped, and I allowed a small smile of my own to slip out, along with some of the tension in my shoulders.

"Now." Abira pulled a knife from her pocket. "Level Two: healing."

Queasy apprehension filled my stomach. "Are you planning to use that on me?"

Her lips firmed. Apparently, I wasn't supposed to talk during the ceremony. "Do you have any other alternatives?"

I sighed. She was going to cut me. Not fair, but I didn't want her cutting anyone else. I walked over. "Arm? Hand?"

"Left forearm." She reached out, holding my arm in a firm grip. "Don't move. This won't hurt much. It's a sharp knife."

Well, that made it all better.

With a quick move, she slashed a shallow two-inch cut on my forearm. I hissed. Fun, fun. Pressing my fingers to the cut, I focused. The foggy mist of healing took over, slowing the minutes until blood clotted and skin mended. When time resumed its march, I held out my arm. Only a thin pink line remained.

Abira smiled. "Very good. Level Two complete."

Again, everyone clapped. But the hardest test was the third level. The one I'd only been practicing for a couple of days. At least no knives or blood were involved.

She picked up the bowl and set it on the ground. "Level Three is comprised of two parts—the removal of fire's heat from water and the removal of fire's heat from earth. Water first. Please proceed."

She released a fireball into the water. As the flames licked across the surface, the bowl of water bubbled at full boil.

I reached in, pulling the heat into my hands. A buzzing sweat streaked up my arms. Removing my hands, I turned to the side and allowed the heat to escape from my fingertips in a rush of flame. I wiped a shaky hand across my forehead. A little too intense.

A tiny voice of doubt whispered in my ear—*epic fail coming up.* I hadn't practiced enough. The last phase, removing heat from the earth, was the hardest and the one I'd practiced the least.

The tattoo's five intricate pieces formed a large flame. I suddenly wanted three of the five pieces more than anything. According to Abira, Level Two was commonplace.

She stood and walked to the circle. Kneeling, she buried both hands in the sandy ground. The dirt cracked, tiny fissures opening in the dry earth. "The last phase of Level Three: heat removal from the earth. Brenna, please demonstrate the final phase."

Taking a deep breath, I walked to the circle and knelt. If the Spierwhit Scorpions returned, I was racing for the house. Uneasiness tightened my shoulders. When Abira pulled her hands out and stepped away, I placed my hands on the ground and took a deep breath. I pulled the heat in, a slow retrieval to make sure I did it correctly. The heat built, licking into my hands, heating my cheeks. But more remained. Leaving my hands on the ground, I eyed the circle.

She'd filled the whole freaking thing.

My brain scrambled. Here it was, what I'd been dreading. Did I discharge what I had or store some of it in my body so I could gather more? Leaving any heat behind felt like a job unfinished. Maybe it would be an immediate fail. But Abira had said holding the heat would warp my gift.

Maybe, maybe, maybe—I didn't know.

In a quick decision, I pulled my right hand away and discharged a fireball. Some of the heat in my left hand discharged as well, returning to the ground. Panicking a bit, I zeroed in and pulled the heat back. I plunged my right hand in to gather more. Then I drew the left hand away and released another round of fire, carefully continuing to gather with my other hand.

Sweat popped up on my neck and slid down my spine. So. Much. Heat.

With a final tug, I filled my palms with the last tendrils of warmth. I again released the flames one at a time while palming the earth to check for lurking heat I might've missed. When I finished, I dropped to my backside, wrung out.

Abira walked over, checked the ground, then stood. "Phase two of heat retrieval has been completed successfully." She grinned and helped me up.

I stood, wobbly and flushed with success. The small group clapped and hooted, Storm giving me a gorgeous grin before putting two fingers to his mouth. His piercing whistle sliced through the air. Tiny slapped his arm before continuing to clap.

Abira held up her hands. "Brenna James has achieved the rank of Level Three Firebrand. We will signify that achievement with the taking of the mark."

She gestured for me to sit under the tent. I stumbled over to the blanket, then sank to my bottom. Crossing my legs, I slumped over, glad I didn't have to support myself anymore. A soft breeze blew, teasing damp hair at my forehead. I closed my eyes and breathed in the fruity scent of blooming cactus.

"That was amazing."

I jerked up, my eyes flying open. Storm crouched in front of me, his eyes filled with admiration. Drawn by his azure gaze, I leaned closer. Something warm flickered in the blue depths.

Blinking, I pulled away and offered him a smile. "Thanks." Was I falling for Storm? No, of course not.

Shiraz approached us. "Little chickadee, you were wonderful. Congratulations!" She reached down to fuss with the pillows nearby. "Here. Get comfortable. Do you know where you'd like the mark?"

Absolutely. Wherever it hurt the least. "Um, I hadn't thought about it."

Shiraz tilted her head. "Abira's is on her arm. I've heard of others getting it on their neck, on a leg. It depends if you want it someplace conspicuous or not."

"I'm more concerned with pain."

The heavyset woman's eyes filled with understanding. "Above a shoulder blade, on the thigh, calf, outer forearm. All good places."

"And you know this how?"

She blushed, her cheeks turning apple red. "I've done some research. Thought about getting a personal one."

"But you never did?"

Chuckling, she shook her head. "I don't like needles."

Me neither.

Abira walked over with a brown bottle in one hand and a box in the other. "I've got the needles, ink, and secatic oil. Are you ready?"

"I think so." I reached up and gathered my hair to the side. "I'd like it high on the back, just above my right shoulder blade."

Her eyes grew flinty. "Are you embarrassed by this mark?"

Sheesh. Not again. "No, I just don't want everyone to know what I'm capable of. The element of surprise is sometimes helpful. Plus, I don't like pain. Shiraz said it's less painful there."

Her stance relaxed. "Fair enough. Lie on your stomach."

Shiraz helped me get situated among the pillows—one tucked between my chest and chin and another nearby to dig my fingers into.

Suddenly, Storm whispered in my ear. "Do you need a hand to hold?"

I jumped and turned to see him smiling at me, close enough for me to see the navy flecks in his eyes. "Um, maybe."

He grabbed my hand. "Squeeze as hard as you need to. I'm tough." His fingers were strong and warm, reassuring.

Abira moved my strap aside and swiped my skin with oil. "If the pain is too much, say something. We can give you a little in some water."

"It's too much."

"Brenna..."

"Really. I don't like pain. I'd like a little extra."

With the exception of Arvandus and Storm, everyone else wandered back to the house. It took more time for her to pour me a glass of water, drip a little oil in, have me drink it, and then allow me to get comfortable a second time, but I didn't care. By the time I was on my stomach again, the oil started to steal through my system. As my vision blurred, I squeezed my eyes shut.

Storm cradled my hand in his once more. "Breathe deep, try to relax."

My breath caught at the first needle prick.

"How about a story?"

"Please," I mumbled.

For the next hour, he shared a story about a brave young man, a beautiful slave, and a callous dragon. Before the ending, Abira interrupted. "Done."

The top of my back stung, though it wasn't bad. Thank you, secatic oil. I sat up. "How's it look?"

She shrugged. "Like you just got the mark. It's inflamed a bit. I'll give you some oil to wipe around the edges to help with healing."

Storm pushed my hair aside. "Very nice. Only two more pieces to go."

His breath was warm on my neck, and I shivered.

Abira pulled out several cloth pads. "Let me wrap it for today and tonight. After you unwrap it, wipe it with oil, then let air get to it so it heals."

I turned to Storm. "So how does the story end?"

He grinned. "You didn't recognize it?"

"Sorry, no."

"It's the story of Aideen Siriol, the famous Firebrand."

The name was immediately familiar. "I have his sword. Emperor Rexson gave it to me last year."

He looked super impressed—and surprised. "Yet you don't know the story?"

"Well, I know some of it, minus the ending." I nudged his arm.

Storm laughed. "You'll have to wait to hear the ending."

"Oh, come on." I tried a pout, which just made him laugh harder.

Tiny came to the back door and called across the yard. "Lunch is ready."

Apparently, work and pain made me ravenous. I ate seconds of everything—fruit salad, sandwiches, roasted veggie casserole, followed by the promised pupkissberry pie—and washed it all down with rainfruit juice. I sat at the head of the table, Storm on my left and Abira on my right. From the corner of my eye, I noticed Storm's glances. One look from his blue eyes and my heart fluttered. Big time. And although I wasn't sure why, a trickle of guilt followed.

As we finished, a low, short howl came from the front of the house.

Abira's eyes widened. "A foslykos?" She left to check and soon called me to the living room. "Brenna, the fo-li is for you."

I made it to the living room in record time.

Sitting on the porch was a light wolf. Shimmering colors—blue, green, gold, soft red—swirled through his fur, like the aurora borealis. My breath caught. Such a beautiful animal. I touched his fur, and light stirred around my fingers, spiraling like oil and water.

She pointed to his collar. "Your name is on the band. The message is tucked inside."

Sure enough, *Brenna James* was written on the wide, leather strap. I found a small pocket inside the collar and fished out the message.

BRENNA,

YOUNG LADY, YOU HAVE NO IDEA HOW UPSET I AM! LEAVING LIKE THAT WITHOUT SECURITY? I DON'T KNOW WHAT YOU WERE THINKING. THE GUARDS I SENT DIDN'T FIND YOU—AS A RESULT, I SPENT TOO MANY NIGHTS WORRIED ABOUT WHERE YOU WERE AND IF YOU WERE SAFE. RECEIVING ABIRA EDAN'S REQUEST TO TRAIN YOU WAS VERY WELCOME INDEED.

I KNOW HER—WE MET A FEW YEARS AGO. SHE IS A DETERMINED WOMAN AND AN EXCELLENT INSTRUCTOR. AFTER YOUR TIME IN GINSELWYN, RETURN DIRECTLY TO ABIRA'S TO CONTINUE YOUR TRAINING. I BELIEVE YOU WILL BE SAFER THERE.

IF I COULD, I WOULD SEND A BODYGUARD TO KELDA HILLS. UNFORTUNATELY, THAT IS IMPOSSIBLE AT THIS TIME. I MISS YOU, SWEETIE. STAY SAFE.

I LOVE YOU,

MOM

A hologram of the eight-pointed Linnean star winked in the message's lower corner under her name. Attached at the bottom was a piece of paper requiring my signature. I signed it, then looked at Abira. "What do I do with this?"

"Fold it and put it back in his collar. He'll return to the sender."

Abira left while I added an *I love you* to my signature before folding the paper and putting it inside his collar.

She returned with a bowl of water. The light wolf drank deeply before turning and leaving.

I watched him go. "How did you know what to do?"

She grinned. "I've used them many times. Besides, didn't you see the directions on the back of that slip?"

I sighed. Of course not. "Well, it's official. My mother has given her approval for you to train me."

"Excellent." She squeezed my shoulder and walked inside.

My brain had grabbed at the mention of it being safer here and held on. What did that mean? Why was Kelda Hills suddenly safer than Linneah? Homesickness mingled with worry washed through me.

After lunch was cleared away, Abira turned to me. "Your griffin says you're leaving now."

"I am?"

Arvandus spoke from his corner of the room. "We need to be on our way to Ginselwyn."

"Don't you need to get back to Astraya?"

"No, the cubs were born last week."

I beamed at him. "Oh, congratulations! I can't wait to see them. But what about Tiny and Storm?"

"If we leave at the same time, they will arrive shortly after us. We can wait for them outside the city gate."

Storm frowned.

Tiny rose from the couch. "That works. We'll meet you as soon as we get there."

We gathered our bags and said our goodbyes. Tiny and Storm left first with promises to hurry through the travel portal.

After Shiraz gave me a bone-crushing hug, Abira pulled me aside. "Come back when you're finished visiting Tiny's family. We'll begin your training."

The tattoo tingled like a reminder. "Will you be safe here? Rune won't, you know, come back or anything?"

"No, one of his primary tools is fear. I won't give him that satisfaction. I'll be fine." Her gray eyes were grave. "And while you're in Ginselwyn, don't do anything stupid, like get married."

I choked out a laugh. "If I can prevent Tiny's arranged marriage, the trip will be a success."

She shook her head. "It's not up to you. Just support her."

My shoulders fell. That was it? Support didn't seem like enough.

Digging into my pocket, I pulled out two money chains. One chain was worth about one hundred dollars. "Here." I thrust them into Abira's hand.

"What's this for?"

"For housing both of us, the clothes, the help, everything. Buy yourself a watering system for your garden."

"It's unnecessary."

Grinning, I grabbed my bag off the floor. "I know."

A small smile played around her mouth, but she shook her head and said nothing.

Arvandus and I took to the air, burdened with a hefty snack from Shiraz. The golden air turned cooler as we gained altitude. Arvandus left me alone with my thoughts until we stopped two hours later for a break.

Ho Mountain loomed, its craggy surface highlighted by the sun at our backs. I stretched my tight muscles, breathing in the warm breeze of sunbaked earth and blooming cactus.

After a long drink of water, my griffin settled on the ground. "Raven, how serious are you about Storm?"

I gave him a wary look. "Why?"

"The Weldens have a very patriarchal society. You would not do well there."

Defensiveness crept into my tone. "We're just friends."

His tail flicked. "I am not sure he views you that way. Are you sure you are not encouraging Storm?"

"No. He's a nice guy. I tend to like nice guys."

"I am only asking you to behave the way you would like Baldwin to behave if the situation was reversed. Remember—fly true."

"It's over between us."

He fixed me with a golden stare. "And he has told you this?"

Frustration bloomed in my chest. I fisted my hands on my hips. "So you expect me to behave with integrity even though he didn't?"

"This is not about getting even. It is about being true to yourself and treating others with respect."

I dropped the subject. He was worse than my mom.

After another thirty minutes of flying, we flew past Ho Mountain, which separated the rolling Kelda Hills from Ginselwyn. I gasped. The landscape glowed. A carnival of multi-colored lights lit the main area of the city while white and yellow pinpricks sparkled around the outside. *Do they have electricity?*

They have learned to harness various gases. They use them to light their buildings, including their homes. It is beautiful.

We landed outside the city gate. A lone guard stood watch. "I guess Tiny and her brother haven't arrived yet."

I didn't want to have to explain who I was waiting for and why, so we withdrew before the guard questioned us. We settled among a cluster of small evergreen trees, a sweet scent tickling my nose. "What are these, anyway?"

"Sweet nessian trees." Arvandus nosed my bag. "Anything else edible in there?"

"Sure." I pulled out a sandwich for myself and several thick slices of roast Shiraz had wrapped and labelled with Arvandus's name. We ate supper while the sun continued its descent. When it touched the horizon, I stood. "We've got to see if we can get in. I don't want to camp outside the city gate."

He stood and stretched. "Do you have money?"

"Yeah, Abira cashed in my stars before we left. I kept a few pieces as a memento. And although I paid her back, I have enough to get in."

"Excellent. Remember, Raven, you are the daughter of a queen. Be confident."

We walked toward the gate, tension tightening my shoulders. Beyond it, a main road unrolled past buildings lit in blues, greens, reds, and golds. Some had signs above doors reading *Inn* or *Butcher*, while the others' only decoration was a large globe or tube to light the entrance. Colored gases swirled and smoldered, the light mesmerizing.

The houses were white cubes with roofs slanted to one side, as if someone forgot to add the other half. Connected to the buildings were living areas, some with roofs and some without, like an outdoor family porch.

The guard watched us approach, his eyes narrowed.

"Greetings," I said. "I am here to visit a friend."

His eyes flickered over my face before running down my body. Ew. After one glance, I felt the need for a hot shower. His eyes met mine again. "And who is this friend?"

"I'm here to see either Shaynedel Lee or her father."

Apparently, the name carried some weight. The guard's face went white. "Uh, yes, um, of course." He unlatched the gate.

Confidence. Daughter of the queen. I held my head high as I walked through, Arvandus at my side.

I turned when the guard spoke. "He's a beautiful creature. Is he for sale?" The guard scrutinized Arvandus.

With a growl, Arvandus bared his teeth and prowled forward, his wings throwing silver sparks.

The guard scrambled to pull his sword from its scabbard.

"No. Griffins aren't sold. Ever. And if you so much as slice one of his whiskers with that weapon, I'll encourage him to eat you for supper."

He sheathed his sword, his hand trembling.

This was so much fun. Not.

The guard gave me another once over. "Where's your guardian?"

I wanted to tell him what he could do with the idea of a guardian, but I bit my lip, hard, before speaking. "I don't have one, but I have money for my entrance."

With a smirk, he stepped closer and held out his hand.

Chapter Sixteen

"Brenna!" Storm hurried toward the gate.

Relief washed through me.

He drew close, his hand catching mine in a possessive grip. The guard didn't miss the action. "We hurried here as quickly as we could. Shaynedel is meeting with Father, but I told her I'd make sure you got in. I'm sorry I'm late." His smile sent liquid warmth through me.

"No problem. I'd like to pay my entrance fee."

"Allow me."

"No, Storm." I drew my hand from his. "I can afford this."

"Of course you can, but as my guest—"

"Actually, I'm Tiny's guest."

Storm laughed as if I were comedian of the year. "That's ridiculous. Shaynedel is not permitted to have guests. You're my *father's* guest."

"But..." And then it hit me. Women had no rights. They were property. I pursed my lips. Welcome to Bizarro World.

Still, I scrounged for my dwindling confidence. "I'm paying for my entrance fee. Period. How much?"

He frowned. "One hundred fifty zoharet nomas."

I didn't know who Storm had turned into, but I kind of didn't like him. Doing the math in my head, I pulled three money chains from my bag. Each chain held fifty zoharet silver nomas, comparable to one hundred American dollars. We were expensive.

The guard snatched them from my hand and with a leer said, "Enjoy your visit."

I scowled at him. Yeah, right.

Storm led me away from the guard, a protective hand under my elbow, as we walked the white gravel sidewalk toward the city. The houses on each side glowed ghostly pale in the twilight, radiant tubes and spheres lighting entryways. Arvandus remained silent behind us, his presence reassuring.

Once we were out of sight of the guard, I pulled my arm from Storm's grasp. Irritation sharpened my voice. "I'm ridiculous, huh?"

"I'm sorry, Brenna. That behavior was for the guard. I'm expected to set an example of a typical Welden, especially because of my family."

That distracted me from the tirade about to explode from my mouth. "Who exactly is your family? I mentioned Shaynedel Lee's father, and the guard couldn't open the gate fast enough."

His eyes begged me to understand. "Father is the governor, the overseer of Ginselwyn. Because of his position, we must uphold traditions in public, regardless of what we practice in our home."

Whoa. Tiny had never mentioned her father's job. She hardly ever mentioned Ginselwyn at all. After being here for less than five minutes, I was beginning to understand why.

I pulled my thoughts back to the present. "And treating women like garbage is tradition?"

"Not garbage. But men make the decisions, handle the money, vote." He hitched a shoulder. "Although the government expects it from most families, ours doesn't think it's acceptable. Mother is permitted to be a very progressive Welden."

Permitted. The word rankled. It sounded pretty hypocritical to me.

Relax, Raven. I told you it would be like this.

Yes, he had. So had Tiny. But I hadn't been prepared for it.

Raised voices drifted on the breeze. As we turned the corner, half a block away, a crowd filled the street. Women, young girls, and a few men paraded toward us. As a drum began a low, booming cadence, they raised their arms. The chant was simple. "E-qual rights, e-qual rights, e-qual rights!"

Storm slowed before leading me down a smaller street. "Let's take this way home."

I craned my head around to keep looking. "Is that a women's rights march?"

"Yes, I'm sorry you had to see that. That group has been protesting for as long as I can remember."

The chants grew fainter as we continued down the side street.

"At least it was a peaceful protest."

"They usually are." A frown grew on his handsome face, his gaze drawn to other houses and front yards.

"What's wrong?"

He gestured to the brown grass. "In the few short days I was gone, the drought has worsened. I passed a couple of farms on the way here. One family slaughtered half their animals."

After two more turns, we returned to the main road and drew closer to the center of the city. The houses here sported longer pathways, expansive windows, more lights. But there were no colorful flower boxes or overflowing urns or decorative plants edging the walkways. At least the colored lights helped beautify the area.

Storm gestured to a massive house on the right, complete with two guards. "This is home."

The house was a beautiful two-story stone structure, its entryway framed with a long, curved glass tube of amber light. Buttery yellow warmth spilled from the windows, beckoning to me. Stellara and Silver, Tiny's little sisters, played on the covered wooden deck to the right.

Storm pointed to the girls. "Aside from the two sisters you've met, I also have an older brother, Sloane, and an older sister, Saeth, although she's married and lives across town."

"Six kids in your family, right?" I stopped at the door, wondering if chaos would be on the other side.

"Yes, although Mother confirmed she's expecting number seven in seven months."

"Wow." The big house made sense.

"Don't you have any brothers or sisters?"

I shook my head. Talus was dead. And I wasn't sure I wanted to claim him anyway.

Arvandus messaged me. *Please ask about overnight accommodations when you get the chance. I will wait for you by the front door.*

I'll do that. Do you need anything else?

No, thank you.

One guard opened the front door and allowed us to enter. The entryway flowed into a big sitting area, filled with stuffed gray chairs around a low white table. Deep-rose pillows and a rose throw were tucked on a gray loveseat. Near the window, a full pot of ivy sat, its once-glossy leaves browning. Several well-placed mirrors made the room appear larger.

Mrs. Lee peeked around the kitchen doorway, her delicate features flushed. "Hi, Brenna. So glad you got here safely. Tiny's with her father in the backyard, but she'll be in soon. I just pulled coffeecake out of the oven. Would you like a piece?"

"Yes, please." The smell of cinnamon drifted into the room. Tiny's mom was a fantastic cook, and I never turned down her creations.

Hope brightened Storm's face. "I'd like a piece, too."

"Both of you come on in, then."

I followed him into the kitchen. White cabinetry contrasted with honey-toned wood walls and ceiling, while several globes hanging from the ceiling provided warm light, the gas inside twirling.

The warm coffeecake's cinnamon-sugar topping melted on my tongue. While I enjoyed the sheer deliciousness, I mentioned sleeping arrangements for Arvandus.

Mrs. Lee nodded. "We have a second-story deck ready he could use, if that's sufficient."

"Thanks, that'd be great."

Tiny peeked into the kitchen. Her face was blotchy, her eyes rimmed in red. She jerked her head to the left. "Come to my bedroom when you're done. End of the hall."

She disappeared.

I pushed back my chair. "Thanks for the cake, Mrs. Lee. It was delicious."

"You're welcome, Brenna." Her smile slipped from her face as she sighed. "And thanks for coming."

"Thanks for having me." As I left the kitchen, I messaged Arvandus. *The second-story deck is waiting for you, big guy. See you in the morning.*

Thank you, Raven.

Passing a set of stairs leading to the second floor, I hurried to the end of the hall, which ended at two doors. Paintings done by smaller, inexperienced hands hung on the one door. A bundle of dried flowers and ribbon hung on the other—Tiny's room, displaying her love of nature. I stared at it for a second, hoping whatever news waited on the other side wouldn't be too bad, before I pushed it open. Tiny sat in the middle of her bed, a shredded tissue clenched in her fist.

"Hey. Everything okay?" Dumb question. Obviously not.

Tiny lifted her head. "No. It's over. My life is over." The anxiety lurking in her blue eyes nearly drowned me. "I'm not here to meet my fiancé. I'm here to marry him."

Shock pulled me onto the bed next to her. "But I thought you'd have a chance to negotiate, or at least have your mom negotiate, or—"

She fell back onto her pillow. "There's a lot more going on my dad didn't tell me. Three weeks ago, Ginselwyn was hit with a drought, but it's gotten worse in the past week. Now there's not enough water. Sloane brought water from the coast, but it's very expensive. But my fiancé"—her mouth twisted on the word—"arrived in town with a solution. And he'll do it, as long as he gets me in the bargain."

I frowned. "That sounds like blackmail."

She lifted a shoulder. "Well, it's working. In less than a week, I'll be his wife."

Panic swelled in my stomach like bread dough. "That's not right. There's got to be something we can do."

"There isn't. It's done. If I don't get married, the inhabitants of Ginselwyn will starve."

I just couldn't believe that. "So how's this genius going to fix the problem?"

"He claims the ground's cursed. On the day of the wedding, he'll cure the land."

I rolled my eyes. "And your father believes him?"

Hopelessness echoed in every word. "He's already proven he can. Shortly after he arrived, he restored a local pond. Besides, we don't have a choice, Brenna. If you had a chance to save hundreds of suffering Linneans, wouldn't you do it?"

"Well, yeah, but—"

Her features hardened. "And that's what I'm doing."

"Have you met him yet?"

She dropped her gaze to the tissue she was shredding. "Tomorrow morning. My father's arranged an early morning hike for the two of us to see the sunrise and get acquainted."

I was at a loss. Any chance to save her from an arranged marriage was nonexistent, snuffed out before we'd arrived. "I'm sorry."

We sat on her bed, not talking, until her mother peeked in to say goodnight.

The next morning, I woke to the sun slipping past the curtains. I rolled off the tiny daybed in Tiny's room. Her bed lay empty, neatly made, the cover pulled up next to a fluffed pillow. At my memory of last night, anger shoved aside the despair lurking in my stomach. I didn't care what city we were in—women shouldn't be used for bartering, blackmail, or anything else. Finding a stick of fypex gum in my bag, I stuck it into my mouth.

I threw on an outfit and left the room. When I got to the kitchen, Storm was already there, drinking what looked like a juice smoothie. Stellara and Silver sat at the kitchen table, talking while they drew pictures.

He gave me a slow smile. "Good morning, gorgeous."

My cheeks heated. What a flirt. "Hi. Can I talk to you for a second? Privately."

"Absolutely." He wiggled his eyebrows. "Privately? Sounds promising."

I slapped his arm. "Stop it. I'm serious. It's about Tiny."

"Oh." His expression turned thoughtful. "You want privacy in a house of eight? The only private place is on the front deck."

"That works." Maybe Arvandus was awake. *Hey, are you awake? Meet me and Storm out on the deck. I'm going to need your help.*

A growl whispered through my mind. Great. I'd woken him up. Now he'd be grumpy.

Storm left the kitchen and turned right. We passed two bedrooms before exiting onto the deck. Plopping onto a wooden chair, I took a deep breath. This conversation would take tact, finesse, luck. I was doomed.

He dropped into the chair opposite me and ran a hand through his hair. "I'm not fully awake, but I can listen. What's so important?"

"This is about Tiny's marriage."

He dropped his head back and studied the roof's underside. "This is the way things are done, Brenna."

"No, they aren't, not like this. This guy's blackmailing all of Ginselwyn for marriage to the governor's daughter. Doesn't that sound shady to you?"

Sadness pulled at his normally smiling face. "Father is at a loss. Shaynedel knows her duty and understands."

I clenched my fists. Arvandus arrived, giving me a chance to think about what I said for a change. He gave me a look that said, *This had better be good.*

"Sorry, Arvandus." I cleared my throat. "I need your advice. Tiny told me last night she's here to get married. Her fiancé is blackmailing her father. If she marries him, he claims he can end Ginselwyn's drought, although—"

Storm interrupted me. "Why are you so concerned about this?"

The memory of Tiny and me talking in Abira's spare bedroom flitted through my mind. "I want her to marry someone she loves and who loves her. It should be her choice."

"But my parents had an arranged marriage and they're happy, very much in love."

"Good. But that doesn't always happen. And I don't think blackmail's a good start to a solid relationship."

He leaned forward to say something, but I kept talking.

"Put yourself in her position."

"What?"

"Let's play a game. Close your eyes." I waited until he did so. "Imagine things are different in Ginselwyn. Men are the ones with no rights."

He grinned, one eye popping open. I glared at him until he closed it.

"I'm not kidding. Imagine you have no say in your marriage. She could be old with no teeth. Or maybe she's really young, like twelve, or maybe she curses all the time. But you're not worried because it's years away. You go home for a visit to discover it's all arranged. Your marriage is in less than a week and might be the answer to the city's drought—maybe. If you're lucky. It might also be an elaborate deception. Even if she's an old hag and beats you, you'll save the city. Maybe."

Storm opened his eyes. "He's not old. He's probably in his twenties."

I gritted my teeth. "That's not my point."

He sighed and slumped in his chair. "I don't like it, but I understand."

"You don't—wait. You understand?"

"But I don't see any alternative."

Silence settled into the spaces of our conversation.

Arvandus flicked his tail. "There is always a choice. What if Shaynedel would choose to end the engagement?"

Storm's brow rose. "Well, she won't be forced into it. But if a man offers, it's poor form to refuse."

Sheesh. It was like the Dark Ages here. "Poor form?"

"All respectable females are expected to marry."

His words sparked the beginning of an idea. "What about the unrespectable ones?"

Arvandus tilted his head. "Unrespectable, Raven?"

"Uh, irrespectable? Disrespectable? You know what I mean. What about them?"

Storm dismissed them with a wave of his hand. "They don't usually marry. Some become prostitutes or beggars."

"*All* of them?"

His expression darkened. "What's your point? This is my sister we're talking about."

Arvandus straightened, his gold eyes bright. "Storm, I have heard about a faction of women who are unhappy with things in Ginselwyn. We saw a protest last night. Who are they?"

"The Avanti. Several times a year, they march for equal rights. The right to vote, to run a business alone, to stay unmarried..." His voice trailed off as comprehension stole over his face.

"That's it!" I squealed. "She could join the Avanti."

"No." Storm stood, hands fisted. "What would people say? She's the governor's daughter."

I glared at him. "The people can take a long walk off a short pier. They're not the ones being blackmailed into marriage."

Storm sighed and began pacing. "What about the drought?"

I crossed my arms. *Yeah, don't work with me or anything. Just allow your sister to marry some creep.* If this guy was so wonderful, why wasn't he helping the starving, dying people anyway? Why did he have to wait until he was married to Tiny to lift a finger? My opinion of him plunged lower every time I thought about it.

Arvandus interrupted my gloomy thoughts. "Where does your water come from?"

Storm answered absently, still pacing. "The Calder River, which comes from the spring outside the city."

I bit my lip. "Has anyone checked the spring?"

"Two weeks ago. The spring's closely guarded. But the water level downstream has never been this low. No one can explain it. Many believe the city or the river's been cursed."

I snorted. "Yeah, sure." When he didn't laugh, I looked up at him. "You don't believe that, do you?"

"Well, no. But what else would cause the river to run dry?"

Arvandus spoke. "Maybe, Raven, it would be a good time to view the spring and river. Besides, I need to stretch my wings."

"I haven't had breakfast yet." My stomach rumbled, emphasizing my words.

"You'll need a guardian. I'll come with you." Storm turned away, his decision made.

I stood. "No, we'll just do a flyover." I turned to Arvandus. "Let me grab some breakfast, and I'll get something for you. Be right back."

Ignoring Storm's dark expression, I walked past him and into the house. I couldn't deal with his irrational arguments on an empty stomach.

CHAPTER SEVENTEEN

HE CAUGHT UP WITH me in the kitchen. "You need a guardian."

"Not if we're only flying." Leftover coffeecake sat on the counter. Ravenous, I cut myself a generous piece. "Is there any meat for Arvandus?"

From the white cabinet, Storm pulled out a package of dried meat. "Sprinkle some water on it, and he'll be fine."

I prepared the meat and took it to the front deck where Arvandus waited patiently.

As he began eating, Storm returned to the previous topic. "For this trip, a guardian is a good idea." His aura brightened to a strong amber.

So annoying. "It's unnecessary. Why would I need one? Is it illegal for me to fly over the spring?"

"No."

"Then I don't need one." I took the last bite of coffeecake, hoping we were done with this stupid argument.

A reluctant grin played at his lips. "Has anyone told you you're stubborn?"

"All the time."

He leaned forward, his grin growing. "You've got crumbs on your mouth." His thumb brushed my lower lip, and his eyes heated to blue fire. "There. All gone."

"Thanks." My voice didn't sound like my own.

Arvandus growled a little, and I stepped back.

Winking, Storm crossed his arms before his expression turned serious. "The spring is fine. But after it passes through Calumbra Cave, the water level drops."

"And what did they find in the cave?"

"Her fiancé and his men thoroughly examined the cave. They found nothing unusual."

I blinked. "What?"

He shrugged, his eyes sliding away from mine. "His report was complete, and Father appreciated the time he took to investigate."

"You didn't verify the report?"

"Father trusts him. There wasn't much more we could do."

Anger flared. "Not more you could do? Everyone's so willing to let Tiny sacrifice herself to some thug who's blackmailing the city. Doesn't that bother you?"

"Yes!" Storm snapped, his cheeks flushed.

I stepped back, surprised at his reaction.

He ran a hand through his hair, mussing up the blond strands. "But this is the deal we were given. I'm not going to tell my father how to do his job, regardless of how I feel. And forgive me, but it's easy to waltz into another city and offer solutions."

"Excuse me? That's not what's happening here. I want my best friend to be loved and to have a choice. That's it."

He crossed his arms. "Well, your goals are a little shortsighted."

I turned and walked to the other end of the deck. Maybe I was missing the big picture, but my intentions were good. That should count for something.

At the soft touch on my shoulder, I turned. Storm offered a small smile. "I'm sorry."

"Don't be. It probably does come across as criticism, but I keep thinking there's got to be a better way."

He gave a mirthless chuckle. "When you figure it out, let me know."

"I will. For right now, though, I need directions to Calumbra Cave." Someone needed to get in there and explore. I just loved dark, eerie, small spaces cluttered with bugs and bats.

He tilted his head. "Why? It was already examined."

I gave him a patient smile and spoke slowly. "I don't believe them."

"It's been cleared. Besides, many people report noises coming from the cave. There's something in there. Maybe something dangerous."

"We'll be fine. I mean, just look at him." I pointed to Arvandus. "Do you think I need to be afraid with him along?"

"Well, no, but—"

"Exactly." I waited.

He sighed, his aura dimming to pale yellow. "Follow the Calder River to the base of Ho Mountain. You'll pass over the cave on the way to the spring. You can't miss it."

I offered him a reassuring smile. "Thank you. We'll be careful."

Tiny glided onto the deck. Her blue eyes sparkled.

"Hey, how are you?" I frowned. "You look...happy."

Her cheeks flushed. "We need to talk. Excuse us." She shooed Storm away. "Go get something to eat. Or bother mom. Or something."

He rolled his eyes. "Yes, princess."

After he left the deck, she turned to me, her aura brilliant. "I met him."

"Your fiancé?"

A dazzling smile burst onto her face. "He's unbelievable, Brenna. Remember the miracle we talked about? I got it."

"That's great." My words sounded lackluster, even to me.

She blushed again and giggled. "He's such a gentleman and so nice. I was upset about the deal with the spring, but he said there's no requirement of marriage for his help. It was all a misunderstanding. And although it's not a big deal, he's cute, too."

I tried to smile for her sake. "See? You had nothing to worry about."

She pulled me toward the backyard. "Come meet him."

"Um, okay, but—"

Tiny chattered on. "His name is Jakeb Damyan. Do you know he's been here for over two weeks waiting for me? He said he kept busy, helping Dad and looking for a place to live."

Yet he was too busy to help with the water shortage? The words stuck in my throat.

We rounded the corner of the house and passed through a white stone archway. A matching stone fence encircled the yard. Several trees offered shade near one corner while the other held a garden plot in full sun. A man stood with his back to us, digging with a shovel. His shirt was off, his toned muscles glistening with sweat.

"Jakeb, meet Brenna."

He turned and thought fled. He. Was. Gorgeous. His dark hair was cut short, and fashionable stubble covered his strong chin. High cheekbones and blue eyes framed by long, dark lashes rendered me silent. I offered him a smile and a wave.

He smiled back. "So nice to meet Shaynedel's closest friend."

My smile froze. There was something weird about his aura. The lighted area went indistinct and fuzzy, and I blinked. Tiny walked over to him, and he leaned down to kiss her cheek. I stared at the yellow blur. Why did it keep wavering like a hologram? Maybe he was sick...

"Is it lunchtime yet?" he asked.

"Not yet." Tiny gave him another sweet smile. "But if you're hungry, I can get a sandwich for you."

"No, I'm only teasing you, my sweet."

Gag. I smiled instead. "Well, it was nice meeting you, but I've got to run."

Jakeb's voice stopped me. "Before you go, I'd like to invite everyone to a picnic supper tonight." He turned to Tiny. "Plan a delicious menu, darling, and we'll celebrate. I'm sure you can do that."

Tiny's mouth made a little O. "Well, I suppose. I'd better get started."

"I'll look forward to seeing you there, Brenna." Without waiting for my reply, he turned and began digging in the garden.

Coffeecake soured in my stomach. Tiny had just been relegated to servant status.

She worried her lip as she turned toward the house. "What can I make on such short notice?"

"I could help." Or try to. My kitchen talents were underdeveloped.

"No, I can definitely do this after all the practice I had at Abira's. I'll see you later." She hurried into the house.

I walked back to the porch where Arvandus sat waiting. "Let's fly to the cave. Or do you want to check out the spring first?"

"We can investigate the cave from the southern opening and then continue to the spring if we do not find answers."

"Sounds like a plan." I climbed onto his back.

He sprang into the air. His massive wings unfurled and carried us high, his silver wingtips glinting in the afternoon sun.

On the short flight, I replayed my encounter with Jakeb and Tiny while the scenery rushed past. Why wasn't I thrilled for her? Maybe it was jealousy. My relationship with Baldwin was nonexistent, and Tiny was happy, giddy over a new romance. But I didn't want a relationship like hers. I wanted the one I'd lost, the one that had evaporated in a crowded restaurant.

I leaned against Arvandus, suddenly tired of thinking and needing to talk. *I met Tiny's fiancé, Jakeb Damyan. She's over the moon about him.*

Is that a good thing? Being over the moon?

I snorted. *Yeah, it's a good thing.* I gave him a brief rundown of the meeting. *So here's my question. Why am I going to check out Calumbra Cave? It was checked. She doesn't need to be rescued from a bad situation. She'll get married, and the river will return to normal.*

The cave in question appeared below, a mound of gray rock amid a tan landscape. The breeze snagged my hair, pulling it straight back as Arvandus dropped to land.

Because it is a puzzle, and you like knowing why *things happen, not just that they do.*

But I hate feeling unnecessary. And that's what I am—unneeded. Tears ached for release, building in the back of my throat. I was disposable. Baldwin had just figured it out before Tiny had. I slipped off Arvandus' back and brushed away a rogue tear.

Do not believe that lie, Raven. Arvandus nudged my hand with his damp nose. "You are valuable. You do not need to be involved in a romantic relationship or enmeshed in a victorious battle or to heal a battalion of soldiers to be so. Remember that. Tiny will be glad to have her best friend at her wedding."

"Thanks." Patting his neck, I allowed his words to sink deep and soothe the confusion inside.

The flat, parched landscape held a few trees, their leaves barely stirring. Dry air pressed in as the unforgiving sun blazed. We hiked toward the cave entrance, dry grass and cracked earth crunching underfoot. The river—well, what was left of it, anyway—flowed over the pebbled streambed toward the city. Aside from the soft trickling of the stream, the area remained quiet. No birdsong, no buzz of insects. A sudden, pulsing squeak rent the air, over and over, before fading.

I buried my hand in Arvandus' fur as Storm's warning whispered in my mind. "You're hearing it, too, right?" I kept my voice low.

He nodded and stalked just inside the entrance, me trailing behind. My eyes adjusted to the dim interior. Crystal-clear water filled the cave. A few feet in, the small trail we stood on dwindled to nothing. Small fissures in the cave walls allowed sunlight to spear through, lighting the river's path. Farther in, a craggy platform rose above the water.

I turned to Arvandus. "So how are you at swimming?"

Chapter Eighteen

Arvandus drew back and slit his eyes.

"Don't give me the royal look. I just asked."

He sniffed. "Please. I am an excellent swimmer."

"Good." Wow. Touchy. I peeled off my shirt, leaving on my tank. Walking back outside, I pulled off my boots and socks, bundled them with my shirt, and stowed the wad behind some long grass.

I stepped into the stream, bracing for icy water and a strong current. Instead, the warm flow curled lazily around my ankles, a soft caress. Weird. I took a closer look at the stream. "Does the water smell?"

He leaned near the water, his nose quivering. "It is fine, although strangely warm."

We waded deeper into the cave, the water climbing higher and the current growing stronger. I swam the last few feet to the platform and hauled myself up. A natural outcropping extended into the darkness where sunlight didn't reach. While I gathered my hair and wrung it out, Arvandus climbed onto the platform. He shook his head, ears flopping and water spraying.

"Come on, dude." I wrinkled my nose. Wet cat. Lovely.

Eek-erk, eek-erk, eek-erk...

A groan followed the pulsing squeak. My skin prickled. Arvandus growled and took half a step forward. I held out a hand, producing a flame. The water on my skin sizzled, evaporating. I held the fire aloft, illuminating our surroundings.

Are you ready for some exploring? Arvandus asked.

As ready as I'll ever be.

We ventured deeper into the cave. The walls dripped with a quiet *plop-plop*, and the river lapped against rocky walls. My light caught a strange shape to my right, and I raised my hand to see it better.

Against the rock wall sat a table surrounded by half a dozen chairs. Holding my hand higher, I allowed the flame to grow. More objects came into view. Pallets away from the river's edge, a few shelves with food canisters labeled "flour" and "sugar," a cold fire pit. The scent of wood smoke tickled my nose.

"Stop!" A powerful female voice rang out from beyond the flame's glow. "Don't come any farther unless you want to be carved open."

"We do not wish to harm anyone, youngling." Arvandus's quiet voice echoed through the cave.

Frowning, I shot him a look. "Youngling?" I asked under my breath.

"Your pretty words mean nothing to me. Hold out your hands so I can see you're unarmed."

Biting the inside of my cheek, I did, but I also allowed flames to flash in both palms.

She gasped. "Remove your fire!"

"Yeah, not happening."

"Raven..."

I ignored his warning. "One, that fire allows me to see. I don't like being blind. Two, this fire is a warning. We won't be intimidated. Treat us fairly, and we'll return the treatment."

"And what if I bury a flying sun in your chest?"

Then I'd make sure she regretted it. "My griffin will tear your throat out. My guess is he can see you, even if I can't."

"I can see all three of you." His gravelly purr was nonchalant.

A beat of silence, then three auras flared to life. Three females, one my age, one a little younger, and one a little older, stood braced for trouble. They were all dressed in worn black and gray tanks. Their long, gauzy skirts with knotted hems had been tucked into their waistbands. Two carried daggers while the youngest carried a sword as big as she was. A throwing star glittered in her gloved hand.

The youngest strode forward, her dark eyes narrowed, and placed the sword point at my throat. "Why are you here?"

So help me, I wanted to throttle her. "We're investigating the reason for the low water level."

She sneered. "So the government finally decided to look here? You won't find anything in this spot. Move along."

I frowned. Decided to look...apparently, Mr. Fantastic Fiancé had lied.

"Kefira, stop." The oldest female stepped forward. Now that she was closer, I could see she was probably in her twenties. "Who asked you to look here?"

Lowering my arms, I kept the flame alight. "No one. My best friend is being forced into a marriage because of the drought. Her fiancé says he'll fix the water problem after the wedding."

The three shot each other wordless looks.

The other girl, a redhead who hadn't spoken, gestured behind her. "Come in and have a seat. And please don't try anything foolish. Kefira's very good with her weapons."

The girl lowered her sword, her smirk setting my teeth on edge.

The redhead struck a match, setting fire to the wood in the pit. The fire's glow lit a living area strewn with pillows and cushions.

Near the water's edge was a wooden oar stuck in a bracket. I walked around it, wondering if that had caused the strange squeaking.

Kefira saw my glance. "Usually the sound is enough to make the smartest walk away. I noticed you didn't."

Little brat.

Reaching up to an indentation in the wall, the redhead slid open a small, hidden window and peered out. "Did anybody see you come in?"

"No. I have a friend who knows we came here, but I believe he's afraid to come by himself."

"Fee, nobody's been this way in days. But I'll keep watch if it helps you relax." The woman smiled as she settled near the small window. "Allow me to make introductions, but first names only. I'm Rachel, this is Fee, and the youngest is Kefira."

"Nice to meet you." Well, except Kefira. "I'm Brenna, and this is Arvandus."

My griffin gave them a small nod.

I continued. "Can I ask why you're living in a cave?"

Fee pulled back a little, her bright-red locks shining in the firelight. "Our location is compromised now. We'll have to find another site."

"Maybe not." Rachel leaned forward. "Maybe if you answer a few questions, we can establish trust. You're not a Welden, but a Linnean, is that right?"

"Yes." Of course. There was no hiding my hairstreak.

She smiled, her gray eyes friendly. "You said you're visiting a friend, for her wedding. Do you have a guardian?"

"Oh no, I paid my own way in. I'm staying with the Lee family."

"Convenient," Kefira muttered. She shot me a glare. "I say you're a spy for the governor."

"And I say you're a brat, so we're even." Ignoring Kefira's sputtering, I turned to the other two. "Now that we've got the name calling out of the way, I'd like to investigate the rest of this cave. Is it possible to walk the length of it and go out the other side?"

Fee's eyes danced with amusement. "You'll have to swim out the other side."

I tilted my head. "Is it far?"

Rachel stood. "We have company."

"Brenna? Arvandus?"

I shot to my feet, recognizing the voice. "It's Storm."

Kefira drew her sword, her eyes wild. "You brought him here to find us. I won't go!"

"No!" I held out my hands as if my bare palms could stop the blade. "You three stay quiet and hidden. Arvandus, stop Storm at the entrance."

Kefira gave me a vicious glare. Good thing looks couldn't kill.

Rachel waved a hand, a shadow swallowing their auras. Fee doused the fire, plunging the area into darkness.

I walked closer to the entrance yet stayed in the shadows. "We'll take care of this, I promise."

Someone snorted—most likely Kefira—before she was hushed by the others.

Arvandus, we need to get rid of Storm. I want answers, but I won't get them if he's here. Convince him I'm using the cave to take a bath so he'll leave.

As Arvandus slipped into the water, his chuckle filled my mind. *I am unsure that will work. I will try.*

The few seconds it took him to leave the cave were the longest ever.

"Arvandus." Relief filled Storm's voice. "Where's Brenna?"

"She is indisposed."

"What do you mean? Is she hurt?"

Arvandus sighed. "She is well but bathing herself. She needs privacy to finish."

"She's bathing? In the cave?" After a brief pause, Storm continued. "I must see her. There's an emergency."

"Halt immediately." Arvandus gave a warning growl. "She is fine, but it is not right for you to intrude. I will give her your message. What is your emergency?"

"Father is sick."

Arvandus said nothing. The silence pressed on. Finally, my griffin spoke. "I am sorry to hear that. I will give her the message."

"You don't understand." Storm's normally smooth voice cracked. "The people of Ginselwyn never get sick. The Stones of the Spring protect us. But now Father's ill. Why is this happening? What do we do?"

I stole from my position to get a better look. Storm stood at the river's edge, shoulders slumped, blond head in his hands.

Arvandus moved closer to him. "Send a runner to get a healer from your nearest town. Your father will need it."

He lifted his head, his face tear-streaked. It broke my heart to see him so vulnerable. Something told me he wouldn't want me to see him that way, but I couldn't look away.

My griffin continued. "Do not share this information with anyone outside of family. Keep the citizens peacefully ignorant. If your father cannot do his job, have someone else take over."

Storm grunted, neither agreeing nor disagreeing. "As Tiny's fiancé, Jakeb would be next in line."

What? No!

Easy, Raven. Arvandus shifted, his tail flicking. "Why would Jakeb be next and not your older siblings?"

Storm shrugged. "Because they told Father they were uninterested in the position. Saeth's husband builds boats, and he's successful. And Sloane refused, saying he had no interest in politics."

"What about you?"

Storm jerked, his eyes meeting Arvandus's. "Jakeb said, um, I mean, he'll do a fine job, I'm sure."

"Storm?"

When he averted his eyes and said nothing, Arvandus tilted his head. Storm was in for a long wait. That griffin could out-wait anyone.

Finally, Storm's shoulders slumped. "In return for lifting the curse, he had two requirements. Shaynedel and the position of father's successor."

I pressed my fist against my mouth to stifle my groan. How were they all okay with this?

Arvandus shook his furry head. "It would be best to keep this news within the family until after the wedding. If there is not an assistant governor, you or Sloane can take temporary control until your father recovers. Involving Jakeb is unnecessary at this point. He is not family yet."

Storm blew out a quiet breath and stood. "Thank you. Would you please inform Brenna the picnic has been post-poned until my father improves?"

Arvandus swished his tail from side to side. "Yes. I am not sure of our plans. Please notify the others we may return late."

"Again, thank you." Storm set his jaw, his eyes already far away on new responsibilities before he pivoted and walked away from the cave.

Although I returned to the girls sitting mute in their living area, Arvandus stood at the entrance for a long while before joining us. "He is gone."

Kefira humphed and turned her back to us.

I rolled my eyes.

Rachel leaned against the cave wall and released a long breath. "Thank you. We've used this spot for some time—we were hoping to keep its location secret for a while longer."

While Arvandus had been talking to Storm, I'd been spin-ning information in my brain. "You're part of the Avanti, aren't you?"

The three exchanged glances before Rachel nodded. Fee grinned, her smile beautiful. "We are few of many and have grown by leaps and bounds. Soon, the government will listen or—" She stumbled to a stop.

"Or what?"

Kefira tested the sharp point of her sword with her thumb, and a spot of blood bloomed. Her smile was just as sharp. "Or we'll make them."

I turned away from her lethal smile. "So do you all live here?"

Rachel sat on the couch. "Some of us are full-time residents of the cave, like Kefira. I live on the outside and organize meetings, marches, membership. Some have jobs, like Fee, yet sleep here. And we all take turns staying here in shifts. It's a haven for girls who have nowhere else to go. We hunt, fish—"

"Don't forget steal." Kefira offered a proud smile.

Fee pressed her lips together. "We're not supposed to do that."

The young girl smirked. "Yet you ate last night's bread without a problem."

"It's still wrong. And I felt guilty afterward."

Kefira shrugged. "My god doesn't have a problem with it. Can't help it if yours does."

Ignoring the disagreement, Rachel frowned. "Did he say his father was sick?"

Uh-oh. "Um, not exactly, I mean—"

Rachel shook her head. "We heard what he said. If you keep our secret, we'll keep yours."

Fee toyed with a thick curl of red hair. "That's not good. There must be something wrong with the Stones of the Spring."

I leaned forward. "What do they do exactly?"

Fee ticked off her list on her fingers. "They filter out sicknesses, viruses, bacteria that could sicken the people of Ginselwyn. Someone falling ill is unheard of. It happened many, many times ago

before the Stones were installed, but if it's happening again..."
Fee's voice trailed off, her frown still in place.

I tried not to sound too excited. "Is there a way to get to
them?"

Fee shrugged. "They are underwater. And the spring is
guarded by day, and the gates locked at night."

I bit down on a grin as I glanced at Arvandus. *A night mission, then.*

Arvandus groaned. *Please do not plan anything reckless. I am
not a young cub anymore.*

"We need to get going." I stood and gave them a smile. "But
thanks for trusting us. I won't give away your hiding spot."

Kefira stood, a challenge already in her eyes. "If you do, I'll
hunt you down."

Of course she would. I bit the inside of my lip. "I have a friend
who might be interested in joining."

Fee smirked. "The governor's daughter? The one who has to
get married? I don't think that'll happen. She'll get married like
a good Welden and serve appropriately."

My spine stiffened.

Fee held up a hand. "I'm sorry. That was uncalled for. I hope
she loves the man who will be her husband and that he respects
her and loves her in return." The sheer sorrow in her voice and
face stole my reply. Whatever Fee's experience had been, the
incident had left invisible scars.

Kefira stepped forward. "Well, this has been lovely, but we
need to eat."

Rachel patted her arm. "Relax. There are berries near the
mountain."

"I'll come too." Fee retrieved three buckets from the kitchen
area.

We said our goodbyes, and I swam out of the cave. Arvandus
glided out and landed next to the bank. I glared at him as I sloshed

out of the river. "You could've offered me a dry trip out of there, you know."

"Yes, I could have." I swear he smirked.

In the bright sunlight, I retrieved my things hidden in the grass. After squeezing the excess water from my hair, I plopped on the ground, amazed my clothes had already begun to dry. I tipped my face to the sun's warmth and thought about my next move. Supper at Tiny's house, but the picnic had been canceled. So something quick, and then...

Arvandus interrupted my planning. "Please share your thoughts with me. I assume you are scheming. You have that look on your face."

"What look?"

Amusement danced in his golden eyes, yet he said nothing.

"We fly to Tiny's, get supper, then rest. Then we fly to the spring when it gets dark."

"How do you plan to get into the spring?"

"Um, well, I haven't gotten that far."

"We also failed to discover the reason for the drought."

His question drew me up. "You're right."

In all the chaos of meeting the Avanti, getting rid of Storm, and finding out about the governor's illness, I'd forgotten. I looked around the dry landscape. Brittle leaves broke into tiny pieces in the wind. Plants wilted in the scorching sun. Grasses grew spindly and yellow. Even the dirt under my hands was like powder. I stuck my fingers into the earth, the soil crumbling at my touch. Heat stirred, seeping into my fingers. What the—? I pulled out my hand and studied it.

I tried again, this time forcing my fingers deeper. Heat climbed into my fingers, crawled past my knuckles, and trickled into my wrists. I pulled out my fingers and studied them. A flame leaped to life on my fingertips before collapsing.

"No way."

Arvandus looked up from cleaning his paws. "Raven?"

Excitement built in my veins. "This ground isn't cursed. It's packed full of heat, just like Abira did for my test."

Chapter Nineteen

As I scanned the landscape, wonder and dread fought for space in my chest. "That's why everything's so dry. This heat is evaporating water, literally leaching it from the soil. And that's why the river is so warm, too."

"But the river is fine as it approaches the cave."

"So it starts in the cave?" I gazed at the landscape, helplessness overwhelming me. "Arvandus, there's no way I can remove all of this heat. It would take me weeks or months. Probably more."

He tilted his head. "Perhaps we should explore the other side of the cave."

"Do you want to do that now?"

"We have more than enough time to study the other side."

I pulled on my socks and boots and tied the extra shirt around my waist. "Fly us there?"

"Climb on."

He rose into the air, his powerful wings scaling unseen ladders. Warm air gusted across my cheeks, and I shaded my eyes. Below, near the mountain's base, Rachel, Fee, and Kefira walked among the bushes. The landscape rippled by, trees and rocks flashing, before Arvandus dropped in altitude and landed near the river.

I slid off his back and stepped to the river's edge. Clear, cerulean water revealed a bottom pebbled with rocks. The water streamed into the cave, skimming past boulders.

I pulled off my shirt, socks, and boots like before, storing them behind a tree. Standing on the bank, I dipped a foot into the water and gasped.

"It's freezing. Let's make this a quick trip." Stepping into the river, I sucked in a breath as the icy current grabbed my legs. "C-c-cold." My teeth chattered.

Arvandus slid in next to me, his warmth dispelling some of the chill. "Stay close, Brenna. And please alert me if you need help."

"H-h-h-help, s-sure." I forced my arms to move. In seconds, each stroke became a goal met. *One more, just one more.* But the cold seeped deeper, glazing my mind with lethargy, as the frigid water pulled me into the cave. My arms and legs froze, free floating in the glacial water.

"Arvandus?" my voice rasped.

He didn't hear, and my head slipped under. Bobbing up, I pulled in a breath through iced lips. My brain went numb. So tired. I couldn't feel my arms or my legs anymore.

Raven? The word slipped through my mind. Too tired, too much work, nothing mattered. I'd slip underneath the water and rest. Closing my eyes, exhaustion stole over me. With an icy splash to my face, Arvandus appeared at my side. "Swim, Raven."

"Can't," I mumbled.

With a lunge, he surged ahead of me and extended his wing. The wingtip flashed, filling the cave with hundreds of silver sparks. *Grab on to my wing.*

The water's flow carried me onto his wing. Wet feathers rested against my cheek, and I clutched the strong armature of his bones.

After what felt like swimming for months, the stream began to glow with an otherworldly yellowish light. The deeper into the cave we traveled, the brighter it grew. The water and air temperatures warmed, and my blood began to thaw. After a turn in the river, the cave glared bright, chartreuse light blazing from the river's depths.

"What's tha—?" I reached for a nearby boulder, missed, and slammed into the next one.

Oh, that'd bruise a lovely shade of purple. At least I was awake now.

I held on tight to the rough surface, wishing I could rub my sore shoulder, the one already tender from my tattoo. Of course. The water, almost too warm, flushed all cold from my body.

Arvandus managed to stop next to me, his paws braced against the current. "Are you strong enough to climb onto the rocks here?"

"I think so." Or not. My weak arms refused to grab the rocky edge. "Can I just hang out here?"

"No. You can hold on to my neck, and I will tow you out."

Arvandus climbed from the river and shook his head. His ears flapped like tiny pennants, spraying water everywhere. When he lowered his head to the water's edge, I looped my arms around his neck and allowed him to pull me up, then collapsed on the rocky platform.

Arvandus stood guard while I recovered. Finally, I sat up and met his glare. "What?"

"I told you to alert me if you needed help."

"I tried. But you didn't hear me, and I just got so tired."

He growled, fastening his yellow gaze on the far cave wall. "You can never give up, Raven. You are needed and loved."

Hiding a smile, I gave him a hug. "I love you too."

After a moment more, I gestured to the unusual item in the river. "What's that?"

Underneath the clear water's flow, resting on the river's pebbled bottom, lay a wooden box as big as a large duffle bag, like the one my mom used for vacations. She'd stuff a week's worth of outfits in it, plus several pairs of shoes. The box glowed yellow green, almost painful in its intensity. I closed my eyes for a moment before looking at Arvandus.

He stood, his wings throwing off silver sparks as he paced. "It is a Dunamis, a vessel containing enormous power."

My stomach fluttered. "Power? What kind?"

"I am not sure, but it has been heightened with Shadow Power. Can you help me bring it to the surface? We can put it on this platform."

I rubbed my pruney fingers together and eyed the river. "Sounds like a plan."

"Can you swim with your eyes open?"

"Sure. I learned to do that in first grade."

"Raven?" He waited until I looked at him. "Be prepared for anything. A great amount of power is emanating from the Dunamis. You must be careful."

The look in his eyes alarmed me a bit. "Um, sure." Arvandus was usually serious, but not scary-serious like now.

He slipped into the water. I followed him, thankful for the water's warmth. Taking a deep breath, I went under and forced my eyes open. Since he was already way ahead of me, I pushed off the stone edge for an extra burst of speed. The water near the Dunamis was unnaturally hot. My stomach flipping, I placed a hand on my abdomen. Getting sick now would be a really bad idea.

Every time I looked at the box, my eyes hurt, so I averted my eyes and searched for handles or another way to grab the box. A rope loop on one side was buried under heavy stones. Arvandus grasped part of it in his teeth, and I moved rocks. Pressure mounted in my chest, a slow ache building. I needed another breath soon. Moving quickly, I swam to the other side and found the other loop. As the box bobbed in the current, we guided it to the surface. When my head cleared the water's surface, I pulled in a thankful breath.

"Go ahead." I jerked my head toward the ledge. "I'll steady this thing while you climb up. You pull the rope, and I'll push."

He climbed out of the water, grabbed the rope with his teeth, and began to pull. As I placed my hands under the box, piercing pain shot through my hands. I gasped and jerked away. No sign of injury, but my palms and wrists throbbed.

Arvandus tilted his head. *Raven?*

"I'm fine." But a second try yielded the same results. "It hurts to touch it." I considered and discarded a few ideas. At a sudden thought, I held up a hand to Arvandus. "Stay right there. I'll only be a minute."

Plunging back into the water, I dove to the bottom. After a few seconds, I found what I was looking for: two flat, palm-sized rocks. Seizing them, I pushed off the bottom for an arduous trip to the surface. Mental note: *Don't swim with rocks.*

One in each hand, I used them to push the box without direct contact. Three pushes and one forceful shove later, the box rested on the stone ledge. I tossed the rocks aside and flexed my aching fingers. Whatever was in this box was trouble.

I climbed out of the water and squeezed out my hair. "That was fun." My stomach flipped again, and I rubbed it.

His keen eyes caught my movement. "The power is making you ill. Step away. It will pass."

"What about you?"

"I am fine for the moment."

Taking a few steps away, I pulled in several slow breaths. My nausea eased. How would we get the box open if I couldn't touch it? "We need to get that thing open to release the power."

He shook his furry head, his eyes still serious. "The box does not hold the power, but the vessel."

"What do you mean? Is there, like, another box in there?"

"Or something else."

I stepped closer. "Can't we just open it? Waiting's making me nervous."

Using a paw, he released a latch and growled. His wingtips shot a few silver sparks.

Holding up a hand, I moved to the other side. "I'll get the other one." I located the latch, and with a quick flip, opened it. My fingers burned from the brief contact. I sat down and gave it a glare. Getting the lid off would be impossible.

After several long moments, Arvandus sat. "We do not have the correct tools. We will have to return later to finish this."

Exhaustion flooded me at the thought of coming back. "No. Arvandus, I can't handle another trip in here, at least not through that water. We need to open this now. Could we use the rocks to pry it open?" I pointed to the rocks I'd used earlier.

Ears twitching, Arvandus paced the length of the rocky lip before turning and retracing his steps.

"Are you—"

"Quiet. I am thinking."

Right.

After several minutes, he sat, his gaze steady. "Use the rocks, but do not overdo it."

It was crude, time-consuming work. I bloodied my knuckles and broke a nail before the lid budged. Jaundiced light seeped from the opening and filled the cave.

Gripping a stone in each fist, I shoved the lid to the side. It clattered to the ground, the harsh sound reverberating throughout the chamber. Harsh light and heat hit me full in the face, and Arvandus and I fell back from its force. At his growl, I crawled to my knees and looked inside.

In the box lay a young girl, her face serene, eyes closed, glowing with an unearthly yellow light.

I gasped. "No! Oh, no. Is she—is she dead?"

"Not yet. But once the power is used up, it is inevitable."

My vision blurred. "How'd she get here? Why would someone do this to her?" Dread weighed down my limbs. "Why would anyone use a *person*?"

"A life force makes the power stronger and more stable. If heat and energy are placed in an inanimate vessel, the Dunamis would be much weaker."

We sat for several minutes, staring at the glowing Dunamis, my stomach in knots.

Arvandus broke the silence. "We cannot leave her like this. She is emitting too much heat."

"What do you suggest?"

His gaze rested on me and stayed there. "Someone should remove the power. Especially if they have that ability."

Hmm, I wonder who he has in mind. I rolled my shoulders, ignoring the fear tearing through me. Although I felt like throwing up, I couldn't walk away. "How am I supposed to pull that kind of power from her?"

"The same way you pulled heat out of the ground. Find an opening, like her ears or nose, and pull. Then dispose of it as quickly as possible."

He made it sound so easy. I looked at his impassive expression. "Will this kill her?"

"If you do not do this, she will die. If you do it, she may live."

May—the word held no assurances. Just a big, fat maybe.

Her ear openings were too small. And I wasn't poking her nose or eyes. Gross. That left her mouth. Her face was ice cold, which surprised me, because the heat emanating from her was intense, like standing in front of a smithy's furnace. I pried open her mouth and stuck my fingers in, just past her teeth. It kind of grossed me out, but at least I wasn't giving her mouth to mouth. Focusing on the cave wall, I tried to pull out the heat.

Warmth oozed into my fingers. This was a different kind of catch and release than what I'd done for my test. The energy moved like molasses, crawling through my palms and filling my wrists. After pulling my fingers out, I slipped my other hand into her mouth. Cool breath chilled my palm.

Then I pushed, but nothing happened.

The heat thickened, filling me like sludge. Panic rose in my chest. I focused, closing my eyes. Nothing. I pushed again, and a few flames flared to life. Bearing down, I forced the heat into flames. By the time I'd dispelled that energy, more waited in my other hand.

I swapped fingers again.

Sweat broke out on my forehead as I shoved out more heat, slow flickers writhing on my palm. I repeated the action two more times. Sweat poured down my back. My stomach flipped, and I swallowed hard. The sluggish force seeped from my hands too slowly. When there was no more dark energy in her body, I pulled my hands away, still trying to rid my system of the heavy force. Some tendrils of it had crept into my neck and shoulders.

It had to stay away from my heart.

Arvandus watched my struggle, his wingtips throwing sparks. "Raven?"

"It's still inside. I can't get it out!" My panicked voice echoed in the cave. Nausea slammed into me, and I turned, placed my hand on the wall's rocky surface, and retched.

When I stood, tremors took over.

"Concentrate and drive it from your being."

I groaned. The seething energy yanked at my stomach, its claws dragging past my chest, raking my raw throat.

Arvandus' voice became more urgent. "Push, Raven!"

Shoving, I screamed as the power tried to sink its greedy fingers into my soul. With a final thrust, a massive ball of flame exploded from my hands. With a flash and a bang, it collapsed, filling the cave with heat.

Black and red spots danced in front of my eyes, and the floor tilted. My knees buckled. Couldn't breathe, couldn't think. Exhaustion tugged at me.

I crumpled to the cave floor.

CHAPTER TWENTY

"Brenna?" Arvandus' wet nose prodded my cheek, and I shifted, moaning. My head pulsed, knives piercing.

"No." I pushed him away. "Hurts."

"Yes, I know. Can you open your eyes?"

"Ungh." I cracked open an eye. Even my eyelashes throbbed.

"Try to sit up, please. If you fall asleep now, you may not wake up."

I blinked at him. "What?"

"Shadow Power cannot be left unchecked in the body. Did you dispose of all of it?"

Using his solid body as leverage, I pulled myself into a sitting position. Although everything ached, no tendrils lurked in my neck or shoulders or oozed through my fingers. I released a relieved sigh that sounded more like a whimper.

"You need food."

My gaze fell on the girl lying to the side, her form no longer glowing. Even her bottom half's aura was a pale, silvery gray, more of a mist than light. Her chalk-white skin stretched over delicate features. "Is she okay?"

He gave her a cursory glance. "Her breathing is shallow. And her body temperature is far below normal."

"Can we warm her?"

"No, her body must fight the hypothermia on its own. It is up to Elyon alone now." He turned his attention back to me. "It is close to suppertime. I will fly to the mouth of the cave. Perhaps the Avanti have returned and will share provisions."

"Do you have enough clearance?"

He peered through the cave's gloom. "I will find out. Is there anything else you need?"

"A towel or dry clothing maybe?" Now that I was out of the water, the air trickled ice-cold fingers over my skin.

He tilted his head. "I will ask."

Kefira with her sharp mouth and sharper sword flickered through my mind. "Hey, if Kefira is the only one there, don't bother."

With a quick nod, he took a running leap and skimmed above the water toward the front of the cave. The cave ceiling and walls stood taller and wider than the opening we'd just traveled through. Too bad. If it'd been the same, we could've flown in and avoided nearly drowning.

My attention shifted back to the girl. Who was she? I leaned closer to get a better look. She was maybe eight or nine years old, with fine delicate features and long blonde hair. Someone had used a young girl to make a Dunamis. I clenched my jaw and fisted my hands.

A small sigh escaped the girl, and she stirred. But her eyes never opened. I leaned against the slimy cave wall. Removing the Shadow Power-enhanced heat had been terrifying, and mini tremors still shook my body. When it had finally exited, I felt like I'd lost part of myself.

When Arvandus returned, Rachel and Fee sat on his back, a bag between them. He landed and both slid off.

Fee grabbed the bag and joined me. "Arvandus told us what happened. Are you all right?"

Rachel gave my arm an encouraging squeeze before checking on the sleeping girl.

"Well, I hope so. Nothing's broken, and I'm pretty sure all the bad energy is gone." I nearly snickered. *Bad* energy, like it was a misbehaving puppy. I was delirious.

Rachel stood. "We heard the explosion and thought it might be a cave-in."

"Has that ever happened before?" I studied the ceiling. No cracks. And no loose rock piled near walls.

"No, but we couldn't imagine what else it was." Rachel's gray eyes grew wide. "I never would've guessed a Dunamis was hidden here. Nobody ever comes into the cave from this end. Kefira swims every other night or so, but she never comes back this far."

Fee sat next to me and pulled out a few slices of bread, a small chunk of purple-striped cheese, and a bag of liberty berries. "Here. But eat slowly. Too much at once might overload your system."

"Thank you so much." I didn't care about overloading, so I tossed a big handful of berries into my mouth. Juice squirted, flooding my mouth with a spiced, tart sweetness. I closed my eyes, savoring the taste.

Rachel touched my shoulder. "We can find a place for you to sleep tonight."

Sleep sounded great.

Arvandus turned away. "Thank you for your offer, but we must check the spring before heading back to the Lee's."

I groaned. "We must?"

"That was our plan."

Well, it had been until some hinky magic had pulled my spleen from my body. "Maybe the Dunamis made Storm's father sick?"

Arvandus shook his head. "No, the water is fine. His father's sickness is because of something else."

I wilted. "But I'm exhausted." Might as well have some cheese with that whine. I took another bite.

"A short nap, then. To recover after your meal." He turned to Rachel and Fee. "Would one of you stay with her?"

Oh. My. Word. Like I was a toddler who needed a babysitter. "I'm fine."

Arvandus turned toward me so swiftly, I jumped. "I must get a meal for myself, and someone must stay with you while I hunt. Your recovery is precarious. Especially by yourself...on a small cave ledge...next to a river." His intense golden eyes pressed his point home.

Glowering, I leaned against the cave wall and shoved a piece of bread into my mouth so I wouldn't say something I'd regret.

Rachel smiled. "We don't mind at all. We'll both stay in case she wakes up." She returned her gaze to the girl's prone form. She looked so small and helpless.

Arvandus walked to the edge of the rocky lip. "Thank you. I will return." He was gone with a rush of wings.

The redhead gestured to the bread. "Is it good? I made it last night."

"Delicious, actually. Thank you." I took another bite, savoring the crunchy crust and nutty flakiness.

"Oh, I nearly forgot." Fee reached into the bag and pulled out a blanket. "Here. When you're done eating, take off your clothes and wrap up in this. I'll dry your clothes while you sleep."

I nestled the blanket in my lap, appreciating its softness. "Thanks. How long have you been a part of the Avanti?"

She fiddled with a thick lock of red hair. "About six moons."

I did the math in my head. A moon was twenty days, so she'd been a member for about...four months? "Do you have a family?"

"It's just my parents and me, although they don't support my joining. It's shameful, indicating I'm ugly or not marriageable."

I nearly choked on my bread. She was gorgeous with her beautiful amber eyes and all that thick red hair. "Don't tell me someone thought you were ugly. Because that's the dumbest thing I've ever heard."

Fee stared at the far cave wall, her eyes haunted. "It is the way of things here, how women are either sold or given away like property, only useful for marriage."

Rachel spoke from her place next to the girl. "But the tide's shifting, and we've gained more rights. Guardians aren't mandatory anymore, although women must pay a steep fee. And women aren't forced to marry, not anymore, although our options are inadequate. A family can shame a girl into marriage." She sent Fee a sympathetic look.

"Do either of you see your family?"

Fee sat back and fixed her skirt over her glowing aura. "A few of us see family members occasionally. I arrange brief visits with my mother. But we don't talk about where I'm working or living, or anything important, really. Rachel stays in touch with her sister"—she sent Rachel a sly wink—"who sometimes joins our protests." Then she sobered. "Others are not so fortunate. Kefira isn't in contact with any of her family."

Somehow that didn't surprise me.

When I finished eating, Fee directed me to a small nook where I took off my clothes and wrapped up in the blanket. I handed the sodden mess to her. "I'm not sure what you can do with them."

"I'll be able to get the water out of them. They won't be warm, but they'll be dry. We'll also clean up the smell." She nodded to where I'd been sick.

My cheeks grew hot. "Sorry."

"Don't be. It happens." Fee gave me the empty bag. "Here. You can use this as a pillow."

Maybe she'd build a fire to dry out my clothes. At this point, I didn't care. A nap would be paradise, despite the cold cave floor.

With the dry bag folded under my head, I fell asleep with the delicious smell of fresh bread surrounding me.

I woke to the murmur of soft voices. Without opening my eyes, I identified Arvandus' low rumble and the higher-pitched whisper belonging to Rachel.

"The spring is due north from the cave. Enormous stone walls surround it."

"Is it guarded at night?"

"Once full darkness falls, guards lock the gate. Two always patrol the perimeter, and they change shifts every four hours."

I pushed up from my makeshift bed, realizing when the blanket slipped I was still naked. Clutching the blanket for dear life, I shoved my hair out of my face. Fee sat nearby on the rocky ledge, smoothing my tank top with her palms. With each pass, water leaked out and dribbled back into the river.

"What are you doing?"

She gave me a shy smile. "Drying your clothes like I promised. This is the last piece, and it's almost dry." She gave the shirt a few more caresses before sitting back. "There. All done."

"It looks like you're petting my shirt."

She grinned. "I'm a Waterbrand. I gathered the moisture from your shirt and directed it back into the river."

And there was my stupidity out in the open. I'd never seen a Waterbrand work up close. "Wow. That's cool. Thanks."

"You're very welcome."

Arvandus strolled over. "I will be taking Rachel and the girl back to their living quarters. Will you be ready to leave when I return?"

"Sure."

I waved to Rachel who returned my gesture. She carried the little girl to Arvandus. After securing her, Rachel mounted my griffin and left.

Fee returned to my napping area and folded my shirt before putting it with my other clothes. Giving me another smile, she stood. "Arvandus picked up your things outside the cave, too. I'll give you privacy so you can dress."

After she walked a short distance away, I dressed quickly. I yanked the tank over my head and pulled my dry hair out from the neckline. I paused. The smooth strands slipped through my fingers like silk. No rat's nest, even though I'd fallen asleep with damp river-water hair.

I walked over to her. "Did you dry my hair, too? Because it's not all snarled like usual."

Flushing, she shrugged. "I just touched the ends while you slept. I hate it when my hair gets all frizzy."

I gave her a quick hug to ease her embarrassment. "You're a girl after my own heart, Fee. You saved me from a bad hair day."

She bit her lip, a smile peeking through before she spoke. "Phoenix."

"Excuse me?"

"My full name's Phoenix. Fee's a nickname."

"I love your name." And it suited her. Not only the red hair, but also the way she lived for change and renewal.

In minutes, Arvandus returned and knelt for us to climb on. "We must leave, Raven. Rachel agreed to contact us if the child improves."

After Fee got on, I climbed on behind her and stayed close as Arvandus flew through the cavern. Striped rocks, boulders, and stalactites all whizzed by, near enough to touch. When we stopped near the front of the cave, Fee slipped off.

She pointed to the area full of sleeping girls, then held her finger to her lips. "We'll be in touch," she whispered.

I squeezed her hand, knowing I was leaving a new friend. "Thank you so much—for everything."

She smiled and stepped back. Arvandus rocketed through the opening with little room to spare. The night sky glittered with stars, Bella's Comet a spot of radiance as it left Eventyr behind. While the Petrus Rings sparkled silver-blue and gold, the dazzling vista stole my breath.

Arvandus gained in altitude before putting on a burst of speed. *We will be there soon. It would be best to remain quiet.*

Got it.

In the darkness, the edges of the far mountains were black shadows snuffing out the stars. I inhaled, pine mixing with sage and a trace of something floral. Past a stand of trees, stone walls encircling the spring rose three stories. Greenery climbed the walls and graced the enclosure's open top before curling down inside the walls.

Arvandus's wings moved in silent strokes as he flew high around the perimeter. As Rachel had said, two guards marched around the walls. A helli lantern hung above each post, while each guard sported a sword dangling from his belt.

How are we going to get in?

They never look up. We will use that to our advantage.

At that point, a guard looked up and squinted.

I rolled my eyes. Come on. Of all the times to become vigilant, the guard chose now?

Arvandus immediately banked and flew higher.

Now what?

Now we wait and watch. Patience, Raven.

The minutes ticked by slowly, and Arvandus flew to the other side, where that guard still patrolled in blissful ignorance. After a few minutes of observation, my griffin's muscles tensed.

Hold on.

When the guard turned to complete another pass, Arvandus burst forward and entered the spring, slipping in above the stone wall. In a smooth glide, he skimmed the water before landing on the far side of the pool.

My eyes watered as I strained to identify shapes in the darkness. *I need light. Do you think it's safe?*

The walls will block most of the light from a low flame.

I created a flame in my open palm and held it over the water. Walking the cobblestone edge, I searched for irregularities. Water burbled from the natural spring, and wavelets lapped against the stone walls of the pool before flowing over the stone spillway and into the river.

It looks fine to me. Do you notice anything?

Arvandus's reply was cut short by a splash. My flame grew larger. On the far side of the pool, a dorsal fin cut through the water. Fear grabbed my heart and twisted. A shark in the spring?

Suddenly, the "monster" broke the surface. Its body a silver arc, it leaped then splashed back into the water, disappearing from view.

I released a shaky giggle. A dolphin. They were fun and playful, right? I hadn't heard of wild dolphin attacks in the Jasper Territory.

The dolphin resurfaced in front of us. Arvandus gave a warning growl, which didn't seem to disturb it at all. I moved a little closer. The dolphin bobbed its head and clicked before leaping onto the stone walkway next to me.

Water sprayed over my boots as I jumped back. My breath caught. I was wrong. The headline would read, *Queen Sarah's Daughter Killed in Rogue Dolphin Attack.* Did dolphins have big teeth?

Before I could check its mouth, the animal morphed. I stumbled back as it grew taller, its silver skin shifting to peach. Blonde hair sprouted, and the tail divided and became jean-clad legs. When the shifting stopped, I took a breath, opened my mouth, and squeaked, "Anna?"

Chapter Twenty-One

"Brenna! Reefstars! It's great to see you, wavekeeper."
Beaming, she offered me a fist bump.

I grabbed her in a hug instead, relief warring with happiness.
"That was terrifying. I thought you hated shifting in front of
people."

"Salt it down. Don't get used to it or anything."

"What are you doing here?" At Arvandus's growl, I dropped my
voice to a whisper. "I mean, what are you doing here?"

She pulled a hand through her hair and matched her voice level
to mine. "Working, but it feels like chasing sea glass."

"Oh. But—why work in Ginselwyn? And you were shifted..."
Nothing made sense.

"Um, can we talk somewhere else?"

At a sudden noise from the other side of the wall, I froze. Footsteps, coming closer.

My heart thundered. Then the unmistakable tumbling of a lock,
followed by the sliding of a wooden beam.

On. Now. Arvandus' words spurred me into action, and I
jumped onto his back. Anna shifted again, a blur of color becoming a Steen falcon. With a running leap, Arvandus took to the air.

We cleared the walls as the stone gates grated open. Anna already flew several yards ahead.

By the time we were halfway to the cave, I caught Anna's eye and pointed to the ground. *Arvandus, let's land. I need to talk to Anna.*

He set down in a field near the base of Ho Mountain.

Anna landed behind a bush and walked out in her human form. "That was foamed out—the way we escaped? Totally shell fine." She blew out a breath.

"We almost got caught."

"Yeah, but we didn't. Speaking of shell fine, how are you? You know, the last time I saw you, you were lost in the blue. Did you and Baldwin make up?"

The familiar ache bloomed in my chest. My expression must've said everything because pity filled her eyes.

"Oh, I was sure you guys would've caught the shimmer again." She sighed. "I'm sorry."

My voice sounded dead, even to me. "He left the next day with the emperor's men. First deployment. And then Tiny and I left that evening. Which reminds me—I thought you were grounded." Yes, any topic was better than revisiting my wrecked love life in Linneah.

"I told you I'm working."

"Yeah, but I didn't even know you had a job."

We sat on the grass, but Arvandus continued to stalk behind her. Back and forth, back and forth.

Finally, I leaned forward. "Arvandus, what's wrong?"

"While you slept, I captured and ate one squirrel. He was small. And tough." He sniffed, the very picture of dejection.

"Oh, well, go hunt. Your pacing's making me nervous."

He turned and prowled into a stand of trees. His body blended into the shadows.

Anna crossed her legs. "Well, you probably don't know this, since I never mentioned it, but my family is tide-called to guard the Stones of the Spring."

"Tide-called?"

"Sorry. It means destined. We check them every third season."

"But you live on Matana Island."

"Right, but my grandparents lived closer to Ginselwyn. When they danced the drift to the Big Ocean, the job passed to my mother. We will always be responsible for the Stones, unless Emperor Rexson chooses a new family, which is highly likely at this point." She cleared her throat.

"What do you mean?"

"I'm tail-tied."

I raised an eyebrow.

She leaned close, her brow furrowed. "This year was my first chance to inspect the spring. Because I'm female, I shifted into a Steen falcon. I was going to fly in, check the stones, fly out. But the stones aren't there."

My breath caught. "What do you mean?"

"They're missing. I shifted into a dolphin and checked the base of the spring, where the water comes into the pool. They aren't there. Somebody replaced them with regular rocks." She rubbed her forehead. "Have there been any reports of people getting sick?"

"No, not—wait! Storm's dad, but—" Nobody was supposed to know. Me and my big mouth. I turned to Anna. "You can't tell anyone about Governor Lee."

She shook her head. "Are you seaweed spun? It's the Emperor."

"Fine, but the citizens can't know. We don't want mass hysteria. Things are so complicated right now. What do the stones look like?"

Anna held her hands about a foot apart. "Kind of like a huge geode that's been split open. You know what I mean? There are two of them side by side, a hole in the center of each rock to let water through. Crystals line the center—some say they have healing shimmer. My grandfather has heard stories, myths and stuff, but nobody knows what they do if they're not in the spring."

Too many questions. Who had taken the stones? How had they removed them? And why? What could they do with them? "When did you get here?"

"Just today. I was going to stop by Tiny's house when I was done."

Then Anna didn't know... "Did you know she's getting married?"

Her blue eyes grew wide. "I thought she was just meeting her fiancé."

I told Anna everything I knew. "But she seems totally happy with Jakeb, even though something about him doesn't sit right."

"You mean aside from the fact he's a blackmailer?"

I snorted. "Yeah, though Tiny says it's just a misunderstanding."

Anna bit her lip. "He's wind-slick. I don't like the sound of him."

"Join the club. But Tiny's thrilled with him, already running around making meals and being Suzy Homemaker."

Anna shrugged. "But if that's what she wants, it shouldn't matter, right?"

Frowning, I shook my head. "I don't know."

Anna lay down on the grass. "Maybe she's found The One." After several minutes, her breathing became deep and regular. Asleep. I don't know how the girl did it, but she could sleep anywhere.

I watched the night sky. Stars glittered through the Petrus Rings, while wispy clouds played tag with Bella's Comet. Maybe Anna was right. If Jakeb was what Tiny wanted, it shouldn't matter what I thought. As long as he loved her.

When Arvandus came back, I woke Anna. My stomach growled, reminding me it was way past dinnertime. "I need food and then bed. Can we head back?"

Arvandus licked his muzzle. "I could catch a rabbit for you, Raven."

"Ugh. No thanks. I prefer my food well done."

Anna snickered. "I'm gonna skim the blue. See you there?"

"Even if you can find the house by yourself, they'll all be asleep."

She stomped her foot. "Ugh, I wanted a bed tonight."

Arvandus moved closer. "There is plenty of room on the side deck, Anna. Brenna can get some bedding for you." He knelt for me to climb on.

I nodded. "Yeah, just follow us there."

She grinned, then walked behind a bush. A Steen falcon flew out, Anna's favorite flying form. She followed us back to the house, a soaring shadow on my right. The air rushed cool against my cheeks, and I buried my hands deep in Arvandus's fur. His paws touched down lightly at the edge of the backyard.

I climbed off and patted his shoulder. "Thanks, Arvandus."

The falcon landed behind a straggly bush, and Anna walked out.

"Follow me." Arvandus stalked toward the front door to check in, Anna and I following.

At the corner of the house, movement caught my eye. Near the forest bordering the fence, shadows blurred. Who was back there? The backyard security guard had followed us to the front door, and he now talked with the other guard.

I waited. No movement. Maybe I was hallucinating. Lack of food could do that. The gloom stirred, shifting away from the house. My curiosity piqued, I crouched, hurrying toward the shadows. A tall, leafy bush bordering the fence provided the perfect hiding spot. I knelt, bracing one hand on the ground. The faint murmur of voices became clearer as they moved and then stopped. Right on the other side of the bush. Perfect.

"You weren't at our meeting spot."

The other dark figure clasped his hands in front of his body. "Yes, terribly sorry, Lord Rune. I was with the family and then—"

"Silence! I don't need excuses; I need results. And I've told you not to use my name, not until our plans are complete. I'm needed elsewhere, and I've already wasted valuable time finding you. Now, what's your report?"

As I peered through the leaves, my breath caught. What? It was Jakeb and the guy from the spillway in Pennsylvania. My lungs seized. He'd called him Rune.

Jakeb leaned closer. "The family has welcomed me, and I've gained the father's trust. He has agreed to draw up papers naming me successor."

I squinted, trying to see if Rune or Jakeb was wearing my jasper. No sign of it. I must have lost it somewhere in Kelda Hills. Rune's next words jerked me back to the present.

"Excellent. Are there any other obstacles, heirs perhaps?"

"His older children are uninterested. There is a younger son, but he is more interested in girls than leading a country. Shaynedel is beautiful and ready to be married, a fruit ripe for picking." Lust thickened his voice.

I wrinkled my nose. Nasty. Get some help, dude.

"Focus on your objective. Use the girl to get closer to the governor."

Barely daring to breathe, I peeked through the thick leaves. Jakeb and Rune stood close enough for me to touch. A trace of rancid spices wafted past my nose, tickling it. Oh, no. No sneezing. Please not now. I pinched it shut.

"Of course," Jakeb said.

"I will remove the Dunamis after the wedding, but I'll permit you to take credit."

Yeah, good luck with that.

Rune continued. "The governor is weak, but if he fails to die, we will murder him and his aides. The papers will name you his successor. Before long, I will hold two cities in the palm of my hand."

A malicious smile grew on Jakeb's face.

Shock and horror hollowed out my stomach. Two cities? What was he talking about?

Rune waved a hand. "That is all. But if you forget who your master is, I will slaughter you and your household."

"Never, my prince." Jakeb stepped back, and Rune disappeared. Jakeb blinked once, then waved a hand over his torso. His legs misted over, disappearing. As he walked toward the road, an aura grew, lighting up the bottom half of his body. Before I could draw a breath, he appeared fully Welden. I leaned back, my hand over my mouth, while Jakeb moved toward the city.

Stunned, I fell onto my butt. After a moment, I sprinted to the front door and encountered the security guard. "Hi. Remember me?"

He looked at me, then glared at the other security guard. "Get back to your post."

The man mumbled an apology before scurrying to the backyard.

The guard at the front door grimaced. "Where is your guardian?"

"Probably visiting his father at the infirmary. Do you really want to wake and question Mrs. Lee just so I can go to bed?"

With a sigh, he waved me toward the front door. I opened it, taking care to be quiet. In the living room, the gloom was broken only by a small orb glowing with a pale-rose hue.

I made my way to Tiny's bedroom and eased open the door. She was sitting up in bed, reading. "Finally home, huh?"

I stuck out my tongue at her, then grinned. "What are you, my mom? I told Storm we'd be back late."

Her scowl only eased a little. "So sue me. I was worried. Storm disappeared after the picnic was canceled, too."

"He wasn't with me. He's probably with your dad. By the way, how is he?"

228   J.M. HACKMAN

She rubbed the edge of her book, her eyes vacant. "They found a healer on the outskirts of town, but we're not sure how skilled she is. So we sent a runner for Kelda Hills' best." She bit her lip. "He's so sick, Brenna. He's been coughing up blood and sleeping a lot. What if he doesn't make it?"

I gave her shoulder a gentle squeeze. "Hey, he'll fight it off. It's probably bronchitis."

Her voice came out in a whisper. "You don't know that."

Unfortunately true. I flopped onto the daybed, wincing as my freshly tattooed and now-bruised shoulder protested. "By the way, Anna's here. She's sharing the porch with Arvandus."

Tiny sat straight up. "She came? She needs to sleep here with us. It can be an early bachelorette party."

All the new information I had about Jakeb whirled in my brain. I faked a smile. "Sure."

In minutes, Tiny herded Anna into the bedroom. I found blankets and an extra pillow in the hallway closet for her.

Anna arranged them on the floor, and I watched the two of them fuss over bedding. The urge to blurt everything out collected in my throat, but I needed to think. Or eat. Or both.

I stepped over Anna's makeshift bed. "Can I get a sandwich or something? I'm starved."

Tiny waved a hand. "Sure. There are probably leftover muffins on the counter."

"Ooh, what kind?"

"Liberty berries and ginger. Oh, and mixed nut."

Yum. I loved liberty berries' spicy-sweet flavor. I had to try one of those.

Anna's voice stopped me in the doorway. "Brenna, foamed out new ink. No drift about it."

Looking over my tattooed shoulder, I grinned. "Thanks."

I hurried down the hallway and slipped into the kitchen. After pouring myself a glass of rainfruit juice, I searched the kitchen counter and found the muffin basket. Grabbing two, I sat at the table. I needed sleep. Not happening, not with everything spinning in my brain. I had to talk it out with someone.

Grabbing a jar of jelly, I slathered some on half the muffin. At the slight creak of the front door, I froze. Jakeb or Rune had come early to kill everyone in their sleep. Fear propelled me across the room to rummage through the utensil drawer for a butcher knife. I closed a fist around the first thing I touched and whirled around, my back to the wall and my eyes fastened on the kitchen doorway.

A figure appeared in the doorway, and I raised my weapon. Jumping back, Storm lifted his fists. I sagged in relief and lowered my vicious weapon—a wooden spoon.

His lips quirked. "Were you planning on stirring me to death?"

"Ha. Funny guy. It was the first thing I grabbed. I thought you were, uh, never mind." My hands trembled as I put the wooden spoon back in its drawer.

His hands closed over my shoulders. "Hey, relax. Who did you think I was?"

I rubbed my eyes. This day had to be the longest on record. And it was getting longer. "You wouldn't believe me if I told you."

"Try me."

I turned and eyed him, hoping my bloodshot eyes didn't give me a crazed look. "I'll tell you what happened, but you can't tell anyone."

He followed me to the table, sitting next to me.

Maybe in the retelling, things would make more sense. I didn't mention the Avanti, only what had happened with the Dunamis and our discovery at the spring. I finished by recounting what I'd seen in his backyard. Rubbing the back of his neck, he cleared his throat.

I grabbed his hand, and his eyes finally met mine. "It was Rune, Storm. He's behind the drought, the blackmail, and he's planning to kill your father if he gets better. And Jakeb? He's using an illusion to appear Welden. He's partnered with Rune, and they're somehow planning to take down *two* cities, though he never gave specifics."

Storm ran a hand over his face, weariness and worry making him look far older than eighteen. "Are you sure you heard correctly?"

I sucked on my teeth and reminded myself it wasn't nice to hit people. "Yes, all of it. Jakeb's the puppet, and Rune's the puppet master who will run Ginselwyn."

His jaw firmed. "That won't happen. I just finished talking with Father. He agreed to draw up papers for me to be his replacement if he dies."

What an awful situation. I swallowed hard. "And how do you feel about that?"

His gaze fell. "Worried. I want to do a good job and make my father proud, but more than that, I want him to get better."

I squeezed his hand. "I know. And I think your dad will. But I also think you'll do a wonderful job as temporary governor."

With a small smile, he reached out, tracing my cheek. "You make me believe I can do anything."

At his words, a glow unfurled in my heart. The room drew close, his warm hand cupping my cheek.

He leaned forward, his eyes dark-blue pools. "Brenna," he whispered, and then his lips found mine.

His fingers slid to the back of my neck in a gentle caress, his warm mouth tasting of mint.

I pulled away, pleasure and guilt a knot in my chest. "Uh, maybe I shouldn't have done that."

He leaned back in the chair, a slow smile building. "You didn't. I did. And I'll do it again the next chance I get. Now go to bed before I rethink letting you go."

The weight of his gaze followed me as I left the room.

CHAPTER TWENTY-TWO

THE NEXT MORNING, I awoke with a clearer head. The facts I'd spilled to Storm had aligned themselves in a neat pattern.

Now to find a moment alone with Tiny to tell her.

Apparently, Mrs. Lee was on a muffin kick. Fresh breakfast muffins waited on the counter, a scrumptious confection of grains, unidentifiable nuts, and seeds. They were still warm when Tiny, Anna, and I made our way to the kitchen. A note on the table said to help ourselves because Mrs. Lee, Stellara, Silver, and Storm had left for the market.

After we had breakfast, Anna went to take a shower. I helped Tiny carry our dishes to the sink as I gathered my courage. I could do this. "How're things with Jakeb?"

She turned, her aura brightening to a dazzling gold. "Really good."

Of course. Because he was Mr. Wonderful. "Have you guys gotten to know each other better, then?"

"Well, he doesn't like to talk about himself. He's so modest. But I'm sure we'll learn."

"So you know where he grew up? Does he come from good people? Do you know his parents?" Sheesh, could I sound any older?

Her smile froze, cracking at the edges. "No, but children don't always end up like their parents. I'll meet them eventually."

"Oh, well, that's good." I forced the words out with a smile.

"I'm so happy. He's almost too good to be true."

I cleared my throat. "Let's just say, hypothetically, he is. Then what?"

Tiny's eyes narrowed. "Is that supposed to be funny?"

"No, not really. I just, uh, wondered, is all. I mean, in a week you'll be married to a guy you don't know much about. What if he's, you know, working with Rune or something?"

She rolled her eyes. "Yeah, I'm sure he's an evil villain, intent on my destruction."

Yes, exactly that. I flexed my fingers and chose my words carefully. "How did your parents find him?"

"Well, actually, he found them. When he heard about the water problem, he wanted to help. And when he heard about their 'beautiful daughter'—his words, not mine—he wanted me to be his wife. Isn't that romantic?"

No, definitely not. "Um, why hasn't he fixed the water issue?"

She turned, giving me her back. "He's busy."

Yeah, meetings with Rune would suck up a lot of his time. "Right, but he said the marriage wasn't a prerequisite. So how come he hasn't done it?"

Her voice tightened. "I'm sure it's on his list of things to do."

"But what about all the Weldens who don't have enough water? Do you think they mind waiting?"

Tiny rounded on me, her eyes furious. "Why can't you just leave him alone? I thought you'd be happy I'd found someone who loved me. Why are you so determined to find something wrong with him?"

Because he's plotting to take over your city. Because he's working with Rune. Because he's planning to have your father killed. "Because nothing adds up."

"Or maybe you're jealous."

I jerked, my eyes finding hers. "Jealous?"

"You can't stand to see someone find love when your relationship bombed. Sure, you're a friend when things are going well, but as soon as your world falls apart, nobody better have a happily-ever-after waiting for them. Well, get a grip, sweetheart. Because you're not going to ruin this for me!"

Slamming down the mug she was holding, she raced out of the kitchen and past Anna who stood in the doorway, eyes wide.

I sighed and collapsed into a chair.

Anna stepped into the kitchen. "What did you say to her?"

"Just voiced some concerns I had about Jakeb.

"Brenna, you've got to salt it down."

I crossed my arms and lowered my voice to a furious whisper. "That guy isn't just some random guy who fell in love with her. He's Rune's pawn, willing to kill her dad to gain the governorship."

"Shells and shimmer." Anna dropped into a chair next to me. "Why didn't you say anything?"

I waved my hands around. "It makes me sound like a lunatic. 'Hey, you know that guy you're crazy about? Yeah, he's a psychopath.' And I have no proof, only what I overheard."

A knock at the front door halted our conversation. Rising from the table, I hurried to the front door and opened it. A security guard stood holding Fee's arm in a firm grip.

"Fee! Hi." I turned to the guard. "She's welcome to come in."

He gave her an impassive stare before dropping her arm and returning to his post.

She walked in, nervously smoothing her skirt. "I'm sorry to bother you. But we have to talk."

"Sure, come on into the kitchen. Fee, this is Anna."

"Hi." Anna jerked her head. "Want a muffin?"

Fee blinked a few times. "No, thank you. I shouldn't be here, but there's a problem. I spent all night thinking about it."

The front door opened, and Stellara and Silver ran into the living room, singing a children's song. Mrs. Lee and Storm followed.

Fee startled. "We can't talk here. Too many people."

Reaching out, I rubbed her arm. "It's fine. They're nice people."

Mrs. Lee walked in, eyeing my friends. "Hello, girls. I don't believe I've met either of you. I'm Mrs. Lee or Mrs. L or Jenica. Welcome to our home."

I smiled. "This is Anna, a friend of ours from Matana Island. And this is a new friend of mine, Fee."

Storm strolled into the room, slowing when he caught sight of Phoenix. Fee looked at him, then lowered her eyes, blushing.

Hmm, a little irritating, since he'd just kissed me last night. Still, Fee was gorgeous, even in a simple tank and skirt. So why wasn't I upset by the attention they were giving each other? If I was truly falling for Storm, I should be furious and making it obvious we were together. But I felt no urge to hurry to his side.

Fee nudged me, bringing me to the present. Oops. "Sorry, I zoned out for a second. How about, um, we talk on the second-floor deck where Arvandus sleeps?"

She brightened. "That's good. He should be part of the conversation. It was nice meeting you, Mrs. Lee."

Tucking her chin, she left the room. Storm's eyes followed her before his gaze snagged on mine. He flushed. I ignored him and hurried to the porch on the second floor.

Arvandus was absent when we arrived, probably out hunting or exploring. Fee paced the length of the deck before turning and retracing her steps. Over and over. I sat on the floor, my back propped against the inner wall. The warm breeze caressed my skin with the scent of sun-warmed clay.

"You want to tell me why you're upset?" I asked. "Or do we play Twenty Questions?"

She frowned. "I've never played that."

"Sorry, I'm being sarcastic. What's going on?"

"There have been a few recent developments since you left us." She sat next to me and fiddled with the hem of her skirt. "Rachel thought you should be informed."

"What about Kefira?"

"This problem involves her."

Arvandus flew in, landing lightly in the middle of the deck. "Good morning, Raven. Fee." He inclined his head in a brief nod. "Is there a problem?"

I gritted my teeth. All the interruptions were driving me crazy. It'd be a miracle if I finally discovered what was bugging Fee.

She took a deep breath. "Well, there are a few things. One, the little girl woke up. She told us her name is Tally. She's tired and a little confused, but she's doing well and eating. In a day or two, she should fully recover."

Tension drained from my shoulders, and I smiled. "Oh, I'm so glad to hear that. Is she from Ginselwyn?"

Fee gave me a weak smile. "Yes, she's a Welden, so we'll start looking for her family soon."

I let out a long sigh. Finally, something was going right.

Fee paled. "There's more. Did you know Rune abducted her?" Her voice hitched. "Tally told us she was forced into being a Dunamis. She tried to get away, but he poured all that power into her against her will."

My stomach flipped, but I kept my voice even. "And this surprises you? That sounds just like Rune's standard method of operation."

Fee shook her head. "No, he doesn't do things like that. He respects people."

I raised an eyebrow. "You sure we're talking about the same person? Tall, well-dressed guy with weird eyes?"

She wrung her hands. "This is so bad. I'm afraid the Avanti made a mistake."

"What do you mean?"

Her voice was a slip of sound. "We made a deal with Rune."

A sudden wash of cold hit my stomach. "Why would you do that?"

"He agreed to help us in our quest for citizenship. All we had to do was help him remove the governor from power."

I gaped at her. "Yet you're sitting in the governor's house, talking about a coup? Are you kidding me? You know I'm friends with this family, right?"

She flushed before setting her chin. "We don't want him hurt; we only ask that he listen to reason."

"This isn't the way to get it, Fee. And Rune doesn't keep promises." But a plan had begun swirling in my mind, pieces of the puzzle clicking together, snap, snap, snap.

Hope made her voice rise. "He might."

Arvandus' voice was rock hard. "It is a foolish wish. Do not work with him."

Phoenix crossed her arms. "How are we supposed to attain our rights if we don't fight for them?"

I tilted my head. "You're willing to kill people? Because if you join Rune, a lot of people are going to die bloody, violent deaths. That's what happens in a coup."

Frowning, she glanced at the floor but said nothing.

I tried a different tactic. "What would be an ideal situation? What do the Avanti want most?"

She gave a mirthless laugh. "Ideally? Representation in the council. But that will never happen, at least not during my lifetime. We'd settle for citizenship. Vote. Own land or businesses."

"Those are all good things."

Silence descended, then, "There's another problem."

"What?"

Her chin wobbled. "There's another Dunamis."

Arvandus and I looked at each other before I turned to Fee. "Where?"

She twisted her fingers in her lap. "Just beyond our living area. Kefira's been siphoning off power. It's making her crazy. She almost lost it last night when Rachel made a joke. She was just teasing, but K pulled her sword. Could you move the Dunamis to a safer place?"

Arvandus flicked his tail, his gold eyes steady. "It would be wiser to destroy it completely."

Fee avoided his gaze. "We don't need to do that."

I spluttered. "But it's another person!"

Arvandus's ears turned sideways. "Phoenix, these vessels are dangerous."

Fee spread her hands. "But it's helped Kefira enormously. She's so small, but the Dunamis gave her extraordinary strength and courage. She only needs to self-regulate."

Arvandus growled, his wings shooting silver sparks. "A Dunamis is not a plaything. It is a destroyer. Kefira is in danger. As is the vessel."

After a moment, her shoulders drooped. "I was afraid you were going to say that."

Arvandus moved forward. "We can come now and remove it."

I stood. "I have an idea."

"Raven?"

"That Dunamis is a bargaining chip. Let's go visit Governor Lee."

"Does this involve the Avanti?"

"Well, yes, but—"

Arvandus shook his head. "If you visit the governor to discuss the Avanti, there should be a representative present."

"Um." I looked at Fee.

She held up a hand. "No, thanks. But I can get Rachel."

I sighed. "I'll wait for her."

When Arvandus dropped off Phoenix at the cave, Rachel sent a message. She'd meet us in town in front of the fountain. Storm chose to accompany me.

We walked along the main road toward the building used as the infirmary. As soon as Governor Lee had been diagnosed, his aides had found an available building in the business district, cleaned it, and stocked it with whatever medical supplies they could find. So far, no one knew Governor Lee was ill beyond the small circle of aides and the town healer. I wasn't sure how much longer the secret could be kept.

"Why do you want to visit my father?" Storm asked.

The sun shone bright, turning his aura almost transparent. I rubbed the back of my neck, sweat gathering there. "My friend Rachel and I need to talk to him. I've found a solution to the drought. I'd like you to be in the room when I talk to him, if you don't mind."

"I don't, but as your guardian, I'd have to be there anyway."

"You're not my guardian. I paid my own way in."

"Well, you need a male representative."

I rolled my eyes. Of course I did.

Ginselwyn still suffered from the drought. As we walked, a cloud of dust and dirt followed our every step. Brown grass lined the road.

At the outdoor market, the smell of freshly baked bread filled the air. Lines gathered before makeshift tents and stalls in the bare field. Customers surged forward near a tent, yelling for better prices. A few men stood outside the market, begging, their eyes dull. Tension thickened as voices rose. One woman haggled for a bargain from a grain vendor, her face pinched with worry while she held the hands of two dirty toddlers. Over in a corner of the field, a group of women passed out pamphlets and held signs with "Avanti" written on them.

Storm's frown grew as we passed. The fountain near the business district remained quiet, a puddle of sludge near the bottom. Rachel waited nearby. When I introduced Storm to Rachel, he raised his eyebrows. "I know you. You're Rachel Marks, organizer of the Avanti."

"Yes, and you're Storm Lee, son of the governor." Her lips twitched. She gestured to a bench in the shade. "I'd like to talk to Brenna before we meet the governor. Privately."

Storm stepped back. "I'll visit Father and inform the guards to let you in."

I nodded. "Thanks. We shouldn't be long."

After he left, Rachel and I sat on the bench. She gave me a half-smile. "Phoenix tells me you don't agree with our arrangement with Rune."

"Only because he won't keep his side of the bargain."

"He treated all of us with respect when we met."

"Rune is a power-hungry liar and will say and do anything to get what he wants."

She tilted her head. "So how can you help us? What's your plan?"

"A coup will only kill good people. But if I can make a deal to get you what you want and deal with the water shortage too, would you take it?"

She laughed. "Citizenship? Council representation? I'd call you a worker of miracles."

"I'll get what I can for you, as long as you promise not to support Rune. He might give you what you ask for, but you won't have freedom when he's done. He wants to rule Ginsel-wyn, and he'll kill whoever gets in his way."

She raised her eyebrows. "And I'm supposed to pin all of my hopes on a seventeen-year-old girl?"

I shot Rachel a glare. "Well, not to be rude, but you don't have anything to offer the governor. I do."

She tilted her head. "What's in it for you? Or do you enjoy going around putting yourself at risk for people you don't know that well?" She gave me a smile.

Was she being sarcastic? Her unsettling ability to be snarky while smiling made it difficult to tell what she was thinking. "If things go well, he'll agree to your requests, allow me to remove the second Dunamis, and eliminate the requirement of an arranged marriage for his daughter."

"So you're doing this for your friend." Rachel's face was set in solemn lines. "She must be a good friend. But you need to understand how important this is for us, too."

"Sure."

She waved away my response. "You say it, but you haven't lived like property. The Avanti started as a small organization of strong-willed women over five generations ago. Our group has grown and made progress, but the time's approaching for our demands to be heard. We have support from several council members. The governor's stubborn and takes the simple path, what his supporters expect. If he'd step out of his comfort zone, he'd find Ginselwyn is ready for change."

"He might be willing this time."

She shrugged a single shoulder and stood. "We'll see. Give your presentation, and I'll list what we expect as well. May Elyon be with us."

Standing, I followed her to the two-story, white stucco building Storm had entered. The guards waved us through. The lobby's bay windows allowed an expansive view of the street, the market, and the defunct fountain.

A guard waiting at the stairwell stepped forward. "Governor Lee's on the second floor at the end of the hall. His son said to go on up."

I smiled my thanks. Rachel and I climbed the stairs, then turned down the narrow hall to where a closed door waited. After Rachel knocked, an aide with white hair and weak brown eyes answered.

"Hello. I'll let Governor Lee know you're here. His son is with him currently."

He led us into a small room. A cluster of chairs sat opposite a large desk, its top cluttered with papers. After crossing the room, he knocked softly on the door, then opened it a crack.

"Governor, your first meeting is here."

"I'll be with them in a moment." The voice coming from beyond the door was rusty and thin.

The aide gestured to the chairs. "You may sit."

I dropped into an available chair. Pulling out a piece of gum, I popped it in my mouth. The aide sat at his desk. In minutes, he became engrossed with the paper scattered across its surface.

Rachel and I waited, her the picture of serenity while I jiggled my knee and tapped my toes. After the longest wait ever, Storm returned.

I shot to my feet. "Hi. You're back. Can we talk to your dad, I mean, the governor now?"

After blinking a few times, he shook his head. "No. Uh, now's not a good time."

With a shake of her head, Rachel laughed. "Of course. He never intended to see us, did he?"

"He doesn't know why you're here. He's very sick. We can come back when Father improves. I'm sure he'd be willing to see you then."

I blinked, stunned at the turn of events, and we followed Storm to the ground floor. When he hesitated at the bottom of the stairway, Rachel turned, her gray eyes zeroing in on us.

"I have an appointment I'm missing, so I have to go. Let me know if things change. If you can arrange a meeting, I'd still like to talk to the governor." She turned and left, the door slamming behind her.

Guilt spiraled through my chest, even though I hadn't had any control over what had happened. I looked at Storm. "You know, Ginselwyn doesn't have time to wait."

The other Dunamis didn't have time to wait, either.

"The healer's doing all she can." He bit his lip, the action making him look like a little boy.

I put a hand on his arm. "I'm sure she is, but what if it's not enough? I hope I'm wrong, but you don't want to gamble with what-ifs. Please schedule a meeting with him. We'll keep it quick."

He closed his eyes for a split second. "Father's dying. The meeting I just had with him? He transferred all his responsibilities to me, making me the governor. So I'm the one you need to talk to."

CHAPTER TWENTY-THREE

SADNESS CLOGGED MY THROAT. "I'm so sorry. Do you want to talk about it?"

He shrugged. "He's getting sicker. The healer isn't helping. I'm in charge. So what is it you wanted?" His voice sliced the air.

I flinched. "Um, I—"

He cleared his throat. "I'm sorry. It's not your fault."

"It's okay."

Walking the length of the lobby, he stared out the window. "When I was younger, I imagined becoming governor, especially when Sloane and then Saeth's husband declined. I'd help the people, keep them safe, make good decisions. But I never wanted to become governor like this. I'm not ready."

"That's why you didn't tell Rachel."

He nodded but didn't turn. "What's your idea?"

Part of me wanted to run after Rachel and tell her to come back, but she was long gone. I took a deep breath, needing courage, persuasiveness, and eloquence. "Is there somewhere where we can sit and talk?"

He led me out into the bright sunshine and pointed across the street to a restaurant. "Let's get a cool drink. The owners can give us a private table."

I followed him across the street, an extreme case of nerves twisting my stomach. Would Storm listen?

Only a few patrons ate at the restaurant at this pre-lunch hour. Light gleamed from glass tubes running the length of the wall, orange gas shimmering and swirling inside like a lava lamp. The waitress hurried to give us the secluded seating Storm requested, leading us to a corner table. The aroma of fresh bread and bacon scented the air. Once we took our seats and gave the waitress our order, I settled against the plush cushions.

Storm wouldn't meet my gaze until I reached over and tapped his hand. "Hey, why are you acting all weird?"

"Because I'm not used to this. Just give me a moment."

I gentled my voice. "Ginselwyn doesn't have time. I've learned some terrible information, but I can't tell you where I learned it."

His eyes were like flint. "I could make you tell me."

I shrugged. "Well, you could try. But I'd probably become more stubborn than ever and not say anything."

He allowed a grin to slip out. "More stubborn? I can't even imagine."

"Shut up."

The waitress brought our drinks and the coffeecake Storm had ordered. I sat, gathering my thoughts.

After taking a sip of tea, he leaned forward. "Now, what have you learned?"

I kept my voice low. "Remember when I told you about the Dunamis Arvandus and I found?"

"Right."

I took a deep breath. "Tally, the little girl, recovered and confirmed Rune had abducted her and made her a vessel. But there's another one hidden in Ginselwyn. Both of these were literally evaporating your water and drying out your land. One still is. Rune's plan was to remove both of them after the wedding and allow Jakeb to take the credit."

Storm closed his eyes. "Jakeb would look like a hero."

"Right. I also found out Rune offered the Avanti a deal."

His eyes flew open. "What kind of a deal?"

I winced a little. "Rune asked for the Avanti's support in a coup. In return, he promised citizenship."

He rubbed his forehead, his dessert forgotten. "This just keeps getting worse. I don't know what to do for them."

"Really? Storm, you've heard their appeals your whole life. Step beyond what's always been done and think about what could be. How does your father treat your mother? Think about what you'd like for the women in your city—your sisters, your mother, your future wife."

He took another thoughtful sip of tea before replying. "I assume you have a plan?"

Oxygen and hope built in my chest. "Yes. I'll remove the second Dunamis. In return, release Tiny from her required marriage. She gets to choose or reject Jakeb with no fear of shame or dishonor. Second, in order to keep peace in your city and prevent a rebellion, you give the Avanti what they asked for. Give women citizenship and a presence on the council. Your father will be safe, you'll prevent a bloody rebellion, and the position of governor will stay within your family."

He sat back, his eyes narrowed. "It's political suicide."

My jaw tightened. "If you don't, your father will be murdered, and Rune will control Ginselwyn."

"The army alone can prevent the takeover."

"Are you sure about that? The Avanti have grown. But promise them safety, equal treatment? They'll give you their support. I'm sure other women would benefit from this decision. And there are men who'll be pleased their wives are safe on the streets and in the market, as well. They won't have to take time from their schedules to escort them on their errands."

For a moment, he looked like he was actually considering it. "I'd need to increase security."

"Yes, at first." I tried to stay calm. No celebrating yet. "And I have one more request."

He shook his head. "You never give up, do you?"

I ignored his statement. "Give the women who are without options a place to stay, a place where they feel safe. Maybe have them learn a trade or—"

Smiling, Storm placed his hand on mine, his eyes warm. "You're so passionate about this. Your eyes sparkle, and your cheeks are flushed. You're beautiful."

Anger flared, and I yanked my hand away. "This isn't about me. This is about you and your city. Stop flirting. Listen to what I'm saying." To my horror, my eyes stung, and a lump rose in my throat. Pushing back my chair, I stood. "You've got a decision to make. I hope you choose quickly."

Refusing to wait for a response, I stalked out of the restaurant.

Shortly after my spectacular exit, I contacted Arvandus. I always thought better in the air.

Arvandus, I'm in the business district of Ginselwyn and heading back to the Lee's house. Can you pick me up?

I will be there.

Moving quickly, I walked to the main road so he could see me. Arvandus arrived in minutes, people allowing him a wide margin as he landed. I climbed on, leaving behind the frustrating guy who had become governor of a ticking time bomb.

You are upset. Do you want to talk about what has happened?

Storm's the temporary governor of Ginselwyn. I presented my idea. It'll require him to make some tough decisions.

He started his climb. *Where is Rachel?*

She left when Storm's father refused to see us. He was too sick, but she was still disappointed.

The Avanti are frustrated. They have waited a long time for equality.

Arvandus dropped me off at the house before flying to his room, and I walked to the front deck. Sinking into a chair, I put my head in my hands. That hadn't gone well. At all. And Storm's flirting made me wonder if he was even listening.

At a shining light in my peripheral vision, I turned. Tiny sat in the chair next to me, looking over the bright, sun-drenched landscape.

During the few moments of quiet, I waited for the yelling to start. Maybe I deserved it. But if she married Jakeb, she'd regret it forever. I wanted to do everything I could to help her, even if she didn't appreciate it now.

"I'm sorry." Her words pierced the tension. "I hate fighting with you. Even if I don't agree with you, I never should've said those things last night."

"I'm sorry too. I'm not sorry for my opinion, but I could've said it better. I'm lousy with that kind of thing." Quiet settled between us for a moment. "Those things you said...do you think they're true?"

She glanced at me, then away. "No, I don't. I was being mean."

I sat back. "I want you to be happy. That's why I'm asking you to think hard about this. I'm trying to help. If you saw me making a bad decision, wouldn't you do the same?"

She huffed out a small breath. "Yes, although marriage to Jakeb isn't a bad decision."

"A marriage to him wouldn't be what you expected."

"No marriage is perfect."

A lead ball landed in my stomach. If only we could go back to Linneah so Jakeb would be far, far away... "This isn't about perfection. I know stuff about him, bad stuff."

Her teeth worried her bottom lip. "Are these rumors?"

"No. If I tell you, you have to promise you'll share it with no one. And I mean no one. Not your mom. Not your sisters. And definitely not your fiancé."

She tilted her head, her normally smiling face serious. "All right, but just facts."

I looked into the bright, blue sky before peering into eyes of the same shade. I repeated what I'd told Storm, but she didn't ask questions, and her expression didn't change. Creepy.

When I was done, she stood, her face a few shades paler. "I'll think about what you've said."

After she walked away, I put my head in my hands again. I was a lousy communicator. As a result, only Elyon could save Tiny or her father or Ginselwyn.

The next day after breakfast, the family left to visit the governor. I took up residence on the front deck and pondered my next move. Just show up for the wedding, I guess. The thought was totally depressing.

A man walking back from the city crossed the road. As he drew closer, I recognized Storm, his face set in grave lines.

After he climbed the few steps, he crossed his arms. "Do you realize how dangerous it was for you to leave without a guardian yesterday? Thank Elyon Arvandus was able to fly you back."

I crossed my arms in a perfect imitation of his pose. "If you make some of the changes I suggested, you wouldn't have to worry about anyone's safety or whether a guardian's needed."

A muscle ticked in his jaw, and he looked away.

"Storm, what are you so afraid of?"

He swallowed hard. "I'm not afraid. I want my father to see me making good choices. If I make radical changes, he might see it as a betrayal."

"He might. Or he might be proud of his son who saw a problem and took the steps to fix it."

He rubbed the back of his neck, weariness in every line of his body. "After turning the issues around in my head, I called an emergency council session early this morning. If no changes are made, I risk the rebellion of a powerful faction intent on overthrowing the government. If new laws are made, I risk a rebellion of angry civilians intent on overthrowing the government."

Silence filled the space between us.

Heaving out a breath, he pulled a sheaf of papers from his inside pocket and held them out. "Here. This was all I could get. The council voted, and the request for citizenship was approved by a slim margin. The request for council representation? It didn't pass. I'm sorry."

No way. I grabbed them and leafed through the formal English. It was all there—citizenship for all female Weldens and the benefits that went with it. I hoped Rachel wouldn't be too disappointed about the second request being denied.

I raised my eyebrows. "When did you draw this up?"

"After the council meeting. The vote was tight, and a few council members are unhappy and complained. But they don't know about Jakeb and Rune's plan. I wasn't ready to share that. I wrote up this separate agreement regarding your removal of the Dunamis. If you sign it, we'll have a deal."

"Do you have a pen?"

He handed me one, and I signed it and handed the papers back. As he signed the agreement, I failed to keep the delighted smile off my face. Although I wanted to hug him, I settled for a nice, firm handshake, much to Storm's amusement.

With a quick tug, he pulled me close. "What if we replayed the other night to make the contract official?" He grinned, his voice husky.

Pulling away, I swallowed hard. "Yeah, I don't think that's a good idea. And something tells me you don't kiss everyone you have a contract with."

He tried to pull me closer, his eyes lit with a blue flame. "Maybe our contracts would be more successful if we did."

I placed my hand on his chest to keep him from moving closer. "You have a city to lead. And I have a Dunamis to destroy."

Before I could move, he trapped my hand on his chest, his skin warm through his shirt. "I'm not giving up. Sooner or later, you'll have to deal with me."

With a gentle tug, I pulled free and walked away.

That's what I was afraid of.

I headed straight to the second floor and stepped onto the side deck. "Hey, big guy. I signed a contract with the governor. We need to locate the other Dunamis."

Despite my words, it was the last thing I wanted to do. Another round of energy removal with a possibility of death? No, thanks. Maybe we could find someone with thrill issues to destroy it.

Arvandus rose and padded toward me. "We should go now. The sooner the heat and power are removed, the better it will be for the vessel and the citizens of Ginselwyn."

I climbed onto his back, and we took to the sky. The warm air pulled at my hair as we climbed. In the hazy heat, brown and gold dominated the landscape below—brown trees, golden grass, russet rocks, and tan-striped mountains.

When we arrived at the cave, nobody came out to greet us. Too bad. I wanted to tell Rachel what had happened.

I turned to Arvandus. "Fee said it was just beyond their living area."

He padded closer. "Allow me to fly in. If there is room, perhaps you will not need to get wet again."

"Sure." At this point, any delay was a good one.

He flew in, his dark form disappearing into the mouth of the cave.

In minutes, he reappeared. "Nobody is in there, although the Avanti are still using this cave. There is a tunnel just beyond their camp. Because there is no evidence of a Dunamis elsewhere, I suggest we search the tunnel first."

Pushing down the surge of dread souring my stomach, I gave a curt nod. Get in, destroy the Dunamis, get out.

I climbed onto Arvandus's back again, and he launched us into the cave. As my eyes adjusted to the darkness, we flew past the platform serving as the Avanti's living and sleeping area, then Arvandus banked left, swerving into a tunnel hidden in the shadows. He slowed, gliding on hidden currents, and turned another corner. A yellow glow gleamed ahead, growing brighter the deeper we traveled into the tunnel.

Another curve, and bright chartreuse light blasted from the Dunamis's resting place. The light revealed a cavernous flat space with no exits, surrounded by rocky outcroppings and stalagmites. The box's lid had been tossed aside—a much bigger box this time.

Inside, the figure shone with a sick glare.

When Arvandus slowed, I slid off. Hurrying to the body, I squinted against the brilliance. Heat and energy poured off an older woman, her features tranquil yet blazing with a vile power, someone I recognized.

Marziah, the Firebrand instructor from Linneah.

Nausea roiled in my stomach. The last Dunamis hadn't been this strong. This one was worse times ten. Around her neck were two jaspers, chartreuse light radiating from the center of each stone. I looked closer, awareness dawning.

Without looking away from her, I spoke. "It's Marziah. And Rune's using my jasper—and another jasper—to strengthen the Dunamis's power."

Arvandus gave a low growl, his ears flattened against his head. He settled nearby. *That is why this one is more powerful. Take your time, Brenna. This will require all your concentration.*

Anger rose in my chest. Rune had wanted my jasper for this? And why had he picked Marziah? I rubbed my damp hands on my pants and forced the contents of my stomach down. As I knelt near the box, heat seeped through my pants. I placed the fingers of my left hand in her mouth and waited for energy to slither into my arm.

The oily crawl slipped into my fingers and through my wrist. I held out my right hand and pushed.

A flame flickered and died. I tried again, focusing on this hideous job. I closed my eyes, imagining the release of a large flame. With a sudden pop, fire burst from my hand. I heaved out a breath and shook my arm. My wrist ached. I transferred hands and repeated the procedure several times.

Concentrating, I dragged the heat from her body. Flames exploded from my palms. Sweat poured off me. Tremors wracked my body. I focused harder until it was just me and Marziah, caught in a nightmarish bubble. Pulling hard, I squeezed all ten of my fingers into her tiny mouth and captured the last bit of energy lurking deep.

"What are you doing?" a female voice demanded.

My focus shattered, and I jumped. Turning, I faced the intruder.

Kefira. Dripping wet, her compact frame quivered with suppressed rage. Her unsheathed sword glimmered in her aura's glow. "Get away from that Dunamis. She's mine."

Arvandus uncurled from his position, placing himself between us. "It needs to be removed, youngling."

"I may be young, but I'm stronger than you, you mutant freak. Now get out."

"It is not wise to play with this energy. It is causing the drought here. When it is removed, the water level will return to normal."

Rachel and Fee appeared behind her, their auras lighting the dim entryway to the cavern. Rachel stepped forward and laid a gentle hand on Kefira's shoulder. "Let it go, K. You're strong enough."

Kefira's face twisted, and she jerked away from the reassuring hand. "We all need to be stronger, or they'll crush us. The woman has enough power for all of us."

Arvandus prowled closer. "The power will corrupt you. It is inside you now, making you angry, heartless, and cruel."

Kefira growled. "No. With that power, I can do anything. No man will ever enslave me or make me afraid again."

Arvandus' voice was steady. "What if someone could gain freedom for you?"

"I don't need anyone to get it for me. I'm becoming more powerful every day. One day soon, I will draw their blood and take that freedom." She bared her teeth. "Don't make me tell you again. Move."

I shifted so I could keep my eyes on her and placed my hands over the two jaspers. Just a little more...

"No!" Kefira's shriek rent the air, and she charged.

Arvandus spread his wings, hundreds of silver sparks flashing from the tips. With an ear-shattering roar, he dodged her thrust. She swung again, and he knocked her back with a massive paw. Her sword clattered from her hand and skidded across the floor.

I struggled to pull the last bit of power from the pendants while Arvandus engaged Kefira. Straining, I groaned, the struggle sapping my strength. Power seeped into my arms, the last of it leaving the jaspers and turning my portion of the cave dark. But my arms glowed yellowish green. I glanced down dumbly, at a loss.

My energy was gone. I wanted to lie down, go to sleep, forget about Marziah, Ginselwyn, and everything else.

With a frantic scramble, Kefira sidestepped Arvandus and reached for me. "It's mine! Give it to me!"

I shook my head. I couldn't discharge the power—it required effort I didn't have. Rune had won. Kefira's eyes turned black, and she backhanded me. As I fell, she grabbed me and shoved her hand into my mouth, making me gag.

"It's mine, give it back." The sentence became her mantra. Gagging again, I bit her hand. She yelled and yanked it out.

Digging deep, I found my last reserve of strength. As I pressed the power from my arms, the pain grew claws, ripping and shredding my forearms. I screamed, and a massive flame exploded from my palms.

Kefira's shocked face was the last thing I saw.

Chapter Twenty-Four

"Brenna, can you hear me?" Rachel asked.

Then Fee. "She probably can't. My ears are still ringing. I wonder if they heard the explosion in the city."

"Please remain still, Arvandus. And stop growling. That doesn't help anyone."

Comforted by Fee and Rachel's voices, I lay still. My head throbbed, and my arms—I had no words for the way they ached.

Cool water soothed my forehead, and I couldn't prevent a moan of pleasure from slipping out.

"Ooh, she's awake. Brenna, can you open your eyes?" Fee again.

Slitting them open, I immediately regretted it.

Rachel smiled. "Good job. Let's have you sit up."

The girls helped me sit against the cave wall. The Avanti's sleeping area lay to my right. Arvandus sat on my left. I gasped at the bloodied rag tied around his front leg.

"Arvandus?"

He perked up, his golden eyes finding mine. "Raven. Welcome back."

I couldn't take my eyes off the blood. "Your leg! What happened?"

"Kefira is very talented with a sword."

I tried to move his way. Nope, not happening. "Come here. I'll heal it for you."

"You can barely sit unattended. I will wait until you regain your strength."

"But all that blood—"

"It looks worse than it is."

Fear twisted my heart. Arvandus had never been hurt this badly before. Where was that coward Kefira anyway? Attacking an unarmed animal and then running away? Who did that?

I scanned the surroundings, but no one lurked in corners or dark nooks. "Where's Kefira?"

Rachel and Phoenix exchanged sad glances before Fee swallowed, her face pale. "She's dead, Brenna."

My thoughts fuzzed. "What? What happened?"

Rachel's gray eyes glistened with tears. "The power killed her."

Or rather I had. Guilt dragged my heart to my stomach. I'd never liked Kefira, but I'd never wished her dead. "What about Marziah?"

But I knew the truth before Rachel answered. "She never recovered. There was too much power in her."

My eyes gritty, my heart crashed at my feet. Linneah had lost a gifted Firebrand.

Phoenix leaned forward and dropped an object into my open hand. "Here. We retrieved your jasper for you. The other was cracked."

The pendant glittered, but I had no way of knowing if it'd been damaged or tampered with. I slipped it into my pocket to examine later.

Fee gave me some juice and crackers while Rachel changed Arvandus' bandage. At voices outside the mouth of the cave, Fee ran for the hidden window. A few teenage girls swam in while other women came in on a raft. Their excited chatter dwindled to whispers when they saw my griffin.

Rachel gave them a reassuring smile. "Don't worry, girls. This is Arvandus. He's a friend."

Gradually, their voices rose again, and laughter twined through their conversations. While they talked, I pieced together the news. The new governor had issued a decree of freedom for all female citizens. I gave a half-smile. Storm had made the first move to take his city in a new direction.

Rachel dropped to her knees next to me, a smile brightening her face. "When did you ask him to do this?"

"After you left, he admitted he was the new governor. I'm sorry I couldn't get council representation."

"No, it's something to keep striving for. Step by step, we'll get there. Thank you." She gave me a hug, her eyes moist.

The women invited our caretakers to join them in a night of celebrating, which would end at the governor's house. I snickered, imagining the noise at the Lee's house.

I waved the girls on. "Arvandus and I are great. Go have fun."

Fee eyed my arms. "Aside from your griffin's injury, you've also been hurt."

Reddish streaks marred my tan arms, which still ached with a sharp, stabbing pain. I didn't even need to ask, but I did anyway. "It's the Shadow Power, isn't it?"

She bit her lip. "Maybe. It may go away, but it's best I stay as you and your griffin recover."

Rolling my eyes, I crawled over to Arvandus, ignoring his displeased growling. I hesitated to touch his cut. "Can I still heal you?"

He shook his head. "It would be wiser to wait. I am unfamiliar with the side effects of Shadow Power. How do you feel?"

I closed my eyes for a moment and jammed down the disappointment thickening my throat. "I'm tired. Sore. Frustrated because I can't help you."

Fee turned to Rachel. "Go on with the group. I'll catch up later."

"You sure? I could stay..." Rachel tilted her head, her gray eyes questioning.

"You should both go." They ignored me.

Arvandus spoke. "The water level is rising with the Dunamis gone. Although the Avanti's camp is safe from flooding, Rune will come to check the river. It would be good to recover elsewhere."

Fee paled but helped me stand.

The women trailed out of the cave, either swimming or taking the raft back out.

Rachel pursed her lips. "We'll need to find a new location. I have a few places in mind."

I turned to Fee. "You could stay with us at the Lee's house for a day or two."

Rachel tapped her chin with a slender finger. "That'll work. I'll move the others to a temporary site tonight and then let you know where it is."

After she left, Fee's hands shook as she packed a bag. In minutes, we both climbed onto Arvandus. As we left the cave, the late afternoon sun gilded everything with a lovely yellow haze.

When we reached the Lee's house, Arvandus flew in a circle. *They have added extra security.*

Can we just skip it? I don't want to have to explain Fee to the guards.

I'll take you to the deck. He landed with a stumble on the second story, favoring his bad leg. After we dismounted, he walked to the corner of the porch overlooking the backyard. "While you visit, I will take a much-deserved rest." He settled with a flick of his tail, both of us dismissed.

Downstairs, we found Tiny, Anna, Storm, Mrs. Lee, and an older blond man in the living room.

I waved. "Hi, we're back. Mrs. Lee, you remember Fee?"

"Of course, it's lovely to see you again. Allow me to introduce you both to my eldest son, Sloane."

"Oh, you're back from the coast?" I asked.

His smile reminded me of Tiny's. "Yes, but I've heard I won't need to bring water again. Storm says I have you to thank for that."

"The water levels are rising already," Storm said from his spot on the couch.

"That's good news. Hey, not to change the subject, but Fee needs someplace to stay just for a day or two. I know I'm asking a lot, but could you put her up?"

Tiny ignored her mother's worried look. "Sure, she can bunk in my room."

Mrs. Lee frowned. "Shaynedel, you already have two extra in your room."

Tiny shrugged. "We have plenty of blankets, and I don't mind."

The woman hesitated, then threw her hands up. "All right, then. Welcome to our crazy household, Fee."

Fee gave her a smile. "Thank you so much, Mrs. Lee. I appreciate it."

Tiny gestured for Fee to follow her. "Let me show you where you'll be sleeping."

Mrs. Lee turned to me. "Would you be willing to watch Silver and Stellara tonight? The rest of us would like to have dinner at the infirmary with my husband."

"Sure. Tell him we hope he gets better."

Her smile quivered at the edges. "Thank you, Brenna."

Too bad there was no pizza delivery here in Ginselwyn. Anna, Fee, and I decided on burgers for us and the girls.

Before he left, Storm found me carefully slicing rainfruit in the kitchen. "Can I talk to you on the patio?"

"Sure." I wiped my hands on a towel, happy to put the knife down. Occasional tremors still shook my hands.

I followed him to the porch. He ran a hand through his blond hair before facing me. His brows came together. "What happened to your arms?"

"When I destroyed the last Dunamis, it fought back. I'm hoping they'll go away."

He traced one of the streaks. "I can have the healer give you something."

"No, I'm fine." Sort of. My arms still ached, but no salve was going to help. The hurt lurked deep inside. In a day or two, I'd heal it myself.

He took my hand, interlacing our fingers. "I've been thinking about you all day. And I'd like to ask you a question."

"Okay." My stomach dipped. His words from last night came back to me. *You'll have to deal with me sooner or later.* Apparently, this was sooner. Or later.

"You're amazing, Brenna. Beautiful inside and out. I've enjoyed getting to know you, and the best part of my day is seeing you, talking with you. Would you be my fiancée?"

Um...what? The words swirled in the air, making no sense until I took another breath. "Your fiancée?"

Storm gave my hand a gentle squeeze, a small smile on his face.

"I thought that kind of thing was arranged."

"For a woman, it is. A man can choose. And I choose you."

I swallowed hard, knowing I couldn't give him the answer he wanted. "Storm, you're a great guy, and I'm flattered you asked me. But do you love me?"

He reared back, his blue eyes wide. "Well, I like you. A lot."

Shaking my head, I released his hand and walked over to two chairs. "I like you too, but I have unfinished business in Linneah." Baldwin would have to tell me it was over in person.

We both sat. Storm leaned forward. "A real man would never let you go."

Well. Baldwin had just been disrespected. "He doesn't own me. And I should've talked with him. You deserve a woman who loves you with her whole heart. And I think, considering the new law, a Welden woman would be perfect for you."

He began to object, but I held up a hand. "Your city will watch how you treat her—like a person, a woman who's cherished, loved, prized. Not property. They will follow your example."

"I could cherish, love, and prize you."

"But I'm not Welden. And you admitted you don't love me. I won't settle for less."

Storm crossed his arms. "This isn't what I expected."

My cheeks grew warm. "I know, and if I led you to believe differently, I'm sorry. I do like you, but I don't love you. Every marriage should start with love."

He tilted his head. "You wanted that for Shaynedel."

"I still do."

"I told her the choice was now hers, but she still wants to move ahead with the marriage."

Great. Abira had been right. I could only support her, even if her choice was a bad one.

After a long moment, he rubbed the back of his neck. "Can I change your mind?"

"About me? Or Tiny?"

He made a face. "You. We could build a new future for Ginsel-wyn."

"A Welden would be perfect for the job." And I had someone in mind. If I could just get them together...

Sitting back, he released a sigh. "What if things don't work out with your 'unfinished business?'"

I bit the inside of my cheek. Good question. "I don't know. But either way, I'll have to finish my training with Abira."

Mrs. Lee, Sloane, and Tiny came out to the patio.

"Ready to go?" Sloane asked.

Storm stood, his gaze lingering on me. "Yeah, I'm ready."

As they walked out of sight, I rolled my tense shoulders. That had been fun. Fortunately, Storm didn't seem too brokenhearted. In time, he'd find someone else.

After grilled rason burgers and rainfruit for supper, a knock on the door drew us from our game of Bits and Pieces. Silver was killing all of us, evidenced by her towering pile of game tokens.

Anna answered it. "Reefstars! I mean, greetings. Please come in."

Fee and I both got up to see who'd flustered laid-back Anna.

Emperor Rexson walked into the Lee family living room, his silver armor shining and the embossed Linnean star on his chest glinting. "Greetings, my ladies."

CHAPTER TWENTY-FIVE

I DROPPED INTO AN awkward bob, made more obvious by everyone else's elegant curtsies. I really needed to learn how to do that
without falling over.

"Brenna, it is a pleasure to see you. Annalice and Phoenix, it is
good to see you as well. And I am guessing these lovely young ladies
are Silver and Stellara."

The two sisters looked at each other and giggled.

While everyone stood there grinning at each other, I took control. "Emperor Rexson, how can we help you?"

"My men and I are looking for Governor Lee."

"Hmm." We'd kept it quiet for as long as possible. If anyone
outside the family had to be told about the governor's sickness, it
was the emperor. "He's sick, but the people of Ginselwyn don't
know."

"Sick?" Emperor Rexson jerked his head back, and I looked at
Anna. The rest of the story was her responsibility.

"I wiped out," she blurted, her face going red. "It was my job
to check the Stones of the Spring. When I got there, they'd been
stolen and replaced with fakes. I'm so sorry." Tears gathered at the
corner of Anna's eyes, and I reached over and squeezed her hand.

Emperor Rexson raised his eyebrows. "Your apology is unnecessary, unless you were the one who stole them."

"Absolutely not. That's low tide behavior. But I don't know who did."

"I have a few suspects. But I do not hold you responsible for the theft. Has anyone else fallen ill?"

Anna grimaced. "When Brenna told me about the governor, I checked around. A few elderly citizens are sick. Their families are tail-tied. It won't be a secret much longer."

"You have done well. I will notify your family and reassure them of your safety and the completion of your job."

A pink tint covered Anna's cheeks. "Reefstars! Thanks."

Emperor Rexson gave a brief nod and stroked his chin. "Do any of you know where the governor is being treated?"

I raised a hand. "I was there just the other day."

"Could you escort us there? Anna and Phoenix, you both may come too, if you wish."

Anna waved us on. "Fee, you go. I'll wait here with the girls. Maybe we'll make smoothies."

Stellara and Silver squealed and ran for the kitchen.

Phoenix grinned, her face lighting up. "I would love to go!"

After we each grabbed a light jacket, we walked out the door.

Arvandus? I called. *We're heading into Ginselwyn with Emperor Rexson. Do you want to come?*

Absolutely.

In seconds, Arvandus dropped into the front yard next to us. Although his landing wasn't perfect, the wobble was hardly noticeable.

Emperor Rexson smiled. "Welcome, Arvandus."

The griffin inclined his head.

Are you sure you can handle the walk with your injured leg, Arvandus?

I would not miss this for the tenderest, juiciest deer in the forest.

Ew. Gross.

His deep chuckle rumbled through his chest.

We waited while Emperor Rexson consulted with the head security guard. Five Linnean soldiers stood nearby, talking with the security detail assigned to the Lee house. Recognizing Kersen, I smiled and waved. My heart stalled in my throat when I saw the soldier next to him.

Baldwin.

He hadn't seen me yet. His skin had darkened to a deep tan, and he looked even better than he had at Starfall. Kersen nudged him, and Baldwin looked up.

Awkwardness swamped me. I'd dreamed of this moment—the way it would play out. Now that it was here, I wasn't sure how to act. He stepped forward, his eyes never leaving my face.

"Brenna." Hesitation laced his words. "I did not expect to see you here."

Yeah, I showed up in all sorts of unexpected places. "I came for Tiny's wedding."

"She is getting married?"

"This weekend."

He offered me a tentative smile. "I would like to talk with you."

Nerves attacked my stomach, so I settled for a simple head bob.

Emperor Rexson stopped next to me. "Lead the way, please."

I let out a quiet breath. The talk—and Baldwin—would have to wait.

A celebratory mood had gripped the city. Handmade posters praising the governor's new law decorated several homes. Parties were in progress at two homes, and crowds gathered to drink, eat, and sing. People waved to Emperor Rexson, and Fee and I grinned at being seen with him.

When we arrived at the infirmary, no guards or security stopped us. The streets lay empty, quiet. Many of the businesses were closed, their windows shuttered.

My neck prickling, I looked at Emperor Rexson. "Something's hinky. Last time I was here, there was plenty of security."

The emperor scanned the area before turning to Arvandus. "Can you do an aerial perimeter check of the building?"

"Of course." He launched himself high, dark wings spread wide in the twilight sky. After two circles around the building, he landed. "I saw three guards—two enemy guards on the second floor, right side, and one downstairs in the lobby."

My stomach knotted. A trap, had to be.

The emperor gestured to two of his soldiers. "Gather the troops. Be aware of perimeter forces. If I am not outside waiting when you return, send a scouting party inside." He then turned to the three of us. "Stay safe. My men and I will continue from here. How do I reach the governor's room?"

My mind produced the basic floor plan. "Up the staircase. Second floor. Walk down the narrow hallway, and his room is the last door on the left. You'll walk into a waiting room of sorts. The sick room is beyond that."

"Thank you." He gestured to his soldiers and headed inside.

Baldwin glanced at me before he disappeared. I waved despite the worry gripping my heart.

After they left, I turned to Fee. "Can you find more of the Avanti? Something tells me we're going to need help. Take Arvandus."

"Raven—"

"You can't go in there, Arvandus. There's no room, the hallway's narrow, and you're still recovering. You and Fee get help. You'll be able to cover more ground in the air. Besides, I've got a plan."

He growled but allowed Fee to climb on. *Please do not do anything foolish.*

I'll do what needs to be done.

That is exactly what I am afraid of.

I grinned. *Fly true, buddy.*

Arvandus and Fee disappeared into the darkening sky, Fee's aura lighting her fluttering skirt. The city square remained strangely empty, light from globes and tubes on each building moving in sinuous waves. Nerves crawled under my skin, leaving me jittery. Too exposed. I hurried to an abandoned vendor's stall across the street and found it unlocked. From its shadowy interior, I took in my surroundings—no people, no guards. Every atom in my body strained toward the house—run in to help.

Pulling a piece of fypex gum from my pocket, I popped it into my mouth, savoring the raspberry-and-vanilla flavor. Three floors, one front door, several windows, two of which were not an option because of the guards. I rubbed my arms against the dull ache. They still didn't feel right. I held out a palm to produce a flame.

Nothing happened. Weird.

I tried again, this time focusing more. A puff of smoke escaped. My hands trembled, panic rising.

Maybe healing would work. I laid my hand on my forearm and closed my eyes, waiting for the minutes to slow. Nothing. Time marched on, unaware my world had shifted. Where was my talent? I dug my jasper from my pocket and held it up in the dim light. Its facets glittered faintly in the shadows but offered no answers. Swallowing hard, I dropped it into my pocket.

I held out both hands and focused, cupping the air. Nothing.

Slumping against the thin walls, I slid to the ground, hiding in the shadows. I tried again to produce a flame, an ember, a spark of light, anything, still unable to believe the obvious truth.

My gift was gone.

Curling into a ball on the floor of the stall, I wrapped my arms around my knees as tears streaked my face. I should just stay here. After all, what could I do? I was a liability. No sword and no talent. I hiccuped as I lay there, struggling to understand.

I finally wiped my eyes and stood. No. I'd go in there and fight, even if I lost.

Keeping my head averted, I scuttled down the street, staying close to buildings and their shadows. I glanced back at the infirmary and discovered my destination: a patio with a back-door entrance.

After a quick check left and right, I scurried to the patio. My footfalls cat quiet, I tugged the back door open. It swung open on silent hinges.

The empty room held a stairwell, its wooden steps descending into darkness. A door on each side of the stairs led to the lobby. At footsteps from the right, I panicked. I opened the door leading downstairs, stepped onto the first tread, and closed the door. Darkness engulfed me. While my eyes adjusted, I gripped the railing.

Drawing in a lungful of stale air, I inspected the stairwell. Dusty shelves filled with containers and bottles lined the staircase. The footsteps paused on the other side of the door. I grabbed a glass bottle, my makeshift club ready.

Go away, whoever you are.

The door swung open, and a guard waited at the top of the staircase. His uniform wasn't the royal blue of Ginselwyn or the black and gray of Linneah. His faded gray uniform draped thin shoulders, and bony hands poked through frayed cuffs. Matching pants sported hems three inches too high, revealing battered boots. His unblinking brown eyes reflected no emotion as he stared through me. I raised the bottle and smashed it over his head, raining a slick downpour of oil over him.

Instead of stumbling back or wiping his face, he reached for me. Like, no other reaction. I ducked, swiping the jagged bottleneck at his legs. The jagged glass sliced through material and skin. Drab fabric flapped open, exposing slashed gray flesh. No blood. I gagged. What was this guy? A zombie?

As I slipped through an opening under his arm, his bony fingers snagged my hair. Yelping, I ran for the door he'd just come through.

Throwing it open, I rushed for the staircase, my footsteps echoing in the empty lobby. Up and away from the scary, undead dude. My steps faltered when I reached the vacant hallway. Where was everyone? Arvandus had said the guards were in the governor's room at the end of the hall.

I dashed through the first door at the top of the stairs and realized it was a connecting suite. No lock on the door. Of course. A table and four chairs were the only furniture in the room, so I grabbed a chair and shoved it under the doorknob. A door to an adjoining room waited on my right. I cracked it open, checking room number two. Empty. I grabbed another chair and put it under that doorknob. Because, again, no lock. What did these people have against privacy?

I turned. Another door stood open. I stiffened. Was someone inside that room? I crept closer, my heart loud in the quiet. I peered in, then sagged with relief. Only a table. But it was piled with treasure: a sword, two daggers, two helli lanterns, and a handful of matches. I grabbed the sword and knives, tucking the shorter blades under my jacket.

An aural check of the hall alerted me to my undead friend coming up the stairs. Grabbing a third chair, I dragged it to room number three and wedged it under the doorknob. I took a deep breath before walking back to the first room. How did you kill a zombie? Last time I'd checked—because I checked that kind of thing all the time—its head needed to be chopped off. With a swallow, I gripped my sword tighter.

He stopped outside and turned the knob. When the door didn't open, he jiggled it, the racket like rattling chains. I tensed, expecting the door to explode open. When he moved to the next door, I leaned against the wall, unsteady. He moved down the hall, checking each knob and rattling it when it wouldn't open. As I moved into room number three, muted conversation drifted through the walls, and I shifted closer to listen.

"...necessary to kill them?"

"...are a problem. If we kill his daughter or his wife, his son will give us the governorship." It was Rune, his voice frozen steel. I shuddered.

"Killing his wife would be easier."

"Jakeb, you've become attached to the daughter?" Rune laughed. "You can have her as a toy, but you must kill her mother."

"Of course, my prince."

A beat of silence.

"But..."

Rune snapped, "What?"

"Perhaps I could force the old man into signing over the position. Then we could use the family as needed..."

My hands shook as I backed away from the door. Where were Storm and his family? Instinct told me they weren't on this floor. That left the basement. I grabbed a helli lantern and matches and hurried for room number one. Removing the chair from under the knob, I checked the hall. Undead Dude lingered at the other end, staring out the window. I ran on my tiptoes to the stairs. No guards patrolled the first floor, so I sprinted for the basement.

After closing the door, I tried to create a flame to light the lantern. Two tries later, I stopped, swallowing my tears, and used a match. Just in case, I checked the knob. No lock. Of course not. Why would there be?

I hurried down the stairs. At the bottom, more shelves waited, stacked with food containers, as well as two rooms, each with a closed door. I knocked at the first door and heard, "Who is it?"

Opening it, I found Emperor Rexson, Baldwin, and two other soldiers on the floor, hands tied behind them. I gasped and moved toward the emperor.

His initial smile upon seeing me slipped away. "You were to stay safe."

"Yeah, but I wanted to help." I worked on the tight knots with little progress. After pulling the dagger from my belt, I carefully slipped the sharp blade into the small space between his hands and sawed through.

His hands came free, and he rubbed his wrists. "Your talent could soften the rope as well, Brenna."

Not anymore. I handed him my sword before working on the next soldier's ties. "The dagger's quicker."

Baldwin was next, and even in his disheveled state, being close to him made me dizzy. I severed his bonds. My heart swooned when he gave me that special look, but I pulled away to work on the next soldier. No. No swooning now. Maybe later.

After all the soldiers were free, I turned to the emperor. "I need to find Storm's family. Do you know where they are?"

"Next to us. We could hear them through the wall."

Going to the next room, I found Storm, Sloane, Tiny, and Mrs. Lee on the floor, their hands tied as the emperor's had been. Storm had an abrasion on his temple, and Tiny's eyes were red-rimmed. Mrs. Lee remained quiet, an unnatural stillness surrounding her.

As I cut their ties, I turned to Storm. "You need to use your gift. Make an illusion, hide, something. Rune wants Jakeb to kill a member of your family in the hopes you'll cave and give up the position."

Tiny burst into tears. "Why is he doing this to me, to my family? He told me he loved me."

Giving her a hug, I let her tears soak my shirt. "I'm so sorry."

After a moment, she wiped her eyes and inhaled a shuddering breath. "You were right."

There was no pleasure in the knowledge. I squeezed her shoulder.

"I concur with Brenna." Emperor Rexson nodded. "Create an illusion, and do not allow it to break for any reason. Rune must not capture you again."

At a rumble from the floor above us, everyone froze. My heart pounded. Emperor Rexson moved everyone behind him, but the threat never materialized.

He turned back to us. "My men and I will clear a path to the first floor. All of you leave by the back door at the top of the stairs. We will free Governor Lee."

I shivered. "Just stay away from the zombies."

"Zombies?"

"The undead guards. Gray skin, dead eyes. Zombies."

Behind him, Baldwin frowned. Was he remembering the one and only zombie movie we'd watched a few months ago? Both of us had decided never to do that again.

"Ah." Comprehension flooded Emperor Rexson's face. "The Life Shades. They are shells of the men they used to be. That would be Rune's doing."

"Yes, it is my doing." A figure detached from the shadows and moved down the steps.

Sickness swirled in my stomach. Dressed in a tailored black shirt and slim black pants, Rune stopped on the bottom step, his face carved into light and shadow.

"Well, everyone is here. Including the famous Firebrand, Brenna James. I had thought you'd be unable to join us."

Chapter Twenty-Six

HE BACKED OUR GROUP into the corner. The scent of bad spices swirled in the air. "Come forward, Mrs. Lee. I need to speak with you. Your husband was most uncooperative, and I paid him back in kind."

Tiny gasped from the shadows. Mrs. Lee didn't move. The woman was a rock.

Rune allowed a malevolent grin to surface. "It's my hope you'll be more forthcoming. Bring your daughter and both sons, too."

My stomach flipped. I knew what was coming. One of them wouldn't come back.

The Lee family stood at the back of the group. They ducked, using the rest of us as cover. When I turned to look, they were gone. I smothered a grin. *Don't mess with Illusionbrands.* By combining all four of their talents, they'd disappeared.

Rune's ice-gray eyes glittered. "Playing games? Perhaps if I start executing your friends, one at a time, you'll stop hiding like cowards."

He grabbed Baldwin by his collar. "You'll be first."

"No!" I sprang forward, unable to stop.

"You." Snarling, Rune grabbed my collar as well and leaned close, his breath a putrid blast. "You've plagued my plans since the day you arrived in this alternity. I'll take you both."

I gripped my blade tighter. Rune flicked his hand, and a flash of fire seared my wrist. With a yelp, I dropped my dagger.

He waved his hand again, and a ring of waist-high fire sprang up around the three of us, blocking the others. He chuckled. "As a Shadow King, I have many gifts, but my Firebrand talent is the most effective."

How many talents did he have?

Pulling a length of rope from his pocket, he grabbed our wrists and bound them together. As we faced each other, Baldwin's eyes met mine. *It will be okay,* they seemed to say. It was something he often said, and my anxiety lessened despite our grim circumstances.

Rune faced the rest of the group. "Learn from this lesson. Cooperate with me, and you will fare better than these two."

He favored me with a grim smile, and his face flickered, the planes shifting. It reminded me of Jakeb's aura, almost like an illusion...

Rune lifted a hand, a single blue flame dancing in his palm. Terror siphoned the air from my lungs as he moved the flame closer to my face.

"Did you know, Lord Marek, that a Firebrand can be burned with Shadow Power?"

His voice was a rasp. "Leave her alone."

Rune ignored him. Closer and closer he moved the flame, his eyes filled with unholy glee. He stopped an inch from my cheek, heat searing my face. I closed my eyes, trying to breathe while imagining a happy place. Which at this point would be anywhere but here. At a stinging slap to my cheek, I gasped, my eyes flying open.

His ruthless smile filled my vision. "No cheating. My face will be the last thing you see as you burn."

Beyond the ring of fire, Emperor Rexson barked orders. Water pooled at our feet, rain sprinkled from the ceiling, swords slashed through burning flames. None of the talents damaged the fiery circle.

A muscle jumped in Baldwin's jaw. I clutched his hand. I'd hoped my end would be more heroic than burning to death in a basement. Somehow, we'd get out of this. Maybe.

Rune produced a flame in his other palm and moved it close to Baldwin's face. Powerlessness pulled at me. What could I do? Rune moved the flames closer still, but Baldwin leaned back and kicked Rune's thighs. The man buckled.

His flaming hand landed on Baldwin's forearm as he fell.

Baldwin screamed as the door behind Rune flew open. Ginselwyn and Linnean soldiers rushed down the steps, large helli lanterns highlighting us all. Distracted by the chaos, Rune turned, and the ring of fire gutted out. Before he could run, a trio of burly soldiers grabbed him. Others placed blades at his neck.

Emperor Rexson sheathed his sword. "Good job, men. Take him outside."

Soldiers dragged him up the stairs, and Emperor Rexson and other soldiers followed. Baldwin and I collapsed against each other, relief making me giddy. Kersen sliced through our bindings then dashed after the emperor.

Storm moved in to give me a hug but stopped. With a half-smile, he squeezed my hand.

Before he could say anything, Tiny pushed him aside to hug me. "That was terrible. Don't ever do that again."

I hugged her back. "Do what? Get captured by Rune?"

"Yes, don't ever do that again."

Well, I'd have to scratch that off my to-do-again list.

I grabbed a helli lantern and followed the Lee family up the staircase, Baldwin gripping my hand. Whether it was for my benefit or his, I didn't know and didn't care. As we exited the house, the front yard teemed with Avanti, Ginselwyn forces, and the emperor's men. In full view of the city square, Emperor Rexson led Rune and Jakeb from the building, their arms bound with thick black bands. Rune grinned idiotically. What was wrong with that guy? I leaned against the building, sunbaked stucco warm on my back.

"This is where it ends, Rune." Emperor Rexson steered him through the crowd of soldiers toward a rason-drawn wagon.

"Shortsighted as usual, old friend." Rune chuckled. "The Stones of the Spring have strengthened me to near immortality. With Matana Island under my control, I have begun the war that will topple Linneah. And sadly, you've forgotten my greatest accomplishment. I am a Shadow King."

With those words, he disappeared. The black ties fell to the ground, empty, a scorched circle the only evidence Rune had stood there. Jakeb's mouth dropped open, his face flushing dark red. The crowd gasped.

My stomach clenched. Matana. Linneah. Were Mom and Dad safe? Anna's family? The urge to get on Arvandus and fly home nearly sent me running.

"Search everywhere!" Emperor Rexson demanded.

The available troops scattered, some returning to the building while others headed into the city. The Avanti followed in groups of two and three, determined to find Rune.

Hissing out a breath as he pushed away from the building, Baldwin's face blanched. "I must help search."

"Your burn! I totally forgot. Let me see." Not that I could do anything about it.

"It is nothing." On his forearm, the burn was several inches of angry red, blistered in places.

"I'd offer to heal you, but I'm recovering and can't do much."
A big lie. I wasn't ready to admit to anyone what had happened.

Emperor Rexson stopped next to Baldwin. "You are excused,
soldier. Get someone to look at that burn."

"But my—"

"That is an order."

Baldwin dropped his head. "Yes, my lord."

As the emperor walked away, I tilted my head. "What exactly is
a Shadow King?"

"Someone with more than one talent due to Shadow Power.
They are rare."

We headed for a nearby bench overlooking the town square, but
I stopped Baldwin by the white fountain.

"Here." I held his forearm under the clean flow, hoping the cool
water would soothe his burn.

After several moments, he pulled away. "Thanks. It feels better."

I pushed his arm back under the water. "Keep it there."

"Still bossy, I see."

In the shadowed evening, the sound of water splashing relaxed
me. I sighed. "They won't find Rune anyway."

"We can hope."

He finally pulled away from the fountain and patted his forearm
dry with his shirt hem. We walked over to the bench and sat. The
colored glass tubes on each house gave the evening a festive feel.

As silence descended, awkwardness filled the spaces. We needed
this conversation, but I didn't know how to bring up the dreaded
subject.

Baldwin surprised me by asking, "So who talks first?"

I chanced a glance at him.

His green eyes studied me. "Did you read my letter?"

"Oh." The letter resting in my dresser drawer back at the castle.
"Well, no. I was furious. Then Tiny and your mom showed up and

I had to leave." At his hurt look, I threw my hands up. "It doesn't matter. You'd already left."

He glowered. "You should have read it. I apologized."

I tried to remain calm. "Baldwin, after something like that, you apologize in person or not at all."

"That was impossible. I was leaving the next day."

I shrugged. Not my problem.

"Will you at least let me explain what happened without interruptions?"

"Okay, but don't you dare give me the 'it's not what it looks like' spiel. Because it looked bad."

He ran a hand through his dark hair, short strands spiking up. "That evening, I was not interested in wrestling. So I went into the Golden Pickle with Flynn and Adal. They wanted to drink. I wanted a clear head, so I walked to the back room. Gari was there."

"Of course she was."

"You are not supposed to interrupt."

I pressed my lips together.

"I hung out with some friends and tried to forget about my deployment. It was warm in that room, and Gari got dizzy. She almost fainted."

Should've let her faint. I chewed on the inside of my cheek, keeping a lid on the snark box.

"She sat next to me to rest."

"You mean she draped herself all over you."

His cheeks flushed. "No, I mean she almost fell, and I caught her. That is when you saw us."

"I certainly did."

"Allow me to state that what Gari did afterward—"

"Oh, you mean when she stuck her tongue down your throat? That was super entertaining. And you didn't even try to stop her."

"Again, you are interrupting."

I bit my lip until it hurt.

"I did not want or expect that kiss. And I told her so." He stopped and looked at me as if he deserved a gold star.

"That's it?"

"Yes." He frowned. "But then you left. By the time I got around all the people, I couldn't find you. Where did you go?"

"I visited Arvandus."

"If you had stayed, I could have explained what happened."

I held up a hand. "Baldwin, let's just back up for a second. In what alternity would I understand your old girlfriend almost sitting in your lap, kissing you like that? Hmm?"

He stiffened. "It was not my fault."

All the anger I couldn't find earlier came roaring back. "Let's reverse the scenario. You come to visit me, surprise, surprise, and find me snuggled next to an old boyfriend, and he's got his hands all over me, kissing me. But it's not my fault, right?"

Although he didn't move, his green eyes turned nearly black. "This is different."

"How? Explain to me how it's different."

"Gari and I have been friends for a long time, since we were little."

I raised an eyebrow but said nothing.

"We played together, went to school together, have the same friends. She understands that what she did was unacceptable."

I rolled my eyes. "Well, good. I feel loads better. And what happens when she does it again?"

He blinked. "Um, what?"

"Baldwin, she's going to keep doing stuff like this. She's never gotten over you. You were the one who broke up with her, remember? And she's never made an effort to become friends with me. I've tried to be nice, tried to be civil, and nothing. So I expect more behavior like this from her. She will always, always try to come between us. And judging from your response, you're going to let her." I clenched my hands in my lap to keep them from shaking.

His voice deepened, and a muscle ticked in his jaw. "I do not think you understand my situation."

"I understand just fine." I stood. "But I can't do this."

His eyes grew wide, disbelief filling his face.

My heart panged, but I kept going, knowing if I stopped I'd never finish. "I'll always be wondering what she's planning, worrying what you two are doing when I'm not here."

Against the white-stucco building, a shadow with golden eyes moved. Arvandus. His presence gave me courage.

Baldwin's eyes glinted like bits of green glass. "Brenna, my friends are important. And you want to break up? Over one mistake?"

In the shadowed city square, night had laid down a black canvas. The Petrus Rings glittered, stars twinkled, and colored gas swirled in the tubes. I faced Baldwin, who'd gone unnaturally still. "I don't trust her. Not even a little. And because she's your friend, you're excusing her behavior. You want me to pretend that nothing happened and move on."

He stood, his hands flexing. "So, just like that, you are giving up?"

I looked at his hands and suddenly wanted him touching me the way he used to—he'd cup my chin or stroke my cheek or lace his fingers with mine. "I don't know."

Arvandus appeared at my side. "Hello, Baldwin. Brenna, it is late. Perhaps you can continue this conversation later."

Baldwin fell back a step, the intimate, tense space between us dissolving. "I am not sure what Emperor Rexson's plans are for the rest of this mission."

I wiped a rogue tear off my cheek. "I'll be heading home, then on to Kelda Hills. Probably within the week."

He crossed his arms. "Perhaps there is nothing more to discuss."

My heart shattered, a silent explosion.

After climbing onto Arvandus's back, a million emotions flooded me. "Fly true, Baldwin."

The look in his eyes—despair, anger, stubbornness—etched itself on my heart. As Arvandus flew away, I finally allowed my tears to fall.

Chapter Twenty-seven

The next morning, I woke with red-rimmed, puffy eyes and my hair in tangles. Sitting up, I cleared my scratchy throat. Anna and Fee's voices floated down the hall from the kitchen. Tiny sat on her bed, staring at nothing.

"Hey."

She shifted, her face barely twitching.

"Did you sleep well?" Closing my eyes, I rubbed my forehead. Why did I ask such dumb questions?

"My father's dead."

"I know. I'm sorry." I'd assumed as much from Rune's comments. This is what he did—used, tortured, and killed to get what he wanted.

"Everyone went to say goodbye to Father. I can't. I can't see him like that."

"Maybe later you can."

She continued to sit, motionless. "My brother is the governor. And my ex-fiancé is a soulless, conniving dirtbag." She clenched the wad of tissue in her hand tighter.

The knowing made me feel worse. What could I say? It didn't matter because Tiny wasn't finished.

"I'm done." Her voice throbbed with emotion. "My whole life I've been the dutiful daughter, doing what was expected, being the perfect example." She shook her head, fire in her blue eyes. "I'm joining the Avanti."

My mouth dropped open. "But you don't have to. The wedding's off, so there's no pressure. If you took some time—"

"Ginselwyn's about to change. Storm needs people to lead. The Avanti will be part of that. So..." Her voice trailed off.

"Did you talk to Fee?"

She dropped her tissue into a nearby trash basket. "I like her. I'm supposed to meet Rachel later today."

"If you're sure this is what you want, then I think it's great." A sudden thought turned my heart to lead. "I'll never see you."

She tried to smile. "Come on. You can't get rid of me that easily. I'll visit, I promise. Where are you headed?"

I grimaced. Good question. "Probably home. I'm worried about Mom and Dad." Even though Mom had ordered me to Kelda Hills first, I couldn't do it.

"Yeah, Anna's not sure what to do. She's worried about her family, wondering if they escaped."

We dressed and headed to a breakfast of muffins and eggs. None of us talked much, each of us thinking about our next step. My mind kept going to Mom and Dad. Were they safe? Was the portal fixed? Would they fight or escape? With the emperor's men here, how much of the Linnean army was available to keep Rune's forces out? The unanswered questions kept circling until my head ached. Finishing quickly, I carried my dishes to the counter.

Raven, we must talk.

Perfect timing. "I have to go talk to Arvandus, guys. It shouldn't take long."

Fee waved and carried more dirty dishes to the counter.

What did Arvandus have to say this early? I walked up the stairs to the second-floor deck. He'd been pretty quiet last night on the flight back. As the cool night air dried my tears, he'd remained silent. I turned the discussion with Baldwin around in my mind, each replay hurting as much as the first time. With one conversation, our relationship had imploded. That was pure talent, right there.

Arvandus's back was to me when I walked onto the deck, his tail flicking back and forth.

"Morning."

He turned, his keen eyes studying me. "We should leave for Linneah. I assume Shaynedel's wedding has been canceled?"

"Yeah. She's joining the Avanti."

"Then your work here is done. If you tarry, Rune may return to exact revenge."

I tilted my head. "He'd come back to the city where everyone's looking for him?"

He flicked his tail again. "Long ago, I learned never to predict Rune's actions. It would be in your best interest to return home. Quickly."

"Mom wanted me to go to Kelda Hills for training, but I'm concerned about them."

"Do not worry about the queen. She will be protected. Perhaps Rune is lying."

A shred of hope flared while my gut churned. Why would Rune lie? To hurt people, to generate fear. Still, the urge to see my family grew.

"I'll say my goodbyes and pack."

He stood and stretched his wings. "I will hunt before we leave."

I walked down the stairs. There was nothing left for me to do. Both Dunamis were gone. Rune had disappeared. Jakeb remained in Rexson's custody. Tiny's wedding had been canceled, and Storm ruled a city on the verge of revolution. Abira expected me to show up, but I couldn't train without my talent. I traced a thin, red line up my forearm. Sadness swept over me, and my eyes stung. I took a deep breath. Sheesh. Cry much?

My friends sat talking in the living room. I interrupted them. "I've got to go, guys."

Anna stood. "Yeah, I need to skim the blue, too."

Tiny headed to the kitchen. "I'll pack snacks for your trip."

A half-hour later, I crammed my belongings into my bag. My stuff must have multiplied overnight and had a party, because nothing seemed to fit. I shouldered my bag and went to the kitchen.

Tiny handed Anna and me wrapped parcels. "Muffins, fruit, cheese, and a big bag of nuts. Do you want dried rason meat with that?"

I faked a gag. "No, thanks."

She wrinkled her nose. "Yeah, that stuff is bad, but you know, protein."

"Nuts are fine. Thanks." I turned to Anna. "Let me know about your family. Oh, did you know there are invisible fo-lis?"

She rolled her eyes. "Yeah, but I can't afford them. You'll have to be content with a regular fo-li."

I smiled. "Or just come yourself. In person is always better.."

Anna gave us both another hug before climbing the stairs to the porch to shift in privacy and leave.

"Promise to visit?" I asked Tiny.

She leaned against the doorframe. "Abira's just in the next city over."

"It might be a few weeks before I get there."

Shame robbed me of further explanation. Who lost their talent? I'd never heard of it happening before. If I wasn't a Firebrand anymore, who was I? Just a nobody with a freaky red hairstreak.

While Tiny and Fee headed up to the porch to wait for Arvandus, I tried to write a quick note to Storm. But the words wouldn't come. After several attempts, I crumpled the last try into a tiny frustrated ball. Maybe Arvandus could stop before we left the city so I could say my goodbyes in person. I trudged up the stairs to the porch. Fifteen minutes later, Arvandus arrived.

I climbed on and waved goodbye. Then I faced the afternoon sunshine as Arvandus leaped into the air. *Arvandus, can we stop and say goodbye to Storm?*

Do not make it a long goodbye. Rather than climbing higher, my griffin stayed low, skimming trees and housetops before dropping into the city square. "Raven, please hurry."

"I will. Promise."

Ginselwyn soldiers patrolled the doors. Hurrying inside, I found him in room number three, where I'd found the knives and helli lanterns. It'd been cleaned and outfitted with a desk and chairs. I stood in the doorway, watching him confer with an aide who held a large stack of papers.

He looked taller, his shoulders broader, the flirty smile gone. I shook my head. He'd grown into a man, a ruler, in a few short days. He looked up, as if hearing my thoughts.

Giving him a wave, I stepped into the room.

He excused himself and walked toward me. "You're leaving?"

"Yeah, I've got to go home. I'm concerned about my parents."

"I've sent a troop of soldiers to see how accurate Rune's statement was." He took a deep breath. "And as a civilian, you probably didn't need to know that. Sorry."

I smiled. "I won't tell. You'll be a great governor, Storm. Your dad would be so proud of you."

He looked away. "Thank you. I just wish—" Swallowing hard, a muscle ticked in his jaw. "Rune will pay for my father's murder and the invasion of Matana Island. I will see to it."

I squeezed his hand. "He was bluffing. How could he have invaded Matana Island without Emperor Rexson knowing?"

Storm rubbed the back of his neck. "I hope you're right."

Arvandus's words came to mind, and I gave Storm a hug. "My griffin told me to hurry, so I've got to go. When you're in Linneah, stop by and say hi."

"I will make it a priority."

"Oh, and Storm? Get to know Fee, would you? She needs a friend." Not really, but those two would make a great couple.

After giving him a smile, I hurried back outside where Arvandus waited.

Silver sparks flickered from his wingtips. "I said to hurry."

"I did, but you can't just barge in and say hi and bye to the governor."

He didn't reply, but disapproval remained in every line of his powerful body.

As soon as I climbed on, he sprang into the sky. His wings unfurling, he climbed higher until the lights and color of Ginselwyn blurred beneath us. Despite their distance, sections of the Kelda Hills came into view, waiting behind Ho Mountain. It stretched to my right, the craggy brown peak cutting into an impossibly blue sky.

How long until we reach Linneah?

If we make a quick stop for lunch, we will arrive tonight.

Aside from a hurried lunch, we only made one other pit stop at twilight outside Wildamek. An hour later, as darkness fell over the city, the top of the castle came into view. I blinked away tears threatening to fall. I'd never been so glad to see home. Flickering lights caught my eye. Near the Linnean harbor, lights shimmered, and wood smoke floated on the breeze.

Arvandus, can we check that out?

Are you not eager for home?

Yes, but it'll only take a minute.

I felt more than heard his sigh.

Arvandus flew closer, lights growing more visible and more numerous. The entire coastline, from the land bridge that connected to Matana Island during low tide to a section of Arowin Bay's coastline, was blanketed with small fires and tents. Shadowy figures of men in battle armor moved beneath us. Arvandus circled once before flying away.

My stomach pitched. *They were Linnean, right?*

Yes, troops protecting the land bridge.

Protecting it from what? Why would there be troops all the way out here unless—

The burning shred of hope that Rune had lied gutted out. Our soldiers were protecting Linneah from an invading army via the land bridge.

Chapter Twenty-eight

My mind whirled as we flew to the castle. Heavy darkness curtained most of the residential area, leaving it black and quiet. Too quiet. Where was everybody? Usually at this time of night, helli lanterns were lit and people sat on their porches, talking. But the trees remained silent and filled with shadows. Dread slicked my stomach, tying it into tight, hard knots.

We touched down outside the castle. The guard Reggie hurried forward, his earnest face sparking the memory of our meeting so many nights ago. "Lady James, praise Elyon. Your mother will be thrilled you have returned home."

Arvandus stepped back. "I will see you tomorrow, Raven."

"Thanks, Arvandus. Goodnight." I laid a hand on his neck before he turned and took to the air.

I followed the cobblestone walkway to the castle steps. As I walked through the heavy double doors, my shoulders relaxed. I was home.

"Brenna!" My mother hurried down the hall, her royal demeanor slipping. She looked more like the mom I'd grown up with, and my throat thickened.

When she reached me, her hug squeezed the breath right out of me. Breathing was overrated anyway. After a long minute, she pulled away. Tears spilled down her cheeks.

"Oh, baby. Why are you here? You're supposed to be in Kelda Hills."

"I'm sorry, Mom."

She gave my shoulders a little shake. "What were you thinking, leaving like that?"

Helplessness filled me. "But Mariel said she'd clear it with you. Didn't you read my note?"

"Mariel is not your mother. You purposely left without asking. Thank Elyon for Abira's fo-lis. It assured me you were alive and well, not lying in a ditch somewhere."

Why did mothers always think that's where their kids would be?

She pulled me into another hug. "I'm so thankful you're safe. Although I have quite a few questions for you."

It figured. I'd probably be debriefed by one of her aides and then assigned two bodyguards, instead of just Jace.

A small yelp from the hallway captured my attention. "Brenna! You're home! Harrison? She's here." Grandma hurried toward me, beaming. My dad followed her.

Two pairs of arms came around me, and I sank into the hug, the feeling of safety familiar within their arms.

Grandma pulled away. "Well, I can't wait to hear what happened. First question, though—how was the wedding?"

I grinned. "There wasn't one."

She raised an eyebrow. "Ooh, that sounds deliciously scandalous."

"You can talk about that tomorrow," Dad said, "but right now, how about some cookies and milk? What do you say?"

"Sure." Despite my heavy eyelids, I wanted nothing more than to simply sit at a kitchen table with my family.

The cook always kept a full cookie jar. In the kitchen, Dad pulled a few chairs into place while Mom and Grandma found the cookies. Minutes later, the four of us were eating White Velvet Cookies and milk.

I was on my second cookie when Dad spoke. "Rune bombed the portal. Although it's fixed now, Grandma and I used the portal in Ohio to get to Wildamek, then came here."

I rubbed my eyes. Although I was relieved to be home, I was oh-so-tired. "How many portals are there in the U.S.?"

Mom dunked her cookie in her milk. "One for every city in the Jasper Territory. Ohio was the closest one, and we're friends with the people who own the portal."

Dad nodded. "After we arrived, your mother and I had a few long talks about you and your behavior."

The dread of impending doom crushed the air out of my lungs. "I know my punishment is going to be massive and horrible, like being grounded for a year with four full-time bodyguards. I'm really sorry. Can you just tell me so we can get it over with?"

Mom and Dad exchanged a look before Dad turned back to me. "Abira's fo-li was illuminating. And when Gareth returned, he gave us a report, too. You went through a lot in the travel portal. So after much discussion, we're putting you on disciplinary probation for two moons."

"Go easy on the kid," Grandma muttered.

Mom shot her a warning glance. "Mother—"

Grandma mimed zipping her mouth closed before grabbing another cookie.

"Probation? What does that mean?"

Dad leaned forward, his eyes stern. "It means you'll need to be careful. If you behave and don't try any more careless stunts like the one you just pulled, you'll have more responsibility. And Jace will no longer be your bodyguard."

This was a punishment? Unbelievable. In only forty days, I could be rid of Jace. I could do anything for forty days if it meant I wouldn't have a personal babysitter. Nodding, I tried to keep the hope from showing on my face. "All right. I understand."

Mom finished her milk and set the glass aside. "We sometimes forget you're growing up. But no matter what you do, you'll always be our little girl." She offered me a smile and held out her hand.

Putting my hand in hers, I smiled back.

A male voice at the doorway interrupted the moment. "Cookies? And milk too? Count me in."

I turned to see a vaguely familiar man. Deep-blue eyes sparkled above a white beard and mustache. His shoulder-length hair hung loose, his scarlet hairstreak a striking contrast to the white strands. The older guy from the beach? What was he doing here?

Grandma stood up with a sigh. "I'll see you for breakfast, Brenna, and you can share more about your adventure. Although this has been lovely, I'm going to bed."

As she brushed past the man, a look of resignation came and went in his eyes.

He walked in and settled in Grandma's seat. His eyes twinkled as he offered me a smile. "Ah, we finally meet."

"Brenna, meet Takacs." My mom smiled. "He fixed the portal for us. He's also my father. Your grandfather."

My mouth fell open. My grandfather? I didn't even know I had one. Every time I'd asked, Mom had been vague. I grinned, remembering his help finding the travel portal entrance.

"How come I've never met you until now?"

He pulled a cookie from the jar. "I live in the Jasper Territory but travel where my work takes me. Until recently, you lived in Pennsylvania. But, my dear, you look exhausted. Perhaps we should talk tomorrow."

Ridiculous. I had a million questions. "I'm not sleepy." A yawn escaped.

Mom smiled and patted my back. "Why don't we head for bed?"

With a sigh, I got up and put my empty glass on the counter. Bed sounded like the best idea ever.

Dad waved us on. "You two go on. Takacs and I will put everything back."

Mom murmured her thanks and followed me down the quiet hall to the staircase. Was it my imagination or were there fewer people in the castle?

When we reached my room, Mom stopped outside my door. "Honey." Two little lines appeared between her eyebrows.

"What?"

She sighed. "Nothing. We'll talk in the morning. I love you."

"I love you too."

As I crawled into bed minutes later, I sighed. Whoever came up with the idea of sleeping deserved a large, shiny medal.

The next morning, I woke to sunlight streaming into my room. After getting dressed in a clean outfit I found in my closet, I headed downstairs for breakfast. Grandma, Dad, Mom, and my new grandfather sat at a table. Hmm, I'd need to figure out what to call him. Grandpa Takacs? Papa T? I smothered a giggle. That'd be a good name for a rapper.

After filling a glass with rainfruit juice and grabbing two Kunkelsteuchen rolls, I walked over to sit with my family.

Mom smiled. "Well, you look ready to start the day."

"Reminds me of you growing up," Grandma said.

"Or her grandmother." My grandfather smiled at Grandma, who ignored him and pretended great interest in her toast. Weird.

"Speaking of starting the day." Dad set down his glass of juice and pointed at me. "At some point, you'll have to share your story with an aide. We need information primarily about the Scorpion, how Storm came to be governor, and what you saw Rune do or say while in Ginselwyn."

I sighed. "That'll take forever."

My dad smiled but said nothing.

As I finished my breakfast, I noticed the strange dynamic continue between my grandparents. My grandfather would talk to Grandma, and she'd ignore him. He'd look at her, and she'd look away. I felt kind of sorry for him. As my dad and I walked to my room after breakfast, I asked him about it.

"It's a sad story. Takacs and Helen married young and were devoted to each other. After many years, Takacs made a mistake. He had an affair, which he deeply regretted. When he confessed, Helen decided she couldn't trust him and filed a discindia, which is equal to a divorce. Although he asked for forgiveness, Helen couldn't give it to him."

I frowned. "Does he still love her?"

"They love each other deeply. That's the sad part."

After Dad left me at my room, I thought about my grandparents' heartbreaking love story. Would Grandma ever forgive him? And how long had Takacs been brushed off? Because I'm sure it hurt. At a sudden knock, I looked up. My mother stood in my doorway.

"Can I come in?"

"Sure."

She handed me a stack of newly washed clothes. "One of the servants was going to bring these up, but I was on my way anyway."

I sniffed the lavender scent rising from the pile. "Thanks."

"Sweetie, did you notice anything when you flew in last night?"

"Well, I saw troops along Arowin Bay's coastline."

Mom nodded. "Rune invaded Matana Island."

"I know. He mentioned it before he disappeared."

She flinched, her eyes wide. "Disappeared?"

"In Ginselwyn, Emperor Rexson had captured him and Jakeb Damyan, Tiny's fiancé. Well, ex-fiancé now. As the emperor led Rune away, he admitted to taking the Stones of the Spring and invading Matana Island. He said Linneah was next. Then he disappeared."

Mom's face had lost all color. "He has the Stones. Elyon help us."

"Sorry. I thought you knew."

She shook her head. "No, that wasn't in the most recent report. The reason I bring it up is because I got word we're evacuating."

My heart shriveled in my chest. "Why?"

"For the last two weeks, we've encouraged the residents to evacuate because Rune instigates minor battles in the residential areas. We helped get the elderly and sick out five days ago. We can't hold Rune's forces for much longer. At every low tide, we lose more men."

"But Emperor Rexson is heading back now. And Storm said he's sending soldiers."

Mom gave me a sad smile. "It's not enough. We don't have enough troops to fight a long, costly war. We're still weak from the battle months ago. We need to build our army, and we can't do that fighting." As she looked around my room, her eyes filled with tears. "Hopefully, the enemy won't notice the castle's empty until we're far away. Just yesterday, I sent fo-lis to the other rulers of the territory, letting them know."

A sudden fear gripped my heart in its tight, sweaty fist. "But we need to stay and fight. If we leave, Rune will take over."

"If he has the Stones, it's only a matter of time. We're leaving for Syeira. They've agreed to offer us sanctuary while we regroup."

The thought of leaving made my stomach hurt. "Maybe I should've stayed with Tiny's family."

She rubbed my shoulders. "We'll be safe in Syeira. Anyway, I wanted you to know so you could pack everything you wanted from this room." She stood, pulling me up with her and giving me a hug. "Although I'm upset you didn't go to Kelda Hills like I told you to, I'm glad I get to hug you. I missed you."

I gave her a smile and another hug before she left. Then I began the tiresome job of packing. Again.

CHAPTER TWENTY-NINE

AN HOUR LATER, I wrestled with my bag. It already bulged with belongings. Anything left behind would probably be gone if and when we returned. I cast a critical eye over the mostly empty room. The thought of Rune walking these halls made my skin itch.

Out my window, the New River rushed toward the ocean, the impressive Steen Mountains a beautiful backdrop. The sun's rays touched every familiar tree and field, the colors rich. A pang of premature homesickness twisted my heart.

A knock on my open door interrupted my musing. I turned. Baldwin leaned against the doorframe. My traitorous heart leaped in my chest. I drank him in—tousled dark hair, bright green eyes, broad shoulders emphasized in his black and gray uniform.

But in his face was something that hadn't been there the night we talked in Ginselwyn—regret, hope, insecurity. Neither of us was perfect. Even if I didn't feel like forgiving him, should I give the relationship another shot? Did it even still exist?

Baldwin gave me a small smile. "Hi."

"Hey." My voice came out rusty, and I cleared my throat. "I've been, um, thinking about us."

"Yeah? Me, too."

That little gem of information gave me the courage to continue. "Yeah, so maybe our, uh, conversation didn't go so good, I mean, so well, um, last time, you know, when we talked. I'm, uh—" This. Was. Agonizing. Somebody shoot me.

He saved me. "I talked to Kersen. He said I was being stupid." *Thank you, Kersen.* "I've always liked that guy."

Baldwin smirked and walked toward me, close enough for me to smell his scent of leather and citrus. "I talked to Gari this morning before her family evacuated. It was a disaster. She was hoping we would get back together. I assure you, I never encouraged that hope. But maybe my friendship was encouraging enough. I am so sorry I hurt you, Brenna. I should have told you about my deployment."

"Well, I kind of lost it that night at the Golden Pickle. I should've stayed, but seeing her hanging all over you, kissing you...you know."

"Yeah." He rubbed his neck, his eyes downcast. "Do you know about Gari's talent?"

"No." And I didn't care. Why was he bringing this up?

"It is rare. The guard, Reggie, is the only other one known in Linneah. They are both Affecters."

"Which is?"

He looked up. "They're stronger than Sensitives. They influence the emotions and behavior of others."

My eyes widened as the implication sank in. "Does she make you do things you don't want to do?"

"Not directly, but she can impress others to feel and behave in certain ways." He swallowed. "Especially if she touches you."

That lying, conniving witch...

He reached for my hands. "Because of my friendship with her, we had an understanding. It never caused any serious problems. Then you and I paired, and she became more flirtatious. If I could go back and do that day over at the Golden Pickle, things would be so different now." He shook his head. "I am sorry, truly. Can you forgive me? Can we start over?"

"We can never go back, Baldwin."

His face fell, hope dying and turning his eyes dull. "I see."

I held on when he pulled away. "No, you don't. I forgive you. I just miss you. The you I—" *The you I fell in love with.* I swallowed the words I couldn't say. "The you I first met on the balcony. We used to talk all the time."

He cleared his throat. "I know. I miss it too. What if we make time for that when we visit? Just the two of us."

"That's a great idea. Why didn't we do that before?"

He tilted his head. "I have never been paired with someone who did not live in Linneah. Apparently, it takes more communication."

"It's a struggle for me. I'm in my head a lot."

Smiling, he caressed my cheek. "You are totally worth it."

I glanced at him through my eyelashes. "Are you still upset about my ultimatum?"

"No, that was what made me think. I wanted to save my friendship with her and my relationship with you. I was sure I could keep both." He shook his head. "Plus, Kersen said he would ask you to pair with him if we broke up."

I snorted out a laugh. "So you're staying with me so your best friend can't have me?"

He crossed his arms, mock serious. "Absolutely. I cannot let Kersen get the best thing that has ever happened to me."

My heart fluttered. I leaned forward, sliding my arms around his neck. "The best thing? That's what we have—together." I kissed him, relearning the feel of his lips on mine.

His arms slipped around my waist, pulling me closer. "I have missed you." He underlined his statement with another kiss, this one a bit deeper.

When I finally pulled away, my brain began to function better. Kissing him always made me stupid. "Why are you here? Shouldn't you be on your way to Syeira?"

He lifted a shoulder. "I needed to talk to you. I took a chance you would still be here. And…"

"Yes?"

"I used a spiegel globe to keep track of you."

My mouth fell open. "What if I'd been in the shower?"

He gave me a wolfish grin. "How is that bad?"

I smacked his arm as my cheeks heated.

Laughing, he pulled away. "Usually, spiegel globes will not show you something you have not seen before. You need the memory to make it work. Since I do not have that memory, well, it cannot happen."

I gave him a skeptical side glance. "If you say so."

"I do. How is your shoulder injury?"

"Oh, it's good. I hardly feel it. Especially if—" I broke off in surprise. He knew about my injury at Starfall? Busted. "How'd you figure it out?"

"You are beautiful, smart, and brave. But you are a lousy man."

I pursed my lips. "That was my best effort."

"I know you, Brenna. Your eyes, your scent of vanilla and raspberry, and especially the feel of you in my arms. By the time I was sure, Abira had dismissed me."

I *knew* I was a lousy guy. "I'm not planning on doing Starfall again, so hopefully I won't need to be Bob again."

"Too bad. That guy was funny." He chuckled. "You said you were headed for Kelda Hills. Why?"

I hesitated. Good question. Why was I doing that?

His eyes narrowed. "Are you keeping a secret from me?"

I plopped on the bed. "More like keeping a secret from everyone. I planned to go to Kelda Hills to train with Abira, since she's a Firebrand trainer. But I never fully recovered from an accident, and now it appears I don't, uh, have a talent." I tried for nonchalance, but the words came out weak and whiny.

Baldwin sat next to me and took my hand, his simple touch warming me all the way through. "Is that what happened here?" He traced a red line up my arm.

I nodded, hating the streaks a bit more every time I saw them. "Can you be healed?"

"I don't know. I can't heal myself, because I can't even create a tiny ember. That's why I couldn't heal your burn. I'm sorry."

"It is healing on its own." His one eyebrow rose, the look that always made butterflies dive and dip in my stomach. "What is that saying? Stick with me, kid."

"Isn't it, 'Stick with me, kid, and we'll go places'?"

"No." He gave me a quick kiss. "Just stick with me."

I laid my head on his shoulder, content to do just that. After a few more kisses, he left with plans to meet me in the kitchen for supper. I sighed, relieved Baldwin and I had talked and made up.

For the rest of the time before supper, I rearranged my stuff in my bag and nearly cheered when the bag closed. My sheathed sword waited in my closet, and I pulled it out, thankful I'd forgotten it in my rush to the travel portal. Rosa would've taken it when she kidnapped me.

After giving my empty room one last look, I picked up my bag and my sword and headed down the stairs to the first floor.

Travel bags lined the hallway. I dropped my belongings into an available spot. Mom strode over. "I was thinking—we should send a fo-li to Abira so she knows you'll be delayed. You're still planning to train with her, right?"

"Yeah, if she still wants me." Although what could she do with a Firebrand that didn't produce fire? Another thought came to mind—school. I hated to bring it up, but... "What about school?"

She brushed back her hair and gave me a half-smile. "There have been a few new developments. Your father resigned from the college."

"He resigned? Why?"

"With all the dangerous things happening, he wanted to be here, not in another alternity. So he resigned and became my first advisor. But before he left, he picked up some materials for you to finish your schoolwork. As soon as you finish, you'll graduate with a GED. After that, you'll have to decide what you want to do."

My mouth opened and closed, but no sound came out.

Three guards burst through the front door. Two rushed down the hallway while the last one flipped the lock and dropped the hardly used barricade into place over the double doors. "My queen!"

She hurried forward. "What is it, Evan?"

"We must leave. Now." His face remained calm, but his breath came fast.

A deep furrow creased her brow. "Now? But we were going to leave after dark."

"We have no more time. They have broken through our forces at the land bridge."

My heart pounded. In the distance, the battle horn sounded, its warning mournful and desperate.

THE END

Will Brenna burn out, or burn bright enough to prevail? Pick up *Burn*, Book 3 of the Firebrand Chronicles!

Read the following short story, "The Midnight Unicorn," to learn about Anna and Erhardt's daring mission to find new Stones of the Spring.

THE MIDNIGHT UNICORN

ANNALISE WASHED UP IN the spare bathroom, wiping sweat and grime from her body. Her search along the foothills of Ho Mountain had revealed nothing. Her brothers had returned home from the mountain's peak empty-handed as well. Their voices drifted down the hall from the other bathroom.

"...storm tossed Finder talent. We've been searching for over a time. What good is having a Finder in the family if she can't find new stones for the spring?" At Aron's words, anxiety cinched Anna's stomach.

"Salt it down. You know it doesn't work that way," Aidyn responded, his baritone a lower rumble.

Anna felt a spark of warmth for her older brother kindle around the cold dismay.

"How do we know she hasn't drifted? Maybe if she focused better, we'd have the stones already."

Aidyn shushed Aron, but Anna had heard enough.

She pushed the bathroom door until it clicked shut and locked it, wishing she could push away her brother's words. Regardless of what he thought, she'd searched just as hard as everyone else. How long would the search for the stones take?

Ever since she'd seen the crushed crystals in Rune's medallions, she'd known this search would be necessary. Ginselwyn's governor, Storm Lee, had been very understanding, and the city was handling the absence of the stones well. As soon as she had realized the stones were ruined, her whole family had searched in earnest. But every moment without the stones left the Ginselwyn residents vulnerable. She swallowed hard as her stomach sank lower.

Her mom and dad were finishing up their search near the northern edge of Starfall Rim and wouldn't be back until late. Thinking ahead, her mom had started a big pot of stew this morning. It had simmered all day, the delicious aroma wrapping around her like a cozy blanket when she'd returned. She'd get a bowl and eat outside, anything to put some distance between her and her brothers. Aron's disdain felt like a deep current, swirling through the rooms and lurking in the hallway.

Padding into the kitchen, she ladled the stew into a sturdy jasperware bowl. Scents of rosemary and golden garlic teased her nose, and her mouth watered. Fresh bread made this morning waited on the kitchen table. She pulled a hearty piece from the woven bag, then cinched it closed to keep it fresh. Turning to leave, an envelope resting at her place on the table caught her eye. *Anna* slanted across the front in her mother's elegant script.

She flipped it over, surprised to see the unbroken seal. Privacy was a rare thing in this household. If she left it here to read later, her brothers would open it. Anna tucked it into her pocket to read during supper and headed outside to the porch.

The air cooled as the sun slipped toward the horizon. It was easy to miss the sea here with the coast so far away, but Kelda Hills had a unique beauty with its striped rocks and dusty soil. The Petrus Rings grew brighter as she ate the stew, the rich brown gravy thick with root vegetables and meat. She soaked up every drop of savory gravy with the crusty bread.

As she took her last bite, her older brother Aidyn stepped out onto the porch. "You're slick as a reef eel, but I figured you were out here."

"Hmm," she responded. Maybe he'd go away, and she could get a few more moments of peace.

He sighed and dropped into the empty seat across from her. "You heard him." It wasn't a question.

Her face warmed. "Of course I did. You guys were just down the hall, not on another planet."

"Look. Everyone's whitecapped. We didn't think it would take this long—"

"What did you expect with a storm tossed Finder talent in the family, Aidyn?"

"I didn't say that."

She snorted and scanned the desert landscape. "Aron just said what everyone's thinking. 'Why can't Anna find a stupid set of stones? I thought her Finder talent was shimmer.'"

Aidyn was quiet for so long she chanced a look at her older brother's face.

"You know Mom hates it when you use island slang."

Anna shrugged. "You don't look like Mom to me."

Sighing again, he stood. "We'll all keep looking. In time, the stones will find us." He hunched his shoulders. "Are you coming in soon?"

"I'd like to watch the moon rise."

"Okay." He took a woven throw from the back of her chair and draped it around her shoulders. "For what's it worth, Anna, I think you're just as wavewise as any of us. It's your hard head that gets in the way."

He dodged her swing and gave her a mischievous grin as he disappeared inside.

The sun disappeared below the horizon. She lit the helli lamp sitting on the table next to her and pulled out her mother's note.

Anna, I hope your day of searching was profitable. Your father and I plan to look beyond the Starfall Rim, so we won't make it home tonight. We'll stay at Declan Edan's inn before returning home.

If we're not successful in our search, we've been thinking about our next search area. We think the next spot to be explored should be One Maiden Chasm. And because of its history, you're the only one in the family who can search there.

We struggled with this decision, but we've few options left. I know you're responsible with a level head (more so than your brothers), but you're still my baby. It's easy to forget how much you've grown.

Your safety is always in Elyon's hands, but as a female in the Chasm, the danger is less. If you don't feel up to it, we'll work something else out. Think about it, pray on it, and we'll talk tomorrow.

Love you beyond the waves and back,

Mom & Dad

Anna slumped back into the chair. The OMC? Part of her stomach fizzed with excitement while the other part tied itself into a knot. Getting there wasn't hard—anything with wings could get to the bottom of the chasm. But the legend stated only unmarried females or those who were accompanied by one could travel there. In the past, too many brave men made the foolish decision to explore One Maiden Chasm on their own.

She'd never heard of any who returned.

The women who returned told tales so varied, they couldn't all be true—filthy streets of beggars, palaces of gold, vicious beasts, or small islands in a wild ocean.

Her thoughts whirled as the moon rose to play with the stars. What waited in the chasm for her? Was she strong enough to explore such a mysterious place on her own? Was the danger worth it? If she did it, her brothers wouldn't be able to say she wasn't doing her part.

Sighing, she turned off the helli lantern. She really didn't have a choice. It was one of the few places left unexplored. She stood and leaned against one of the porch columns. Cool air slipped down her neck, and she tugged the blanket tighter around her shoulders.

Sometimes when it was this still and dark, she liked to become invisible, just shift into wind. Before she could attempt it, the hair on the back of her neck rose. Her eyes scanned the landscape, noting a large shifting shadow. Dropping to her haunches, she shifted into a Steen falcon, and the blanket puddled to the porch floor. She flew to the railing, blending into the shadows while she watched the shadow move and grow larger.

The shape of a man detached from the night and entered the yard. He didn't seem to be skulking around or trying to hide his approach. Another shadow further back came into view, its wings flaring wide before being tucked to its sides—a griffin.

She focused on the approaching figure again. As the moonlight illuminated his face, her heart lightened. It was Erhardt.

Dropping to the ground behind the porch railing, she shifted and moved toward him from behind. Before he could climb the steps, she spoke. "Hey, stranger."

He whirled, his serious face relaxing with recognition. "Anna."

The way he said her name made her stomach flutter. Which was drift talk. She'd been wave hung on him forever. They'd had meals together, spent afternoons hiking, even gone flying—him on his griffin and her shifted into a Steen falcon. But Erhardt had never made a romantic move.

"Are you lost in the blue?"

He flashed a grin, and her breath snagged in her throat. It wasn't fair. He owned a double-take kind of face, but his smile did amazing things to his handsome features. *Breathe, Anna.*

"No, I got a vacation."

"You don't do vacations." She squinted and crossed her arms. "Your commander made you, didn't he?"

"Does it matter why?"

"Shells and shimmer, Erhardt! Everyone needs a break once in a while."

He stretched out his arms. "And here I am."

She shook her head. "I'm glad to see you, but I wish you'd come because you wanted to, not been forced to."

With a small grin, he stepped closer. "I did come because I wanted to. I distinctly remember your suggestion several months ago. You offered a quiet place to relax. I hoped the offer was still available even though you moved."

For the second time in a minute, her breath caught. He stood close, his marine scent of ocean and wood smoke twirling around her. His intense blue eyes shone black in the moonlight.

"Of course," she said, ignoring the raptors dive-bombing in her stomach. "We have an extra bedroom if you need a place to sleep."

"Maybe you should ask your parents."

She gave him a glare. "I am an adult, fully capable of offering you a room. Plus, they're not here."

The moonlight turned his blond hair gray as he tilted his head. "Where are they?"

"Still searching for the stones. Their search took them farther than expected. They should be home by tomorrow."

He scanned the yard before turning back to her. "Do you have a place for a griffin?"

"We have a storage shed in the back. I could give you some old blankets for him."

"Her. I flew in on Reina."

She grinned, remembering several past flights on the griffin. "Really? I haven't seen her in forever."

"You will see her a lot more in the future. We, uh, bonded."

Her eyes grew wide. "You? When?"

Erhardt hitched one muscular shoulder. "Just after the Jasper Territory War. Although I had assumed I would not bond with a griffin, it is common knowledge bonding can happen at any time."

"*You* bonded with *Reina*?" She covered her amusement with a hand.

"What?"

She swallowed her smile. "You're both opinionated."

He frowned. "I am the epitome of compromise."

Anna snorted.

If anything, his frown grew darker, so she changed the subject.

"Come on in. I'll get the bedding for Reina, and you can meet my blowhole brothers, Aron and Aidyn."

As she opened the door to the house, a vegetable chip hit her forehead.

Aron hooted. "Direct hit!"

Ignoring the living room floor littered with more chips, she grimaced at Erhardt. "Welcome to the insanity."

Turning to her brothers, she barked, "Aidyn and Aron, clean up. We have company. This is my friend, Erhardt. He's staying overnight. Please get the guest bedroom set up."

Aidyn raised an eyebrow, but she didn't pause. "I'm getting bedding for his griffin." And she escaped to the linen closet in the hall.

As she gathered several blankets, Aidyn's and Erhardt's murmured polite conversation floated down the hallway. Due to her older brother's protective streak, that would change to lots of questions once she went outside.

She found Reina near the storage shed. "Reina, I haven't seen you in a long time."

Reina's golden coloring glimmered silver in the moonlight. "Hello, Anna. I was detained before I returned to Syeira and then Linneah. I have decided Linneah is a suitable place for a griffin to live." She released a high-pitched whistle. "Did Erhardt tell you? I have chosen him as my bonded rider."

"That's foamed out. You won't find a better rider than Erhardt." Anna spread out the blanket in the storage shed. As long as Reina didn't have a rave, there was plenty of room.

The griffin paused for a moment as if processing her comment. "He is an honorable man. Despite his somewhat silent nature, he has deep feelings for those he cares about."

Anna nodded and placed a bucket of drinking water in the corner. "I'm lucky to be his friend."

Reina paused again, this silence awkward. "Friend?"

"Well, yeah. We spend some time together when his schedule allows it."

"Hmm. Allow me to offer a word of advice, Anna."

Reina would offer it whether Anna allowed it or not. "What?"

"Men do not have friendships with women. Do not be stupid. You are a bright individual—use that mind." With that, she strutted into the shed, turned around, and settled into the corner. "Thank you for the blankets. Good night."

Leaving, Anna furrowed her brow. Stupid? They were friends. Even though the relationship hadn't developed into more like she'd hoped.

But Reina's words lingered. If they weren't friends, what were they? Her steps slowed as she headed back toward the house. Did he view her as a nuisance? If he did, then why spend time with her?

She thought back over their times together, and her cheeks heated. She always sought him out. He probably didn't know how to put her off. She leaned against the porch railing, her memories turning sour—afternoon hikes, mealtimes, even the evening spent star-gazing after an outdoor meal in Syeira. While she'd been sea spraying, hoping for a romance to develop, Erhardt had been placating her. Her eyes stung.

Reina was right—she'd been stupid. And blind and pathetic and wave hung. Her cheeks burned as she thought of her subtle and sometimes not-so-subtle attempts to spend time with him. Why hadn't he said anything? Yes, it would've hurt, but she would've been fine after a little ice cream and some surf time.

She sighed. Tomorrow, things would change. She'd give him what he wanted—a quiet place to relax. She'd make herself scarce by searching the OMC.

In the house, Aidyn was still in the living room. He propped his long legs up on the table in front of the couch. "Aron's got a new idol, who's in the spare bedroom."

"Thanks."

Her brother nodded, his eyes narrowed. "Where'd you meet him?"

"I met him in Linneah. And he's just a friend." Or something. She wasn't sure how else to classify their relationship now.

"So what's the plan for tomorrow?"

"I'll introduce him to Mom and Dad and then skim the blue to search for the stones."

Aidyn widened his eyes. "You're going to leave him here alone? He came to visit you."

"No." She was sticking to her decision. "He just needed a quiet place to get away and relax. You can't get much quieter than here."

"Anna—"

She turned toward her bedroom. "Ginselwyn's waiting. They're my first priority. Talk to you tomorrow."

Aidyn's instructions on polite behavior and being the proper hostess didn't apply here—any extra time with Erhardt would cripple her. And after month after month of hoping for more, she was done. It was time to move on.

Anna slitted open her eyes to voices downstairs. Sitting up, she pushed aside her tangled hair. A large tree stood sentinel near her window, and sunlight streamed through the branches, creating shifting light and shadow on her walls. She'd overslept.

And judging from the voices downstairs, Mom and Dad were already back. A lower voice mingled with the others. Erhardt, talking to her parents. Earlier, she might have freaked out. Her mouth twisted. Now, it wasn't worth getting whitecapped since nothing was going to happen between them.

After dressing for the day, she strapped her bottomless bag to her leg and headed downstairs to grab breakfast. If she left now, perhaps it wouldn't be too late to head into the chasm.

Her mother and father sat at the table with Erhardt. Her steps faltered. He looked like he belonged there, his blond hair and green hairstreak shining in the sun flooding the kitchen.

Aron was a barnacle, judging by the way he sat close and stared at Erhardt. A large platter of eggs, rason bacon, and a stack of toast graced the table. Rainfruit juice shone blue in a large glass pitcher.

Her mother looked up with a smile. "Morning, dear. I hope we didn't wake you."

"G'morning." Anna grabbed a piece of toast before sitting at the table. On her right, Erhardt filled the available space. His shoulder brushed hers, his heat seeming to radiate down her arm.

She shifted away and focused on spreading the homemade Bora marmalade across the toast's surface. "No. I should've been up way before now. I want to make the chasm before nightfall. Unless you found stones?"

Her mother and father exchanged a look before her father shook his head. "No, we didn't. But we have a solution to the dangerous business of your trip."

Anna waved a hand, wishing she could dispel the butterflies in her stomach the same way. "Dangerous if you're male. And I'm not, so it's shell fine."

Mentally giving herself a high five, she took a bite of toast. She hadn't made direct eye contact with Erhardt once, although she could see him frowning in her peripheral vision. She poured herself a glass of juice.

His voice made her jerk. "Your parents and I talked after they returned. You cannot know all the dangers that wait in the chasm. I can go with you."

"But you're male." As she said it, her eyes lingered on his muscular shoulders and broad chest. She cleared her throat and yanked her gaze back to her toast.

He didn't seem to notice. "If we travel together, it will be safer."

She frowned. "You came to visit and relax, not work more."

Her father looked like he wanted to say something before her mother patted his hand. "It would make me feel better knowing Erhardt was with you."

"I would like to help you." His words seemed loud in the small kitchen.

"What?" She lifted her head and met his gaze. His blue eyes glittered with determination and something...deeper. A flash of warmth crept down her neck.

Aron's voice pulled her away from whatever was unsaid in Erhardt's face. "Do you know how much she talks? No peace and quiet in the chasm today. She'll make you seaweed spun." He shoveled in a last bite of eggs.

"Shut up, you seagull." Her sharp response was automatic.

"*You* shut up," her brother shot back.

"Kids—" Her father's voice had a hard warning in it.

Her mother stepped in. "Aron and Aidyn, clean up. Erhardt, make sure you have supplies for two days. Aidyn can take care of Reina while you're gone."

"Reina can't go with us?" Anna asked.

"Reports are the chasm is too narrow near the bottom," her father said. His tone was final, implying he'd decided on the traveling arrangements. "Reina can take Erhardt as far as possible, then you two can hike in the rest of the way."

Pursing her lips, Anna reevaluated her flight plan. She'd have to shift before she reached the bottom and hike in with Erhardt. As a male, he'd need her presence to stay safe.

"Anna, come with me," her mother said, pulling her thoughts back to the present. "We'll make sure you have what you need for a two-day trip."

As she followed her mother to her room, she mulled over the new development of having Erhardt along. Her parents were being pretty laid back about the whole setup. Weren't they worried since it'd be just the two of them? A week ago, she would've celebrated the change of plans. Now, she just wanted to travel alone.

A sudden thought caused her heart to crack. Erhardt must have said something. What did he tell them? If he mentioned the words "helpless," "vulnerable," or anything like that... The thought stiffened her spine. Hadn't she been all over Linneah and the Jasper Territory on her own? She didn't need his protection, his sword, or his big muscles.

When her mother entered her bedroom, she trailed her and shut the door behind her. "I don't think Erhardt should come with me."

Her mother pulled a warm blanket from her closet. "Why?"

"He'll slow me down. Without him, I could stay shifted the entire time and look for the stones much more quickly. But with him, I'll have to shadow him, make sure he's safe."

"We don't know what's in the chasm, Anna. Erhardt's Warrior ability makes me worry less about you."

"But we'll be alone." Maybe if she threw some good arguing points out there, her mom would flip her fin.

"And I trust you and Erhardt to be mature and realize this isn't a time for a romantic retreat."

Anna almost choked on her own saliva. "It's not like that at all. We're just friends. But I don't need a chaperone."

Her mother's eyebrows rose before she turned and added another thinner blanket to the first. "I didn't say you did. But he assured us he would protect you as if you were his sister."

Her heart dropped to her feet at the comparison. "He doesn't have a sister."

"It's a metaphor, dear." Her mother gave her a smile and left.

Sighing, Anna packed the extra blankets her mother had laid out. A sister? She wasn't sure if that was better or worse than a friend. And she couldn't drum up any brotherly feelings for Erhardt.

After a last-minute gathering of supplies, she met Erhardt downstairs. With a flurry of goodbyes to her family and promises to be back in two days, she hurried outside.

At the bottom of the porch stairs, she turned to him. "Do you want to take the lead or shall I?"

His eyes were intent on hers. "I can. Reina will let me know when she feels she can go no further. Your father said to start at the southern edge of the chasm."

"I'll join you in the air, then."

She walked behind some bushes lining their property. Since they didn't have neighbors, she didn't have to worry about shifting while people watched. While some Merripans didn't mind, she hated that.

As Reina took to the air, Anna in her Steen falcon form wasn't far behind. With a few powerful strokes of her wings, she caught up with them and kept pace all the way to the OMC.

The sun was already heating the air, and a balmy breeze blew, smelling of sage and pine. She caught an updraft and let it carry her toward the chasm. The fissure in the earth came into view, looking like a dark seam in the tan landscape.

As Reina plunged into the crack in the earth, Anna followed the powerful griffin. The bridge from the Kelda Hills portal spanned the chasm, and she flew under it, its rickety planks flashing above her. In another hundred yards, the chasm dead ended, and Reina dove for a large rock ledge about sixty feet from the canyon floor. Anna followed. The undulating layers of colorful rock in the gorge told a story of the ancient land's shifting landscape.

The griffin landed, and while Erhardt dismounted, Anna shifted behind Reina's bulk before coming around to the other side.

"Reina, I will contact you when we finish, at best no more than two days." Erhardt adjusted his bag onto his broad shoulders.

Reina gave a whistle. "Agreed. Be safe." She launched into the sky, her golden wingtips brushing the narrow chasm walls as she climbed toward the patch of blue sky.

A set of steps carved into the rock showed their singular path down. Anna peered over the edge of the ledge. No scary monsters, oceans of water, or filthy beggars. Despite the relief, a vague disappointment swirled in her chest. It was just another chasm. "We should get going," she said.

Erhardt fell into step behind her on the stairs, his presence behind her a mix of safety and excitement.

As they reached the bottom, they headed north where the walls narrowed. There was room for them to walk side by side, but nothing more. Anna dragged a hand over the curving rock formations creating the chasm.

"So, how do you know where to search?" Erhardt's question broke the silence.

"Most of the stones suitable for the spring won't be found lying around on forest floors. They're formed in caves or swept into riverbeds. And all the selections have to be cracked open to be sure they separate the right way."

Erhardt raised his eyebrows. "What do you mean 'the right way?'"

"When we split the rocks, they must separate into four distinct pieces—two useless end pieces and two hollow rings lined with crystals. These hollow pieces allow for the flow of water through the crystal-lined center. Elyon must guide us to the correct stone and guide its breaking, as well."

"Sounds complex. No wonder you have been searching for so long."

She nodded, grateful he understood this wasn't a simple job. They continued walking, talking of trivial matters. As it neared time to stop for lunch, the walls closed in, the curves and cutouts of stone creating optical illusions.

Pinching her nose, Anna squeezed her eyes shut. "These rock formations are gorgeous, but I need a break."

Erhardt pointed to a small nook. "We could stop to eat here."

"Good idea." She walked over and peered into the space. "Hey, this opens up further in."

He followed her, bumping into her when she stopped. A cave yawned before them, complete with a small waterfall trailing into a small rippling pool. The stream meandered away, curving around a rock column before disappearing into a side tunnel. The same striped rock made up the walls with spots of sunlight breaking through the ceiling, a few rays highlighting the cavern floor.

"Wow," she breathed. Deeper in the cavern on the far side, stalagmites reached for the ceiling where the stream disappeared. Water dripped from above, although it was dry at the entrance.

The warm touch of Erhardt's hand at the small of her back caused her to stumble away. "We should eat," she blurted and busied herself finding her lunch in her bag.

Erhardt paused. "Are you okay?"

Ignoring his bemused look, she continued searching. "Fine, just hungry." And heartbroken and confused and sad. But she couldn't say those things, because she'd get better. Once she was done grieving, she'd arrive on the other side of Heartbreak Mountain and move on with her life. This trip with Erhardt at her side was just making that transition more difficult.

She pulled out her sandwich and Bora fruit. If only the weird tension between them would dissipate.

As she relaxed against the wall, she unwrapped her sandwich.

Erhardt settled next to her, his hand slipping over hers. "We should thank Elyon for the food. And his protection."

Looking up, she was struck dumb. He was so close she could see flecks of silver in his blue eyes. "What?"

"We should say thanks."

"Um, right." She bowed her head, still reeling over the safe feeling of his strong hand wrapped around hers. His brief prayer rumbled to a close, although she had no idea what he'd said.

After he pulled his hand away, she dragged in a difficult breath. Why couldn't she turn off her feelings? She frowned and took a vicious bite of her sandwich.

"Are you sure you are okay? You seem—different."

She focused on the waterfall, its silver curtain rippling into the pool. "Sure. I'm great. Sorry this trip wasn't the break you were looking for."

His blond brows lowered. "I came to see you."

She looked down at her half-eaten sandwich, the sentence making her heart ache. "Erhardt, that's foam talk. I'd rather you were honest with me."

"I am being honest."

She yanked her gaze to his. "Look, Reina told me how you felt. About me, I mean."

"What?" Pink suffused his cheeks. "She had no right."

"I'm glad she did."

"I-I wanted to tell you myself." Although he turned to face her, his comment was almost lost under the babbling of the stream.

She shifted away, her stomach churning like rough surf. "I appreciate that, but it's unnecessary now. If you don't want to be friends, fine. Just don't pretend. And I don't want another brother. I have two too many as it is."

The dead calm and stunned look on his face made her scramble up. "Excuse me. I'd like to search the streambed. It looks promising."

Swallowing the rest of her sandwich in two bites, she pocketed her fruit. Erhardt still sat, mute, but her feelings were a tangle as she stalked over to the stream.

Memories of all the ways she'd tried to spend time with him played through her mind. Had he laughed about her pathetic attempts when he was alone or with his buddies?

Blinking hard against the stinging in her eyes, she jumped the stream. While she continued to search, her thoughts whirled.

His expression had told her everything. Despite his words, he'd never intended for her to find out how he felt. Her heart twisted at the thought. A few unproductive minutes later, she stood. Erhardt remained where she'd left him, staring at her with a strange look on his face. It was a combination of befuddlement and intensity, and she was glad for the distance between them.

A sudden sound blended with the bubbling of the small river. Was it an animal? A human? The noise came again, and she crept toward the tunnel.

Before she could venture farther, an animal stepped from the side tunnel and stopped, its fierce golden gaze paralyzing.

Anna's mouth gaped. It was a unicorn, midnight black body, mane and tail, its golden horn glistening in the muted light of the cave.

"The Midnight Unicorn," Erhardt whispered.

The creature whipped its head to stare at him, as if suddenly noticing another person in the cave. *Greetings, Maiden. Who is this?*

The words shifted in Anna's head, not audible, but as real as her surroundings. "Reefstars. I'm Anna. This is my friend Erhardt."

As your friend, he is under your protection. I am sorry to intrude. Excuse me. The unicorn turned back toward the tunnel.

"Wait." Erhardt took several steps toward the animal. "If you are the Midnight Unicorn, you are required to aid us."

The unicorn glanced back, tossed its head, and disappeared.

Anna's eyes rounded. "Where'd he go? What just happened?"

Erhardt grimaced. "I think that was The Midnight Unicorn. According to legend, if a person sees him, they are to approach, touch his mane, and ask for help."

"But I didn't touch him."

He nodded. "I remembered that after I spoke."

She barely refrained from rolling her eyes. "Did you hear the unicorn speak? It was in my head."

"I heard it." Erhardt continued to stare at the spot where the unicorn had disappeared. "We need to find him. He could help you find new Stones of the Spring. All your searching would be over."

The thought was heaven. "Maybe if we follow this tunnel, we'll find him again."

He nodded. "Good idea." He stopped in front of the rock column, still on the other side of the stream. "I can cross here and follow you in. There is more space to walk on your side of the stream."

She backed up, and Erhardt jumped. As he landed, he tripped and put out both hands to catch himself.

It seemed to happen in slow motion—his stumble, his muscular arms stretching out, the stalagmites glistening in the dim light...

Gasping, she reached out but couldn't stop the inevitable.

His eyes wide, Erhardt threw his bulk to the side. A stalagmite still caught his forearm, ripping through the flesh. He groaned and shifted into a sitting position, holding his arm.

Anna knelt next to him and pushed his hands aside. Blood spilled from his arm and dripped off his fingers.

Her vision went hazy, and she swallowed hard. "What do I do?"

Clamping down on the wound with his free hand, Erhardt clenched his jaw and spoke through gritted teeth. "There are bandages in my bag."

She carefully pulled his bag off his back to search the packed contents. The bandages waited near the bottom in a small bag.

He leaned closer to her. "Can you wrap it for me?"

She nodded, still eyeing the blood flowing from the wound. So much blood. "Tell me what to do, and I'll do it."

He directed her through the steps—water for rinsing, a thin layer of salve, wrapping the wound with the right amount of pressure, and at last, medicine for pain. When she finished, Erhardt leaned back against the cavern wall, breathing hard. She walked to the stream and rinsed off her bloody, shaking hands.

When she returned, he opened his eyes as she approached. "We should follow the unicorn. Perhaps he did not travel far."

She shook her head. Pure reef logic. "Erhardt, you're injured. Contact Reina to come and get you. I'll walk you to the pickup site."

Frowning, he pushed to a standing position. "It is a minor injury, not a major one. Come, before it gets late."

She stood her ground. "There was blood, a lot of it. What if you get lightheaded and pass out?"

He gave her an offended look. "I have never fainted. Ever."

"Well, you will if you hike through One Maiden Chasm when your arm's been ripped open."

His jaw flexed. "I am fine." He set off down the smaller tunnel as if expecting her to follow. She shadowed him and grumbled under her breath about shark-bait males.

Erhardt interrupted her mumbling. "You know I can hear everything you are saying, right?"

She pressed her lips into a thin line and didn't say another word.

In the winding tunnel, shafts of sunlight illuminated the interior, so using a helli lantern wasn't necessary. But after several minutes, Anna's doubts overtook her. Chasing after a sleek as a reef eel unicorn would only take longer.

"This side quest isn't worth it. We're chasing sea glass, especially since we already saw him once." Her voice echoed in the tunnel.

"But if we find him again, he can help you—shorten your search time, maybe even direct you to the correct location."

Doubt was a large bubble rising in her chest. "Maybe."

Stopping, he turned to study her face and leaned back against the tunnel wall. "Sorry. I forgot this is your search. It is up to you."

Anna raised her eyebrows. Her seagull brothers always told her what to do—having someone defer to her judgement was a novel experience. "We can look for just a few more minutes."

After a minute of walking, a glow came from ahead and they emerged into a meadow of green grass, a profusion of flowers, and birdsong. It was Eden.

On her right, a large pond glistened. Beyond it lay a forest with paths threading through thick trees. Several boulders tumbled on the left side of the path, before a sheer drop framed the vast ocean beyond. Below, violent waves smashed against the stone cliff, the wind kicking up sea spray.

Erhardt dropped onto a rock near the pond and closed his eyes.

She hurried to his side and knelt. "Are you okay?" Her eyes scanned his bandage. Blood seeped from under the edges.

"We never should've come this way." She stood, concern firming her voice. "Contact Reina."

He shook his head. "The bleeding has almost stopped."

"You need medical care."

His blue eyes glittered, and a soft smile broke across his face. His free hand grasped hers, tugging her closer. "I can think of a few things I need. But right now, I have them all."

Everything faded away, the forest, pond, and meadow disappearing into the background. Her heart pounded. The long moment stretched. His gaze traced her features like a physical touch before stalling on her mouth. At the crunch of brush, she pulled away and turned to face the visitor.

The Midnight Unicorn had returned.

Anna straightened her shoulders. "I'm getting you help." She forced her feet to move to the beast's side and touched his mane. "We need your help."

What do you need?

Erhardt's voice behind her broke the quiet. "Please help us find new Stones of the Spring."

She whirled on him with a glare. "Shells and shimmer, Erhardt! What're you doing?"

"You need the stones."

I need you. The words rested unsaid on her tongue. She altered them. "I need you to stay alive."

"Like I said earlier, I am fine." His jaw jutted, his stubborn streak on display.

The unicorn claimed her attention, his commanding voice thrumming through her head. *I heard the Evil One took the stones. Follow me.*

Before she could move, Erhardt tumbled from the rock onto his uninjured side. A moan slipped from his throat.

Gasping, she flew to his side. "Erhardt?"

He blinked, his eyes narrowing as the unicorn stepped closer. "Do not coddle me. I am fine."

"You keep saying that, but you aren't." Cradling his head in her lap, she brushed back a lock of his hair before looking up at the unicorn. "Can you help him?"

The unicorn stamped a foot. *You have already issued your request. It cannot be changed.*

Her eyes widened. "But he needs help. He'll go into shock."

Erhardt's fingers found her lips. "Shh. The longer you argue, the longer it will be until we return home. Go. I will wait here."

She clenched her fists but slipped Erhardt's head from her lap to the ground. Pulling the blankets from her bag, she placed the thinner one under his head and the heavier one across his chest. She stood and turned to the unicorn. "Will we be gone long? And will he be safe here? Alone?"

The Midnight Unicorn gave a quick nod. *It is not far. And you are both safe here.*

After making sure Erhardt's bag and a cup of water from the pond was within his reach, she faced the unicorn. "Okay, I'm ready."

He took a step closer. *Touch my horn.*

As her fingers touched the gleaming gold spike, the landscape whirled into a blur of color. Her hand clutched the unicorn's single antler, her stomach flipping. One moment later, the world around them steadied, and she found herself and the unicorn next to a babbling stream. A swath of tall grass swayed in the breeze on the other side of the stream. In the middle of the meadow, a lone tree stretched leafy branches into a hard blue sky. The sun warmed her back.

"Where are we?"

Farther from your friend than you would like. As soon as you make your selection, we may leave. The unicorn stepped a short distance away as if giving her privacy.

She dropped to her knees, looking through the rocks gathered near the rushing water. As she sifted through them, her mouth dropped open. She couldn't be sure without opening them, but she'd never seen so many potential specimens in one place.

"Can I open them here?" she asked, without breaking from her search.

Yes, of course. And you may take as many as you need.

As many as she needed? She only needed one, one perfect stone that would crack open in perfect halos to create the set she needed.

Most of the rocks were too big, so she ignored them and looked for one the size of a soccer ball. Methodically, she moved smaller rocks, adding and discarding. One small rock fit in her palm like it was tide-called. She put it aside, then picked it up seconds later, her attention again captured. After the third time, she examined it, letting it warm her palm.

She huffed out a breath. Her Finder talent. Always picking things up for "some time." She never knew when she'd need it, just that someone, somewhere, would need it later on. Why didn't it work for things that were needed right now?

Pushing aside the question, she examined the streambed again. The unicorn said she could take more than one, so she slipped the smaller stone into her bottomless bag and continued her search.

After several more minutes, she'd found three possibilities, the right size and shape with the lightweight heft suggesting it was hollow. She took her hammer from her bag and clutched the handle, her fingers sweaty with hope. Swinging up, she let the head drop with a resounding bang. The rock split into two perfect halves as if someone had taken a sword to it. Inside the two flawless bowls, crystals glittered.

The rock hadn't broken the way she needed. That was okay—there were two more rocks to split.

Moving it aside, she focused on the next. The same thing—a massive swing, the connection with the stone making the vibration snake up her arm and ache a bit. The rock shattered into several dozen pieces, none of them in the needed ring shape for the spring.

She frowned. What if none of these stones broke correctly? She knew it was up to Elyon, but they'd been searching for so long. Didn't He want the people of Ginselwyn to be safe from disease?

She'd have to return with nothing to show for the search except a very weak Erhardt. The memory of his pale face before she left made her set her jaw. If this one didn't work, she'd return home. She could always come back.

Adjusting her hand around the wooden handle, she took a deep breath. "Please," she whispered. "We're running out of places to look. Please."

With a deep inhale, she held her breath and let the hammer fall with a resounding smash. The rock split, the two halves falling away in tandem. She blinked, her heart withering.

So that was it then.

Dropping the hammer on the ground, Anna let her head fall into her hands.

She wiped away the frustration wetting her cheeks. Time to go home. She took a step, but something made her look back. The last stone she'd struck had dark snaking marks on either end.

As she picked up one half of the stone, it shifted into two pieces. Her breath caught. Peering inside, a frisson of excitement curled through her. Daylight gleamed through the stone, glittering crystals lining the inside of the rock. Putting it down, she checked the other half. It split the same way, and she held it up, noting the clear opening on both sides. She bit her lip against a giddy grin. The crystals in these two pieces could easily filter out impurities, providing clean water for Ginselwyn.

The unicorn waited for her in the field.

Slipping her hammer and the stones' end pieces into her bag, she hefted the stones. Because of their hollow nature, they weren't as heavy as a regular stone of this size. Still, she had to be careful carrying them.

The Midnight Unicorn looked up, his gaze steady. *You have found what you needed, then?*

"Yes, thank you so much. I'm ready to skim the blue. But I, uh, my hands are full." How could she return if she couldn't hold the unicorn's horn?

Before she could juggle the stones, the unicorn stepped closer and lowered his horn to her shoulder. As before, colors whirled, blending into gorgeous tie-dye kaleidoscopes. When the vivid colors drained away, she found herself next to the pond.

Erhardt lay still. His tanned face had paled bone-white. His shallow breathing was way too rapid.

"No, no, no." Putting the stones at a safe distance, she hurried to his side. Blood had soaked through the bandage, turning it crimson. He was still losing blood.

"I am *not* doing this alone." But she was, and it ripped her apart. Erhardt didn't stir, wasn't even aware she was at his side.

"If you don't snap your scales and get through this, I'll never forgive you," she said.

Digging into his bag again, she found a sharp knife and sawed through the bandage. Water from the cup cleaned the wound, and she pulled out another clean bandage. But before she could apply it, a nudge in her heart stopped her.

The rock, the one waiting in your bag.

She knew this voice, had heard it a hundred times before—Elyon, the wave wielding, omniscient Finder.

Still, there was no time to experiment with her finds. "I'll take care of Erhardt, then I'll get to the rock, okay?" She pushed aside the urge, but her fingers fumbled with the binding.

Now.

She huffed out a breath. What could be done with the rock? Maybe if she smacked her own head with it, it'd knock some sense into her. She pulled out the palm size rock and stared at its unspectacular appearance. Grayish brown with a slight bulge, it nestled in her palm. Maybe crystals were inside, but so what?

Open it.

For a moment, she squeezed her eyes shut then pulled the hammer out of her bag. Without hesitating, she split it with a quick strike. "So now what?" she muttered.

Put the crystals into his wound.

"What?"

The silence was deafening. A quick glance confirmed her suspicion. A pool of blood grew on the ground under Erhardt's arm, his breath still shallow.

Okay, then. Using the knife, she picked away at the crystals, letting the tiny, glittering shards fall onto the bandage. "This is seaweed spun. It'll make him worse. Won't it slice up his arm? And he's lost so much blood."

Silence met her protests.

But as she continued to sprinkle the crystals onto the bandage, they seemed to dissolve into a glistening substance. Several long minutes later, her fingers fumbled at another command.

Enough.

She had put aside her own reasoning minutes ago and was listening to Someone all-knowing. Putting the rock aside, she picked up the bandage and wrapped Erhardt's arm with the material. He murmured, and his eyes fluttered open.

"Reefstars, you're awake," she breathed. "I rewrapped your bandage, but you need to rest."

"Reefstars?" He gave her a small smile which twisted into a grimace. "Did you find stones?"

"Yes." She waved aside the matter. "But you need to rest. I rewrapped your bandage and um..." She stuttered to a stop.

"Thank you—" He bit off his sentence and muffled a groan. "Is there more medicine in my bag?"

"I-I think so."

As she pulled his bag closer, he groaned again. "Anna?"

"What?" Without glancing up, she continued to search his bag, scattering the contents.

His hand stroked her cheek. Her eyes jumped to his, her hands stilling, the medicine forgotten.

"I am glad I could take this trip with you." His eyes fluttered then rolled back in his head.

"Erhardt?" She felt for the pulse in his neck, noticing he was still breathing. No medicine, then. And what was up with that caress? Not fair, not at all if she was trying to prevent her heart from breaking.

She put everything back in his bag, washed her hands, refilled the cup of water and then sat and watched him sleep. Although it was the best thing for him, it gave her too much time to think, obsess, and worry. And what of Reina and her parents? Was there a way she could contact them to let them know what had happened?

Near the forest, half a dozen unicorns came out to graze. No Midnight Unicorn among them, although these gorgeous animals captured her attention. For half an hour, she watched them nibble on tender grass and drink from the pond before they melted back into the trees.

Standing, she took a walk around the pond. She could still see Erhardt, but it also helped her work off some nervous energy.

After a quick supper of Bora nut bread and pond water, she shivered. As the night air turned colder, she glanced at the heavy blanket draped across Erhardt's chest. After a moment or two of consideration, she shrugged. He'd have to share.

Moving close, she found a comfortable spot on the ground and draped the blanket over them both. In the twilight, she could still study the planes of Erhardt's face without him noticing.

"Even though I love you, I'm letting you go," she whispered. "No matter how it feels when you touch my cheek or hold my hand."

Closing her eyes, she set her jaw. She'd do it too—it would just take a while.

Anna turned her head from the bright light and into the warmth on her right side. Wood smoke with a faint scent of ocean waves made her smile. Best. Dream. Ever. A powerful arm pulled her close, and she burrowed into a muscled chest.

The sleepy feeling drifted away, and she bit back a groan. Dream over. She forced her eyes open, and only inches away, Erhardt's blue gaze pinned her.

"G'morning," he rumbled with a smile.

"Ack!" Throwing off his arm, she bolted up, her cheeks on fire. "Sorry, but it got cold last night. I—"

"Anna."

"—didn't think you'd mind, after all, you were unconscious, although I was glad you were still breathing—"

"Anna."

"And then we only brought the one heavy blanket—"

"Saints and sinners, Anna, shut up!"

She stumbled to a stop. "Okay, that was rude."

Erhardt pushed himself up to a sitting position and gave her an unrepentant grin. "Yes, but you stopped talking."

Giving him a glare, she walked over to him. "How do you feel?"

"Well, it was one of my best waking up experiences."

Her cheeks heated again, and she refused to look at him as she sat. "Your injury?"

He sobered. "Right. My arm feels much, much better. Did you do something different?"

Erhardt knew a bit about her talent, but she offered a little more explanation. "My talent kept telling me to save this small rock I'd found. I did, and when I returned here, well, you were the one who needed it. The crystals in the Stones of the Spring keep the people of Ginselwyn healthy. The crystals in this rock worked the same way."

He took her hand, his thumb stroking the back. "Thank you for taking care of me."

She eyed his hand holding hers before pulling away. "Sure. We should have breakfast."

Ignoring Erhardt's heavy gaze, she pulled out the food stashed in her bag—the last of the nut bread, dried fruit, and a small bag of jerky. Not her favorite, but it was protein. She handed a serving to Erhardt, making sure their fingers didn't touch.

"Are you angry with me?"

She jerked her head up, surprised to see a sad frown mar his handsome face. "No, why would I be angry?"

He shrugged. "Like I mentioned yesterday, you are acting differently."

With a sigh, she closed her bag. This was too hard. Maybe she needed to swallow her pride and explain it all. Embarrassing? Yes, but over time it'd fade. He'd get married, and she would too—maybe—and this would all be some memory they could chuckle over.

She hitched a shoulder. "I was just surprised you wanted to come with me. I'd planned to travel alone."

He nodded. "Your parents were concerned about your safety."

"Yeah, about that." She pointed a finger at him. "I've been searching for quite a few months, many times on my own. Why would I need a protector this time?"

He didn't blink. "One Maiden Chasm is unexplored."

She gritted her teeth. "Did you tell them I was incompetent?"

His eyes went wide. "No! I—" He muttered a curse. "Anna, what exactly did Reina say to you?"

She pursed her lips. "I said I was glad we were friends. And she said a man and a woman are never friends. Which makes me feel seaweed spun, thanks. Like the little girl who always wants to tag along. You should've told me you weren't interested in a friendship." Or in any relationship, for that matter, but she wasn't voicing that thought.

Erhardt shook his head. "No, that is not what is going on here."

She sat back, the early morning sun warming the top of her head. No breeze stirred the still pond, although something floral scented the air. "Just forget it, Erhardt. It's okay." It wasn't, but she didn't want to talk about it anymore.

His blue eyes flared. "I am in love with you, you stubborn woman."

"You—what?" Her thoughts stuttered, spun to a stop.

He linked her hand with his. "I am in love with you, Annalise Annalice. Reina was right. I do not want to be just friends with you. I want to be your husband, your lover, *and* your friend. I want it all—with you."

"But-but—" Her brain had stopped working. She cleared her throat. "You told my parents you'd protect me like your own sister."

He cocked an eyebrow. "I also told your parents that with their blessing, I intended to ask you to twine with me."

"Twine?" Her voice was a whisper.

He reached deep into a pocket and pulled out a small cloth bag. "I did not plan to ask you this way, but I have learned nothing is traditional with you, Anna."

She couldn't breathe, couldn't think. "But I didn't think you were interested. You never made a romantic move or anything."

He raised his eyebrows. "I thought the stargazing nights were romantic."

She nodded in agreement, and he shifted closer, his warmth seeping into her arm. "I had hoped our time together would show I was serious."

"I thought you saw me as a friend, one of the guys."

His eyes rounded. "You were never one of the guys. Ever."

"But how was I supposed to know that?"

He leaned in, his lips a hair's breadth from hers. "Know it now, Anna. I am not interested in a flirtation." He brushed her lips with his. "I want forever."

When he pulled away, a silver ring engraved with a beautiful rolling wave pattern glistened between his fingers. He frowned, his expression unsure. "Will you, Anna? Can you twine with this Warrior?"

Bright joy sparkled like the sun on sea spray, filling her chest and making her giddy. "Yes, of course. I love you, stone deep."

Slipping the ring on her finger, he grinned and asked, "Stone deep?"

"It means 'sincere and heartfelt.'"

He leaned closer. "Then I love you too, stone deep." His lips covered hers, and he didn't pull away until several long moments later.

Giving him a mock stern look, she jabbed him in the chest with an index finger. "I expect many more kisses from you. All that time we spent together feels like wasted opportunities."

With a rakish smile, he pulled her close again and kissed her senseless. After a moment, he raised his head. "Better?"

"That's a good start," she gasped, her head spinning. Pulling away, her hand caught on the edge of his bandage. "We should change this."

He nodded. "And I would like to head back. If you found stones, there is no reason to wait."

After unwinding the bandage, she found the wound looked ten times better than the previous day, the edges clean and pink.

She said a silent, private message. *Thank you. Thank you for healing him and making me listen.* In the future, when Elyon gave her directions, she wouldn't doubt.

After smoothing on salve and rewrapping it, they finished breakfast.

Anna couldn't stop shooting glances at Erhardt, almost as if to convince herself this wasn't a dream. This amazing man loved her, despite her strange talent and island slang.

He caught her looking and gave her hand a quick squeeze. "I will contact Reina and tell her we are leaving now. She can meet us at the ledge."

She nodded, still mulling over the morning's events. All this confusion, just from a simple misunderstood conversation with a griffin. She was going to have a little talk with Reina the next time she saw her.

As they left the clearing to head for the tunnel, Anna looked back. Among the trees, a dark shadow moved, and a glistening golden horn glimmered. With a small smile, she raised her hand in a thankful farewell.

In finding the Stones of the Spring for Ginselwyn, she'd found the love of a lifetime too.

THE END

Anna's Island Slang

- **Chasing sea glass:** searching for the impossible
- **Danced the drift:** died
- **Drift talk:** nonsense, rambling
- **Foam talk:** empty words
- **Foamed out:** excellent/awesome
- **Low tide behavior:** sneaky & underhanded
- **No drift about it:** no doubt
- **Reef logic:** confused thinking
- **Reefstars:** expression of awe/wonder
- **Ride the curl:** travel on/keep going
- **Riprider:** hero
- **Rogue wave:** terrible situation
- **Salt it down:** relax; take a breath
- **Sea spray:** daydreaming/ unfocused
- **Seagull:** obnoxious
- **Seaweed spun:** crazy
- **Shell fine:** good; perfect
- **Shells and shimmer:** exclamation
- **Shimmer:** magic
- **Skim the blue:** take off; leave
- **Slick as a reef eel:** agile & fast
- **Stone deep:** sincere; heartfelt
- **Storm tossed:** bad
- **Surge boss:** attractive guy/girl
- **Tail-tied:** stuck in a bad situation
- **Tide called:** destined
- **Wave hung:** crushing on a guy/girl
- **Wavekeeper:** friend
- **Whitecapping:** angry
- **Wind slick:** charismatic and smooth

PLEASE LEAVE A REVIEW

Reviews can help other readers find good books and can create more exposure for good books by indie authors. Plus, all authors treasure reviews!

If you enjoyed this book, please consider leaving a review on Amazon, Barnes & Noble, Goodreads, or even a post on social media! A line or two is all that's needed. The information below can give you a few more tips.

Writing an Easy Book Review

Writing a book review can be hard, but it doesn't have to be.

Review Template (pick one):

Not sure what to say? Just copy, paste, and fill in the blanks! Your review can be as short or as long as you like – but every word helps this book find new readers.

Option 1: Quick + Easy
I really enjoyed [Book Title] by [Author Name]. If you like [genre/theme], you 'll love this. My favorite part was [a scene, a twist, a character]. I'd recommend it to anyone who enjoys [similar books/authors or vibes].

Option 2: Feelings First
[Title] made me feel [emotion: hooked, heartbroken, hopeful, etc.] I couldn't stop reading because [reason]. I especially loved [character/scene]. I can't wait to read more from this author.

Option 3: Vibe Reader
If you're into books that are [adjective: dark, romantic, twisty, cozy, fast-paced], this one is for you. [Book Title] gave me major [vibe: fairytale, dystopian, small town, enemies-to-lovers] energy.

Option 4: Combo Review
I loved [Book Title] by [Author]. It was a(n) [adjective] tale that left me [emotion]. I loved [scene, character, twist] and can't wait for more from this author. If you like [similar book/vibe], check out [Book Title].

Ready to leave a review? Please go to my Amazon author page (https://www.amazon.com/stores/J.-M.-Hackman/author /B01K9PJMPE), click on the book you want to review, then scroll down to leave a customer review. Thank you so much!

Acknowledgements

There are so many lovely individuals behind the release of a book—supporters, encouragers, prayer partners, and hand-holders. These people are irreplaceable.

To my family. Thanks for putting up with late dinners and unwashed laundry. Your support and encouragement mean everything. I love you all to the moon and back.

To my parents, who taught me I could be anything (even when I said I wanted to be a cowboy).

To my beta readers: Laurie, Vicky, Laura, Jebraun, and Anne. You are amazing! And thanks to Sarah and her daughter Ellie for finessing my blurb. All of you are awesome!

To Kathy Furr, LCSW, for answering all my questions and making sure my ADHD information was correct.

To all my readers and reviewers. Your comments and reviews are so appreciated and make the frustrating days bearable. Thank you!

And most of all, to my Lord and Savior who made me a storyteller. I'm humbled and blessed to share the stories You put in my heart.

J.M. Hackman, the award-winning author of the Firebrand Chronicles and the Stardust Hearts series, loves thunderstorms, fuzzy socks, and thick chocolate milkshakes. Her engaging fantasy and soft science fiction stories are threaded with hope and end with a happily ever-after. While her characters are feisty and fearless, J.M. is afraid of spiders, wasps, and the crowds at post-Christmas sales. When she's not writing, she reads, crafts, watches football, and adventures with her family in the mountains of rural Pennsylvania.

Her short stories have been published in the anthologies *Crowns*, *Encircled*, *Tales of Ever After*, *Mythical Doorways*, and *Realmscapes*. Go to her website at www.jmhackman.com to learn more about her.